D1567721

SHOVELING
Smoke

SHOVELING Smoke

selected mystery stories by
MARGARET MARON

Crippen & Landru Publishers
Norfolk, Virginia
2000

The original dates and places of publication are given after each story. "Prayer for Judgment" is first published in this book.

Cover by Victoria Russell

Crippen & Landru logo by Eric D. Greene

ISBN (trade edition): 1-885941-15-3

Fourth Printing, December 2004

10 9 8 7 6 5 4

Printed in the United States of America on acid-free paper

Crippen & Landru, Publishers
P. O. Box 9315
Norfolk, VA 23505-9315

E-Mail: Info@crippenlandru.com
Web: www.crippenlandru.com

In memory of Lois Fisher,
the high school English teacher who changed my life

Contents

Introduction

I must have been nine or ten before I made a connection between the printed page and walking-around human beings and suddenly realized that writing was a genuine option, even for a kid growing up in the cotton and tobacco fields of central North Carolina.

It's probably no accident that the earliest surviving pieces from the dawn of literature are usually scraps of poetry—when it comes to playing with language, the putting of words in rhythmic order seems to be a primal human instinct. And I was no different at eleven and twelve. The words flowed, the lines scanned, the end-words rhymed. Bliss!

By the time I finished high school though, I knew two basic facts: writing bad poetry is very easy, writing good poetry isn't.

If I couldn't write poetry, short stories seemed the logical progression; and, because I also grew up reading Rex Stout, Agatha Christie, Erle Stanley Gardner, Ellery Queen, et alia, a short *mystery* story was my first sale when I finally started writing for publication.

For twelve years, until the market began to dry up, it never occurred to me to try to write a novel. Indeed, *One Coffee With*, my first book, began as a short story that kept growing.

It's been an interesting experience to reread the early stories, to see how rough some of them are, how derivative, how implausible. Yet I can also see the first soundings of certain themes and interests that would develop almost by accident into that elusive thing I sought at the beginning, a voice of my own.

On the whole, the stories reprinted in this anthology are as they first appeared. I have resisted the temptation to rewrite them completely although I may have tucked in a shirttail here or smoothed a cowlick there. Someone has said that a painting is never finished, merely abandoned. Twenty years from now, I'll be wishing I could rewrite the stories I'm writing now.

Justice Learned Hand used to say, "Doing justice is like shoveling smoke."

So is writing.

Margaret Maron
Willow Spring, North Carolina
February 1997

The Death of Me

In the fall of 1966, I tried to stop smoking.
Again.

I had been quit for about three hours, had gone through two packs of gum and was ready to kill for a cigarette. Which made me wonder, "Would someone really kill for a cigarette? Why?"

I walked up to the corner drugstore, and as I walked back home with a carton of cigarettes tucked under my arm, I finished plotting out this story. It was eventually rejected by Ellery Queen's Mystery Magazine, *but the printed rejection slip carried a handwritten note of encouragement, the first I'd ever received. I was over the moon. In the spring of 1967, Ernest M. Hutter, the editor at* Alfred Hitchcock's Mystery Magazine, *bought it for the magnificent sum of $63.75. Your family may love everything your write, your friends may say you're another Jane Austen, but nothing validates you like a check from an editor you've never met.*

Here's the story exactly as it was first printed in January 1968 under my maiden name.

You know, Father, the most irritating thing about all tired, worn-out, cliché-ridden platitudes and moralistic aphorisms is that they're so infuriatingly, smugly true: haste does make waste; a stitch in time will save nine; and Myrtle, a walking cliché . . . well, Myrtle was right, too.

"Cigarettes will be the death of you," she nagged whenever she had exhausted my other faults. "Not to mention me. Always smelling up the house with those filthy things, leaving ashtrays to be washed and ashes all over the furniture and rugs."

She left magazines in conspicuous places, opened to articles ringed in red which expounded on nicotine-linked diseases or the dangers of smoking in bed; and she took great relish in reading aloud obituaries in which lung cancer was the cause of death.

"You could stop if you tried. It's just simple mind over matter," she'd harangue.

When I had the temerity once to point out that *her* mind wasn't so hot at controlling her own corpulent matter, she flared indignantly, "You know I'm a glandular case. I can't help it if a slight heaviness runs in my family. And don't try to change the subject. It's been proved that smoking takes years off a person's life. Do you think I want to spend my last years a widow?" The thought so depressed her that she consoled herself with another handful of chocolates.

I often wondered why Myrtle was so concerned about my life span. It wasn't as if she loved me; that was over before our first year of marriage, eighteen years ago. My insurance would more than keep her clothed, sheltered, and sated with chocolates, so perhaps she thought worrying about my longevity (or lack of it) was the proper wifely thing to do, or that she would genuinely miss my being around to nag.

Why did I stay with her? Habit, I guess. Too, she kept the house immaculate, cooked delicious meals, and was so fat that I didn't have to worry about unfaithfulness.

If she hadn't been such an obese harpy, I suppose we could have jogged along as happily as any other married couple, but she just wouldn't understand that I haven't the least desire to stop smoking. It's my one real enjoyment. We had no children, my job is boring, I don't make friends easily, and I have no hobbies except reading.

Do you smoke, Father? No? Then you don't know the pleasure of sipping a second cup of hot, black coffee after a good breakfast, the newspaper opened to an interesting editorial, as you strike a match to light your first cigarette of the day. That first whiff of sulfur as the match flares and catches the end of the cigarette—what perfume to a smoker's nose! A few tentative puffs to get it going, then you inhale deeply and your whole body relaxes. At work, it eases the pressures, helps you concentrate; at night, it's soothing to sit in an easy chair with a book in your lap watching the transparent ribbon of smoke curl and undulate upward in thin blue swirls. With a cigarette in my hand I could even shut out Myrtle's droning complaints, as she was well aware.

I must have ignored her once too often because last winter she really became determined to make me quit. Until then, she'd only sniped at me; now it became serious guerrilla warfare. She began to keep the ashtrays in the kitchen on the pretext that she'd just washed them and hadn't gotten around to putting them back in the livingroom, forcing me to go hunting for one. She kept "forgetting," where she'd put the matches, and disavowed any knowledge of the disappearance of the last two or three packs in each carton.

"Am I to blame if you're smoking so much you can't keep track of how many packs you have?" she would ask with an injured expression.

So I began secreting them around the house, and as quickly as Myrtle would find one hiding place, I'd discover a different one. It became almost a game. My best cache was in the box of dietetic cookies she once bought in the vague hope of reducing. She never did find that particular place.

I don't know how long we'd have kept up that cat-and-mouse farce if I hadn't broken my leg while standing on a rickety stepstool to reach a pack of cigarettes hidden on the top shelf of the linen closet behind some blankets.

The crash brought Myrtle waddling upstairs and, as the pain closed in on me, I heard her half-satisfied wail, "I told you cigarettes were going to be the death of you!"

When I came to, I was lying in bed and Dr. Mason was putting the final touches on a very heavy plaster cast. "A few weeks in bed, a month or two on crutches and you'll be good as new," he told me cheerfully. "It's just a simple fracture and you're lucky it was your leg and not your neck. I'll check in on you in a few days."

Then he was gone—my last link with the outside world. Still dazed and groggy, I didn't realize what it meant until Myrtle brought me my breakfast tray the next morning.

"It was delicious," I told her truthfully, reaching for a new book by one of my favorite authors which she had picked up from the library for me. I actually felt a wave of affection for her, Father.

"You're really a very good wife in many ways, my dear," I said appreciatively, indicating the breakfast tray, the steaming coffee, the book, my fresh pajama shirt. "I know it's going to be a lot of extra work for you."

Myrtle stood by the door, smiling, silent, while I opened the book and fumbled for cigarettes on the night table. Realizing they were missing, I met Myrtle's exultant eyes.

"This is no time for fun and games," I told her quietly. "Bring me my cigarettes."

"No!" she cried triumphantly. "Haven't you learned anything from that fall? What caused it? Cigarettes!"

"I fell because you made me resort to hiding them," I yelled back. "I should have slapped you down the first time you took them!"

"You would hit me, would you?" She leaned over the foot of the bed and shook a thick finger at me, her face mottled with rage. "You listen to me! I'll cook for you, I'll fetch and carry, I'll try to make you comfortable, but I will not give you cigarettes!" Smoothing her dress down over her nonexistent waist, she added, "I just can't be a party to your getting lung cancer and now is a perfect time to quit."

She collected the dishes, lumbered out of the room, and that was that. Neither pleading nor cursing moved her. She was as firm as the Rock of Gibraltar which she so much resembled; and on the issue of cigarettes, she would not be budged. After that first day, pride kept me from trying. If only I had broken something less handicapping than a leg!

True to her word, Myrtle did make me as comfortable as possible. She lugged the portable television up from the den, kept me supplied with books and magazines and served new delicacies, but the sheer physical craving for cigarettes gnawed at my nerve ends, and everything reminded me of them.

I'd never realized before how much television time is devoted to cigarette commercials. I would lie helpless and immobile, watching an actor demonstrate how enjoyable his brand was, and break out in envious sweat.

Every magazine carried at least a dozen ads for different forms of tobacco, and every chapter in every book described a character puffing a cigarette "nervously," "disdainfully," "confidently," or "lazily," while I longed to puff one "avidly."

The next two days dragged though Myrtle kept refilling the dish of lemon drops with which she had replaced my ashtray. I munched and nibbled constantly but grew more and more irritable from the sudden withdrawal.

"You'll get over it and someday you'll thank me," said Myrtle complacently.

"Thank you! If I hold onto my sanity, I'll divorce you as soon as I'm on my feet again!"

Before, I'd felt nothing for her but indifference. Now she became the embodiment of all my frustrations,

On the fourth day, my pride shattered and I groveled before her. "Just one!" I pleaded. "How will one cigarette hurt me?"

"It'll get you right back where you were before," she panted, stooping heavily to pick up the papers I'd scattered on the floor beside my bed. "You don't realize it, but you're over the worst part now."

She was so smugly self-righteous that I couldn't bear her any longer. Without thinking, I swung my broken leg, and sixteen pounds of plaster cast smashed down on her bent head. Howling with pain and pent-up frustration, I hit her again and again even after she lay still. Finally, my leg throbbed so unbearably that I fainted.

The insistent peal of the doorbell brought me to, and then I heard Dr. Mason calling from the hallway, "Anybody home?"

❖ ❖ ❖

My lawyer pleaded temporary insanity under mitigating circumstances; and although one is entitled to be judged by his peers, you'll never convince me that there were any smokers on my jury. Well, they do let you have a few last cigarettes on Death Row.

The most discouraging thing, though, Father, is how right Myrtle was. At least she's not around to say, "I told you so!"

Just a minute more, Guard; I haven't finished my cigarette yet.

Alfred Hitchcock's Mystery Magazine, January 1968

A Very Special Talent

This was my fourth published story and I was still in my Donna Reed mode of housewife and mother first. (When you grow up in a father-knows-best society, some ideas change very slowly.)

"**B**ut he used to hit me," Angela explained, rubbing her shoulder in memory of past bruises. "What else could I do?"

"You could have divorced him," I said firmly.

"He wouldn't let me. You know what the grounds for divorce were in this state then. Don't you care that he beat me?"

Of course it enraged me that that brute had hit my lovely, fragile-looking wife, even if it had been before I'd met her. "Nevertheless," I said, "it's the principle of the thing. It just isn't done."

"It was his own fault," she insisted. "I told him it was dangerous to have the radio that close to the bathtub when he'd been drinking, but that was like waving a red flag at a bull. He would have done it then or died."

She giggled suddenly, remembering that he had, indeed, died.

I was appalled. What does a man do when, after seven blissful years of marriage and two lovely children, he discovers that his adorable little fluff of a wife is a cold-blooded murderess who goes around killing people who aren't nice to her?

"I am *not* a cold-blooded murderess," Angela flared indignantly, "and I would never, never kill anyone who wasn't nasty to a whole lot of other people, too."

At this point the back screen door banged and Sandy, my five-year-old replica right down to a cowlick of red hair and a faceful of freckles, burst into the room and angrily demanded, "What's the matter with you guys? Can't you hear Matt crying? Georgie hit him and he's all bloody!"

Angela whirled and followed Sandy from the room at a trot, with me just behind them.

Four-year-old Matt sat sobbing on the back doorstep. Blood trickled from a split on his lower lip onto his white T-shirt while Sandy's best friend, Chris Coffey, awkwardly patted his shoulder.

One of the things I love about Angela is her absolute cool whenever one of the boys is hurt. I tend to panic at the sight of their blood, but she remains calm and utterly soothing.

She swooped Matt up in her arms, assessed the damage and cheerfully assured him that he wouldn't need stitches. In the kitchen, she applied a cold cloth to his swollen lip and soon had him tentatively smiling again.

The screen door banged again and Jill Coffey, our next door neighbor and Angela's closest friend, came charging in. "That Georgie! I saw it all! Matt hadn't done a thing to him and Georgie just hauled off and socked him!"

"Yeah, Dad," Sandy chimed in. "He won't let us swing, and it's our jungle vine. Chris and me, we built it."

Matt started to cry again, Jill raged on, Angela began to shoot sparks, and Sandy's shrill indignation pierced the chaotic din.

"Hold it!" I shouted. "One at a time."

With many interruptions, a coherent story finally emerged.

When our development was built, the creek which used to cut through our back yards had been diverted, leaving an eight-foot gully overhung with huge old willows which the developers had mercifully spared. With so much of the area bulldozed into sterility, the gully lured kids from blocks around.

Depending on the degree of danger, various stretches of it attracted different age groups: the pre-adolescents usually congregated a block away, where the banks were somewhat steeper and the old creek rocks larger and more jagged. In the section between our house and the Coffeys', the bank was more of a gentle grassy slope and there were fewer rocks, so the pre-school set usually played there.

It seemed that Sandy and his cronies had tied a clothesline rope to one of the overhanging willow branches and had been playing Tarzan, swinging out over the gully as if on jungle vines, experiencing a thrill of danger more imaginary than real. Then Georgie Watson had come along and, as usual, destroyed their fun by taking over the rope swing and hitting Matt.

An overweight nine-year-old, Georgie was a classic neighborhood bully, afraid of boys his own age and a terror to everyone under six. No neighborhood gathering was complete without a twenty-minute discussion of Georgie's latest bit of maliciousness and a psychological dissection of his motives which usually ended with, "Well, what can you expect, with parents like that?"

I suppose every suburban neighborhood has its one obnoxious family; it seems to be written into the building code. At any rate, the Watsons were ours: loud, vulgar, self-righteous, and completely heedless of anyone else's rights and desires.

They gave boisterous mid-week parties which broke up noisily at one in the morning, or they would come roaring home at two from a Saturday night on the town and Mr. Watson would lean on the horn to bring the baby-sitter out.

After such a riotous night, you'd think the man would have the decency to sleep in on Sunday morning nursing a king-size hangover, but no. There he'd be, seven o'clock the next morning, cranking what must be the world's noisiest lawn mower and carrying on a shouted conversation with Mrs. Watson in the upstairs bedroom.

Mrs. Watson was just as bad. Georgie had been born after they had given up all hope of having children and she doted on him. Though quick enough to complain when any boy Georgie's age or older picked on him, she was completely blind to his faults.

If confronted by an angry parent and bleeding child, Mrs. Watson would look the enraged mother straight in the eye and say blandly, "Georgie said he didn't do it and I find Georgie to be very truthful. Besides, he never provokes a fight."

"That kid is a menace to the neighborhood!" Angela fumed, after the three boys had settled down in front of the TV with a pitcher of lemonade.

We had moved out to our screened back porch and Angela was still so angry that her paring knife sliced with wicked precision as she frenched the string beans for dinner.

"But the doctors must love him," Jill said wryly. "Five days into summer vacation and he's drawn blood at least four times that I know of."

She stopped helping Angela with the beans and ticked off the incidents on her fingers. "Dot's boy had to have three stitches after Georgie threw a rock at him; he pushed little Nancy Smith onto a broken bottle; my Chris got a cut on his chin when Georgie tripped him yesterday, and now your Matt. How we'll get through this summer without having all our kids put in the hospital, I don't know."

"Somebody ought to do something about him," Angela said, giving me a meaningful look.

"Not me," I protested. "The last time I complained to Watson about Georgie, he waved a monkey wrench in my face and told me adults ought to let kids fight it out among themselves."

"I know!" Jill exclaimed brightly. "Let's hire a couple of twelve-year-olds to beat him up!"

"The Watsons would sue," said Angela glumly.

"Maybe they'll send him to camp or something this year," I offered hopefully.

"Not a chance," Angela said. "Mrs. Watson couldn't be separated from him that long."

She finished the beans, wiped the paring knife on the seat of her denim shorts, then gazed out through the early evening twilight toward the gully, absentmindedly thwacking the handle of the knife on the palm of her hand.

"Think positively," she said suddenly. "Maybe Georgie did us a favor just now."

Jill and I looked at each other blankly.

"Maybe that rope isn't safe to swing on," she said.

"But it's good and strong, Mrs. Barrett," Chris volunteered from the doorway. Their program over, the three boys had drifted out to the porch.

"Yeah, Mom," Sandy added. "I tied it with a square knot, just like Dad showed me."

"He did," echoed Matt with all the assurance of one who hadn't even mastered a granny knot yet.

Angela grinned at him and tousled his hair, a gesture he hated. "Just the same, I'd feel better if your father and I took a look at it."

So out we all went, across the already dew-dampened grass to the gully, and while I examined the rope for signs of fraying, Angela swung her lithe hundred pounds up into the willow tree with catlike grace. Matt and Sandy are the envy of their peers with a mother who thinks nothing of dropping her work and her dignity to shinny up a tree for a tangled kite or to clamber onto a roof to get a ball lodged in the rain gutters.

"It seems strong enough," I said. "What about the knot, Angela?" Between the leaves and the fading light, I could barely see her.

She poked her neat little pointed face through the willow leaves. "I really don't think it's safe, Alex. Maybe you could pick up a stronger rope tomorrow."

She dropped to the ground, barely panting with the exertion. "It's a fine knot," she said to Sandy, "but the rope *is* old. Dad'll get you another tomorrow; but until he does, I want your solemn promise that you won't swing on it or let any of your friends swing on it."

"That goes for you, too, Chris," Jill said.

"Well it doesn't go for me!" sneered a juvenile voice.

We whirled, and there was dear old Georgie, cocky in the security of knowing that we were too civilized to smack the impertinence off his face.

"Oh, yes, it does," Angela contradicted coldly. "If it isn't strong enough to hold the little ones, it isn't strong enough to hold you."

Georgie flushed at this allusion to his weight. It seemed to be his only sensitive spot. "You're not my mother," he yelled, "and I don't have to mind you!"

I took a step toward him, my civility rapidly retreating before a barbarous desire to flatten him, but Angela restrained me.

"It's dangerous, Georgie, so you'll just have to stay off of it," she said, and took the end of the rope and tossed it up into the tree.

"I can still get it," Georgie taunted, but be showed no inclination to do so, with me blocking his path.

At that moment, Mrs. Watson called him in for the evening. Jill suddenly remembered that she'd forgotten to take a steak out of the freezer and headed for home with Chris, while Angela, Sandy and I gave Matt a head start before racing to our own back door.

The prospect of a long summer spent coping with Georgie Watson, together with the usual mayhem of feeding, tubbing and bedding our two young acrobats, blotted out the interrupted conversation I'd been having with Angela until we were in bed ourselves. I remembered it with a jolt.

"Didn't the police suspect anything?" I asked in the semidarkness of our bedroom.

"The police were very sympathetic and nice," Angela murmured sleepily. "They could see he had locked the bathroom door himself. Actually, all I had done was balance the radio too close to the edge of the shelf and hoped for the best." As if that ended it, she rolled over and put the pillow over her head.

"Oh, no, you don't!" I muttered, lifting the pillow, for I had just recalled something else. "What about 'The Perfect Example'?"

"Sh!" she whispered. "You'll wake the boys."

"Well, did you?" I whispered hoarsely.

In that city neighborhood where we had spent our first two years of marriage, home had been a second floor walkup in a converted brownstone. Its age, dinginess and general state of deterioration were somewhat ameliorated by the low rent and large, relatively soundproof rooms, and it attracted several other young couples.

We were all blithely green at life and marriage, determined to succeed in both, and that old house would have exuded happiness had it not been for the constantly disapproving eye of our landlady.

She lived on the third floor of the house, and every time the outer vestibule door opened she would appear on the landing, lean over the wobbly old mahogany railing and peer down the marble stairwell, hoping to catch someone sneaking in a forbidden pet or leaving a shopping cart in the vestibule.

She bullied her husband, tyrannized her three timorous daughters, and took a malicious delight in stirring up animosity among her tenants. "I don't care what that snip in 2-D says," she would confide to her innocent victim, "I think your clothes are very ladylike."

It was only after you had lived in the house a couple of months that you realized she was putting lies in your mouth, too. It was like an initiation to a fraternity, that first two months. Afterward, you would laugh with the more experienced tenants and compare the lies as they recalled, with amusing mimicry, how they knew by your icy expression exactly when she had slandered them to you.

She was such a perfect example of everything the young wives never wanted to become that we all called her "The Perfect Example" behind her back.

It was bad enough when she pitted couple against couple, but it stopped being funny when she managed to slip her knifed tongue into a shaky marriage, as happened twice while we lived there. The first marriage probably would have crumbled anyhow, but the second was a couple of teenagers deeply in love but handicapped by parental opposition and the sheer inexperience of youth.

When she discovered what was happening, Angela broke the rule of silence and tried to make them understand how "The Perfect Example" was destroying them, but it was too late. The girl went home to her parents and the boy stormed off to California.

Never had I seen Angela so blazingly angry. "She's like a big fat spider, leaning on that railing, watching us flies walk in and out, spinning her web for the defenseless midges!" she raged, almost in tears. "Why aren't there laws against people like that?"

So it had seemed like divine vengeance when, two days later, the decrepit mahogany railing had finally pulled loose from the wall and collapsed under her weight, and "The Perfect Example" had plummeted to the marble tiles of the vestibule three floors below. As soon as the police had declared her death a regrettable accident, her husband had put the house up for sale and happily removed himself and the three dazed daughters back to the corn fields of his native Kansas.

"What about 'The Perfect Example'?" I repeated, shaking Angela.

"Oh, Alex," she pleaded, "it's after midnight."

"I want to know."

"She knew the house was old, but she was too miserly to spend a cent

in repairs. That rail would have collapsed sooner or later—you heard the
police say that—and I just helped it along a bit. And don't forget that I told
her it wasn't safe to lean against all the time."

"That was sporting of you," I said bitterly. "Just because you warned
those two—that is all, isn't it—you think that justifies everything!

"Tell me something, Angela—*Angela!* Boy, your parents had some
sense of humor when they named you!—how do you see yourself? As an
avenging angel or Little Mary Sunshine scattering rays of joy through
oppressed lives?"

"I'll tell you how I see myself, Alex Barrett," she said in exasperation,
propping herself up on one slim elbow. "I see myself as the very tired
mother of two boys who are going to be awake and wanting their break-
fasts in about five or six hours! I see myself as the wife of a man who wants
to hash over every petty little incident that happened *years ago* when I am
exhausted!"

She fell back upon the bed and plopped the pillow over her head again.
I didn't think it prudent to take it off a second time; she might decide to
tell me it wasn't safe. "Petty little incident," indeed!

The night was broken by restless dreams in which I defended Angela
before massed benches of irate judges and policemen who demanded
adequate reasons why she should not be taken out and hanged. They were
unmoved when I argued that she was a perfect wife and tender mother, and
it only seemed to infuriate them when I added that she in no way *looked*
like a murderess. Through it all, a hooded hangman with a frayed
clothesline rope looped around his shoulders swung back and forth on the
chandelier chanting, "We're going to give her the rope! The rope! We're
going to give her the rope! The rope!"

Shreds of the dream clung to me all day. I couldn't rid myself of a
feeling of apprehension, and when I stopped at a hardware store after work
to buy Sandy's new rope, it seemed as if I were somehow adding to
Angela's guilt.

As I drove into the carport late that afternoon, I saw Sandy rummaging
in the toolshed. "I got your Tarzan rope for you," I called.

"Thanks, Dad," he said, dragging out an old tarp, "but we're going to
play army men. Can me and Chris and Matt have this for a tent in the
gully?"

"O.K., but aren't you afraid Georgie will tear it down?"

"Oh, we don't have to worry about him anymore," Sandy said cheerfully, and disappeared around the corner of the house before I could find
my voice.

Oh, no, I thought, and roared, "*Angela!*" as I tore into the house, nearly ripping the screen from its hinges. No answer.

"Surely Sandy would have thought it worth mentioning if the police had carted his mother off to jail," I jittered to myself, trying to look at the situation coolly. "Angela!"

Then I heard her voice: "Alex! I'm over here at Jill's. Come on over," she called.

"Hi, Alex!" Jill caroled as I pushed open their screen. "We're sort of celebrating. Want a drink?"

Women! Were they all so cold-blooded that they could murder a child, obnoxious as that child had been, without turning a hair? I sank down on the porch glider, unable to speak for the moment.

"Poor dear," said Angela solicitously. "Did you have a bad day? You look so drained."

"What happened to Georgie?" I demanded, glaring at Angela.

"Didn't Sandy tell you?" asked Jill as she handed me the tall cool drink that I so desperately needed. "He was swinging on the boys' Tarzan rope and it broke with him. He fractured both legs, one in two places," she added with satisfaction.

"He wasn't killed?" I croaked weakly.

"Of course not, Alex," said Angela. "How could he have been? There weren't any rocks under the rope and that stretch of gully is mostly grass."

"I hate to seem ghoulish," Jill said, "but it really does make the summer for us. By the time he gets out of those casts and off his crutches, school will be open again."

She grinned at Angela. "I just can't believe it! A whole summer without Georgie Watson beating up every little kid in sight!"

"Just a lucky break for everyone," I murmured sarcastically. There was no point in asking if the break had occurred up by the knot which Angela had examined last night.

"Well, it is," Jill insisted stoutly. "And as I told Mrs. Watson, it was his own fault. Angela very specifically warned him not to swing on that old rope till you could get a stronger one."

"Angela's very thoughtful that way," I observed.

At least she had the grace to blush.

The next day, a Saturday, even I was forced to admit that if it were any indication, it was going to be a very relaxed summer. The boys peacefully slaughtered the bad guys all day in the gully without once running in to us with tearful tales of Georgie's latest tyranny.

After all, I thought as I watched an afternoon baseball game undisturbed, *maybe a summer of enforced solitude will be good for Georgie's character.*

When I awoke early Sunday morning, my subconscious had completed the job of rationalizing the situation: don't some wives occasionally bring unusual talents to their marriages? If a woman loves to tinker with machinery, is it wrong to let her clean the carburetor on the family car? If she wants to paint the house herself, take up tailoring as a hobby, or learn how to fix the plumbing—if, in short, her oddball talents add to the comfort and serenity of her family—should her husband make an issue of it if it doesn't get out of hand?

That settled, I turned over in bed and began drifting off to sleep again when the loud spluttering roar of a lawn mower exploded on the morning quiet. I shot up in bed, examined the clock and groaned: 7:02 a.m.!

I buried my bead under a pillow, but the racket rose in volume. There was no way to escape it.

Sighing, I leaned over and kissed Angela's bare shoulder. "M-m?" she murmured drowsily.

"Angela," I whispered, "do you suppose you could give Mr. Watson a reason why it isn't safe to mow his lawn before nine a.m.?"

Alfred Hitchcock's Mystery Magazine, June 1970

The Beast Within

We were still living in Brooklyn when our young son found an abused and probably brain-damaged kitten in the alley and talked us into letting him keep it. It grew into a malevolent creature that would scratch if you stroked it more than once. I was downstairs alone late one night, immersed in a book, when I suddenly realized that I was being watched. My eyes went instantly to the front drapes, but they were pulled tightly together. Uneasily I glanced around and saw the cat sitting six feet away. His eyes seemed to catch the lamplight and he stared at me with an eerie hostility that I have never forgotten. When he ran away, I did not put up placards around the neighborhood and this story was written to exorcise his memory.

E arly summer twilight had begun to soften the city's harsh outlines as Tessa pushed aside the sliding glass doors and stepped out onto the terrace. Up here on the twenty-sixth floor, dusk blurred the sharp ugly planes of surrounding buildings and even brought an eerie beauty to the skeletal girders of the new skyscraper going up next door. Gray-haired, middle-aged and emotionally drained by her last confrontation with Clarence, Tessa leaned heavily fleshed arms on the railing of their penthouse terrace and let the warm night air enfold her.

From the street far, far below, muffled sounds of evening traffic floated up to her and for a moment she considered jumping. To end it all in one brief instant of broken flesh while ambulances screamed and the curious stared—what real difference would it make to her, to Clarence, to anyone, if she lived another day or year or twenty years?

Nevertheless, she stepped back from the railing unconsciously, the habit of life too deeply rooted in her psyche. With a few cruel and indifferent words, Clarence had destroyed her world; but he had not destroyed her will to live. Not yet.

She glanced across the narrow space to the uncompleted building. The workmen who filled the daylight hours with a cacophony of rivets and protesting winches were gone now, leaving behind, for safety, hundreds of small bare light bulbs. In the mild breeze, they swung on their wires like chained fireflies in the dusk.

Tessa smiled at the thought. How long had it been since she had seen real fireflies drift through summer twilight? Surely not more than half a dozen times since marrying Clarence all those years ago—God! Was it really almost forty years now? She no longer hated the city, but she had never forgiven it for not having fireflies—nor for blocking out the Milky Way with its star-quenching skyscrapers.

When he first brought her away from the country, Clarence had probably loved her as much as he was capable of loving anyone; yet even then he hadn't understood her unease at living in a place so eternally and brilliantly lit. When his friends complimented them on the penthouse and marveled at the size of their terrace (enormous even by those booming postwar standards of the Fifties), he would laugh and say, "I bought it for Tessa. Can't fence in a country girl. They need 'land, lots of land 'neath the starry skies above!' "

It hadn't taken her long to realize he'd bought the penthouse to feed his own vanity, not to still her unspoken needs. Eventually, she stopped caring. If this terrace weren't high enough above the neon glare to see her favorite stars, it at least provided as much quiet as one could expect in a city. She could always lie back on one of the cushioned chaises and remember how the Milky Way swirled in and out of the constellations; remember the dainty charm of the Pleiades tucked away in Taurus the Bull.

But not tonight. Instead of star-studded skies, memory forced her to relive the past hour in every humiliating and painful detail.

She was long since reconciled to the fact that Clarence did not love her; but after years of trying to mold herself to his standards, she had thought that he was comfortable with her and that she was necessary to him in all the other spheres that hold a marriage together after passion fades away.

Tonight, Clarence had made it brutally clear: not only was she not necessary, she was a boring encumbrance. Further, the woman she'd become, in her efforts to please him, was the antithesis of the woman he'd chosen as her replacement.

Tessa had followed him through their apartment in a daze as he packed his suitcases to leave. Mechanically, she had handed him clean shirts and underwear; then, seeing what a mess he was making of those perfectly tailored suits, she had taken over the actual packing as she always did when he went away on business trips. Only this time, he was going further than he ever had before, to a midtown hotel, out of her life.

"But why?" she asked, smoothing a crease in his gray slacks.

They had met Lynn Herrick at one of his sister-in-law's parties. Aggressive and uninhibited, her dress was blatantly sexual and her long black hair frizzed in a cloud around her bare shoulders. Tessa had thought the young woman brittle and obvious, hardly Clarence's type, and she had been amused by Ms. Herrick's brazenly flirtatious approach. "Why this one?" she demanded again, knowing there had been other, more suitable women over the years.

A fatuous expression spread across Clarence's face, a blend of pride, sheepishness and defiance. "Because she's going to bear my child," he said pompously.

It was the ultimate blow. For years Tessa had pleaded for a child, only to have Clarence take every precaution to prevent one.

"You've always loathed children. You said they were whining, slobbering nuisances!"

"It wasn't my fault," Clarence protested. "Accidents happen."

"I'll bet!" Tessa muttered crudely, knowing that nothing accidental ever happens to the Lynn Herricks of the world.

Clarence chose to ignore her remark. "Now that it's happened, Lynn's made me see how much I owe it to myself. And to the company. Another Loughlin to carry our name into the next century since it doesn't look as if Richard and Alison will ever produce an heir."

Richard Loughlin was Clarence's much younger brother and only living relative. Together they had inherited control of a prosperous chain of department stores begun by their grandfather. Although Tessa had heard Richard remark wistfully that a child might be fun, his wife Alison shared Clarence's previous attitude toward offspring; and her distaste was strengthened by the fear of what a child might do to her size eight figure.

With Clarence reveling in the newfound joys of prospective fatherhood, Tessa had snapped shut the final suitcase. Still in a daze, she stared at her reflection in the mirror over his dresser and was appalled.

In her conscious mind, she had known that she was well past fifty, that her hair was gray, her figure no longer slim; and she had known that Clarence would never let her have children—but deep inside, down at the primal core of her being, a young, half-wild girl cried out in protest at this old and barren woman she had become.

The siren of a fire engine on the street far below drew Tessa to the edge of the terrace again. Night had fallen completely and traffic was thin now. The sidewalks were nearly deserted.

She still felt outraged at being cast aside so summarily—as if a pat on the shoulder, the promise of lavish alimony, and an "I told Lynn you'd be sensible about everything" were enough to compensate for thirty-six years of her life—but at least her brief urge toward self-destruction had dissipated.

She stared again at the bobbing safety lights of the uncompleted building and remembered that the last time she'd seen fireflies had been six years ago, after Richard and Alison returned from their honeymoon. She and Clarence had gone down to Pennsylvania to help warm the old farm Richard had bought as a wedding surprise for Alison.

The hundred and thirty acres of overgrown fields and woodlands had indeed been a surprise to that urban young woman. Alison's idea of a suitable weekend retreat was a modern beach house on Martha's Vineyard.

Tessa had loved it and had tramped the woods with Richard, wind-blown and exhilarated, while Alison and Clarence complained about mosquitoes and dredged up pressing reasons to cut short their stay. Although Alison had been charming and had assured Richard that she was delighted with his gift, she found excellent excuses not to accompany him on his infrequent trips to the farm.

Remembering its isolation, Tessa wondered if Richard would mind if she buried herself there for a while. Perhaps in the country she could sort things out and grope her way back to the wild freedom she had known all those years ago, before Clarence took her to the city and "housebroke" her, as he'd expressed it in the early years of their marriage.

A cat's terrified yowl caught her attention. She looked up and saw it running along one of the steel girders that stuck out several feet from a higher level of the new building. The cat raced out as if pursued by the three-headed hound of Hell, and its momentum was too great to stop when it realized the danger.

It soared off the end of the girder and landed in a sickening thump on the terrace awning. With an awkward twist of its furry body, the cat leaped to the terrace floor and cowered under one of the chaises, quivering with panic.

Tessa watched the end of the girder, expecting to see a battle-scarred tom spoiling for a fight. Although cats seldom made it up this high, it was not unusual to see one taking a shortcut across her terrace from one rooftop to another, up and down fire escapes.

When no other cat appeared, Tessa turned her attention to the frightened animal. The night air had roused that touch of arthritis that had begun to bother her this year, and it was an effort to bend down beside the lounge chair. She tried to coax the cat out, but it shrank away from her hand.

"Here, kitty, kitty," she murmured. "It's all right. There's no one chasing you now."

She had always liked cats and, for that reason, refused to own one. It was too easy to let a small animal become a proxy child. She sympathized with Richard's mild disapproval whenever Alison called their dachshund "baby."

Patiently, she waited for the cat to stop trembling and to sniff her outstretched hand; but even though she kept her voice low and soothing, it would not abandon its shelter. Tessa's calcified joints protested against her crouch and creaked as she straightened up and stepped back a few feet.

The cat edged out then, suspiciously poised for flight. From the living room lamps beyond the glass doors, light fell across it and revealed a young female with crisp black-and-gray markings and white paws. Judging from its leggy thinness, it hadn't eaten in some time.

"You poor thing," Tessa said, moved by its uneasy trust. "I'll bet you're starving."

As if it understood Tessa meant no harm, the cat did not skitter aside when she moved past it into the apartment.

Soon she was back with a saucer of milk and a generous chunk of rare beef which she'd recklessly cut from the heart of their untouched dinner roast. "Better you than a garbage bag, kitty. No one else wants it."

Stiff-legged and wary, the young cat approached the food and sniffed; then, clumsily, it tore at the meat and almost choked in its haste.

"Slow down!" Tessa warned, and bent over heavily to pull the meat into smaller pieces. "You're an odd one. Didn't you ever eat meat before?" She tried to stroke the cat's thin back, but it quivered and slipped away from her plump hand. "Sorry, cat. I was just being friendly."

She sank down onto one of the chaises and watched the animal finish its meal. When the meat was gone, it turned to the saucer of milk and drank messily with much sneezing and shaking of its small head as it inadvertently got milk in its nose.

Tessa was amused but a bit puzzled. She'd never seen a cat so graceless and awkward. It acted almost like a young, untutored kitten; and when it finished eating and sat staring at her, Tessa couldn't help laughing aloud. "Didn't your mother teach you *anything*, silly? You're supposed to wash your paws and whiskers now."

The cat moved from the patch of light where it had sat silhouetted, its face in darkness. With purposeful caution, it circled the chaise until Tessa was between it and the terrace doors. Light from the living room fell full in its eyes there and was caught and reflected with an eerie intensity.

Tessa shivered uneasily as the animal's luminous eyes met her own with unblinking steadiness. "Now I see why cats are always linked with the supernatu—"

Suddenly it was as if she were a rabbit frozen in the middle of a back-country road by the headlights of a speeding car. Those feral eyes bored into her brain with a spiraling vortex of blinding light. A roaring numbness gripped her. Her mind was assaulted—mauled and dragged down and under and through—existence without shape, time without boundaries.

It lasted forever; it was over in an instant; and somewhere amid the splintered, whirling clamor came an awareness of another's existence, a being formless and desperate and terrified beyond sanity.

There was mingling.

Tessa felt the other's panic.

There was passing.

Then fierce exultation.

There was a brief, weird sensation of being unbearably compacted and compressed; the universe seemed to tilt and swirl; then it was over. The light faded to normal city darkness, the roaring stopped, and she knew she was sprawled upon the cool flagstones of the terrace.

She tried to push herself up, but her body responded queerly. Dazed, she looked around and screamed at the madness of a world suddenly magnified in size—a scream which choked off as she caught sight of someone enormous sitting on the now-huge chaise.

A plump, middle-aged, gray-haired woman held her face between trembling hands and moaned, "Thank God! Thank God!"

Shocked, Tessa realized that she was seeing her own face for the first time without the reversing effect of a mirror. Her shock intensified as she looked down through slitted eyes and saw neat white paws instead of her own hands. With alien instinct, she felt the ridge of her spine quiver as fur stood on end. She tried to speak and was horrified to hear a feline yowl emerge.

The woman on the chaise—Tessa could no longer think of that body as herself—stopped moaning then and watched her warily. "You're not mad, if that's what you're wondering. Not yet, anyhow. Though you'll maybe go mad if you don't get out of that skin in time."

She snatched up a cushion and flung it at Tessa.

"Shoo! G'wan, scat!" she gibbered. "You can't make me look in your eyes. I'll never get caught again. Scat, damn you!"

Startled, Tessa sprang to the railing of the terrace and teetered there awkwardly. The body had begun to respond, but she wasn't sure how well she could control it, and twenty-six stories above street level was too high to allow for much error.

The woman who had stolen her body seemed afraid to come closer. "You might as well go!" she snarled at Tessa. She threw a calculating glance at the luxurious interior beyond the glass doors.

"It's a lousy body—too old and too fat—but it looks like a rich one and it's human and I'm keeping it, so scat!"

Tessa's new reflexes were quicker than those of her old body. Before the shoe even left the other's hand, she had dropped to the narrow ledge that circled the exterior of the penthouse. Residual instinct made her footing firm as she followed the ledge around the corner of the building to the fire escape for an easy climb to the roof. There, in comparative safety from flying shoes and incipient plunges to the street, Tessa drew up to consider the situation.

Cat's body or not, came the wry thought, *it's still my mind.*

Absently licking away the dried milk that stuck to her whiskers, she plumbed the sensations of her new body and discovered that vestigial traces of former identities clung to this brain. Mere wisps they were, like perfume hanging in a closed room, yet enough to piece together a picture of what had happened to her on the terrace below.

The one who had just stolen her body had been young and sly, but not overly bright. Judging from the terror and panic so freshly imprinted, she had fled through the city and taken the first body she could.

Behind those raw emotions lay a cooler, more calculating undertone and Tessa knew that one had been more mature; had chosen the girl's body deliberately and after much thought. Not for her the hasty grabbing of the first opportunity. Instead, she had stalked her prey with care, taking a body that was pretty, healthy and, above all, young.

Beyond those two, Tessa could not sort out the other personalities whose lingering traces she felt. Nor could she know who had been the first or how it had all started. Probing too deeply, she recoiled from the touch of a totally alien animal essence struggling for consciousness—the underlying basic catness of this creature whose body she now inhabited.

Tessa clamped down ruthlessly on these primeval stirrings, forcing them back under. This must be what the girl meant about going mad. How long could a person stay in control?

The answer, of course, was to get back into a human body. Tessa pattered softly to the edge of the roof and peered down at the terrace. Below, the girl in her body still cowered on the chaise as if unable to walk into the apartment and assume possession. Her shoulders slumped and she looked old and defeated.

She's right, thought Tessa. *It is a lousy body. Let her keep it.*

At that moment, she could almost pity the young thief who had stolen her most personal possession; but the moment was short-lived. With spirits soaring, Tessa danced across the black-tarred roof on nimble paws. Joyfully she experimented with her new body and essayed small leaps into the night air. No more arthritis, no excess flab to make her gasp for breath. What bliss to think a motion and have lithe muscles respond!

Drunk with new physical prowess, she raced to the fire escape, leaped to the railing and recklessly threw herself out into space. There was one sickening moment when she felt she must have misjudged, then she caught herself on a jutting scaffold and scrambled onto it.

Adrenalin coursed in her veins and her confidence grew with each step that carried her further and further away from familiar haunts. She prowled the night streets boldly, recapturing memories and emotions almost forgotten in those air-conditioned, temperature-controlled, insulated years with Clarence. Never again, she vowed, would she settle for less than this.

Freed of her old woman's body, she felt a oneness again with—what? The world? Nature? God?

The name didn't matter, only the feeling. Even here in the city, in the heart of man's farthest retreat into artifice, she felt it, and a nameless longing welled within her.

What it must be to have a cat's body in the country! Yet even as the thought formed in her mind, Tessa shivered in sudden fear. It would be too much. To be in this body with grass and dirt underneath, surrounded by trees and bushes alive with small rustlings, with uncluttered sky overhead—a human mind might well go mad with so much sensory stimulation.

No, better the city with its concrete and cars and crush of people to remind her that she was human and that this body was only temporary.

Still, she thought, descending gracefully from the top of a shuttered newsstand, *how dangerous could a small taste be?*

She ran west along half-deserted streets, heading for the park. On the crosstown streets, traffic was light; but crossing the avenues scared her. The rumble and throb of all those motors, the many lights and impatient horns kept her fur on end. She had to force herself to step off the curb at Fifth Avenue; and as she darted across its wide expanse, she half expected to be crushed beneath a cab.

The park was a haven now. Gratefully she dived between its fence railings and melted into the safety of its dark bushes.

❖ ❖ ❖

In the next few hours, Tessa shed the rest of the shackles of her life with Clarence, her years of thinking "What will Clarence say?" when she gave way to an impulsive act; the fear of being considered quaint by his friends if she spoke her inmost thoughts.

If Pan were a god, she truly worshiped him that night! Abandoning herself to instinctual joys, she raced headlong down grassy hills, rolled paws over tail-tip in the moonlight; chased a sleepy, crotchety squirrel through the treetops, then skimmed down to the duck pond to lap daintily at the water and dabble at goldfish turned silver in the moonbeams.

As the moon slid below the tall buildings west of the park, she ate flesh of her own killing. Later—behind the Mad Hatter's bronze toadstool—she crooned a voluptuous invitation and allowed the huge ginger male who had stalked her for an hour to approach her, to circle ever nearer . . .

As he grasped her by the scruff and began to mount, the alien animal consciousness below exploded into dominance, surging across her will in wave after roiling wave of raw sexuality with every pelvic thrust. Thrice more they coupled in excruciating ecstasy, and only when the ginger tom had spent himself into exhaustion was she able to reassert her will and force that embryonic consciousness back to submission.

❖ ❖ ❖

Just before dawn, a neat feline head poked through the railing at Fifth and East 64th Street and hesitated as it surveyed the deserted avenue, empty now of all traffic save an occasional bus.

Reassured, Tessa stepped out onto the sidewalk and sat on narrow haunches to smooth and groom her ruffled striped fur. She was shaken by the night's experiences, but complacently unrepentant. No matter what lay ahead, these last few hours were now part of her soul and worth any price she might yet have to pay.

Nevertheless, the strength of this body's true owner was growing and Tessa knew that another night would be a dangerous risk. She had to find another body, and soon.

Whose?

Lynn Herrick flashed to mind. How wickedly poetic it would be to take her rival's sexy young body, bear Clarence's child, and stick Lynn with a body which, after last night, would soon be producing offspring of its own. But she knew too little about that man-eating tramp to feel confident taking over that particular life.

No, she was limited to someone familiar, someone young, someone unpleasantly deserving and, above all, someone close. She must be within transferring distance before the city's morning rush hour forced her back into the park until dark—an unthinkable risk.

The logical candidate sprang to mind.

Of course! she thought. *Keep it in the family.*

Angling across Fifth Avenue, she pattered north toward the luxurious building that housed the younger Loughlins. Her tail twitched jauntily as she scampered along the sidewalk and considered the potentials of Alison's body. For starters, it was almost thirty years younger.

The deception might be tricky at first, but she had met all of Alison's few near relatives. As for surface friends who filled the aimless rounds of her sister-in-law's social life, Tessa knew they could be dropped without causing a ripple of curiosity—especially if her life became filled with babies. That should please Richard. *Dear Richard!*

Dear Richard? Tessa was intrigued. When had her brother-in-law become so dear? Richard was a small boy when she and Clarence married, and she had always considered the tenderness he roused in her a sort of frustrated maternalism, especially since he was so comfortable to be with. Somewhere along the line, tender maternalism had apparently transmuted into something earthier; and all at once, wistful might-have-beens were exciting possibilities.

❖ ❖ ❖

Behind the heavy bronze and glass doors of Richard's building, a sleepy doorman nodded on his feet. The sun was not yet high enough to lighten the doorway under its pink-and-gray striped awning, and deep shadows camouflaged her own stripes.

Keeping a low silhouette, she crouched outside and waited. When the doorman opened the door for an early-rising tenant, she darted inside and streaked across the lobby to hide behind a large marble ash stand beside the elevator.

The rest would be simple as the elevator was large, dimly lit, and paneled in dark mahogany. She would conceal herself under the pink velvet bench at the rear of the car and wait until it eventually stopped at Alison and Richard's floor.

Her tail twitched with impatience. When the elevator finally descended, she poised herself to spring.

The door slid back and bedlam broke loose in a welter of shrill barks, tangled leash and startled, angry exclamations. The dog was upon her, front and back, yipping and snapping before she knew what was happening.

Automatically, she spat and raked the dog's nose with her sharp claws, which set off a frenzy of jumping and straining against the leash and sent his master sprawling.

Tessa only had time to recognize that it was Richard, taking Liebchen out for a pre-breakfast walk, before she felt herself being whacked by the elevator man's newspaper.

All avenues of escape were closed to her and she was given no time to think or gather her wits before the street doors were flung open and she was harried out onto the sidewalk.

Angry and disgusted with herself and the dog, Tessa checked her headlong flight some yards down the sidewalk and glared back at the entrance of the building where the dachshund smugly waddled down the shallow steps and pulled Richard off in the opposite direction.

So the front is out, thought Tessa. *I wonder if their flank is so well-guarded?*

It pleased her to discover that those years of easy compliance with Clarence's wishes had not blunted her initiative. She was not about to be thwarted now by any little canine frankfurter.

Halfway around the block, she found an alley that led to a small service court. From the top of a dumpster, she managed to spring to the first rung of a fire escape and scramble up.

As she climbed, the night's exertions began to pull at her physical reserves. Emotional exhaustion added its weight, too. Paw over paw, up and up, while every muscle begged for rest and her mind became a foggy treadmill able to hold but a single thought: paw in front of paw.

It seemed to take hours. Up thirteen steps to the landing, right turn; up thirteen steps to the landing, left turn, with such regular monotony that her mind became stupid with the endless repetition of black iron steps.

At the top landing, a ten-rung ladder rose straight to the roof. Her body responded sluggishly to this final effort and she sank down upon the tarred rooftop in utter exhaustion. The sun was high in the sky now; and with the last dregs of energy, Tessa crept into the shade of an overhanging ledge and was instantly asleep.

When she awoke in the late afternoon, the last rays of sunlight were slanting across the city. Hunger and thirst she could ignore for the time, but what of the quickening excitement that twilight was bringing?

She crept to the roof's edge and peered down at the empty terrace overlooking the park. An ivied trellis offered easy descent and she crouched behind a potted shrub to look through the doors. On such a mild day, the glass doors had been left open behind their fine-meshed screens.

Inside, beyond an elegant living room, Alison's housekeeper set the table in the connecting dining room. There was no sign of Alison or Richard—or of Liebchen. Cautiously, Tessa pattered along the terrace to the screened doors of their bedroom, but it too was empty.

As she waited, darkness fell completely. From deep within she felt the impatient tail-flick of awareness. She felt it respond to a cat's guttural cry two rooftops away, felt it surfacing against her will, pulled by the promise of another night of dark paths and wild ecstasy.

Desperately, she struggled with that other ego, fought it blindly and knew that soon her strength would not be enough.

Suddenly the terrace was flooded with light as all the lamps inside the apartment were switched on. Startled, the other self retreated; and Tessa heard Alison's light voice tell the housekeeper, "Just leave dinner on the stove, Mitchum. You can clear away in the morning."

"Yes, Mrs. Loughlin, and I want you and Mr. Loughlin to know how sorry I am that—"

"Thank you, Mitchum," came Richard's voice, cutting her off.

Tessa sat motionless in the shadows outside and watched Liebchen trot across the room and scramble onto a low chair, unmindful of her nearness.

As Richard mixed drinks, Alison said, "It's so horrible. Poor Tessa. Those delusions that she's really a young girl—that she's never met Clarence or either of us. Do you suppose she's trying to fake a mental breakdown?"

"How can you say that? You saw her wretchedness. It wasn't an act."

"But—"

"What a shock it must have been to have him ask for a divorce after all these years. Did you know about it?" His voice was harsh with emotion. "You introduced Lynn to Clarence. Did you encourage them?"

"Honestly, darling," Alison said scornfully. "You act as if *Tessa's* been victimized."

"Maybe she has." Richard sounded tired now and infinitely sad. "In more ways than either of us can possibly know. You should have seen her when they were first married—so fresh and open and full of laughter. I was only a kid, but I remember. I'd never met an adult like her. All our stodgy relatives were snide to her. They said she was a gold-digging country hick. *I* thought she was like an April breeze blowing through this family and I was proud of Clarence for breaking out of the mold."

He gazed bleakly into his glass. "After Father died, they sent me away to school and it was years before I really saw her again. I couldn't believe the change; all the laughter gone, her guarded words. Clarence did a thorough job of cramming both of them back into the Loughlin mold. First he kills her spirit and then he has the nerve to call her dull! No wonder she's retreated into her youth, to a time before she knew him. You heard the psychiatrist. He doesn't think she's faking."

"Perhaps not," Alison said coolly, "but you seem to keep forgetting: Clarence may have killed her spirit, but Tessa's killed him."

In the shadows outside the screen, Tessa quivered. So they had found Clarence's body! That poor thieving child! At the sight of Clarence lying on the bedroom floor with his head crushed in, she must have panicked again.

"I haven't forgotten," Richard said. "And I haven't forgotten Lynn Herrick either. If what Clarence told me yesterday is true, I'll have to make some sort of arrangement for the child out of Clarence's estate."

"Don't be naive," said Alison. "I'm sure she merely let Clarence believe what he wanted. Trust me, darling. Lynn's far too clever to take on motherhood without a wedding ring and community property laws."

"You mean the divorce—his death—Tessa's insanity—all this was based on lies? And you knew it? You did! I can see it in your face!"

"Oh, please!" Alison snapped. She stood abruptly and stalked across the room. "Yes, I introduced them, but you can't blame me for your brother's stupidity. Clarence was sixty-three years old and Lynn made him feel like a young stud again. If Tessa couldn't hang on to him, why shouldn't Lynn have tried to land him?"

Richard stood, too, and freshened his drink. "Is that what marriage is to you? A hanging-on?"

But Alison had gone into the kitchen and appeared not to have heard when she returned with a large tray. As she began to arrange dishes and food on a low table in front of the couch, Liebchen put interested paws on the edge of the table, but Richard shoved him aside.

"There's no need to take it out on Liebchen," she said angrily. "Come along, baby. Mummy has something nice for you in the kitchen."

On little short legs, the dachshund trotted after Alison and disappeared into the kitchen. Relieved, Tessa moved nearer to the screen.

When Alison reentered the room, she left the kitchen door closed and her flash of anger had been replaced by a mask of solicitude. She made sandwiches, poured hot tea and spoke in soothing tones.

Richard ate mechanically, then stood up and reached for his jacket.

"Must you really go out again tonight, darling? Can't things wait till morning?"

"You know lawyers," he sighed. "Everything's going to be doubly complicated by the way he died."

"That's right," Alison said thoughtfully. "Murderers can't inherit from their victims, can they? No, don't pull away from me like that, darling. I feel just as badly for Tessa as you do, but we have to face up to it. Insane or not, she did kill him."

"Sorry." Richard straightened his tie. "I guess I just can't take it all in yet."

He went down the hall to his study and came back with his briefcase. Alison remained on the couch with her back to him. As Richard sorted through some papers, she said with careful casualness, "If they decide poor Tessa did kill him while of unsound mind and she later snaps out of it, would she then be able to inherit?"

"Probably not legally," Richard answered absently, his mind on the papers. "Wouldn't matter though, since we'd feel morally obliged to see she's fairly provided for."

"Oh, of course," Alison agreed, but her eyes narrowed.

Richard leaned over the couch and kissed her cheek. "I don't know how long this will take. If you're tired, don't wait up."

Alison smiled up at him, but once he was gone and the outer door had latched shut, her smile faded and was replaced by a look of greedy calculation.

Lost in thought, she gazed blindly at the dark square of the screened doorway, unaware of someone watching. Slowly, slowly, Tessa eased up on narrow haunches until lamplight hit her eyes—eyes that were slitted and glowed with abnormal intensity . . .

It was after midnight before Richard came home again. Lying awake on that wide bed, she heard him drop his briefcase on the floor inside his study, then continue on down the hall to the dimly lit bedroom. She held her breath as he opened the door and whispered, "Alison?"

"I'm awake." She turned between the linen sheets. "Oh, Richard, you look absolutely drained. Come to bed."

When at last he lay beside her in the darkness, she touched him shyly and said, "All evening I've been thinking about Tessa and Clarence—about their life together. I've been as rotten to you as he was to Tessa."

Richard made a sound of protest, but she placed slim young fingers against his lips. "No, dearest, let me say it. I've been thinking how empty their marriage was and how ours would be the same if I didn't change. I want to become a whole new person. Will you let me? Let me pretend we just met and that I barely know you? Start new? Please?"

"Alison—"

"No, let me finish. As soon as the funeral's over—as soon as we've arranged for the best legal and medical care that we can give Tessa—could we go away to the farm for a few weeks? Just the two of us?"

Incredulous, Richard propped himself on one elbow and peered into her face. "Do you really mean that?"

She nodded solemnly and he gathered her into his arms, but before he could kiss her properly, the night was broken by an angry, hissing cry.

He sat up abruptly. "What the devil's that?"

"Just a stray cat. It's been out on the terrace all evening." With slender, eager arms, she pulled Richard back down to her, then pitched her voice just loud enough to carry through the screen to the terrace. "If it's still there in the morning, I'll call the animal shelter and have them take it away."

Alfred Hitchcock's Mystery Magazine, July 1972

When Daddy's Gone

My tenth mystery story was the first to draw explicitly on my Southern roots.

Every evening if Daddy wasn't there, soon as it started to get dark, Mama would sneak around to all the doors in the house and lock up: first the screens on the front and side porches, another on the back porch and then the kitchen door itself. She tried to act casual and like it didn't really matter if they were locked or not, but I was eleven that summer and I could tell.

Barefoot like Kessie and me those hot still nights when the chuck-Will's-widow called from the edge of the woods, she'd wander down the wide-planked front hall. "Thought I heard a car," she'd murmur, peering through the screen as if to see Daddy parking his car beyond the long veranda, while all the time her fingers were fitting the brass hook into its little eye.

Then she'd say something about wanting ice water, but she didn't fool me. If she was really thirsty, she'd go down the front hall into the back one and straight to the kitchen. Instead, she took the long way—through the living room and sitting room, where me and Kessie were watching TV, then into the dining room to hook the side door. I always heard the bolt slip home on the kitchen door before she opened the refrigerator.

Kessie never noticed the dark outside all the windows. She was only five and still a baby. Small help she'd have been if somebody tried to come in on us.

Once in a while, when Daddy was gone, I almost wished we lived in a new brick house with such skimpy little windows that we'd need air conditioning. Then we could lock all the wooden doors, pull the drapes tight, and nobody could get in or look in. Instead, our big old house has eight-foot windows and ceilings so high Daddy used to say it'd cost a fortune to air condition. That's why everything's screened and left open to catch the night breezes.

Most times I like it. When Daddy's here, I feel I'm part of the house, all open and comfortable. Besides, we're Thorntons and Thorntons have always lived here. It's not the biggest house around, but it's done us for a hundred and fifty-three years. After Granddaddy died and Daddy married Mama, Grandma Thornton moved in with Aunt Flossie on the other side of the farm.

"You're the lady here now," she told Mama, "and you'll fare better without a mother-in-law watching every change you make."

Except that Mama didn't change anything but her and Daddy's bedroom. She said the house was too big and old-timey to mess with and she used to plague Daddy for one like Aunt Flossie's till he told her to shut up about it.

When Aunt Flossie married Uncle Billy, Granddaddy deeded her that little field where cotton used to grow and built her a nice big brick house on it. Two bathrooms and air conditioned, too, but Aunt Flossie talked spiteful once in a while because she really wanted this house.

She had no cause to be jealous of Daddy getting it, along with most of the land. He was the only living Thornton man, wasn't he? I'd not have been spiteful if Mama'd had another baby like Daddy wanted and it was a boy instead of one more girl like Kessie and me.

But Mama said she wasn't going to ruin her figure having a yardful of daughters just to get Daddy a son, so he treated me like his boy and he put down in his will that someday this would all be mine.

Of course, when Daddy was home, Mama never locked up and the house felt nice and safe; but when he was gone, she jumped at every little noise and even got me to thinking someone might be hiding in the bushes outside, looking in.

Mama was a town girl and I guess she never got used to not having street lights and car noises all night long. She tried to get Daddy to rent out the farm and live in town after they got married, but he wouldn't. He said she'd never have to help out in the fields, but he couldn't live no place else. Mama didn't know that special belonging Daddy and I felt because she was a Riggs and Riggses never owned a pea nor a pot to put it in till Mama was almost grown. We used to drive around town and little bits of her life were scattered all over the place amongst the different houses they'd rented.

Maybe it was her lonesomeness for town noises that made all the night sounds around our house so scary when Daddy wasn't there.

❖ ❖ ❖

Even with the TV going, it was creepy and quiet that night. Kessie's eyes were stuck to the screen tighter'n a tick to a hound's ear and Mama wasn't talking to me again. Some nights, me and Mama and Kessie used to have a ball. She taught us all the yells she did when she was head cheerleader at the town high school and Aunt Flossie said she could hear us all the way across the farm. But ever since my body started changing and Mama started fooling around with Joe Rex Austin, we seemed to hate each other. That night Mama was still mad at me for getting Daddy mad at *her,* so she just sat there staring at the TV till it was Kessie's bedtime.

Like always, Kessie whined it wasn't time yet, but Mama turned off the TV and scooped her up and by the time they reached the stairs, Kessie was giggling. Mama always liked her better than me, but I didn't care. Kessie's got her curly red hair and pale skin, but I'm just like Daddy and the rest of the Thorntons—straight brown hair and skin to match.

As Mama came back down, we heard a car drive up outside and a door slammed. I turned on the front light and there was Joe Rex Austin running up the veranda steps.

"Are you all right?" he asked Mama. "If that madman hurt you—"

"My daddy's no madman," I snarled at him, "and he's never once raised his hand to her!"

"That's enough out of you, Miss Blabbermouth!" said Mama, her green eyes flashing, so I marched upstairs like I was going to bed, but instead I sneaked out to the balcony over the veranda where they sat talking on the swing.

Joe Rex said Daddy'd been all over town threatening to bash his head in if he didn't leave her alone. Then Mama said I'd blabbed about her letting him buy us milkshakes and hamburgers at the Hardee's that day and Daddy'd got in another of his black rages.

"Sammy's right though. He's never hurt me with his hands, Joe Rex, just his tongue. After he says all the nasty things he can think of, he goes over to Henry's Garage and gets drunk. Sometimes he'll spend the whole night there and then, next day, act like nothing happened."

She sounded so sorry for herself that he said, "Damn it all, Debby, why do you put up with it? When're you going to leave Sam and marry me?"

"If only I could," she said in a soft little-girl voice.

It was quiet for a couple of minutes, then the swing gave a loud squeak and she said, "Stop it, Joe Rex! Don't you know they branded a big T on me the day I married Sam? I'm the Thornton wife and I'm going to live in the Thornton house and keep having Thornton children till one of us dies. He'd kill me before he let me go. Especially if he thought I'd be going to you."

I got mad then and even if his voice hadn't dropped too low to hear, I wouldn't have stayed to listen. I stomped downstairs and turned on the TV. I could've shot them both. Joe Rex Austin may be rich and own both drugstores in town and one at that strip mall out at the bypass, but Mama made her choice back in high school and she should've stuck to it. Folks still talk about that time and how, almost overnight, Mama went from being a scrawny little carrot-top to the prettiest thing in three counties, with all the boys swarming after her. Joe Rex had the edge because he was in her class in town and captain of the basketball team she cheered for, while Daddy played for a country school. They were both big and dark-haired and they both wanted Mama so bad they nearly killed each other on the ball court whenever the two teams played.

Joe Rex had the best prospects, him being an only child and Mr. Austin owning two drugstores and dickering for the third. But Mr. Austin squeezed every dollar three times before he turned it loose and he kept Joe Rex on a short rope. Granddaddy Thornton wasn't much better, but he went and died just before they all finished high school. That made Daddy a man and owner of a big farm while Joe Rex was still an errand boy, so Mama married Daddy right after graduation.

For a time, they stayed friendly. When Daddy'd tease Joe Rex about getting him a wife, Joe Rex would say, "No way, Sam. You stole the pick of the crop right from under my nose and I'm going to wait till you fall under a tractor or something."

They'd all laugh and laugh, but Daddy quit laughing about a year ago and told Joe Rex he wasn't welcome at our place any more. That was right after old Mr. Austin died of a heart attack and Joe Rex suddenly had a shiny new car and lots of money to splash around. Rumors started that Mama had been seen riding in Joe Rex's new car, some of it got back to Daddy, so whenever he heard about them talking to each other in town, even if it was nothing but "Hey" or "How you doing?" he'd get in a black rage and light out for the back room of Henry's Garage.

If I live to be a hundred, I'll never understand why he didn't take a firm hand just once—either beat some sense into her or throw her out. We didn't really need her here. I knew enough about cooking to take care of him and Kessie.

Besides, Mama purely hated living on the farm. She wasn't lazy in the house, but she wouldn't even walk out with us on a Sunday afternoon to see how the tobacco and corn were growing. She acted like the land had nothing to do with her pretty clothes and new car. And every time Daddy said something about trying one more time for a son, then *she'd* get mad and say she wasn't a brood sow. "You'll have to make do with Sammy. You've turned her into such a tomboy she's never going to get a husband."

As if I cared about a husband! I could drive a tractor, shoot a copperhead through the eye and already knew as much about growing and curing tobacco as most full-grown men, but Daddy wanted a real son and it wasn't fair of Mama.

It was almost an hour before Joe Rex left. When Mama came back inside, I couldn't help thinking how much prettier she was now than in those pictures of when she was head cheerleader. I didn't mind how all the men still turned around to look at Sam Thornton's wife when we drove into town, but the way Joe Rex looked at her like she was his special Christmas present or something just burned me up.

"You going to run off with him like he wants?" I asked.

When she didn't answer, I said, "Daddy won't let you. He'll come after you and kill Joe Rex and everybody'll say good enough 'cause you belong to Daddy and you always will whether you want to or not!"

She slapped me hard. "You've got a fresh mouth, Samantha Thornton and a mind as dirty as your daddy's! Get to bed!"

I wanted to answer her back about throwing off on Daddy, but something in her face made me stop.

Lying in bed, I started to feel edgy again. It was the wrong time of month for the moon and the sky had clouded over so that there wasn't even any starlight. Everything was pitch black and all the noises I never heard when Daddy was across the hall came back to plague me—the creak of a shutter sounded like a someone on the veranda steps, the sudden hush of the crickets. Was someone creeping around the house?

I could hear Mama tossing on her bed in the front room and I hoped it was because she was afraid. That made me feel better. Maybe she'd think twice before she gave Daddy cause to get mad again. I hoped she'd lie awake all night feeling scared and sorry.

As I drifted off to sleep, I decided that if Mama was nice to me at breakfast, I wouldn't tell Daddy about Joe Rex coming out tonight.

It seemed like I'd only slept a minute when I felt Mama's hand on my shoulder and came wide awake.

"Sh-hh," she whispered. "Get up quietly and come on."

"Where're we going?" I whispered back. "What's wrong?"

"Somebody's prowling around out back. I'll get Kessie and we'll sneak out the front and run over to Aunt Flossie's."

"It's probably just an old dog," I said, but I was scared, too. You don't have to be born in the country to tell the difference between a stray hound scrounging for scraps and a man trying not to wake anybody up. "We can't just let him steal anything he wants."

"Will you stop being Miss Know-it-all and do what I say just once without arguing?" Mama hissed. "There's nothing in this whole damn house worth fighting for even if I knew how. I've never shot a gun."

"Well, I have!" She made me so mad I forgot to be scared. "Daddy didn't teach me how to shoot just so I could kill snakes."

I slipped away from her hand and ran tiptoe down the hall. Daddy kept the guns on a rack at the head of the stairs and I grabbed the .22 repeater which was always loaded for emergencies.

As I crept down the stairs with it, I half expected Mama to call me back. Probably too scared to raise her voice.

I hated her for being a cheating town girl with no backbone and I hated Daddy for being drunk at Henry's Garage instead of home with us where he belonged, but most of all I hated whoever thought he could just walk into our house and take whatever he wanted.

It was too dark to see when I reached the kitchen, but I could hear him trying the back door. After a minute, he gave up and started creeping around the house toward the front. From window to window, I tracked him by the sound of small twigs breaking beneath his feet and when he came up the front steps, I was waiting at the end of the hall.

A big tall man was briefly framed against the dark sky. Joe Rex Austin! Coming to get Mama to run off with him.

Red hot rage poured through me. Did he think Thorntons wouldn't keep what was theirs?

As his pocketknife ripped the screen beside the hook, I steadied the .22 against my shoulder and let him have it right through the chest three times.

Slowly, Mama came down the stairs, took the rifle from me and turned on the outside lights.

"Oh, Sammy," she said in her little-girl voice. "You've killed your daddy!"

"No!" I screamed and pushed her aside. "You lie!"

But she wasn't.

Not Joe Rex all crumpled up on the veranda.

Daddy.

And then, by the veranda lights, I saw Daddy's car parked down the drive, right under their bedroom window and all at once, I knew what Mama had done to me.

She knelt beside him, still clutching the .22, and she looked like she was about to cry, but she was never going to fool me again. She'd deliberately tricked me into shooting Daddy and suddenly, like in a vision, I could see her married to Joe Rex and all of us living in his new house in town while our house stood empty.

That's why when Aunt Flossie and Uncle Billy and the sheriff got there, I told them Daddy woke me up begging Mama to unlock the door. "He said he was sorry for getting mad and that he loved her, but Mama said she loved Joe Rex and she was going to marry him and Daddy said it'd be over his dead body and Mama said that suited her and then she shot him. When I ran down, she tried to get me to take the rifle and say I'd done it because I thought he was a robber trying to break in."

Aunt Flossie put her arms around me and said, "There, there, honey."

"Liar!" screamed Mama. "She's lying!"

They took her away in the sheriff's car and she was still screaming, "She's lying! That's not how it happened!"

That was two months ago. Kessie and me'll probably stay here at Aunt Flossie's till the trial's over, but her brick house is too little to hold us all for long and we'll soon be back where we belong.

Our big old house will never be scary again with so many kinfolks around all the time, but it's always going to feel lonesome with Daddy gone.

The Executioner Mystery Magazine, August 1975
Revised version, June 1996

Deadhead Coming Down

I'm often asked, "Where do you get your ideas?" This story came out of a routine eye examination when my optometrist and I were wondering if a recent car wreck was an accident (official police version) or suicide (the grapevine version). This was at the height of the CB craze and there are no more Datsuns, but we still have eighteen-wheelers and we still have questionable highway deaths.

Funny thing about this CB craze—all these years we trucking men've been going along doing our job, just making a living as best we could, and people in cars didn't pay us much mind after everything got four-laned because they didn't get caught behind us so much going uphill, so they quit cursing us for being on the roads we was paying taxes for too and sort of ignored us for a few years.

Then those big camper vans started messing around with CB radios, tuning in on us, and first thing you know even VWs are running up and down the cloverleafs cluttering up the air with garbage and all of a sudden there's songs about us, calling us culture heroes and exotic knights of the road.

What a crock of bull.

There's not one damn thing exotic about driving an eighteen-wheeler. Next to standing on a assembly line and screwing Bolt A into Hole C like my no-'count brother-in-law, driving a truck's got to be the dullest way under God's red sun to make a living. 'Specially if it's just up and down the eastern seaboard like me.

Maybe it's different driving cross-country, but I work for this outfit—Eastline Truckers—and brother, they're just that: contract trucking up and down the coastal states. Peaches from Georgia, grapefruit from northern Florida, yams and blueberries from the Carolinas—whatever's in season, we haul it. I-95 to the Delaware Memorial Bridge, up the Jersey Turnpike, across the river and right over to Hunt's Point.

Fruit basket going up, deadhead coming down and if you think that's not boring, think again. Once you're on I-95, it's the same road from Florida to New Jersey. You could pick up a mile stretch in Georgia and stick it down somewhere in Maryland and nobody'd notice the difference. Same motels, same gas stations, same billboards.

There's laws put out by those Keep America Pretty people to try to keep billboards off the interstates, but I'm of two minds about them. You can get awful tired of trees and fields and cows with nothing to break 'em up, but then again, reading the same sign over and over four or five times a week's a real drag, too.

Even those Burma Shave signs they used to have when I was driving with Lucky. We'd laugh our heads off every time they put up new ones, but you can't laugh at the same things more'n once or twice, so we'd make up our own poems. Raunchy ones and funnier'n hell some of 'em.

Those were the good old days, a couple of years after the war. WW Two. I was a hick kid just out of the tobacco fields and Lucky seemed older'n Moses, though now I look back, I reckon he was only about thirty-five. His real name was Henry Driver, but everybody naturally called him Lucky because he got away with things nobody else ever could. During the blackouts, he once drove a load of TNT across the Great Smokies with no headlights. All them twisty mountain roads and just a three-quarter moon. I'd like to see these bragging hotshots around today try that!

Back then it took a real man to truck 'cause them rigs would fight you. Just like horses they were. They knew when you couldn't handle 'em. Today—hellfire! Everything's so automatic and hydraulic, even a ninety-pound woman can do it.

Guess I shouldn't knock it though. I'll be able to keep driving these creampuffs till I'm seventy. Not like Lucky. Hardly a dent and then his luck ran out on a stretch of 301 in Virginia. A blowout near a bridge and the wheel must've got away from him.

Twelve years ago that was and the company'd quit doubling us before that, but I still miss him. Things were never dull driving with Lucky. We was a lot alike. He used to tell me things he never told anybody else. Not just the things a man brags about when he's drinking and slinging bull, but other stuff.

I remember once we were laying over in Philly, him going, me coming down, and he says, "Guess what I saw today coming through Baltimore? A red-tailed hawk. Right smack in the middle of town."

Can you feature a tough guy like him getting all excited about seeing a back country bird in town? And telling another guy about it? Well, that's the way it was with me and him.

✤ ✤ ✤

I was thinking about Lucky last week coming down, and wishing I had him to talk to again. 95 was wall-to-wall vacation traffic. I thumbed my CB and it was full of ratchet jaws trying to sound like they knew what the hell they were saying. It was *Good buddy* this and *Smokey* that and *10-4* on the side, so I cut right out again.

I'd just passed this Hot Shoppe sign when the road commenced to unwind in my head like a moving picture show. I knew that next would come a Howard Johnson and a Holiday Inn and then a white barn and a meadow full of black cows and then a Texaco sign and every single mile all the way back home. I just couldn't take it no more and pulled off at the next cloverleaf.

"For every mile of thruway, there's ten miles on either side going the same way," Lucky used to say and, like him, I've got this skinny map stuck up over my windshield across the whole width of the cab with I-95 snaking right down the middle. Whenever that old snake gets to crawling under my skin, I look for a side road heading south. There's little X's scattered all up and down my map to keep track of which roads I'd been on before. I hadn't never been through this particular stretch, so I had my choice.

Twenty minutes off the interstate's a whole different country. The road I finally picked was only two lanes, but wide enough so I wouldn't crowd anybody. Not that there was much traffic. I almost had the road to myself and I want to tell you it was as pretty as a postcard, with trees and bushes growing right to the ditches and patches of them orangy flowers mixed in.

It was late afternoon, the sun just going down and I was perking up and feeling good about this road. It was the kind Lucky used to look for. Everything perfect.

I was coasting down this little hill and around a curve and suddenly there was a old geezer walking right up the middle of my lane. I hit the brakes and left rubber, but by the time I got her stopped and ran back to where he was laying all crumpled up in orange flowers, I knew he was a sure goner, so I walked back to my rig, broke on Channel 9 and about ten minutes later, there was a black-and-white flashing its blue lights and a ambulance with red ones.

Everybody was awful nice about it. They could see how I'd braked and swerved across the line. "I tried to miss him," I said, "but he went and jumped the wrong way."

"It wasn't your fault, so don't you worry," said the young cop when I'd followed him into town to fill out his report. "If I warned Mr. Jasper once, I told him a hundred times he was going to get himself killed out walking like that and him half deaf."

The old guy's son-in-law was there by that time and he nodded. "I told Mavis he ought to be in a old folks home where they'd look after him, but he was dead set against it and she wouldn't make him. Poor old Pop! Well, at least he didn't suffer."

The way he said it, I guessed he wasn't going to suffer too much himself over the old man's death.

I was free to go by nine o'clock and as I was leaving, the cop happened to say, "How come you were this far off the interstate?"

I explained about how boring it got every now and then and he sort of laughed and said, "I reckon you won't get bored again any time soon."

"I reckon not," I said, remembering how that old guy had scrambled, the way his eyes had bugged when he knew he couldn't get out of the way.

Just west of 95, I stopped at a Exxon station and while they were filling me up, I reached up over the windshield and made another little X on my road map. Seventeen X's now. Two more and I'd tie Lucky.

I pulled out onto 95 right in front of a Datsun that had to stomp on those Mickey Mouse brakes to keep from creaming his stupid self. Even at night it was all still the same—same gas stations, same motels, same billboards.

I don't know. Maybe it's different driving cross-country.

Mike Shayne Mystery Magazine, April 1978

Guy and Dolls

The idea for this story came straight out of the fashion pages of our local newspaper when it reported on a new sales gimmick.

They were tearing up the parkway again the day Harry and I drove out to see Guy. The doctors had said Guy was coming along nicely enough to see relatives and Harry was the closest thing Guy had to that, but his car was in the shop and the place is seventy miles out on Long Island, so I said I'd drive him. About halfway there, we had to detour around several yellow bulldozers and dump trucks and a cluster of workmen propped on idle shovels. Beside a big SLOW sign stood a flagman waving a bright orange flag with a bored steady motion. He was dressed like all the others in a dirt-stained blue shirt and jeans, and we were nearly past him before I did a double-take which twisted my head around so abruptly I nearly ran off the pavement.

Harry noted my reaction and chuckled. "Is that the first time you've seen one of those?" be asked. "It gives you a weird feeling, doesn't it?"

"What was it?" I asked. "A robot?"

"Nothing that sophisticated. Just a machine modeled like a man with a simple motorized gear to keep the flag arm moving."

"It's too lifelike for me," I said. "What's the point?"

"Someone did a study showing that drivers will slow down for men quicker than they will for signs or blinking lights. A mechanical man waving a caution flag costs less than hiring a real man, of course. Good thing Guy can't see it. He'd probably drive back and run the thing over three or four times."

An automatic toll booth ahead made me slow down. I tossed a coin in the plastic basket, the red light changed to green, and the device blinked a courteous THANK YOU as we drove past.

"Sometimes I think Guy had a point," I muttered. "It's not natural to have machines thanking you or waving flags." I thought of electronic door openers and banking facilities that talk back to you and I said to Harry, "It's no wonder Guy went berserk. Machines should stay machines. They deserve what they get if they try to act human."

"Still, murder's a little excessive," Harry said dryly. "Not to mention mutilating all those baby dolls."

"That part was never clear to me," I said. "What caused his hangup, about dolls anyhow?"

"In one word—Clara," said Harry. He'd been married to Guy's sister briefly, which was how he knew about Guy's childhood. Harry's testimony had been a big help to the psychiatrists and even more help to Guy's lawyers, who had used it to get the murder charge reduced due to temporary insanity. Except that Guy's insanity wasn't proving very temporary. It had been nearly a year now.

"When you and I were kids," said Harry, "dolls just lay there and looked cuddly."

I objected. "My sister's dolls used to make disgusting mewling noises, as I recall."

Harry brushed my objection aside. "Those were simple gravity cry boxes: turn the doll over and the crier said 'Ma-ma.' Still you have a point. Guy had cut the crier out of one of Clara's older dolls and that made her mad enough to scare him into leaving them alone. Remember that Laurel and Hardy movie they used to show on television, *Babes in Toyland*? Remember the scene when all the toys came to life and the wooden soldiers start smashing the villains? Well, Clara told him that's what dolls did to naughty boys who cut open their sister's dolls. Guy was always a nervous lad and she kept it up till he was howling with terror. She got herself spanked good and hard for scaring her little brother, and that made her even more furious. She blamed him and was determined to get even."

There was a contemplative note in Harry's voice. Apparently he was recalling the grown-up Clara's disagreeable methods of keeping her males in check.

"That was around the time toy makers started going crazy with animation. They had dolls doing everything—crying, wetting, growing hair, waving their arms and legs, as well as walking and talking—and Clara must have owned one of each. That night she sneaked into Guy's room and lined them all up around his bed, then wound them or pulled their strings or whatever one does to get them started. When Guy woke up, half groggy with sleep, he opened his eyes to see a dim gaslight playing over that writhing mass of arms and legs and to hear Clara's disguised voice whispering the most appalling threats.

"He nearly screamed the house down and Clara got another spanking, but Guy never touched her dolls again. In fact, Clara occasionally blackmailed him with them. If he started to tease or tattle, she'd threaten to sic the dolls on him. Do you know, I've just realized that Clara's probably the reason Guy left home at fourteen. How fortunate for him that it was Jasper who took him in. Did you two ever meet?"

I nodded. I'd known Jasper when he was fleecing the golden coast of California before arthritis slowed him down, but he'd come east several years before me.

"Remember how smooth he was?" Harry said. "Fastest fingers in the state at one time, with a touch as light as a butterfly's kiss. After they started stiffening up, he needed an innocent-looking boy like Guy to stop a mark in the fight crowd or at the basketball game, wave an old wallet at him and ask, 'Did you lose this mister?' The mark slapped his hip or chest pocket and Jasper knew exactly where to dip. That extra couple of seconds means a lot when your fingers are going, right?"

I flexed mine around the steering wheel. Still supple. Still good for a few more years of extracting credit cards and bills from the wallets of unsuspecting men.

"Wasn't long," said Harry, "till it was Jasper shilling for Guy. He taught the lad everything."

"And then came Nellie?"

"And then came Nellie," Harry agreed. We were silent for a couple of miles, thinking of poor Nellie. What a lovely child she was. Elegant and chic, Nellie loved beautiful expensive silks and furs with a sensual extravagance. More than actually being locked up, she must loathe wearing those coarse and ugly prison-issue clothes.

"I can see that Guy might have ripped up all those dolls because he'd once been frightened by your ex-wife's collection," I said, "but I'll never understand why he killed the clerk." Sleight-of-hand artists like Guy—or like Harry and myself, for that matter—almost never do anything more violent than run like startled gazelles when actually caught in the act.

"But she wasn't a sales clerk," said Harry. "Surely you knew that?"

I reminded him that I'd just left New York to follow the King Tut exhibit around the country when Guy fell apart and so I'd missed the details. The well-heeled crowds jamming the museums to see the boy Pharaoh's possessions had kept me busy and prosperous, and many of them came wearing solid-gold reproductions of Egyptian jewelry—golden fleecings indeed.

My eyes were on the parkway, which was now winding through beautifully landscaped terrain, yet my attention was fixed on Harry's tale. In our business, you can't afford ignorance of something which might trip you up too someday.

"It seemed the usual piece of cake," Harry said. "Chesterman's jewelry department was on the left side of the up escalators, if you recall, and a boutique for designer dresses was on the right. Two inspection trips and Guy had decided that after lunch would probably be the best time. There's a lull around then when the lunch-hour crowd's gone back to work and shoppers thin out enough to let the senior jewelry clerk slip off for a break. Guy was delighted to see that the junior clerk looked new and green, which was just more icing on that piece of cake.

"He browsed through the boutique, impersonating a young man bent on surprising his wife with a dress, all the while watching the junior jewelry clerk across the expanse of carpeted aisle. He was staring so intently at the clerk that he bumped into someone. He started to excuse himself, then recoiled, so frightened he was speechless. It was one of those lifelike mannequins and it bobbed and swayed until for a horrible moment, he thought he was back in his childhood nightmares with Clara's dolls menacing him again. Then a salesgirl popped her head around the thing and apologized. They were rearranging her section, putting new wigs and dresses on the dummies, and setting up a new display. Guy was so unnerved that he cleared out immediately. He'd seen enough by then anyhow.

"The next day, he and Nellie stepped from the escalator just after the senior jewelry clerk had gone for her break. Eight or ten shoppers— more than Guy would have preferred—had paused to examine that new dress display directly across from the jewelry counter. Nellie was puzzled. Chesterman's isn't quite Saks, of course, but its customers are usually too sophisticated to gawk at a perfectly ordinary grouping of three or four mannequins wearing blandly stylish costumes. Nellie knew clothes and she simply couldn't see what the fuss was about, but Guy wouldn't let her stop. They only had fifteen minutes before the senior clerk was due to return. In any event, nothing could have induced him to linger over what was essentially a bunch of large dolls.

"As they turned toward their quarry, they heard a smothered burst of laughter and Nellie glanced back curiously. The small crowd was dispersing and all had smiles on their faces. As did the young clerk at the jewelry counter. 'Cute idea, isn't it,' she grinned. 'Quite,' said Guy, cutting her off as he went into his act."

On the parkway shoulder I saw a sign for our exit, so I signaled and eased over into the right lane. It seemed incredible that Guy should be out here in what Harry euphemistically called a rest home.

I remembered the last time I'd seen them on their way to a job. Guy could never conceal his high-strung nerves, but somehow that seemed to transmit an air of over-breeding. He became a poor little rich boy who'd spent so much time in executive boardrooms or rarefied art galleries that he didn't quite know what to do with such a strange new emotion as love. Young clerks felt tender and protective when Guy asked their advice on selecting the perfect dinner ring for his lady love.

Nellie looked equally well bred, of course, but with just enough over-bearing arrogance to keep a clerk on her toes. Eager to please the one, anxious not to offend the other, a poor green clerk had no chance. Anyhow, young Guy could look so honest a cynic would have left him alone with the Hope Diamond without a second's hesitation.

I maneuvered our car through the intricacies of the cloverleaf and made the turn onto a broad avenue, sighing as I imagined how handsome and correct Guy and Nellie must have looked that last day. What a waste of genuine talent.

"It was the classic switch job," said Harry. "The old ways are sometimes the best, don't you find? A whole generation has never seen them. Guy immediately pushed aside the gold-plated desk set on the counter and pointed out the tray of rings he wished to examine. The clerk unlocked the case and brought it out. That was Nellie's cue to act bored with such unimaginative baubles and to drift a few feet down the counter to the bracelets. The clerk was distracted just long enough for Guy to palm five or six of the choicest rings and replace them with similarly styled imitations before drifting down himself to join Nellie.

"Few clerks know the contents of every tray in their cases. Only if there are empty slots in the black velvet will the clerk look at it twice before locking it up. Days might pass before the switch is discovered and suspicions will be well distributed by then."

"So what went wrong?" I asked, braking gently for a red light.

"Nellie said everything was a blur after that. They heard a voice cry 'Thief!' Guy jerked around and saw only a few equally startled shoppers. Then, to his utter horror, he watched his most terrifying nightmare come true—one of the mannequins in the new dress display across the aisle came to life before his very eyes. She moved stiffly at first, but determinedly, and when she stepped down from that low stand and headed for him Guy backed into the jewelry counter. She kept coming at him and started yelling, 'Call Security! I saw him put those rings in his pocket!'

"Nellie thought she meant to take them away from him and that's when Guy gave way to gibbering terror. He grabbed the gold-plated paper knife from that desk set on the counter and slashed out at her. He caught her in the jugular, poor thing.

"The next thing Nellie knew he was racing up the escalator. She tried to slip away at that point and ran right into the arms of a security guard. Meanwhile, Guy had made it to the next floor where he found himself smack in the middle of the toy department."

"Dolls?" I asked.

"Dolls," he said heavily. "They'd just gotten in a new shipment of the old-fashioned kind that did nothing but cry 'Ma-ma,' and when Guy sailed around the corner he upset a whole counter full. He was so surrounded by crying baby dolls he just sat down on the floor and methodically started to work with his paper knife. He'd eviscerated the criers from a couple of dozen before they finally caught up with him."

"But the mannequin that started it all," I said. "You're not going to tell me that a clothes dummy really did come to life? What was it, a robot of some kind?"

"No—that's the irony of it. Instead of a mannequin wired to act human, it was a human hired to act like a mannequin. She was a freeze model, one of those girls who can hold a pose for minutes without blinking an eye. It's a sales gimmick, something to make the customers do a doubletake and then look more closely at the clothes."

"So Guy didn't know he'd slashed the throat of a real girl?" I asked as I pulled the car into a nearly empty parking lot. A prison for the criminally insane doesn't draw many visitors.

"Of course he didn't know," said Harry. "Guy's the most gentle person in the world. I'm convinced he thought he was cutting out a doll's voice box."

Alfred Hitchcock's Mystery Magaizne, June 1979

Let No Man Put Asunder

We once knew a wildly mismatched couple. I couldn't help wondering what would have happened if they hadn't prosaically gotten a divorce.

The house was like a handful of baby's blocks clumped down upon an exclusive hillside above town—wood and glass blocks, loosely connected by a multi-angled roof with only trustingly simple snap-locks to protect the contents from the naughty world. A piece of cake.

Louie flashed his penlight around the luxurious room, gratified by all the easily-fenced, delightfully-portable objects which met his eyes—the porcelain figurines, a small French clock, the heavy silver table lighter and he blessed their owners' fine traditional taste. Too often, modern architecture meant no ornaments beyond Mexican pottery, chunky wood carvings or some outlandish conglomerate of chains and old plowshares welded together in the name of Art. The little thief preferred dainty miniatures which he could slip into the capacious pockets of his favorite working jacket.

Thick trees and shrubs had so screened the house from the road that he would never have noticed the unmarked drive had his attention not been directed to it. And to think he'd almost decided not to push his luck in this neighborhood anymore!

Moving noiselessly to avoid waking the woman who lay sleeping several wings away on the far side of the house, Louie pencilled his light into the adjoining room. He liked to examine all the merchandise before filling his shopping bag; and when he first saw the shelves of bright loving cups, he thought he'd struck gold, which—considering the price of silver these days—wasn't a bad analogy. But when he lifted one, he didn't need to read the recent date etched on the surface. By heft alone, he could tell these were made of cheap alloys and not the sterling of long ago.

His back to the door, Louie had replaced the cup and was just turning when two things happened simultaneously: a low voice said, "I really didn't think it'd be this simple!" and his right arm suddenly blazed with pain.

A light snapped on and Louie staggered around to see a young woman in the doorway, calmly fitting another arrow to her bowstring. Horrified, he stared down at his arm, at the point of a steel arrow head piercing the front of his jacket sleeve. Before he could speak, the girl looked up from her task and her eyes widened in shocked surprise "Why, you're a *burglar!*" she gasped and hastily stretched the bowstring to its tightest.

"Well what the hell did you think I was?" Louie cried, outrage mingling with fear at the way she kept that arrow pointed at his heart. His arm throbbed with every syllable and when he touched it, his hand came away wet and red. Unnerved at the sight of his own blood, Louie fainted dead away without waiting for her answer.

As he regained consciousness, Louie gradually became aware of the girl's calm voice: "—guess that's why I jumped the gun. Or should I say the arrow? With so many break-ins in the area lately, you can understand my nervousness, Sergeant."

He was dismayed to hear the familiar tones of his old nemesis, Sergeant Thaddeus Dixon, answer her, "Of course, Mrs. Harris. No way for you to know that Louie's as harmless as a fly."

Louie stiffened at the insult and the policeman noticed his movement. "With us at last, are you, Louie? How does the arm feel?"

Groaning, the little thief glanced down and was relieved to see that the arrow was gone. A professional-looking bandage covered his flesh wound and eased the pain. "Thanks, Sarge," he muttered.

"Not me." Sergeant Dixon was clearly amused. "Mrs. Harris already had the arrow out before we got here. You can thank her for the first aid treatment."

"*Thank* her!" Louie made his voice that of an indignant citizen. "Here I try to help her and what thanks do I get? This—this Pocahontas shoots me full of arrows!" He glared at Mrs. Harris.

"Hold on," said Dixon. "You're getting your story confused. This is where you usually tell me about your car trouble and how you just let yourself in to phone for help because you didn't want to disturb anyone."

"Go ahead and sneer, Sarge; there are others who believed me."

"Only once," Dixon reminded him. "That second jury wasn't quite as gullible. Three to five the judge gave you, but I suppose you got time off for good behavior. If I'd known you were out, I'd have had you in for questioning before now."

"Then he's the one who's been breaking into all the houses around here?" asked Mrs. Harris, interestedly. She was tall and tanned and her bright golden hair had been cut short to form a smooth, sleek cap. Her green eyes blazed with quick intelligence.

"Has someone been working this area?" Louie asked innocently. "You know, that must have been the guy I saw drive off about ten minutes before she started using me for target practice."

"Sure, sure," said the big police officer, genially.

"I *did!*" Louie insisted. "Listen, I was out driving around tonight, and I stopped for a smoke at the top of the hill there."

"And suddenly your car wouldn't start again?" suggested Dixon.

"Would you just lay off about car trouble?" Louie snarled. "There's nothing wrong with my car! My car goes just fine! That's not why I'm here. I was just sitting there, see, when *another* car drove up the hill and pulled into some bushes just across from this driveway; and I saw this guy pop out and sneak across the road like he didn't want anybody to see him. I wanted to see what he was up to, so I tailed him."

"And *he* was the one who broke in?"

Louie wasn't quite ready to touch upon that delicate issue yet, so he ignored Dixon and doggedly continued. "There were some lights from back of the house and I could see every move he made. He went straight around to the back and stopped outside the brightest window where she was sleeping."

Sergeant Dixon was skeptical. "A peeping Tom?"

Louie shrugged and let a doubtful note creep into his voice.

"Who knows? He was more interested in the time than the lady—kept looking at his watch like he was late for a bus. A real weirdo. After a few minutes, he sneaked on around the house and I took a look myself. Not peeping, you understand," he assured the girl, who was following every word intently. "Just to see what he'd been looking at. You could've gone to sleep with a book like it seemed, but for all I knew, he might've been there earlier and you were dead."

"Now, Louie," grinned the sergeant.

"Anyhow, I started to follow the peeper, but I got tangled up in a bush and he got ahead of me. That must've been when he opened the door around on this side." Dixon raised a disbelieving eyebrow at that, but Louie hurried on with his story. "I thought at first he was still inside, but then I heard his car start up on the road like he was in a big hurry. Well, what could I do?" he asked virtuously. "He might've been a firebug. The lady could've been roasted in her sleep. It was my civic duty to come in and make sure she was okay, wasn't it?"

Before Dixon could answer that, Mrs. Harris stood up and smoothed her long skirt. "If you'll excuse me, Sergeant, I want to call again and see if they've located my husband yet."

Shelley Harris was not only slim and lovely, but she moved with an athlete's easy grace, and the two men watched in silent appreciation as she left the room.

Louie's arm had begun to throb again and Dixon shook his head sympathetically. "You were asking for it when you tried to rip off an archery champion," he said, gesturing at the loving cups she'd won in competition. "Too bad it wasn't her husband who caught you."

"What's he champion of?" Louie asked sourly. "Knife throwing?"

"Bridge," chuckled Dixon. "He writes a column for the newspapers. The worst he could have done was hit you with a deck of cards."

"Funny, Sarge, very funny. But I wasn't ripping them off. There really was another guy sneaking around here first tonight." Having produced that story, Louie stuck with it even though Dixon clearly wasn't buying.

"My husband should be here any moment now," said Mrs. Harris when she re-entered the room. "The tournament director said he left as soon as they told him, so you don't have to stay, Sergeant."

"It's no trouble," said Dixon. "Besides, I want to check under your window outside."

"Surely you don't believe this man's absurd story?"

"We have to go through the motions. Come on, Louie. Show me where your peeper stood."

Louie led the way around the house. In the darkness outside, the girl's bedroom was a brilliant stage, but the grass beneath her window was so thick and springy a whole platoon of peeping Toms could have tiptoed past without leaving a trace. "Better go back to your engine trouble story," Dixon advised genially.

As they returned to the house, car lights swept up the drive and a dapper, middle-aged man of medium height rushed from the expensive sedan. "Are you all right, darling? They said someone broke in. Thank goodness you're safe! He could have killed you!"

Louie winced and Shelly Harris laughed outright. "Don't be silly, Winston. You should know by now I'm quite capable of defending myself." She started to introduce Sergeant Dixon, but the big policeman stepped forward and put out his hand.

"Glad to see you didn't suffer any permanent injury, Mr. Harris."

Winston Harris looked blank and the girl said, "You didn't mention that you knew my husband."

Before he could answer, Harris had placed him. "Of course!" he smiled. "Sergeant Dixon, isn't it? You were the officer who radioed for a wrecker. You remember, dear—the night I cleaned out both ditches at the bottom of Daredevil Hill? This is the policeman who was so helpful after he realized my brakes had failed and that I wasn't roaring drunk. You seem to be Johnny-on-the-spot lately, Sergeant."

"We've had extra patrols in this area because of all the pilfering," said Dixon. "You'll be seeing a lot less of us now that your wife's caught him for us."

"Where were you tonight?" she asked curiously. "They couldn't find you the first time I called."

"You must have phoned in the middle of intermission. Jake and I finished our boards early and I'd gone out on the terrace for some fresh air."

"I hope you didn't have to leave an important tournament," Dixon inquired courteously.

"Oh no. The club has a duplicate match every week. Less than fifteen tables. It gives me a chance to experiment with a new bidding convention I'm developing."

Dixon nodded and beckoned to Louie, who'd been sitting near the door nursing his sore arm. "Let's go, " he said and herded the little man into the patrol car waiting outside. Winston Harris stood silhouetted in the doorway as they drove off and Louie said, "Now wait a minute, Sarge! You gotta believe me!"

"Later, Louie," Dixon said wearily. "You can give it to me from the top as soon as we get back to the station."

❖ ❖ ❖

The following night, Winston Harris was working on his weekly column in the glass block which constituted his study in the modernistic house. Several bridge hands lay face up on the felt tabletop before him and he was studying them intently when a small noise made him glance around. He expected to see his wife, but the open doorway was vacant and he could hear the faint sound of a television several rooms away as she watched the delayed broadcast of an archery tournament. Then a movement beyond the sliding glass door caught his eye and he saw Louie signaling to him.

Puzzled, Harris obeyed the silent entreaty and closed his study door before approaching Louie. "You have a nerve coming here again," he observed as he let the little man in. "I thought you were in jail."

"I'm out on bail," Louie said hoarsely. He'd never attempted anything like this before and he was nervous. "I figure you and me've got business to discuss."

Harris was disdainful. "What possible business could we have in common?"

"You get your wife to drop the charges against me, and I won't tell her it was you I saw sneaking around here last night!"

The bridge expert frowned haughtily and Louie rushed on. "I didn't recognize you till we were driving away last night. I got to thinking: Mister, I don't know what kind of game you and Minnehaha are playing, but when she let fly with that arrow last night, she thought I was you."

Winston Harris resumed his seat at the felt-covered Queen Anne table, gathered in the cards and began to shuffle them thoughtfully.

"The way I figure it," said Louie, "last night had to be a trial run. You were seeing if you had time to get up here and back before that intermission was over and somebody missed you."

"Don't be ridiculous."

"*Me?* What about you? You may fool the police, but you didn't fool me, and you sure as hell don't fool that wife of yours. She's on to you, Mister, and she plays rough. That accident you had the other night—did the brakes really quit all by themselves?"

The question hit home.

"Do you play bridge?" Harris asked. "No? Too bad. You seem to possess the necessary rudiments of deductive insight to make a fair beginner." He squared the edges of the cards and placed the decks in neat alignment. "What did the police say about your allegations?"

Louie snorted. "I didn't waste my breath. It'd be my word against yours; and even if they believed me, there's no law against a man walking around his own house."

"But awkward if dear Shelley should hear of it," and Harris; "which brings us to your proposition."

"Just get her to drop the charges and I won't breathe a word."

"Oh, I think we can finesse her together," Harris said easily; and when Louie looked blank, he complained, "I do wish you knew bridge terminology. As you've guessed, Shelley and I are indeed playing a rather deadly game. You, Mr.—ah, Louie, shall be my trump card."

"You want *me* to kill her?" Louie squeaked. "No dice!"

"Dice are for fools who depend on luck and happenstance!" snapped Harris. "*We* shall play with skill and certainty. The police will have no reason to suspect a petty thief of murder, and I shall take care to be surrounded by witnesses at the time. In return, I'll see that this charge against you is dropped and give you enough money to abandon your nocturnal activities for quite some time."

"*I* think his activities should be stopped right now!" Standing in the half-opened doorway with a loosely-strung bow in her left hand, Shelley Harris looked like a young Diana, sun-bronzed and invincible.

Without moving, she smiled wickedly at her husband. "How's this for a game plan, darling? I'm quietly checking over my bows for next week's tourney when suddenly a shot rings out in your study. Alarmed, I fit an arrow into the string and rush to your aid. Imagine my horror when I find that you've tried to fend off this insanely persistent intruder with your pistol and have been mortally wounded in the struggle. At the loss of my beloved husband, I'm angered beyond madness. I take aim at the fleeing culprit—*stay right where you are!*" she warned sharply as Louie edged for the door "—and before I realize what I've done, I've pierced his heart with my griefstrung arrow. Like it?"

"It has a certain panache," Harris admitted. "But as usual, my dear, you've forgotten to draw all the trumps." His hand groped inside the table drawer which he'd eased open and came out empty.

"Is this what you're looking for?" she asked sweetly. She pushed the door fully open and a gun's dull metal glinted in her right hand. "I've always known precisely how many arrows were in your quiver, darling. In case you were tempted to use this on me, I planned to make a few adjustments. The next time you pulled the trigger, it would have exploded in your face.

She came closer, pointing the gun at his chest. "I do wish I could say it's been fun, Winston."

"Hold it right there!" thundered Sergeant Dixon. The study was suddenly full of policemen, who quickly confiscated the girl's gun and bow. Louie's legs had turned to rubber and he sank down on the nearest chair. "I thought you were going to let her do it," he grumbled.

Dixon flashed him a wide smile and turned to the Harrises. "You're both under arrest," he said and began to read them their rights.

"On what charge?" Harris said haughtily.

"You, for conspiracy to commit murder; your wife for attempted murder."

"Nonsense!" Harris cried, placing a husbandly arm around his wife. She glared at him and tried to resist, but he held her implacably until she regained her composure and relaxed, against his shoulder. "Surely you don't believe that little charade you just saw was for real? It was a Mississippi Heart Hand. Shelley and I were simply having a bit of sport with this fellow. Tell him, darling."

"That's all, Sergeant." The girl's green eyes were guileless and innocent. "Winston saw me crack the door right after he let that man in. He gave me our special wink which meant to play along with his joke."

"You may be the bridge expert," said Dixon, "But I've played enough poker to recognize a bluff when I see it, and you're both lying. When Louie told me it was you sneaking around here last night, Harris, I thought he was trying to wiggle out of trouble; but when he told me what your wife said when she shot him, I began wondering about your brake failure. I pulled some well-placed strings today, and it's very odd: none of your friends can understand why you've stuck it out this long, but nobody's taking bets on you two ever celebrating a silver anniversary together. There was even some talk about two moderate, private incomes which could become one very comfortable fortune if either of you died.

"It was obvious from the moment Louie put the idea it my head— young wife, older husband. One athletic, the other intellectual. Even this house: modern design, antique furniture. I wonder how long you've been playing Russian roulette with each other?"

Winston Harris smiled coolly. "An interesting hypothesis, but one you'd have difficulty presenting to a judge if neither of us cooperates."

Dixon stared at them a long frustrated moment, then ordered his man back to town.

"What about me?" asked Louie, who'd been ignored till then.

"You're home free this time," Dixon said grimly. "They're not going to risk having you talk in court."

"Oh, I think he's learned his lesson," Shelley Harris said lightly, her glance touching the newly-mended sleeve of Louie's jacket.

"But the games stop here and now," Dixon warned. "If anything ever happens to either of you, the other had better have the mayor himself as an alibi, because I'll be there, taking your story apart bit by bit. No more free accidents or mistaken identity!" He glared at them again and then turned on his heel. "Come on, Louie."

Driving down the steep hill, Dixon was silent; but as they swerved toward town and Louie complained about his arm, he chuckled sourly, "Count yourself lucky that a flesh wound's all you got for getting between those two and almost breaking the eleventh commandment."

"Eleventh?" Louie surreptitiously patted his pocket wherein lay the spade-shaped paperweight he'd taken when no one was looking. From tip to base, it was only six inches long, but from its heft, pure sterling silver.

"Yeah," said Dixon. " 'What God hath joined together, let no man put asunder.' " She almost sundered *you!*"

It was a typical cop joke, and Louie didn't bother to laugh.

Mike Shayne Mystery Magazine, May 1980

A City Full of Thieves

Another "what if?" story triggered by police warnings not to leave our keys in the car with the engine running while we dashed into a convenience store. (To think we had to be warned!)

"This stinking rotten city!" Mike growled as he placed a ham sandwich beside Peter's gin and tonic. He gave the polished counter an angry flick of his bar cloth and Peter grinned.

"Maybe you ought to change the name. *Mike's Bar and Grill* would be a lot cheaper."

"I'll roast in hell with the devil playing darts on me backside before I'll change it!" Mike roared stubbornly. "*The Red Feather* it is and *The Red Feather* it stays!"

"Except that it doesn't," Peter said, taking a bite of his sandwich.

"That's for sure," Mike agreed glumly. "This city's full of loonies; but in the name of all that's holy, what does a body want with me feathers?"

He referred to the sign which hung outside his tavern. Attached to that sign was supposed to be a five-foot-long red feather, a graceful contrivance of plastic and fiberglass which was apparently irresistible to thieves. The feathers weren't expensive—some guy over in Brooklyn made them for less than twenty-five dollars—but last night's loss was the second this month.

"I thought when I moved the brackets up higher, it'd stop. You'd expect it in a slum, but a busy street like this, good neighborhood—" He flicked the counter again. "A doorman around on Eighty-second told me somebody stole the trees right out in front of his building. Concrete pots and all! Can you believe it? Jeez!"

"Anything's possible in this city," Peter agreed, thinking of a certain thief with golden eyes. He slid his empty glass towards Mike. "How about a refill, and is it time for the news yet?"

"Five past six," Mike said and switched on the color set over the register. It was a slow Tuesday evening and Mike liked to gab, but he'd been tending bar long enough not to get insulted when a customer felt like being alone. He brought Peter's drink and moved to the far end of the bar where another regular had just sat down.

As the stolid face of a network reporter filled the screen, Peter sipped his drink and let his thoughts blank out the words. A tall muscular man in his mid-thirties, Peter's eyes were often filled with distant dreams, a quality which irritated such movers and doers as his wife.

Tracey barely came up to his shoulder and her small body was sweetly formed, not that it did him much good anymore since Tracey's delicately erotic body harbored enough driving ambition to forge empires. She never came with him to the tavern these days. If she didn't have a meeting like the one she was due at tonight, Tracey filled her evenings with studies and reports. On Wall Street, a woman had to be twice as sharp as a man, she told him. Her not-too-subtle implication was that any male body could hold Peter's job.

Soybean futures were Tracey's specialty and the brokerage firm where she worked had steadily promoted her until her salary was larger than Peter's, another source of irritation. "If you'd only stop daydreaming and apply yourself," she nagged. It wasn't enough that Peter enjoyed his job at one of the city's largest banks, that he was in line for department head. "You should already be a vice-president," she would say angrily, glaring at him through oversized glasses.

At first it had amused him that fortunes could be built on the future yield of a small white bean before it was even planted, much less harvested. He tried to imagine Tracey walking through a field of soybeans, but the image failed. She hated the smell of freshly-turned earth. Orchids from a florist were as close as she cared to come to nature. Peter wondered if there weren't something dishonest about devoting so much work and time on a gummy little bean she'd never soil her fingers with; but he kept that observation to himself, just as he never voiced his growing anger and frustration when she rebuffed his overtures by pleading paperwork or tiredness. As far as Peter could tell, all of Tracey's carnal desires were centered around a growing lust for money and power.

Outwardly, they still seemed a normally happy couple; even though, as soybeans became more and more time-consuming, Peter found himself stuck with a larger share of household chores. Tracey grudgingly paid for a weekly cleaning woman, but all the other bills—her clothes, rent, the car—came out of Peter's salary while most of hers went into a growing portfolio of stocks and bonds. "Our security for the future," she said, but everything was in her name alone. "Be sensible, Peter, and remember that most women do live longer than their husbands. If they were in both our names and you died first, I'd have to pay an enormous inheritance tax."

How unemotionally she could consider that possibility!

"See? More of the same, right?" said Mike as he rang up a drink at the cash register.

Peter blinked and realized that the TV was detailing kickbacks which a local politician had taken on a federal project.

"Thieves everywhere. Want your drink freshened?"

Peter glanced at his glass and shook his head. "Not just yet," he answered. Thieves everywhere. The hoods in the street and crooked politicians in office didn't have a monopoly. Everybody had a streak of larceny and would yield to it without a qualm, given the safe opportunity, thought Peter. Look at that golden-eyed thief who'd stolen something no longer of value to Tracey. Three months ago it'd been and in a supermarket, of all places.

Until then, Peter had tried to be reasonable and non-chauvinistic; but that evening, as he loaded his grocery cart with tasteless frozen dinners, he was suddenly overcome by a thoroughly sensuous longing. Not for Tracey's body—she no longer aroused his desire—but for one of those mouthwatering stews she used to concoct in the early days of their marriage when their incomes barely stretched from one paycheck to the next. Nowadays, if it couldn't be broiled or thawed, she didn't bother.

Bitterly, he had just decided on frozen turkey for his solitary dinner (Tracey was in Chicago attending a seminar on the market potential of soybean derivatives) when another cart banged into him from behind.

"I'm *so* sorry!" said a breathy voice as he turned. "Why, Mr. Helms! What are *you* doing here?"

She seemed limned in gold in that first confused glance; a cascade of blonde hair trailing over a tawny jacket, long slender legs encased in golden brown slacks. Even her eyes were a deep golden topaz. Peter groped for her name, certain that held seen her behind a desk somewhere in the bank's labyrinth of offices. "Trust Department?"

She nodded shyly. "I'm Priscilla Ackerman, Mr. Russell's secretary."

"Of course. Well, Miss Ackerman, I'm shopping for my dinner. Which would you recommend? Turkey or chopped steak?"

"Neither," she shuddered and then, impulsively, "Look, I left a chicken roasting. Why don't you come and share it? You look as if you could stand a home-cooked meal." She hesitated a moment. "Unless there's a Mrs. Helms?"

Such youthful, golden warmth coupled with a real made-from-scratch dinner left Peter helpless with temptation.

"Does it matter?"

Her topaz eyes were thoughtful. "No," she said slowly; "I guess it really doesn't." As simply, as openly as that, Priscilla had stolen him from Tracey.

"Hiya, Pete! I had a feeling you'd be here. Scotch, please, Mike," said Cal Morris, sliding onto the barstool beside him. Cal was in the car pool Tracey had organized to lower the costs of driving back and forth between Wall Street and the East Eighties and he was as good-natured and friendly as an overgrown puppy.

"Let me guess," Peter grinned. "Sally's having a hen party and decided to let you out for the night." Cal's wife was a devoted homebody who kept him on a very short leash.

"Nope. As a matter of fact, she sent me looking for you. As soon as I'd dropped you and Tracey off, I realized I should've invited you over for dinner since Tracey said she had to rush out for that meeting. I tried to call you, but you'd already left."

"Oh, yes. Tracey said she heard the phone ringing after she'd already locked the door. We were there just long enough for her to change clothes while I got the car out for her and then she dropped me off at the corner." Peter kept a calm face, but inwardly he was jubilant. What an unforeseen stroke of luck that Cal had been the caller and could confirm the exact time! He felt like clapping good old Cal on the shoulder and ordering a round of drinks for everyone.

"I told Sally you'd probably get Mike to fix you a sandwich and that was all she needed to hear. She's keeping a plate warm for us in the oven." Cal beamed as he looked around the aggressively masculine tavern. Although he adored Sally, he continually grumbled about never getting a night out. "How about a quick game of darts?"

"Won't Sally be waiting?"

"Let her! A half-hour won't make that much difference."

But Cal carefully noted the time on his watch, then flushed when he realized Peter had seen him and was smiling. He gave a sheepish shrug. "You don't know how lucky you are, Pete, old boy, having a wife like Tracey—independent, not hovering over you every minute."

"No, Tracey's not much of a hoverer," Peter agreed dryly and was deeply grateful that even Cal, his closest friend, had noticed no change in his and Tracey's relationship. Priscilla didn't hover either and she hadn't asked him to divorce Tracey, but he'd known from that first night that she was the wife he needed. The wife he meant to have, no matter what.

"You've got a great marriage: equal partners, no responsibilities, no kids." Cal signaled for another drink. "Don't get me wrong, though, Pete; I love those kids."

"I know you do," said Peter. Once, he'd wanted Tracey to forget soybeans long enough to bear a child. Now he dreamed of tall, golden-eyed children every night and was glad she'd refused.

"The thing is," said Cal, "Sally thinks the city's a lousy place for them now that they're getting older. She wants to move out to the Island. What do you think?"

"Sounds sensible. I've tried to get Tracey interested in a piece of land upstate, but she thinks commuting would be impossible."

As Cal talked about Long Island, Peter thought of that wooded lot a few miles up the Hudson. Was it still available? The price had probably doubled, but the setting was perfect for Priscilla. Office work smothered her. She was made for a home and children and Peter intended giving her both.

It wasn't that he hated Tracey, just that he'd caught a glimpse of heaven and there was no other way to scrape up a down payment on paradise. Tracey would have divorced him without a quibble, no doubt; but also without a dime from the stocks and bonds she'd squirreled away all the years he'd supported her. In her name, yes; but thanks to her efficiency, they had signed mutually beneficial wills long ago; and unlike Tracey, he wouldn't begrudge inheritance taxes.

It had taken only twenty minutes. Twenty minutes between the time Cal could swear he had dropped them off in front of their apartment and the time Mike could confirm he'd walked into The Red Feather three blocks away. Time for Tracey to hurriedly change for her dinner engagement and meet him in the deserted basement garage. Time for him to—no, try not to remember how easily that slender little neck had broken beneath his fingers, the way her eyes had—

"I guess we'd better be going before Sally sends one of the kids after us," Cal said reluctantly. "What time's Tracey due back? Maybe you could call her to come over for a nightcap."

"Good idea. It'll probably be early; around ten. With all the muggings these days, she's gotten a little nervous about driving through the city alone too late at night." Peter handed Mike a twenty and while he waited for his change, he wondered how soon he should start his concerned husband act for Cal and Sally. For that matter, he also wondered just where the car was now. He'd left the motor running when he pulled in beside a corner drugstore on the busy avenue two blocks away—something the cops were constantly warning everybody not to do.

His faith in the basic dishonesty of the city had been fully rewarded. He'd barely reached the drugstore door when, from the corner of his eye, he'd seen his car jerk away from the curb and merge with heavy traffic. It had looked like a kid. Peter hoped it was. A youthful, inexperienced car thief who would panic and abandon the car way the hell across the city—Brooklyn or the Bronx, he didn't care where as long as it was so far away that not even the most suspicious cop on the force could accuse him of dumping it there and getting back to Mike's in only twenty minutes.

"Something funny?" Cal asked as Mike returned with Peter's change.

"Oh, I was just thinking about Mike's feather thief," Peter said. "Did you notice he'd lost another one?"

"Sulphurous spawns of the devil!" Mike roared. "Next they'll be robbing graves!"

Cal laughed and Peter, picturing the surprise of a certain young car thief when he got around to looking under Tracey's mink cape which he'd so carefully draped over the front seat, joined him.

Skullduggery, June 1980

Mrs. Howell and Criminal Justice 2.1

In order to sound as if I know what I'm writing about, I have occasionally taken classes in criminalistics at the local community college. Mrs. Howell's classmates were much like some of mine. So were the things she learned. (And by this time, I was no longer a Donna Reed clone.)

Jeff Dixon watched with jaundiced eyes the dozen or so students drifting into his classroom. After three years, he could almost predict why each person had signed up for this summer course in criminal justice.

Take that clean-shaven young man in off-duty chinos and Izod shirt, for instance. He was probably capital police, bucking for plainclothes; an associate degree from Colleton County Technical College would almost cinch it.

Dixon was privately amused to note that he already had the textbook. Some of the guys never bothered; thought they could get through the course on sheer machismo. Like the blond kid strutting through the door now, his tie loosened, the top button of his blue uniform undone, and, even though he wore a wedding ring, already coming on strong to a couple of very pretty women ahead of him.

Dixon shuffled through the enrollment cards. They must be the pair of SBI clerks from the ID lab outside the capital. Those two stocky black guys behind them he remembered from previous classes. CCBI. (Like the uniformed police departments, both the State and City-County Bureaus of Investigation gave their people time off from work for classes that would upgrade their ratings.)

"Excuse me, please?"

Hovering in the doorway was a well-dressed, slightly plump woman with smart gray hair and inquisitive green eyes. Probably looking for Needlecraft on the next floor, thought Dixon. Colleton Tech drew a lot of older women who took up new hobbies when their children left home.

"Criminalistics?" chirped the woman.

Nonplussed, Dixon nodded.

"Oh, good!" She clicked into the room on thin high heels and took a desk near the two SBI women.

Several nondescript males wandered in. Lower echelon patrolmen from some of the surrounding small towns, no doubt; encouraged to attend by their sergeants, but more motivated by VA stipends.

Last through the doorway was a thin, freckled woman in full summer uniform. A sleeve of her crisp blue shirt carried the identifying patch of the Lockton police department.

Lockton was a bedroom suburb, and he'd heard about Officer Janet Jones from the captain there. The only woman in a twenty-man department, Jones was a divorcée, mid-thirties, who had talked her way onto the force after several years with the county rescue squad. She had a reputation for competence and hard work, and the captain was pushing her to advance.

The bell rang, and Dixon called the roll. The older woman's enrollment card carried a social security number and a name, Mrs. Marie Howell, but nothing to indicate why she was there.

As usual, Dixon began with a quick description of the course. "Welcome to Criminal Justice 2.1," he said. "Better known as Criminalistics 1. We cover the fundamentals of investigation in this course—crime scene search, recording, collection and preservation of evidence, with investigation of specific offenses such as arson, narcotics, sex crimes, larceny, burglary, robbery, and homicide. The main thing I'll be stressing is the importance of common sense, thoroughness, and teamwork."

"If we're gonna form teams," said Blair, the blond hotshot, "I wanna be on her team." He leered at Sue Lee, the prettier of the two SBI women.

There was a snicker from some of the men in the rear, and the three professional women in the room exchanged here-we-go-again looks, but Mrs. Howell smiled at Blair as if she hadn't quite understood his remark.

Dixon brought them to order and continued his introductory lecture. Everyone began taking notes except Blair, who not only lacked notepaper, but had somehow lost his pen. Mrs. Howell lent him both.

❖ ❖ ❖

By the end of the three-hour class session, Dixon had seen most of his first impressions confirmed. The discussion period brought intelligent comments from the SBI women, who were experienced in identifying partial fingerprints; thoughtful questions from the capital police officer and Janet Jones about why detectives took certain actions; and a running stream of smart-aleck remarks from Blair. Only Mrs. Howell had contributed nothing; and as class ended amid general conversation, Dixon said, "Mrs. Howell?"

She paused with a bright smile. "Yes?"

He held out her enrollment card. "There's a space here for noting if you're connected with a law agency. Yours is blank."

"Oh, I'm not anything official," she said. "Heavens, no! Do I have to be?"

"Not really, but I wondered . . ."

"Why I'm here?" Mrs. Howell looked self-conscious. "I thought it was a writing class."

"I beg your pardon?"

"I've always loved to write," she said shyly. "I write poems. Not very good ones, I'm afraid. And poetry's not very popular unless you're Robert Frost or Rod McKuen or somebody. Then I noticed that there are lots of mystery books on the newsstands and I thought they might be easy to write, only I don't know a thing about guns or poisons; so when I saw Criminalistics in the catalog, I hoped it meant the technical parts of crime-writing. Well, I see now that it didn't, but it sounds awfully fascinating and I hope you don't mind if I stay."

Dixon suppressed a smile. "Not at all," he said.

❖ ❖ ❖

In the weeks that followed, Dixon was rather pleased with the way the class shaped. The women were more conscientious about assignments, and they plunged into experimental crime scene searches with so much enthusiasm that pride spurred the men into keeping up. Blair became the class kvetch, grumbling about tests and papers. He was the only one to pass out at the autopsy they attended. "Try to pretend he's just cutting up a chicken," Mrs. Howell advised.

Mrs. Howell brought a distinctly domestic touch to the course. Despite some elementary consciousness-raising from the younger women, she persisted in calling herself "just a housewife" and in seeing things in that light.

When they mixed plaster of Paris to cast shoe tracks, she likened it to making cream waffles. "Mr. Howell's terribly fussy about his waffles. Cook never gets them right so I always have to do it, and this is the exact consistency of my batter."

She was enchanted to learn of the chemicals available to crime labs: chemicals that could lift a gun's filed-off serial numbers, that would react with microscopic traces of blood, that could develop fingerprints several years old.

Janet Jones took her under her wing, explained police procedures and terminology, and let the older woman examine the handcuffs and gun she wore on her belt.

Mrs. Howell reciprocated with home-baked cookies; and during coffee breaks in the canteen, she tried out arcane plot devices on her classmates and pretended not to mind when they picked flaws in her motives and methods.

"Black widow spiders aren't all that deadly," one of the CCBI guys told her. "And even if they were, putting some in a man's bed wouldn't necessarily do the trick. He'd probably roll over and crush them before they bit."

"Then what about a rich woman who can't sleep because it's a scorching hot night and the air conditioner is broken," Mrs. Howell postulated. "She goes out to the car, cranks it up, switches on the air conditioner, and goes to sleep in the back seat. Her husband sneaks out, closes the garage door and stuffs rags in the exhaust pipe so that she dies of carbon monoxide poisoning."

"There would be smudges on the tailpipe," said the policeman from the capital.

"Maybe if he'd just replaced the exhaust system?" she asked hopefully.

"That'd make him the number one suspect. He'd be accused of premeditated tampering."

When Dixon discussed paraffin tests to determine whether someone had recently fired a gun, she was excited to hear that handling bologna would give an inconclusive reading.

"So a killer could conceal a gun in his lunchbox, shoot the victim, and then eat a bologna sandwich! Mr. Howell loves bologna," she confided. "He says people wouldn't be so snooty about it if it cost as much as roast beef. We have it for lunch all the time. It doesn't quite agree with me and Mr. Howell's really not supposed to have so much smoked meat, but you know husbands. They love to have their way."

She said it without the least trace of irony or resentment. Sue Lee sighed and once again began to explain some of the basic gains that women—even "just housewives"—had made in the last twenty years.

Dixon tried to be patient; but one day, after listening to yet another zany murder plot in the canteen when he really wanted to talk to Janet Jones, he couldn't resist expounding the cold hard facts of life to his naive student.

"It's not *Columbo* or *Kojak* and half the time it isn't even *Hill Street Blues*," he said, ignoring Janet's frown. "Read the textbook, Mrs. Howell. There's only a seventy-three percent clearance rate on homicide, and it wouldn't be that high except that most murders are domestic and the killers don't even try to deny it. More murders go unsolved because of dumb, lazy detectives than because of smart killers."

Mrs. Howell's face fell, and Janet Jones glared at him. To take the sting from his words, he grinned at them both. "Look," he said, "go ahead with your plots. They'll make good reading; but just remember that in real life, there are more Blairs around a station house than Kojaks."

Mrs. Howell smiled back gamely. "The KISS system you tell us to follow—Keep It Simple, Stupid?"

"Oh now, I didn't mean—"

"No, you're probably right. I suppose it *is* stupid for a fifty-year-old housewife to try to write anything."

Blinking back tears, Mrs. Howell fled from the canteen and left Dixon alone at the table with a seething Janet Jones.

"You probably kick cats, too," she said fiercely.

"I didn't mean to hurt her feelings," Dixon said. "Look, Bob Reed told me you were his most level-headed officer. Doesn't that nonsense she spouts get under your skin?"

"She's a neat lady doing what she has to to get by," said Janet, her blue eyes snapping.

"What's that supposed to mean?"

"Forget it," she said and crushed her foam cup into a ball. "You wouldn't understand."

She strode from the canteen, and Dixon sprinted after her.

"That sounded suspiciously like a chauvinistic remark, Officer Jones."

The policewoman paused.

"Yes," she admitted.

"Chauvinistic, male-directed anger with a feeling of sisterhood toward Mrs. Howell," Dixon said thoughtfully. "Does her husband beat her or run around on her?"

"Captain Reed said you were good," said Janet Jones, impressed in spite of herself. "Mr. Howell owns Lockton's second-largest bank, so I know his car."

"And?"

"It's parked at a motel out on the bypass several times a week. The woman's one of his tellers."

"Does Mrs. Howell know?"

"I don't think so. Anyhow, you've heard her. She's so pre-ERA she'd probably think it was her fault. He's the reason she's here, though. He told her she writes rotten poetry, and she wanted to impress him with something better. Now you've shot her down, too."

"I'm sorry about that. Look, if I tell Mrs. Howell I think her luminol and Clorox plot has possibilities, will you have dinner with me tonight?"

Janet Jones smiled and a small dimple appeared in each freckled cheek. "What else did Captain Reed tell you?" she temporized.

"That you're brilliant and beautiful and that if he weren't happily married, he'd ask you out himself except that you're too sensible to see anyone in the department. What did he say about me?"

Her smile became a laugh, and her blue eyes danced impishly.

"That you were the best investigator the SBI ever had, that you went into teaching because you were so exasperated with the level of incompetence on most police forces, that you'd probably ask me to dinner, and that I should say yes."

"A good officer never questions her captain's judgment," Dixon said.

"Okay, but you have to give Marie some encouragement."

They returned to the classroom, but Mrs. Howell had not come back after the coffee break. "Next time," Dixon promised.

Unfortunately, there was no next time for Mrs. Howell.

Classes were canceled for a week when a severe wind and lightning storm hit the area, uprooting trees and knocking out power lines. Some parts of the county were without electricity for two days.

Like others in her department, Janet Jones had worked double shifts, directing traffic around fallen power lines, assisting in medical emergencies, and patrolling business areas where store windows had been broken by flying debris.

There were still dark circles under her eyes when the class finally met again. Everyone had tales of damage the summer storm had wrought, and it was several minutes before Dixon could call the class to order.

Even then, Janet interrupted him. "Did anybody hear about Marie Howell?"

The others looked around, suddenly realizing that Mrs. Howell was missing. "Was she hurt?" someone asked.

"Not her; her husband," said Janet. "A fallen limb broke one of their storm doors—left glass all over their brick patio. He was picking up the pieces when he slipped on some wet leaves and fell on a jagged edge." Janet's fingers touched her neck. "Marie found him too late."

"He bled to death?" asked one of the SBI women, shocked.

Janet nodded. "The funeral was two days ago." She pulled out a sympathy card she had bought. "I thought we could send this to her as a class."

The card went around, and everyone signed it. Dixon added a note expressing their hope that she would soon rejoin them.

A few days later, a black-bordered envelope appeared in his mailbox at Colleton Tech. He showed it to Janet at dinner that night.

"Mrs. Howell isn't coming back," he said and handed her the letter.

Dear Fellow Classmates and especially Mr. Dixon,

> *Thank you so much for your sympathy upon my recent bereavement. You'll never know how much the class has meant to me and how much I learned. You are a good teacher, Mr. Dixon. Most of all, you helped me see that I have no talent for complicated murders. Poetry is my first and deepest love, and I shall not wander from my field again.*
> > *Kind friends who helped*
> > *I thank you so.*
> > *Sorrow's cares are gone*
> > *Since you I know.*

> > > > *Marie Howell*

Janet's blue eyes were misty in the candlelight. "Poor dear," she said.

" 'Poor dear,' my Aunt Fanny!" Dixon said. "Your department must have handled Howell's death. Are you sure it was an accident?"

"According to the autopsy report, he fell on a piece of glass and it pierced his jugular. Why?"

"Did anyone print the glass?"

"Of course we did, and it was just his fingerprints and hers."

"Hers?"

"She pulled it out of his neck. He was her husband, Jeff. She tried to save him. You can't possibly think—"

"Can't I? Read her letter again: how much the class meant, how much she learned! She's thumbing her nose at me. Look at that poem, dammit!"

Puzzled, Janet scanned the letter again. "Those are things people say at a time like this," she said helplessly. "You can't read double meanings into a thank-you note."

Her smile was rueful as she reread Marie Howell's poem. "I'm afraid her husband was right, though. She's certainly not a very good poet. 'Sorrow's cares are gone/Since you I know.' Awkward."

"Awkward but accurate," Dixon said. "Since knowing us, she's managed to get rid of a wealthy, cheating bully of a husband. I told her to keep it simple, and she did."

"Oh, honestly, Jeff! It's just bad poetry."

"But good acrostics," he said bitterly. "It wouldn't stand up in court, but read the first letter of each line, dear Janet, and tell me she shouldn't get an A in the course."

Alfred Hitchcock's Mystery Magazine, April 1984

On Windy Ridge

As a child I loved those old black-and-white B movies about angels coming back to earth. I seem to recall one in which a horse and a dog assumed human shapes to help a beloved master. (If anyone remembers the title, please let me know.) This is my homage to those movies. But Flannery O'Connor once scolded a friend for seeing symbolism everywhere—"Sometimes the fork of a tree is just the fork of a tree"—so maybe this dog is only a dog.

Waiting is more tiresome than doing, and I was weary. Bone weary. "Seems longer than just yesterday those two went up to Windy Ridge," I said. "Two went up, but three were there, you know."

"Now what's that supposed to mean, Ruth?" asked Wayne.

Wayne's my cousin and a good sheriff. What he lacks in formal training, he makes up in common sense and a knowledge of the district that comes from growing up here in the mountains and from being related by birth or marriage to half the county. Our grandmothers were sisters and we've run in and out of each other's houses for forty years. I knew he was wondering if my queer remark came from tiredness or because I half believe some of the legends that persist in these hills.

He walked over to the deck rail and looked down into the ravine, but my eyes lifted to the distant hills, beyond trees that burned red and gold, to where the ridges misted into smoky blue. The hills were real and everlasting and I had borrowed of their strength before.

When I built this deck nearly twenty years ago, I planned it wide enough for a wedding breakfast because Luke Randolph and I were to be married as soon as he came home from Vietnam. It was May, wild vines grew up the pilings, and the air was heavy with the scent of honeysuckle and wisteria the day Luke's brother Tom came over with the crumpled telegram in his hand.

The hills haven't changed since then, but the red cedar planks have weathered to silver-gray and Wayne looked at me uneasily across their width.

"You're not going ghostie on me, are you, Ruth? This isn't the first time a man's been shot up on Windy Ridge, and it won't be the last. Hell, Sam's already put in two complaints."

Feisty Sam Haskell owns a small dairy farm on the edge of Windy Ridge, and trying to keep his herd from being shot out from under him every year makes him a perennial source of tall tales. In exasperation once, he'd painted C-O-W in bright purple on the flank of every animal. Two were promptly shot.

Wayne sighed. "That's what puzzles me. Gordon Tyler was a furriner, but Noah knew better than to go into the woods the first day of deer season when all those city folk show up, blasting away at anything that moves without waiting to see if it's got two legs or four. Why'd he go?"

"Gordon wanted to try his new rifle, and he talked Noah into it," I said.

Yesterday had been one of those perfect October mornings with barely a hint of frost in the air. We'd just finished a late breakfast here on the deck: Noah Randolph, who was Luke's nephew, my niece Julie, and me. Julie had bubbled like liquid sunshine that morning, her red hair flaming like a maple tree. After a summer of flirting around with Gordon Tyler, she'd finally decided that Noah was really the one she wanted to marry, and her brand-new diamond sparkled in the crisp air.

Noah was so much like my Luke—a mountain man, tall and solid, with clear brown eyes and a mane of sandy hair. Not handsome. His features were too strong and open. But a good face. A face you could trust your life with. Or trust with a niece who's been your life for fifteen of her twenty years after her parents died in a plane crash.

They were arguing over the last cheese biscuit when Gordon Tyler came up the side steps carrying a gleaming new rifle. Dark and wiry, he moved with the grace of a panther, and most women found him magnetic.

"I never liked Gordon," I told Wayne.

"Then why did you encourage him?"

"Because Julie didn't appreciate Noah. Remember how I dithered over Luke so long? Wondering if I loved him only because no one more romantic was around? It took that damn war—knowing he could be killed—to make me realize. Julie was me all over again, and Gordon had money, glamour, and the surface excitement she thought Noah lacked.

I thought if she got a good dose of Gordon, she'd wake up to Noah's real value."

"It's usually a mistake to play God," Wayne said.

Which was exactly what I had thought as I fetched Gordon a cup from the kitchen and urged him to pull up a chair and how about a slice of ham? I knew I'd acted shabbily in using him to help Julie finish growing up, and I tried to ease my conscience by being overly hospitable when the pure and simple truth was that I wanted Gordon Tyler to go away. To get off our mountain and out of Julie's life now that he'd served his purpose.

Until then, I'd rather enjoyed the seasonal influx of wealthy people who bought up our dilapidated barns and farmhouses and remodeled them into sumptuous vacation homes. Old-timers might grumble about flatlanders and furriners and yearn for the days when Jedediah's store down at the crossroads had stocked nothing more exotic than Vienna sausage, but it's always amused me to step around a flop-eared hound sprawled beside the potbellied stove and ask Jedediah for caviar, smoked oysters, or a bottle of choice Riesling.

Now I felt like one of the old-timers, and I wished all flatlanders and furriners to perdition, beginning with Gordon Tyler, who'd bought the old Edditon orchards as a tax shelter and play-pretty last year. We'd heard he'd inherited right much money, and he never mentioned any commitments to work beyond occasional board meetings up north. That gave him a lot of free time. Especially after Julie caught his eye this summer.

Julie said she'd been frank with him about Noah, but I was sitting across from Gordon when Noah and Julie announced their engagement out at Taylor's Inn, and something about the way he went so white and still made me think he really hadn't expected it. The moment passed, though, and he was the first to jump up and offer a toast.

Before the engagement, Gordon had barely noticed Noah; yet in less than two weeks he transformed himself from Julie's rejected lover into Noah's good ol' pal. When Noah could get away from the farm he'd inherited from Luke, they even went squirrel hunting and fishing together.

"It always sort of surprised me that Gordon could shoot so well," said Wayne, "him being a city boy and all."

"Gordon never did anything in public unless he could do it best," I said bitterly. "He always had to win. By hook or crook."

"He won the shooting medal fair and square," Wayne observed.

"Only because the Anson boy couldn't enter."

"Come on, Ruth! You don't think Gordon had anything to do with Tim Anson's falling through his barn roof, do you?"

"I don't know what I think anymore," I said crossly. "Gordon was up there with him, pointing out the rotten spots he wanted reshingled. Maybe he didn't know that section of roof was so far gone. All I'm saying is that Tim's the best shot around, and Gordon didn't enter the match till after Tim had broken his arm."

"No, honey," Wayne said gently, "you're saying a lot more than that."

Wayne has known me all my life. Did he realize I'd spent the last twenty-four hours brooding over all that had happened since Julie and Noah became engaged?

❖ ❖ ❖

When Gordon had interrupted our breakfast on the deck, I'd marked down the faint unease his presence aroused as a product of my own guilt pangs. Unlike Noah and Julie, I wasn't happy that he'd taken their engagement so well. Good-natured resignation seemed out of character.

Yet, as I brought out a fresh pot of coffee, there was Gordon showing Noah his new rifle. All morning the surrounding woods had reverberated with gunshots as deer season opened with its usual bang, and Gordon was anxious to test the gun. "It should stop a whitetail," he said.

"Oh, it'll do that," Noah agreed dryly. His big hands held the expensive, customized Remington carbine expertly, and as he laid his cheek against the hand-carved stock and sighted along the gleaming barrel, a strand of brown hair fell across his eyes. Julie brushed it back with a proprietary hand, her ring flashing in the sunlight.

Gordon's eyes narrowed, but he smiled and said, "I know you don't like to go out opening day, but this may be my only chance. I'm flying to Delaware tomorrow on business, and there's no telling when I'll get back. Of course, if you're afraid to come, I can go alone."

"Common sense isn't fear!" I snapped, and Julie said, "Noah's staying right here. Too many fools show up the first day."

If we'd kept our mouths shut, he probably would have put Gordon off; but with both of us jumping in, Noah naturally stood up, tousled Julie's red-gold hair, and told her to quit acting like a bossy wife.

"How far do you feel like walking?" he asked Gordon.

"Why don't we try Windy Ridge? I saw a nice buck up there the other day."

As Noah grabbed his jacket and started to follow Gordon down the steps, he looked back at Julie. There were times when she could look very tiny and crushed, as if all the sunshine had gone out of her life, and she was doing it then. I'd have sworn that even her hair had gone two shades duller. Hurt tears threatened to spill over her sandy lashes, and Noah returned, wiped her eyes with his handkerchief, and gently cupped her face in his strong hands.

"Quit worrying, honey. I'll wear my orange hunting cap. Nobody's going to take me for a deer, so cheer up and give me a kiss."

Brightness flowed back into her and she kissed him so thoroughly that it took an impatient horn blast from Gordon in the driveway below to tear Noah away.

"You be careful, Noah Randolph!" Julie called. She saw me grinning and smiled ruefully. "Was your Luke as pig-headed as Noah?"

"Never," I lied airily. "Any Randolph can be led around by the nose if you know how."

"Yah! And cows can fly," she gibed, but she was content again and it did give us a chance to work on the wedding. By mid-afternoon we were well into the invitation list when we heard a car door slam on the drive below.

Julie pushed the papers away and rushed to the rail to peer over. Mild disappointment in her voice, she said, "It's only Cousin Wayne. Gordon's with him, but where's Noah?"

I joined her at the rail and as soon as I saw Wayne's face, my arms went around her instinctively, as if I could shield her from what I knew he would say.

The next few moments were a blur of kaleidoscoping time. I heard Wayne's words, but they seemed overlaid by those other words twenty years ago.

". . . some trigger-happy hunter (*Vietcong sniper*) . . . up on Windy Ridge (*on midnight patrol*) . . . happened so quickly . . . I'm sorry, Julie." (*Luke's dead, Ruth.*)

"I was up ahead in some thick brush," Gordon said shakily. "There was another party working the west slope, but we didn't think anyone else was up as high as we were. I heard the shot, and when Noah didn't answer, I ran down and found him lying there. Someone went crashing through the bushes. I fired my gun and yelled at him to stop, but he didn't. Thank God for those guys on the west slope. I didn't even know they were there until I heard their dog bark."

One of them was a doctor from Asheville, and he had stanched the wound and applied first aid while the others rigged a stretcher. Together they got him down from the ridge and into a truck. Using CB radio, they had called for an ambulance that met them halfway into Asheville. Even so, it didn't look good.

"He's lost too much blood," Wayne told me quietly.

While Gordon drove us to the hospital, Wayne remained behind to direct the hunt for whoever had shot Noah. It was a forty-minute drive, and Gordon kept blaming himself all the way. "If he dies, it'll be my fault," he kept saying.

"He won't die!" Julie said fiercely.

"Whatever happens, it won't be your fault," I told him. "Noah's a grown man. He went with you of his own free accord."

❖ ❖ ❖

Tom and Mabel Randolph were in the intensive care room when we arrived, along with her sister and cousins. The news had traveled fast.

Noah was still in surgery, we were told. There was nothing to do but wait. "And pray," said Mabel Randolph, her eyes swollen from so much crying. "Please pray for him."

Time dragged. There was a snack area next to the waiting room, and hospital volunteers kept the coffee urn filled. More kinfolk arrived to share the wait and to offer the homely comfort of fried chicken, ham biscuits, and stuffed eggs. Everyone kept trying to get Julie and me to eat, but Julie couldn't seem to swallow either.

Six hours after Noah had been rushed into surgery, the doctor came to us, still dressed in his operating greens, the sterile mask dangling from his neck. Clinically, he described the path the bullet had taken through back and lung, just missing the spinal column, but nicking the heart and finally coming to rest in the left lung.

He talked about shock and trauma and blood pressure that wouldn't stabilize, and Mabel Randolph listened numbly until he'd finished, then said, "But he'll be all right, won't he?"

The doctor's eyes dropped and I liked him for that. Till then, he'd been so full of facts and figures that he could have been talking about soybean yields or how he'd gone about mending a stone wall. But he still had enough feeling that he couldn't look a dying boy's mother straight in the face and tell her, sure, he was going to be just fine. "Maybe, if he makes it through the night," he told Mabel and his voice trailed off.

He seemed relieved when Wayne's sturdy form advanced across the waiting room. "Here it is, Sheriff," he said, and gave Wayne a small packet. "I tried not to scratch it any further."

It was the slug he'd removed from Noah's lung, and Wayne passed it over to one of his deputies, who left in a hurry for the state lab.

"We blocked the roads and impounded every gun that came down the mountain," Wayne told us. "Then we did a sweep to make sure nobody was hiding up there."

❖ ❖ ❖

By morning, Noah's threadhold on life was stretched cobweb thin and Wayne had the lab report. Noah had been shot with a .30 caliber bullet.

Now, I like to trail along behind a pack of bell-voiced coon-hounds on a moonlit night, and I can knock a possum out of a persimmon with my .22 as well as anybody, but such things as calibers, rifling, bores, and grains were beyond me. All I knew was that after the roads were blocked, every gun that came down from Windy Ridge, even Noah's old Winchester and Gordon's new Remington, was impounded, and all the rifles that could shoot a .30 caliber load were test fired.

No match.

"What about the three men who helped carry Noah out?" I asked.

"All cleared," Wayne said.

It had been a long, tense night, and when he offered to take Julie and me home, I was ready to go, but Julie wouldn't be budged.

She promised to nap on one of the empty couches if I'd bring her some fresh clothes that afternoon when I returned. We left with Gordon trying to persuade her to go down to the cafeteria with him for breakfast and Mabel telling her she needed to keep up her strength for Noah's sake.

As we drove home along winding mountain roads, Wayne said, "We found his white handkerchief up there where he fell, Ruth. Warm day like yesterday, a man works up a sweat tramping the woods. Guess he forgot and pulled it out to wipe his brow."

I looked puzzled so he spelled it out for me. "Say you've never done much hunting; say you've got an itchy trigger finger, and you spot something white, flickering in the underbrush. You gonna wait till it turns around and shows antlers? Hell, no! A patch of white means a whitetail deer to you, so *bang!*"

At home, I showered and lay down, but tired as I was, sleep was a long time coming. I drifted in and out of troubled dreams in which Noah blended into Luke—Luke in his army uniform manning a lonely sentry post in a thicket of red-berried dogwoods and golden poplars. I saw the Vietcong sniper snaking through the underbrush and tried to cry out, but Luke couldn't hear me. He fell slowly into the leaves, and the sniper covered his face with a white flag.

"But Luke doesn't have a white flag!" I cried, and came awake as the telephone rang.

It was Julie with a list of small items she wanted me to bring. She said they'd persuaded Mabel Randolph to let Gordon take her home for a few hours while she and Tom kept the vigil. There was no change in Noah's condition.

"No change is probably a good sign, don't you think?" Julie quavered. "It means he's holding on."

I said it did seem hopeful, but my heart grieved for what she still might have to face.

My dream of Luke had left me too restless and disoriented to sleep again. Instead, I found myself pacing the deck as I had twenty years ago, until—like twenty years ago—I got into my car and drove aimlessly, until despair finally eased off again and I realized that I was at the end of one of the old logging trails that crisscross Windy Ridge.

The trees had begun to shed, and a cool gust of wind stirred the fallen leaves. I got out of the car and walked up a slope where Luke and I had often walked together. Squirrels chattered an alarm, a pair of bobwhites exploded into flight at my feet, and, from further up the ridge, a dog greeted me with sharp, welcoming barks.

I thought I knew every dog in the area, but I couldn't place the pointer that came crashing down the hillside so recklessly. For some reason, dogs lose all dignity with me. I'm not particularly fond of them, but through the years, I've become resigned to having them act the fool whenever I'm around. This one was no exception. He came prancing through the leaves, paw over paw, as if I were his long-lost friend, and tried to jump up and lick my face.

"Down, boy!" I said sternly and he sat obediently enough. He was white with the usual rust-colored markings, flop-ears, and intelligent brown eyes. His long, thin tail whipped the air to show me how happy he was for company, and I remembered that Gordon said he'd heard a dog bark just before Noah was shot. This dog, probably. He wasn't wearing a collar, but I was willing to bet he belonged to the party that helped Gordon with Noah, though I'd never heard of anyone using a pointer to hunt deer.

"Your people go off and leave you in all the excitement?" I asked, scratching behind his floppy ears.

More tail-whipping and another attempt to wash my face.

It was so peaceful there that I sat down on a nearby tree stump and let silence wash over me. The dog sprawled at my feet, his big head resting on my shoe. Bluejays played Not-It in the treetops, and scarlet maple leaves drifted down around us. Beyond the ridge, I heard the lazy tinkle of Sam Haskell's cowbells. It seemed unreal that Noah's life could halt amid such peace and beauty. Winter winds had stripped these flaming trees and spring rains had reclothed them in green twenty times since Luke and I had raced each other up these slopes looking for chinquapins or wild violets, and now Luke's nephew might soon be gone, too.

I buried my head on my knees and the dog nuzzled my ear sympathetically. When I stood at last, I heard him frolicking on the rise above me.

Those city hunters had given Noah Good-Samaritan help; I could at least keep their dog for them. He answered my whistle with a woof but didn't reappear.

Wayne told me he'd closed Windy Ridge to hunters, so we had the woods to ourselves, I thought. Except for the cowbells and birds and the sound of the dog running ahead through dry leaves, the place seemed silent and watchful.

I followed the dog up past a clump of red-leafed dogwoods until we were just below the last steep incline to the crest. Pulling myself around an outcropping of rock, I was startled to realize that this must have been the very spot where Noah fell. The ground was scuffed, and cigarette butts and bits of paper from an instant camera's film pack lay discarded from where Wayne's deputies had photographed the site.

Then I heard the dog bark further up. He had stopped by a large fallen log; and when I approached, he pawed at the hollow end and whined as if he'd cornered something. Field mouse or chipmunk, I hoped. It was a little late for snakes, but you never know.

I found a stick and raked aside the leaves that stopped the hole. As I probed, my stick touched something soft that crackled almost like dry leaves. Gingerly, still thinking of timber rattlers, I pulled it out.

The bundle was long and heavy, wrapped in several layers of waterproof plastic, and it was worse than rattlesnakes. Even before I unwrapped it, I think I knew it was a rifle that had been bought for just one reason.

Abruptly, I was pushed aside, and Gordon Tyler snatched the gun from me, his eyes blazing with anger and fear.

"How the devil did you know?" he cried. "You weren't even here."

"The dog—" I said.

"What dog?" he snarled. "You came around the rocks and went as straight to that log as if you'd watched me yesterday."

I looked about and the dog was nowhere in sight; but in the horror of the moment, one more oddity didn't register because I was suddenly remembering.

"Noah couldn't have pulled out a handkerchief! He left his with Julie. You dropped one there after you shot him, Gordon, to make Wayne think some trigger-happy fool saw a flash of white."

"And this evening, he'll think you stumbled across the killer hiding up here and got yourself shot for meddling."

The rifle barrel gleamed in the sunlight as he swung it up to aim. After that, everything seemed to happen in slow motion. The gun swung up; but before it could level, there was a blur of white and brown fur springing for Gordon's throat, then both plunged backwards onto the rocks below.

By the time I slipped and skidded down into the ravine, the gash on Gordon's temple had quit bleeding and there was no pulse.

I thought the dog would be nearby and I whistled and called, fearful that he might be lying somewhere among the rocks, hurt and dying, too.

Eventually, I had to give up and climb out of the ravine; yet, though dazed from my brush with death and from learning that Gordon had shot Noah deliberately, I was vaguely soothed by a sweet fragrance and was even able to wonder what autumn-blooming plant could so perfume the air.

❖ ❖ ❖

Now Wayne and I waited on my deck and watched twilight deepen the blue mountains while Gordon's body and Gordon's gun were examined in distant laboratories.

At dusk, one of Wayne's deputies stopped by. "Sorry, Miss Ruth, but we looked under every log and rock in that ravine and there's no sign of your dog."

"I appreciate your looking, but he wasn't mine," I said. "He belonged to those other hunters yesterday."

"They didn't have a dog with them," Wayne said gently. "I asked. And Sam Haskell says he hasn't seen any stray pointers up that way, either."

I shrugged and didn't argue. Gordon had denied the dog, too. Maybe I was getting senile.

Once more, Wayne called the lab, and this time he learned that a test bullet from Gordon's second gun matched the one removed from Noah's lung. Ten minutes later, the medical examiner phoned to report that Gordon's death was from a broken neck and, no, except for the gash on his temple, no other marks; certainly no teeth marks at his throat.

The phone rang again and this time it was Julie. "Noah's blood pressure's stabilized and they think he's coming out of the coma!"

Her voice sparkled with radiant thanksgiving, and a huge weight rolled off my heart.

I've heard that people often don't remember the actual moment when they were hurt; but someday soon I will ask Noah whether or not he heard a dog bark just before Gordon fired at him. *Something* up there had thrown Gordon's aim off just enough to save his life.

Yet, even if Noah doesn't remember, it won't really matter because I suddenly identified the sweet fragrance I'd smelled earlier. All around me, trees and vines flamed with October colors; but in that ravine up on Windy Ridge, the air had been heavy with the honeysuckle and wisteria of May.

Alfred Hitchcock's Mystery Magazine, Mid-December 1984

Lieutenant Harald
And the *Treasure Island* Treasure

One Coffee With began as a short story featuring a Lt. Peter Bohr. By the time it'd been doubled and redoubled and then doubled again into a full-length book, Lt. Bohr had morphed into Lt. Sigrid Harald. This was the first of her short adventures to see print and, since Alfred Hitchcock's Mystery Magazine *made it their cover story, it was also the first time an artist had tried to render her likeness.*

The old blue copy of Treasure Island *is one I still own. In that introductory essay, Robert Louis Stevenson also wrote that he used to look upon full-length novels "with a sort of veneration, as a feat—not possibly of literature—but of physical and moral endurance and the courage of Ajax"— sentiments with which I heartily agreed. I couldn't imagine myself filling three hundred sheets of paper with consecutive words and I'm still a little surprised to realize I've now done it fourteen times.*

"**I** thought you liked puzzles," argued Oscar Nauman's disembodied voice.

"I do," Lieutenant Sigrid Harald answered, balancing the telephone receiver on her shoulder as she struggled with a balky can opener. "That's one of the reasons I joined the NYPD. I get paid for it, Nauman. I don't have to waste a free weekend."

"But this is a real buried treasure. One of my former students is going to lose her inheritance if it isn't found soon, and I told her we'd help."

As one of America's leading abstract artists, Oscar Nauman could have sold one or two paintings a year and lived in comfortable retirement on some Mediterranean island. Instead, he continued to chair the art department at Vanderlyn College over on the East River where Sigrid first met him during a homicide investigation. The end of the case hadn't been the end of their acquaintance, though. He kept walking in and out of her life as if he had a right there, lecturing, bullying, and keeping her off balance. Her prickly nature seemed to amuse him, and Sigrid had quit trying to analyze why he persisted.

Or why she allowed it.

"We can drive up tonight," said Nauman. "Unless," he added craftily, knowing her aversion to sunrises, "you'd rather leave around six tomorrow morning?"

"Now listen, Nauman, I don't—" The can opener slipped. "Oh, damn! I just dumped soup all over the blasted stove."

"Throw it out. I'll pick you up in thirty minutes and we'll have dinner on the way."

"I am *not* going to Connecticut," she said firmly, but he had already hung up.

❖ ❖ ❖

Fourteen hours later, she sat on the terrace of Nauman's Connecticut house and placidly bit into a second Danish. A good night's sleep had removed most of her annoyance at being dragged from the city and hurtled through the night at Nauman's usual speed-of-sound driving. The sun was shining, the air was warm, and she had found an unworked double-crostic in an elderly issue of the New York *Times*.

She looked contented as a cat, thought Nauman. Her long dark hair was pinned at the nape more loosely than usual, and her faded jeans and cream-colored knit shirt were more becoming than those shapeless pantsuits she wore in town. Thin to the point of skinniness, with a mouth too wide for conventional beauty and a neck too long, her cool gray eyes were her best feature, but these were presently engrossed in her paper.

He'd been up for hours and was so impatient to be off that he swept cups, carafe, and the remaining sweet rolls back onto the large brass tray and carted it all away without asking Sigrid if she'd finished.

"I thought your friend wasn't expecting us before ten," she said, following Nauman to the kitchen where she retrieved her cup and refilled it while he loaded the dishwasher.

"It'll take us about that long to walk over." He took her cup and poured it in the sink.

"*Walk?*" Sigrid was appalled.

"Less than a mile as the crow flies. You walk more than that every day."

"But that's on concrete," she protested. "In the city. You're talking about trees and snakes and briars, aren't you?"

"It used to be an Indian trading path," Nauman coaxed, leading her out through the terrace gate. "It'll be like a walk through Central Park."

"I hate walking in Central Park," Sigrid muttered, but she followed him across a narrow meadow to a scrub forest. As Nauman disappeared behind a curtain of wild grapevines, she hesitated a moment, then took a deep breath and plunged in after him.

Ten minutes later, sweaty, her ankles whipped by thorns, a stinging scratch on her arm, she was ready for mutiny. "No Indians ever walked through this jungle."

"Not this part. We're taking a shortcut. The path is just past those tall oaks."

"If it isn't, I'm going back."

But it was; and once they were on it, the walk became more pleasant. Sigrid was used to covering twenty-five or thirty city blocks at a stretch, but she was deeply suspicious of nature in the raw. Still, it was cooler under the massive trees in this part of the forest. The path angled downward and was so broad that no branches caught at her clothing. She began to relax. They crossed a small stream on stepping stones and the path rose gently again.

As Nauman paused to re-tie his sneaker, a large black bird lazily flapped along overhead in their general direction.

"That crow of navigational fame, no doubt," said Sigrid.

Her smiles were so rare, thought Oscar, that one forgot how they transformed her face. She was more than twenty-five years younger than he and nearly as tall and she photographed badly, but perhaps a painting? He hadn't attempted a portrait since his student days.

"Hi, Oscar!" came a lilting voice from the top of the path. "Welcome to Treasure Island."

To Sigrid, Jemima Bullock looked like a thoroughly nice child as she ran down to meet them in cut-off jeans. She was sturdily built, athletic rather than buxom, with short reddish-blonde hair, an abundance of freckles on every inch of visible skin, and an infectious grin as Nauman effected introductions.

"Jemima's the art world's contribution to oceanography."

"What Oscar means is that he's eternally grateful I didn't stay an art major at Vanderlyn," Jemima explained cheerfully. "My technical drawing was good, but I bombed in creativity."

"At least you had the native wit to admit it," Nauman said.

At the top of the path, they rounded a hummock of wisteria and honeysuckle vines to find an old cottage of undressed logs. A wide porch ran its length and gave good views of rolling woodlands and of Jemima's battered VW van, which was parked on the drive beneath an enormous oak.

"My uncle was caretaker for the Rawlings estate," said Jemima, leading them up on the porch and pulling wicker chairs around a bamboo table. "The main house is farther down the drive, but no one's lived there for years. Uncle Jim mostly had the place to himself."

What looked like a small telescope on a tripod stood at the far end of the porch. "He called this Spyglass Hill but that's really a surveyor's transit."

"Nauman said his hobby was Robert Louis Stevenson," said Sigrid. "Is that why you welcomed us to Treasure Island?"

"Partly, but Uncle Jim was nutty about only one of Stevenson's books: *Treasure Island.* He was my mother's favorite uncle, see, and their name was Hawkins; so when he was a kid, he used to pretend he was Jim Hawkins in the book. Mom named me Jemima Hawkins Bullock after him, and, since he never married, we were pretty close. I used to spend a month up here every summer when I was growing up. He's the one who got me interested in oceanography, though it started off with treasure maps. Every summer he'd have a new one waiting for me." She darted into the house and reappeared a moment later with a book and a large leather-bound portfolio of charts which she spread out on the porch table.

"This is a survey map of the area," she said. Her finger stabbed a small black square. "Here's this cottage." She traced a short route. "Here's Oscar's house and the path and stream you crossed. See the way the stream comes up and intersects the creek here? And then the creek runs back down and around where a second stream branches off and merges again with the first stream."

"So technically, we really are on an island," said Sigrid, obscurely pleased with that idea.

"A body of land surrounded by water," Nauman agreed. He pulled out his pipe and worked at getting it lit.

"The freaky thing is that it's actually shaped like the original Treasure Island," said Jemima. She flipped the book open to an illustration. To Sigrid's eyes, the two were only roughly similar, but she supposed that wishful thinking could rationalize the differences.

"Uncle Jim made all these treasure maps for me. So many paces to a certain tree while I was small; later he taught me how to use a sextant and I'd have to shoot the stars to get the proper bearing. He didn't make it easy, either. It usually took two or three days and several false starts to find the right place to dig. It was worth it, though."

Sigrid leafed through the sheaf of hand-drawn charts. Although identical in their outlines, each was exquisitely embellished with different colored inks: tiny sailing ships, mermaids, and dolphins sported in blue waters around elaborate multi-pointed compasses. Latitude and longitude lines had been carefully lettered in India ink, along with minute numbers and directions. Sigrid peered closely and read, "Bulk of treasure here."

"He never made much money as a caretaker," said Jemima, "but the treasures he used to hide! Chocolates wrapped in gold and purple foil, a pair of binoculars I still use, maps and drawing pads and compasses so I could draw my own." There was a wistful note in her voice as of a child describing never-to-come-again Christmas mornings.

"Tell her about the real treasure," Nauman prompted, bored with the preliminaries.

"I'm coming to it, Oscar. Be patient. She has to understand how Uncle Jim's mind worked first—the way he liked making a mystery of things. It wasn't only his maps," she told Sigrid. "He never talked freely about his life either. He'd trained as a surveyor but seldom held a steady job till after his leg was hurt—just bummed around the world till he was past thirty. I guess he might've seen or done some things he didn't want to tell a kid; but when he was feeling loose, he'd talk about a treasure he brought home from England during World War II. Nothing direct, just a brief mention. If you asked too many questions, he'd cut you off. I used to think it might be gold, then again it'd sound like jewels. Whatever it was, he got it in London. He was on leave there and the building he was in was hit by a buzz bomb. Crushed his left leg.

"That London hospital was where he really got into the *Treasure Island* thing. The nurses kept bringing him different editions of the book. Because of his name, you see. He'd always had a flair for precision drawing—from the surveying—and when he started mapping the wards on scrap paper, they brought him sketch pads and pens and he was off to the races. I think they made a pet out of him because they knew his leg would never heal properly. Anyhow, he let it slip once that if the nurses hadn't liked him, he never would have recognized the treasure when it appeared."

She looked at Sigrid doubtfully through stubby sandy lashes. "That doesn't sound much like gold or diamonds, does it?"

"He never revealed its nature?"

"Nope. Anyhow, Uncle Jim knew it takes an M.S. to get anywhere in oceanography. That means an expensive year or two at some school like Duke, and I just don't have the money. In fact, I haven't been able to get up here much these last four years because I've had to work summers and part time to stay at Vanderlyn. Uncle Jim said not to worry, that he was going to give me the treasure for graduation and I could sell it for enough to finance my post-graduate work.

"When he called three weeks ago to make sure I was coming, he said he was drawing up a new map. The heart attack must have hit him within the hour. I drove up the next morning and found him slumped over the table inside. He'd just finished sketching in the outline. It was going to be our best treasure hunt."

An unembarrassed tear slipped down her freckled cheek, and she brushed it away with the back of her hand.

"The trustees for the Rawlings estate have been very understanding, but they do need the cottage for the new caretaker. Uncle Jim left everything to me, so they've asked if I can clear out his things by the end of the month. You're my last hope, Lieutenant Harald. Oscar said you're good at solving puzzles. I hope you can figure out this one 'cause nobody else can."

Sigrid looked at Nauman. "But I don't know a thing about sextants or surveyor's transits, and anyhow, if he died before he finished the map—"

"Nobody's asking you to go tramping through hill and dale with a pickax," Nauman said, correctly interpreting her horrified expression. "Jemima doesn't think he'd buried it yet."

"Come inside and I'll show you," said the girl.

In essence, the cottage was one big room, with kitchen equipment at one end and two small sleeping alcoves at the other end separated by a tiny bath. A shabby couch and several comfortable-looking armchairs circled an enormous stone fireplace centered on the long rear wall. A bank of windows overlooked the porch, and underneath were shelves crammed with books of all shapes and sizes. Most were various editions of—"What else?" said Jemima—*Treasure Island*. In the middle of the room was a round wooden table flanked by six ladderback chairs, one of which was draped in an old and worn woollen pea jacket with heavy brass buttons. A rusty metal picnic cooler sat beside one chair with its lid ajar to reveal a porcelain interior.

"Things are pretty much as Uncle Jim left them. That cooler was our treasure chest because it was watertight. As you can see, there was nothing in it."

Sigrid circled the table, carefully cataloguing its contents: an uncapped bottle of India ink, a fine-nibbed drawing pen, a compass, a ruler, four brushes, a twelve-by-eighteen-inch block of watercolor paper with the top half of the island sketched in, a set of neatly arranged water colors and a clean tray for mixing them. Across from these, a book was opened to a reproduction of the map Robert Louis Stevenson had drawn so many years ago, and several more books formed a prop for two framed charts. Sigrid scanned the cottage and found the light oblongs on the white-washed walls where a chart had hung on either side of the stone chimney.

"Uncle Jim often used them as references when he was drawing a new map," explained Jemima. "The right one's a copy of the survey map. It's the first one he drew after he took the job here and realized that the stream and creek made this place an island almost like the real Treasure Island. The other one's the first copy he made when he was in the hospital. I guess he kept it for sentimental reasons even though the proportions aren't quite right."

Sigrid peered through the glass at the sheet of yellowed watercolor paper, which was frayed around the edges and showed deep crease lines where it had once been folded into quarters. It, too, was minutely detailed with hillocks, trees, sailing ships, and sounding depths although, as Jemima had noted, it wasn't an accurate copy.

She turned both frames over and saw that the paper tape that sealed the backings to the frames had been torn.

"We took them apart," Jemima acknowledged. "A friend of mine came over from the rare book library at Yale to help appraise the books, and he thought maybe the treasure was an autographed letter from Stevenson or something like that which Uncle Jim might've hidden inside the matting."

"None of the books are rare?" asked Sigrid. That had seemed the most likely possibility.

"He thought they might bring a few hundred dollars if I sold them as a collection," said the girl, "but individually, nothing's worth over forty dollars at the most. And we thumbed through every one of them in case there really was a letter or something. No luck."

Sigrid's slate gray eyes swept through the large, shabby room. Something jarred, but she couldn't quite put her finger on the source.

"Not as simple as a double-crostic, is it?" Nauman asked.

Sigrid shrugged, unnettled by his light gibe. "If a treasure's here, logic will uncover it."

"But we've *been* logical!" Jemima said despairingly. "Last week my mom and I and two cousins went over every square inch of this place. We looked behind knotholes, jiggled every stone in the fireplace, checked for loose floorboards, and examined mattress seams and cushion covers. Nothing. And my cousins are home ec majors," she added to buttress her statement.

"Mom even separated out all the things Uncle Jim might have brought from England." She gestured to a small heap of books stacked atop the window case. "Luckily he dated all his books. My Yale friend says none of those is worth more than a few dollars."

Sigrid lifted one. The blue cloth binding was familiar, and when she read the publication date—1932—she realized it was the same edition of *Treasure Island* as the one her father had owned as a boy and which she had read as a child herself. Memories of lying on her stomach on a window ledge, munching toasted cheese sandwiches while she read, came back to Sigrid as she paused over a well-remembered illustration of Jim Hawkins shooting Israel Hands. Inscribed on the flyleaf was *A very happy Christmas to our own Jim Hawkins from Nurse Fromyn and staff.* Underneath, a masculine hand had added *12/25/1944.*

The other four books in the heap carried dates which spanned the early months of 1945. "Mom said he was brought home in the summer of '45," said Jemima, peering around Sigrid's shoulder.

"What else did he bring?"

"That first map he drew," she answered promptly, "a shaving kit, that jacket on the chair, and Mom thinks that leather portfolio, too." She fetched it in from the porch and carefully removed the charts it held before handing it over. It measured about eighteen by twenty inches.

The leather was worn by forty years of handling, but when Nauman turned it over, they could still read the tooled letters at the edge of the case. "Bartlelow's," he said. "They're still the best leather goods shop in London. And the most expensive."

Sigrid found a worn spot in the heavy taffeta lining. Carefully, she slipped her thin fingers inside and worked the fabric away from the leather. Had any slip of paper been concealed there, her search should have found it. Nothing.

The shaving kit and threadbare pea jacket were equally barren of anything remotely resembling treasure. "My cousins thought those heavy brass buttons might be worth five dollars apiece," Jemima said ruefully. She looked around the big shabby room and sighed. "If only Uncle Jim hadn't loved secrets so much."

"If he hadn't, your childhood would have been much duller," Oscar reminded her sensibly. He knocked his pipe out on the hearth. "You promised us lunch, and I for one am ready for it. Food first, ratiocination afterwards. Lead us to your galley, Jemima Hawkins, and if it's water biscuits and whale blubber, you'll walk the plank."

"It's cold chicken and fresh salad," Jemima giggled, "but we'll have to pick the greens ourselves. Uncle Jim's garden is just down the drive."

Sigrid looked dubious and Oscar grinned. "Don't worry. I know you can't distinguish lettuce and basil from poison oak and thistles. You stay and detect; we'll pick the salad."

❖ ❖ ❖

Left alone, Sigrid circled the room again. Although spartan in its furnishings, the area itself was so large that another thorough search was impractical. One would have to trust the home ec cousins' expertise. As a homicide detective with her own expertise, she told Nauman that logic would uncover a treasure if it were there to be found, but perhaps she'd spoken too soon.

If there were a treasure . . .

She stared again at the forlorn table where Jemima's uncle had died so peacefully. At the drawing paraphernalia and the uncompleted map. At the empty chest on the floor, its lid ajar to receive a treasure as soon as old Jim Hawkins had mapped its burial site. She lingered over the two framed charts and a sudden thought made her measure the older one against the leather portfolio.

Jemima said this had been the very first *Treasure Island* map her uncle had attempted and that he'd kept it for sentimental reasons. But what if this were the map Robert Louis Stevenson had drawn himself. Wouldn't that be a real treasure? And what better place to hide it than in plain sight, passed off as Hawkins' own work?

She strode across the rough-planked floor and pulled two likely books from the shelves beneath the windows. One was a fairly recent biography of Stevenson, the other a facsimile copy of the first edition of

Treasure Island. Both contained identical reproductions of the author's map, and the biography's version was labeled *Frontispiece of the first edition as drawn by RLS in his father's office in Edinburgh.*

She carried the books over to the table, but there was no denying the evidence of her eyes: the embellishments were different and the map Hawkins had brought home from London was misproportioned. The uncle's island had been drawn slightly longer and not quite as wide as Stevenson's original version.

Disappointed, Sigrid returned the books to their former slots and continued circling the room. Surely that expensive portfolio had something to do with the treasure. Or was it only a bon voyage gift from the nurses when Hawkins was shipped home?

She paused in the door of the tiny bath and inspected the battered shaving kit again. Had such a homely everyday pouch once held diamonds or gold?

Nothing about the cottage indicated a taste for luxury. Devising modest treasures and drawing exquisitely precise maps for his young namesake seemed to have been the caretaker's only extravagance. Otherwise, he had lived almost as a hermit, spare and ascetic, still making do with an ancient pea jacket whose eight brass buttons were probably worth more than everything else in his wardrobe.

She paused by the chair which held the jacket and again tried to make herself take each item on the table top separately and significantly.

And then she saw it.

When Jemima and Oscar reentered the cottage, hilarious with the outrageous combination of herbs and salad greens they had picked, they found Sigrid standing by the window with her finger marking a place in the blue clothbound book she'd read as a child. Jemima started to regale her with their collection, but Oscar took one look at Sigrid's thin face and said, "You found it."

Her wide gray eyes met his and a smile almost brushed her lips. "Can you phone your expert at Yale?" she asked Jemima.

"Sure, but he checked all the books before. Or did you find a hidden one?"

Sigrid shook her head. "Not a book. The map." She pointed to the older of the framed charts.

"What's special about Uncle Jim's map? Its not the original, if that's what you're thinking. Charlie told me that one was auctioned off in the forties and he's pretty sure the same person still owns it."

Nauman had found a reproduction of the original and silently compared it to the faded chart on the table. "Look, Siga, the proportions are wrong."

"I know," she said, and there was definite mischief in her eyes now. "That's precisely why you should call him, Jemima."

"You mean the books are all wrong?" asked the girl.

Sigrid opened the blue book to the forward. "Listen," she said. With one hand hooked into the pocket of her jeans, she leaned against the stone chimney and read in a cool clear voice Stevenson's own version of how he came to write *Treasure Island*, of how, in that rainy August of 1881, he and his stepson, "with the aid of pen and ink and shilling box of water colours," had passed their afternoon drawing.

> On one of these occasions, I made a map of an island . . . the shape of it took my fancy beyond expression . . . and I ticketed it "Treasure Island". . . the next thing I knew, I had some papers before me and was writing out a list of characters.

Sigrid turned the pages. "The next is familiar territory. The story was written, serialized in a magazine, and then was to be published in book form." She read again,

> I sent in my manuscript, and the map along with it . . . the proofs came, they were corrected, but I heard nothing of the map. I wrote and asked; was told it had never been received, and sat aghast. It is one thing to draw a map at random, set a scale in one corner of it . . . and write up a story to the measurements. It is quite another to have to examine a whole book, make an inventory of it, and, with a pair of compasses, painfully design a map to suit the data. I did it; and the map was drawn in my father's office . . . but somehow it was never Treasure Island to me.

Sigrid closed the book. 'If you'll look closely, Jemima, you'll see the handwriting on that map's a lot closer to Stevenson's than to your uncle's."

Oscar compared the maps with an artist's eye, then lifted the phone and wryly handed it to Jemima. "Call your friend."

It took several calls around New Haven and surrounding summer cottages to chase Jemima's expert to earth. While they waited, Oscar created an elaborate dressing for their salad and sliced the cold chicken.

Lunch was spread on the porch and Sigrid was trying to decide if she really approved mixing basil and parsley together when Jemima danced through the open doorway.

"He's going to call Sotheby's in New York!" she caroled. "And he's coming out himself just to make sure; but if its genuine, he says it'll bring thousands—enough to pay for at least two years in any M.S. program in the United States!"

Oscar removed an overlooked harlequin beetle from the salad bowl and filled Jemima's plate. "Admit it, though," he said to Sigrid. "It was the coincidence of remembering that passage from your childhood book that made you suspect the map, not logic."

"It was logic," she said firmly, forking through the salad carefully in case more beetles had been overlooked. She was not opposed to food foraged in a garden instead of in a grocery, but Nauman was entirely too casual about the wildlife.

"Show me the logic," Oscar challenged, and Jemima looked at her expectantly, too.

"All right," said Sigrid. "Why would your uncle acquire an expensive portfolio if not to bring home something special?"

"It didn't have to be that map."

"No? What else was the right size?"

"Even so," objected Oscar, "why not assume he was taking pains with it because it was the first copy he'd drawn himself?"

"Because it's been folded. You can still see the crease lines. If he'd ever folded it up himself, why buy a leather case to carry it flat? We'll probably never know exactly how the map disappeared in the 1880's and reappeared during the Blitz, but I'd guess one of the publisher's clerks misfiled it or maybe an office boy lifted it and then was afraid to own up."

"So that it rattled around in someone's junk room until it caught a nurse or corpsman's eye and they thought it would cheer up their Yank patient? Maybe," Oscar conceded. He cocked a skeptical eye at Sigrid. "So, on the basis of some old crease marks, you instantly deduced this was the original Stevenson-drawn *Treasure Island* map?"

"They helped. Made it seem as if that paper hadn't been carefully handled from the beginning." She peered at a suspicious dark fleck beneath a leaf of spinach. "Too, he'd told Jemima that if it hadn't been for the nurses, he wouldn't have recognized the treasure when it appeared. Lying there in bed, he would have read the book they'd given him from cover to cover, wouldn't he? Including the foreword about the missing map? I'm sure it would have interested him because of his own mapping skills. That' s really what made me look twice: the map was all wrong.

"Jemima's uncle was far too skillful to have miscopied a map with the book right there in front of him. I don't care how sentimental he might later have been over a first attempt, I couldn't see him framing and hanging a misdrawn, ill-proportioned copy.

"And *that*," she concluded triumphantly as she presented Oscar with a potato beetle done in by his dressing, "is logic."

Alfred Hitchcock's Mystery Magazine, September 1989

Out of Whole Cloth

I've always enjoyed stories in which the biter gets bitten and when Marilyn Wallace started editing the Sisters in Crime *series, this seemed an appropriate contribution.*

Cait Fabrics' annual banquet had always been one of Turlton's most glittering galas; but after tonight, the Cait sisters would be officially retired, so this year's celebration was expected to out-glitter all previous banquets. And since Cait Fabrics affected businesses far beyond the city's booming economy, the banquet had even occasioned a few inches in *The Wall Street Journal:*

> *Turlton, NC—Control of a small but prosperous company passes tonight to a new generation. Named president of Cait Fabrics is Lucinda Ashley, granddaughter of Sarah Cait Engles and great-niece of Naomi Cait, co-founders of the North Carolina firm.*
>
> *The Cait sisters inherited a run-down gingham mill in 1930, and expanded it to a leading producer of high-quality industrial textiles by an early recognition of the automotive industry's need for rugged but attractive fabrics.*
>
> *A graduate of Harvard Business School, Ms. Ashley follows the family tradition of aggressive marketing. Cait recently signed contracts to furnish all fabrics for the new multi-million-dollar convention center in Stuttgart, West Germany.*

In her private suite high above the hotel ballroom where other Cait Fabrics personnel were gathering for pre-banquet cocktails, Sarah Cait Engles lifted a crystal goblet with a hand that was wrinkled but steady. "To Stuttgart!" she said.

"To Lucinda!" Naomi Cait smiled fondly.

Gowned in apricot silk, her dark hair braided with gold ribbons, Lu Ashley looked like a fashion model as she accepted their tribute, but her brown eyes held executive wariness when her brother raised his own glass and said, "To the New York Stock Exchange."

"And just what is that supposed to mean?"

"Oh, Lu," their mother said with a sigh. "Nicky didn't mean a thing."

Sally Engles Ashley had spent thirty years explaining her firstborn to her mother and aunt. Now it began to look as if she'd spend the next thirty explaining him to her daughter. "What Nicky meant—"

"I know what he meant, Mother, and he can forget it! Cait Fabrics isn't going after the private home market."

"Don't count on it, baby sister," Nicky mocked, sipping his champagne as he lounged on his grandmother's velvet sofa. An unrepentant grasshopper, he had sneered at his sister's antlike devotion to work too often to expect the company presidency; but being passed over rankled, and he did not look forward to tonight's public coronation. "I'm not the only stockholder who thinks dividends would be larger if the company diversified."

Fearing fresh arguments, Sally Ashley peered at her diamond watch in pretended alarm. "Oh, dear! We're late for our own party. Come down with me, Nicky? I promised the senator you and I would have a drink with him before dinner."

Nicky started to argue, then gave a what-the-hell shrug and stood up.

Relieved, Sally adjusted her mink stole. "I'll tell everyone you'll be right down," she told the others, and hurried Nicky out to the private elevator before he could further antagonize them.

As the door closed behind her daughter and grandson, Sarah Cait Engles held out her glass for more champagne. "They can't start dinner without us," she said serenely.

Even with silver hair, the two sisters were still slim of body and straight of spine. Sarah had been nineteen, Naomi twenty, when they were left to run the broken-down mill.

"Nicky's an ass," said Lu, "but he could stir up the stockholders."

"You'll manage," Naomi said. "Cait women have always been a match for Cait men. Remember how we managed dear Uncle Bob, Sarah?" Her voice put quotation marks around *dear Uncle Bob*.

"Your father's brother?" asked Lu, vaguely remembering. "Didn't he try to take over the company back at the beginning?

"Nicky's very much a Cait man," said Sarah, and Naomi nodded.

"Papa and Uncle Bob inherited the mill from their father but Uncle Bob was so taken with the novelty of airplanes and flying that Papa bought him out with Mama's dowry. When she died, Papa started drinking and would've let the mill go under, only Uncle Bob talked him into flying around the world in his new hydroplane. They both disappeared, the Depression worsened, and we almost lost the mill."

Lu was familiar with their long hard struggle—the skepticism of their customers, the reluctance of bankers to lend dwindling funds to mere girls, the loyalty of their workers. Gradually, however, the red ink had begun to blacken.

"If Sarah hadn't talked Continental Motors into using our fabric in their new runabouts—"

"Your designs sold themselves," Sarah said generously.

Six years after the two men disappeared, the sisters had toasted their first real profits with the last bottle of Grandfather Cait's pre-Prohibition brandy. A week later, their small piece of the sky fell in.

Sarah had looked up from her desk to see a man striding across their office. "Sarah!" he cried. "Naomi! My little girls!"

"Papa?" they'd asked wonderingly.

Edward Cait had left with black hair and mustache. This man was clean-shaven and completely gray. According to him, their plane had floundered off the coast of France. Bob drowned, but Ed had been picked up by a homeward-bound Japanese steamer and it had taken him this long to work his way back from Tokyo.

"Six years?" asked Lu, watching champagne bubbles effervesce in her glass.

"He kept getting sidetracked," said Sarah; and Naomi murmured, "A large Hawaiian woman, a cook in L.A., and wasn't that Kansas woman who kept writing him letters a librarian?"

He had toured the renovated mill and generously praised what the sisters had achieved. "But now that Papa's home, my little girls can be ladies again." He smiled. "You'll go to parties, go to dances . . ."

The sisters exchanged horrified glances. "Who'll run the mill?" they asked.

"It needs a man's firm hand on the stick. Things young ladies can't understand. Making cloth for car seats is just a start. This is 1936! Aeroplanes carry people almost as regularly as trains. Bob was right: The future's in flight and Cait Mills will move with the future!"

The analogy of a man's firm hand on the stick confirmed the sisters' worst fears.

That night, after the fatted calf had been eaten and the prodigal had retired to an early bed, Naomi and Sarah asked one of his guests to remain behind. Judge Sims had considered himself a sort of substitute father to the two young women during his friend's long absence, but his indulgent smile changed to a frown when they said, "He's not Papa."

The judge had spent the evening reminiscing about boyhood days with Ed and Bob Cait, and now Ed's daughters were saying he was an impostor?

"Rubbish," said Sims. "He knew about our Haw River mud slides and snatching ice chunks from the ice wagon and—"

"He's Uncle Bob," Sarah said. "It must have been Papa who drowned, and now that Uncle Bob's tired of bumming around the world, he wants to come back and take over *our* mill."

"Would our own father abandon us for six whole years?" asked Naomi.

If the judge remembered a streak of irresponsibility in both Cait boys, he suppressed it. "I suppose Bob *could* pass himself off as Ed," he said, rubbing his long chin judiciously, "but proving it might be difficult."

"*Prove?*" roared a voice from the hall. "*Prove?* You know who I am, Sims. Naomi, Sarah—why?"

"We're sorry, Uncle Bob, but we cannot let you take our papa's place," they told him firmly.

❖ ❖ ❖

The story swept through Turlton and within days everyone in town had chosen sides. Pulp thrillers had popularized the infallibility of fingerprints; unfortunately, neither brother's had ever been recorded. Doc Harris recalled cutting out Bob's appendix, but not Ed's. If this was Ed, let him show a smooth belly.

The returnee admitted a scar but claimed it had been done in Tokyo. Doc Harris said he recognized his own stitch marks, and Cait called him an old fool. Those who saw the scar said it looked fairly new.

Dental records might have helped, but hoping to cover his stock-market losses, Dr. Todd had burned down his office for the insurance money and was now serving time for arson.

Judge Sims remembered that one of his boyhood chums had a webbed little toe, but was that Ed or was it Bob?

"Ed!" cried half of the old swimming-hole gang. "Bob!" shouted the other half.

Turlton might still be divided if Flossie Lanigan hadn't gone to Judge Sims and reminded him of the nights Ed Cait had drowned his sorrows down at Sullivan's speakeasy after his wife died. Flossie was a woman "no better than she ought to be," and what she whispered in Judge Sims's ear was soon snickered about all over town.

That was when Cait gave in. He was willing to take off a shoe and sock and he didn't mind lifting his shirt, but he'd be damned if he was going to drop his pants so the whole town could verify what he swore was a dirty lie in the first place.

He took the small allowance Naomi and Sarah offered and left them in undisputed control of Cait Fabrics. It was thought he ended his days in Hawaii, half a world from Turlton's ribald laughter.

"What did that Lanigan woman *say?*" asked Lu, amused.

"We were never quite sure," Sarah said primly. "Nice young ladies didn't know about such things back then."

"Well, I just hope I have your luck when the showdown with Nicky comes," said Lu, gathering up her wrap.

"It wasn't luck, dear," said Naomi as Sarah daintily swallowed the last of her champagne. "We knew Flossie wanted a respectable job at the mill."

"You mean you gave her a good job because she convinced Judge Sims that Uncle Bob wasn't your father?"

"Oh, no, dear." Her grandmother beamed. "We gave her a *very* good job because she convinced Judge Sims that *Papa* was dear Uncle Bob."

Sisters in Crime 2, 1990

My Mother, My Daughter, Me

All of my stories have been set in the current "now" of when they were written—all except this one. The World War II flashback was important to the story, which meant it had to be set in the Sixties to work properly. It was interesting to try to think myself back to that mindset.

It isn't just me, is it? Surely other mothers of little girls experience this uncanny sensation when time overlaps and folds back, when they feel they've lived this incident before in another body or seen it through different eyes?

For instance, when I tell five-year-old Beth, "You're not going out in shorts in the middle of winter" and she glares at me a long level moment before she stalks off to change, then I know—I mean I really *know*—exactly what she's feeling. More than that, I *am* her, whirling away from my mother and biting back the rebellious words that would get me a spanking.

I flounce upstairs and yank open the dresser for those ugly woolen slacks, banging my anger, but not hard enough to bring Mama up with the fly swatter. (And how come *that* never gets put away for winter?)

With an almost physical jerk, I pull myself back to the present of 1965. I'm me again and getting irritable and if Beth slams the drawer just one more time, she's going to get a smack on the bottom.

You see? It's been like this since she was a toddler. My husband doesn't understand; but a girlfriend said recently, "I never liked my mother much till my daughter started glaring at me every time I spoke to her. Suddenly I understand." Yes.

And yet, somehow, that isn't exactly it. Not all of it anyhow. Even though I'm an adult now, safely married with a successful husband, comfortable house, and daughter of my own, it's only the child I once was that I fully understand, not Mama. I was probably no more aggravating than Beth, but these day-to-day flashes of irritation don't make me stop loving Beth. So why did Mama stop loving me?

Perhaps if she hadn't died the year I married Carter, Beth's birth could have bridged the unspoken distance between us. Or is the apparent warmth between most mothers and their grownup daughters only a mutual pretense while the politeness between Mama and me is the unavoidable reality?

Must Beth and I come to that?

I was four, almost five, when I learned not to take Mama's love for granted. Her moods were as uncertain as that war-time spring of 1945. There were moments of unquestioned security, but too often I would look up from play and see her watching me from a window, her eyes bleak with foreboding—almost as if I were a Nazi hand grenade primed to explode in her face.

Eventually, as the larger world groped its way back to sanity, so did my small one. My father came home from the Merchant Marine to stay, and, by the time I was an adolescent, the stiffness between Mama and me was taken for granted. Yet even now, twenty years later, when Beth touches in me a sense of déjà vu and I look at myself/Mama through Beth's/my eyes, I yearn for that barely-remembered closeness and again I wonder . . .

❖ ❖ ❖

Today I sit before the mirror in my bedroom, intent on getting my makeup exactly right. I'm meeting my husband for dinner and, like most men, Carter feels flattered when he thinks I've taken special pains just for him. Except for slipping into my new mini-skirted A-line, I can leave as soon as our teenaged neighbor gets home from school to sit with Beth.

Beth sprawls across my bed as she watches me in the mirror and whines halfheartedly about being left behind. She knows I won't relent and that Karen will indulge her most outrageous demands, but she has to keep her hand in. Her restless fingers flip the dial of my clock-radio, and as the serious tones of a newscast fill the room, I lift my hand to keep her from changing it. My favorite cousin is with the Seventh Fleet, but it isn't mentioned; and when I drop my hand, Beth turns to a rock station, muttering, "Why do they always have to have wars?"

Why? I echo silently. The newest Beatles song floods the room, but I'm lost in sudden memories of the staccato war bulletins that used to burst from our old radio and transfix the grownups in alert uneasiness. The words, urgent and tense and half-obscured with static, meant nothing to me; but that sudden adult fear made me afraid, too, without knowing why.

After "God bless Mama and Daddy," I was taught to pray, "and bring Uncle Paul home safe from the war." But that was as much a part of the ritualistic ending as "and-make-me-a-good-girl-amen." Uncle Paul,

Mama's younger brother, had been in Europe for three of my four years and I did not remember him. He was killed at Bastogne in December of 1944, although it was March before we knew for sure. When Mama put down the phone, I was appalled. I'd never seen her cry, had never realized there were things that *could* make an adult cry.

Someone—I forget just who—put an arm around Mama and shooed me off to the candy store with a handful of pennies. That night Mama interrupted my prayers harshly. "Didn't you understand? Uncle Paul is *dead!*" And so I stopped praying for him, even though his deletion left a gap in the singsong formula that bothered me for months.

❖ ❖ ❖

Eyes finished, I begin on my lips and Beth draws near to watch. She stands on one foot and leans against my bare shoulder, staring at me in the mirror objectively while her lips arc in unconscious imitation. Amused, I recall watching Mama put on her blood-red lipstick; but this is only another of those surface memories that color all our familiar actions when our children watch.

Bored, Beth goes to the window to look for Karen, then returns to play with the dozen or so perfume vials on my dressing table, souvenirs of all the foreign ports my cousin's ship has visited.

A schoolbus rumbles to a halt outside and the little glass bottles tinkle as Beth whirls away, dancing across the room to the window.

"Karen! Wait! I'm coming now!" she shrieks, and kisses me hastily. I hear her light footsteps patter on the stairs as I, too, call down to Karen with last-minute instructions.

Beth waves up to me as I stand at the window in my lace-trimmed slip; and although her smile is gay, though she leaves me without another backward look, skipping up to Karen and draping the older girl's sweater around her thin shoulders as she follows Karen across our wide lawn, I am suddenly filled with unbearable anguish and something colder.

Guilt?

Guilt at deserting my child?

Ridiculous! I'm as good a homemaker as Donna Reed, as devoted a mother as June Cleaver. Surely the few hours I'm away each week take nothing from Beth. Her father and I will be home before nine thirty. Carter doesn't like late hours or any music that rocks harder than Pat Boone's, and after six years of marriage, we don't exactly linger over candlelit tables.

But the feeling of guilt persists, overshadowed now by a growing sense of desolation so strong that I sit down before the mirror again, perplexed. Absently I straighten the perfume bottles Beth has muddled and see that one has come unstopped. It's a small cube of dark green porcelain, sprigged with minute red roses, and its heavy fragrance permeates down through layer after layer of suppressed memories . . . *how incredible that I could have forgotten so completely!*

❧ ❧ ❧

It arrived on a cold dreary day in early March when it seemed that winter would last forever. Mama took the box from the postman and knelt on the living room rug to tear it open. It'd been months since Daddy's last short leave, and presents trickled back to us in lieu of the letters he never wrote.

I realize now that those presents must have been a pledge more to himself than to Mama and me that there was a time and world unbounded by gray North Atlantic waters and deadly U-boats. In later years he was such a silent, preoccupied, just-there father that I forgot how perceptive his gifts had been.

I asked him once to tell me how mermaids ran and was crushed when he explained the difference between the glittering mermaids I'd imagined and the grim actuality of the Murmansk Run. But weeks later, he sent back a tiny wooden mermaid scaled with golden sequins.

That day, Mama lifted the square green bottle from its nest of tissue and let me touch the exquisite ceramic roses. Then she smoothed some perfume on her bare white arms and lay back upon the rug, her eyes closed; and while chill March rains streamed down the windowpanes, the room filled with the heavy, languorous scent of full-blown roses under a hot June sun.

"What does this say?" I asked tickling her nose with the note that had fallen out. She opened her eyes, crossed them for my benefit, and read, " 'This reminded me of the day we met.' "

"Didn't you always know Daddy?' I asked, as much in surprise as to prolong her mood.

"I was the original farmer's daughter," she answered fliply. She gazed around the spacious rooms with their deep rugs and polished tables and Sadie clattering out in the kitchen beyond many closed doors. "Luckily for me, he wasn't a traveling salesman."

I held my breath, hoping she would go on. She so seldom forgot that I was a child. She lay on the rug looking up at the ceiling with dreamy eyes and let me see her as she'd been that hot summer day when Daddy drove by in the first yellow convertible she'd ever seen.

Sweaty and barefoot, she'd just hoed to the end of a long tobacco row when Daddy tapped his horn and asked if he were on the Raleigh road. He wasn't but before he could turn the car, its radiator boiled over.

"Your Uncle Paul was only sixteen and practically pushing his mule and plow down the furrow, just dying to see that car up close."

One good look at Mama with her long black hair hanging free beneath a faded straw hat, and Daddy couldn't seem to get his yellow convertible started again.

He accepted Grampa's invitation to a cold glass of sweet tea and would have maneuvered to stay for supper if Uncle Paul, tempted beyond the limits of good manners, hadn't slipped down the lane in the growing dusk and started the car with no trouble. Mama walked down the lane with him, pausing in the twilight to pick a cluster of Gran's climbing roses.

"They were still warm from the sun and your daddy took them and said he was sure he could get lost again the next week if he tried. Anyhow, we got married right after barning season."

She was eighteen.

It was better than a fairy tale and Daddy was Prince Charming. I was so full of love for them both that I hugged Mama hard. She squeezed me absently, then got up and stood before the mirror above our marble fireplace. She tucked stray ends of her black hair into its smooth pageboy.

"I'm twenty-five years old and just look at me! My life's half over and nothing's happening. Oh, Libby, your daddy's been gone so long and this old war's never going to end. I'm so tired of being lonesome!"

I could have wept for her; but Sadie came in just then, her small frame draped in a long raincoat, to tell Mama our lunch was ready. With Daddy gone, there wasn't enough work to fill Sadie's day, so Mama made her leave at noon.

She would have dispensed with Sadie altogether if Daddy'd let her because she felt Sadie blamed her for all the changes the war had made: Daddy's absence, the parties no longer given, the other maids lured away by higher factory wages. But things had been changing for our family long before the latest war. Once the whole northwest quadrant of town had been Watson land; now our house stood on less than a hundred acres of scrub woodland. A hundred acres out of all those thousands, and what had been an isolated country estate was increasingly threatened by gas stations, factories, and truck-filled highways as the town pushed north and west and began to act like a city.

As the youngest Watson, I didn't mind the encroachment. A ten minute walk along neglected bridle paths brought me out to the highway where a small general store sat between two truck depots. Sugar rationing or not, one glass case was always heaped with penny candy, and if I didn't have a penny, one of the drivers lounging there between runs would usually treat a little girl if she looked wistful enough. At four-going-on-five, I'd barely heard of Shirley Temple or Margaret O'Brien, but already I knew instinctively how to lift my blue eyes to those male faces and get what I wanted.

That's where I met Jethridge. He gave me cinnamon jawbreakers and dizzying heart-stopping rides on his Harley-Davidson motorcycle. In one truck yard, around the store, and back through the other yard. Most of the truckers were too old for the army, but Jethridge was youth and laughter and swaggering masculinity in a black leather jacket studded with bright nailheads and chips of red glass. He made a pet of me, and as I ran through the lane, jumped the ditch, and darted across the cement road, I always hoped he'd be there, back from Nashville, Atlanta, or Lexington.

He was there the day after Daddy's perfume came, and when I tripped on the doorsill and fell sprawling on the planked floor with a skinned knee, it was Jethridge who picked me up and took me home.

He placed me on the back of his glittering machine as if I were a princess and I clasped him tightly around his waist and laid my cheek against the cold leather of his jacket. It smelled of motor oil and hair tonic as we roared along the highway. He throttled down as we came to the end of our long driveway into the yard, but Mama heard and came out onto the porch.

"Carry me," I coaxed and was swooped up in his arms again. For one aching moment, I longed for my own daddy; then Mama was there with worried questions as Jethridge carried me into the house.

She removed the splinter and cleaned my knee, but before she could ease him out of the house with polite dismissive thanks, I put on my prissiest Watson manners, which always amused her. "You must allow us to repay your courtesy, Jethridge."

That was the first time, and if Sadie didn't approve of serving coffee to leather-jacketed truck drivers in our living room she kept it to herself.

Or tried to.

Jethridge must have noticed, though, for when he stopped by to ask how I was the next day, it was after Sadie had gone.

Mama sparkled that afternoon, gayer than I'd seen her since Daddy left, and her dimples flashed when Jethridge said, "Now I see where Libby gets her charm." I made him tell her my favorite trucking stories, and Mama laughed as much as I did.

I was central and necessary those first few days until the phone call about Uncle Paul made Mama cry. When I returned from the store with my candy, something in the relationship had shifted—a sudden tension in the air which didn't include me. Later, though, as I lay in bed, their voices floated up the stairwell and I could hear Mama's careless laughter and the familiar swagger in Jethridge's tones. The whole house seemed to drift on a sea of warm June roses and I fell asleep reassured.

❖ ❖ ❖

April set a new pattern for our days: Mama no longer let me go to the store, but Jethridge made up for it by spending most of his layover times with us. Soon after Sadie left each day, we'd hear the pop of his motorcycle and I'd race across our wide porch and down the steps to fling myself upon him and rifle his pockets for the jawbreakers he kept stashed for me. Then he'd swing me up behind him, and we'd roar through the old bridle paths, avoiding Sadie's cottage on the far side of the land, to end up in a skid by the porch where Mama waited with mocking laughter. "Four-year-olds, the both of you!"

At first Mama refused to ride behind him. "It's not ladylike," she protested; or, "Can you imagine what Sadie would say if she saw me?"

We hooted at the thought of Sadie's face, but Jethridge teased her and eventually she even managed to ride alone—never very expertly, but she could wobble down to the end of our long drive, circle awkwardly, and return without falling. She was so competent with the little red coupe Daddy had given her when I was born that I couldn't understand her ineptitude, but Jethridge seemed charmed and corrected her mistakes indulgently. Then Mama would shrug prettily and declare that only a man could handle such a monstrous machine.

Late in April, he left for a four-day haul to Nashville, and as Mama and I waved goodbye from the porch, I squeezed her hand and said, "Aren't you glad I found Jethridge? You're not lonesome any more, are you?"

She jerked her hand away with a strange look, then kneeling beside me and talking very fast, she explained that Jethridge was my friend—that she let him visit only because I liked him so much. Did I understand? Her hands hurt as she grasped my shoulders, and I nodded, too scared by her sudden intensity to speak.

Mama changed after that. The house no longer smelled of warm roses. Spring was upon us and soon Daddy would be home again, but I felt confused and often caught Mama looking at me as if I were about to do something horrible.

Jethridge changed, too. He still came, but he had no laughter and no time for me. I was turned out of the house to play in the sun or hide myself under the Cape Jessamine bushes and brood on what I'd done to make them hate me.

One early May night, a roll of thunder from a spring storm awakened me. It sounded like Nazi bombers, and I'd just opened my door to go to Mama when I heard her voice, no longer low and sweet but edged with the new sharpness she used on me. Jethridge's words were soft and coaxing but hers shrilled above them. "Leave all this for some white-trash bungalow while you're on the road half of your life? Don't be as childish as Libby!"

Lightning flashed outside as matching anger rose in his voice. I crept back to bed, pulled the covers over my head to shut out both storms, and wished that the next roll of thunder really would be Nazi bombers so Jethridge could be brave and rescue us and make Mama like him again. I must have dozed off, because when next I sat up in bed, all was quiet downstairs. The rain had dwindled to a steady drizzle, but I heard the sound of Mama's car as lights swept briefly across my bedroom ceiling. From my window, I heard the motor go silent in the drive below and the door quietly open and close. I waited to hear her come up the porch steps but long minutes passed. Suddenly I realized that Jethridge, too, must have been there in the dark shadows beyond her car, for I heard his Harley-Davidson splutter several times before catching.

Kneeling by the window, I saw its red taillight wobble unsteadily down our long straight drive and disappear in the rain.

And still Mama did not appear. At last I crept out to the landing, feeling strange and lonely. Viewed through the railings, the big rooms below were shadowy and frightening in their emptiness, and one of Grandmother Watson's Chinese lamps was lying on the floor, its silk shade torn and the bulb splintered upon the rug.

I huddled on the landing, afraid to go down and even more afraid to go back to my dark room. I must have slept again because Mama woke me as she was tucking me into my bed. I clung to her, sobbing, and felt her hair hanging in cold wet strings like a soaked floor mop. Her cool skin smelled faintly of gasoline.

"You left me," I sobbed. "You and Jethridge went away and I was all alone."

"Little goose," she soothed. "Jethridge left *hours* ago, right after you went to bed. And I didn't leave you. I just ran outside to bring in the lawn chair cushions before the rain spoiled them."

"But the lamp," I quavered, confused. 'I didn't break it, Mama. It was just lying there. Honest."

"There's nothing wrong with the lamp. You've had a bad dream. You always have bad dreams when it thunders. Remember? Go back to sleep now and forget all about it."

In the bright sunlight of morning, the night's strangeness really did seem like a bad dream. The Chinese lamp was in its accustomed place, bulb intact; and if there was a neatly mended tear in the silk shade, well, many things had been repaired instead of replaced during the endless war. By the time Sadie arrived that morning, Mama had begun a sudden orgy of spring cleaning. Even after Sadie left, Mama kept cleaning, and Jethridge did not come.

That afternoon I sneaked over to the store with the last pennies he'd given me. Afterwards, Mama heard me crying under the Cape Jessamines. At the store they'd talked of Jethridge's death—how his beautiful Harley-Davidson must have skidded at the bad curve on Ridge Road during the thunderstorm and plunged down the hillside. A terrible accident, they said. Just terrible.

Mama's hand clenched my arm as I sobbed out my news. One of her pretty red fingernails was broken to the quick and I remembered that it was broken like that when she soothed away my bad dream. Yet as soon as I told her what the men said about Jethridge's terrible accident, the tightness went out of her fingers and she forgot to spank me for going to the store.

By the time Daddy came home, she was almost her old self; but if her face froze when I was prattling to my father, then I would choose my words with care.

Fear that she would tell him whatever it was that I'd done wrong those past few months made me avoid any references to that time and I buried Jethridge so deeply that only the smell of sun-warmed roses could—

"Aren't you going?" asks Beth from the doorway and before I think, I hiss, "What are you doing here, you sneaking little—"

Suddenly everything snaps back into focus.

"Sorry, honey," I smile. "I was daydreaming and you startled me."

She hugs me in relief. We find the toy she came back for and I kiss her goodbye again.

So *that's* all it was!

Poor stupid Mama! How incredibly careless to let a four-year-old witness her one shabby little affair. But what a stroke of luck for her that Jethridge was killed when their romance turned sour, before Sadie found out for sure. Remembering the man's swagger of confidence, I doubt if he'd have let Mama go back to being a proper Watson wife without a messy scandal.

If it weren't so pathetic, I could almost laugh with relief to know finally, after so many years of wondering, that the coldness between Mama and me wasn't something Beth and I need ever endure.

I'll have to be careful, though, about lashing out at Beth like that again. She's not me and I'm not Mama, but neither is she a baby any more. I mustn't let her become puzzled or uneasy—she and Carter are much too close.

I glance at the diamond-rimmed watch Carter gave me on our fifth anniversary. Nearly four. Already?

Carter expects me at seven. Even if I hurry, I'll only have two hours with Mitch and he'll probably spend most of it sulking and going on and on about how I put my reputation above his love. He's really getting tiresome. I could almost wish *he* had a Harley-Davidson so I could . . .

Oh my sweet Jesus!

Mama?

Alfred Hitchcock's Mystery Magazine, March 1990

Small Club Lead, Dummy Plays Low

Since I majored in bridge in college, it seemed appropriate to structure at least one story around the game.

Arriving home from a bridal luncheon that Saturday afternoon, Milly Duncan hummed a soft tune and the car, a recent gift from her husband, hummed back. She knew she was supposed to be lulled by its sleek power, but life with Randall necessitated alertness and over the years she'd learned to gauge the intensity of his affairs by the gifts he bestowed on her at the beginning of each new one. If gold earrings implied a one-night stand and a mink jacket had meant he was temporarily playing house with someone in the city, what was she to make of such expensive conscience salve as this shiny new car?

If only she could just ask him! Out of the question, of course; a violation of the rules by which they'd both been reared, rules which said a wife should ignore her husband's affairs as long as they took nothing from his family.

"But that's disgusting!" Karen Drew had objected when Milly once spoke of this over morning coffee. Milly had prudently kept the discussion hypothetical because those same rules prevented one from hanging out the family undies before a next-door neighbor. Besides, at home, among their friends, Randall *was* a loving husband and father—why spoil a good illusion?

"You honestly think you'd keep quiet if you knew Randall was sleeping with someone else?" Karen had demanded indignantly.

"As long as he behaved discreetly and it didn't affect our child, I'd certainly try," said Milly.

"Well, not me! If I ever caught Charles tomcatting around, he'd hear about it and fast!"

Which was why she and Karen no longer shared morning coffee. Milly was certain that the redhead had been a momentary aberration for Charles, a flame no hotter than a birthday candle and one that would have died from want of wax and wick if Karen hadn't built it into a bonfire.

Such a stupid mistake and so sad for the Drew children. Deprived of their father, they now made do with a part-time mother. (Despite property settlement and child support, Karen had found that three could not live as cheaply as four.)

"At her age, she was lucky to find a job," said Joan when Milly told them about Karen. The four women—Milly, Joan, Prue and Meg—played bridge once a week. Each lived in a separate suburb and had never met the others' neighbors, but years of weekly gossip made them familiar with many of the details.

"She's only twenty-nine," protested Meg, who was thirty-seven.

"Which makes her ten years older than half the bright young things who flood all the entry-level jobs," said Prue as she competently shuffled the cards.

At forty-two, Prue affected a cynicism that went well with her short, stocky figure and strong face. "What would you do, Meg, if Frank divorced you? What would any of us do? I'd loathe being someone's junior assistant nothing, yet where would I get the money to go back to school while the kids are going? Between women's lib and no-fault divorce, decent alimonies are a thing of the past."

"Women's lib," snorted Joan. "It's all very well for those who want a career instead of children, but what about *us*? Marriage was preached from the cradle up and our husbands were damn well pleased with what they got out of it. Look at me: I dropped out of school to support him through med school, was father and mother to the boys while he established a practice, and now, when he finally has time to notice us, what happens?"

The other three nodded, knowing Joan's husband had begun noticing his cute young office nurse.

"The dreariest job might be worth the freedom," sighed Meg, who was married to a jealous and abusive man.

Milly won the deal and bridge had occupied their conversation the rest of the afternoon. Despite chatter and gossip, the four took the game seriously and each played to win.

Originally, they had anted five dollars on the side, winner of three rubbers taking the pot; but while victory itself remained the sweetest prize, the five dollars had grown to ten, the ten to twenty, and just this week, the stakes had been raised again.

Remembering the radiant face of that young bride-to-be at lunch, Milly felt a little sad as she turned the car onto her street. Once upon a time, she and Randall had been that deliriously happy, had counted the days till they would be alone with each other forever. These days he acted as if he couldn't bear to be left alone with her an hour. Their daughter was away for the weekend, so they had planned dinner at their country club where unsuspecting friends would help fill the silences that had grown between them.

Milly pulled into the driveway and cut the motor. Beyond the shrubs that divided their wide lawns, she saw Karen Drew with a trowel in her hand. Gardening had been Karen's joy before the divorce, now weeds sprouted freely in all her flower borders.

Karen stood to wave, with a wistful smile for Milly's crisp linen dress and air of leisure. "Playing bridge today?" she called.

"No, that's Wednesdays. Today was a luncheon for Randall's niece. She's marrying the man of her dreams this month."

Milly caught herself being bitter, consciously suppressed it, and smiled back at her neighbor. "Karen, it's been ages. Why don't you take a break and come have a drink with Randall and me?"

Karen's tired face lit up. "I shouldn't stop, but just give me a minute to freshen up.

"Good. I'll go break out the ice." Touched by the other's eagerness, Milly entered the house by the side door, filled the ice bucket and then went to call Randall.

After a morning of golf, he usually spent Saturday afternoon in his study, but he didn't look up from his papers as she entered. She circled the desk, saw the bullet wound in his chest and dissolved in screams.

❧ ❧ ❧

It was Karen who called the sheriff and it was Karen who remembered seeing someone enter the Duncan house around two, the approximate time of death. "I was busy weeding and didn't look closely. He wore dark green coveralls, I think, and he carried a toolbox. I thought he was a repairman."

"Height, weight, hair color?" they asked, but Karen shook her head. "Not much over five feet and a stocky build, I think, but I really wasn't paying attention."

When she was calm again, Milly gave the police a list of their usual repairmen and admitted that they usually left the side door unlocked during the day.

In the days that followed, the police learned enough about Randall Duncan's discreet affairs in the city to make them look at Milly again. No matter how perfect suburban friends and neighbors may say a marriage was, any wife who suddenly inherits a sizeable estate, especially one that sizeable, must be able to bear close scrutiny.

Fortunately, the bridal luncheon had been attended by most of Milly's female in-laws and all vouched for her unbroken presence. In fact, she had driven Randall's mother home afterwards and stayed for a glass of sherry. Not even the police could question an alibi furnished by the victim's grieving mother.

❖ ❖ ❖

Two days after the funeral, from her cool and spacious veranda, Milly watched Karen leave for work. It was going to be a scorcher today and already Karen's dress looked wilted by the heat as she herded her children out to the car to be dropped off at a summer day camp.

Poor Karen! Milly couldn't help comparing their conditions. She truly grieved for Randall's death; but if one must lose a husband, how much better widowed than divorced.

Later, she telephoned the minister to thank him for his comfort. The service had been so moving.

She called Randall's mother. Certainly Randall would have wanted them to be brave, and yes, *of course* his niece's wedding should continue as planned.

Last of all, she called Prue to thank her for the wreath she and Joan and Meg had sent. "You'll understand if I don't play bridge this week?" "Certainly, dear," said Prue. There was a short pause and then she said thoughtfully, "You know, Milly, I keep thinking about that last hand we played. If only I had gone up with my ace! I was ahead of you till then."

"I'm sure you'll win next time," said Milly. "I was just lucky last week."

"Serves me right," Prue said briskly. "I should have *known* your king would drop."

New Crimes II, 1990

Deborah's Judgment

When I first began to contemplate a new series, Sara Paretsky asked if I'd contribute a story to her anthology. I'd had the germ of this plot for years but could never seem to bring it into focus. It wasn't a Sigrid Harald situation, but what if I gave it to a young Southern attorney? Or what if she were a district court judge? Or an attorney running for judge? Before I knew it, Deborah Knott strolled into my head and began telling this story. I shall always be grateful to Sara for giving me a chance to "test-drive" Deborah's first-person voice before tackling Bootlegger's Daughter.

"*A*nd Deborah judged Israel at that time."

An inaudible ripple of cognizance swept through the congregation as the pastor of Bethel Baptist Church paused in his reading of the text and beamed down at us.

I was seated on the aisle near the front of the church, and when Barry Blackman's eyes met mine, I put a modest smile on my face, then tilted my head in ladylike acknowledgment of the pretty compliment he was paying me by his choice of subject for this morning's sermon. A nice man but hardly Christianity's most original preacher. I'd announced my candidacy back in December, so this wasn't the first time I'd heard that particular text, and my response had become almost automatic.

He lowered his eyes to the huge Bible and continued to read aloud, "*And she dwelt under the palm tree of Deborah, between Ramah and Bethel in Mount Ephraim; and the children of Israel came up to her for judgment.*"

From your mouth to God's ear, Barry, I thought.

Eight years of courtroom experience let me listen to the sermon with an outward show of close attention while inwardly my mind jumped on and off a dozen trains of thought. I wondered, without really caring, if Barry was still the terrific kisser he'd been the summer after ninth grade when we both drove tractors for my oldest brother during tobacco-barning season.

There was an S curve between the barns and the back fields where the lane dipped past a stream and cut through a stand of tulip poplars and sweetgum trees. Our timing wasn't good enough to hit every trip, but at least two or three times a day it'd work out that we passed each other there in the shady coolness, one on the way out to the field with empty drags, the other headed back to the barn with drags full of heavy green tobacco leaves.

Nobody seemed to notice that I occasionally returned to the barn more flushed beneath the bill of my baseball cap than even the August sun would merit, although I did have to endure some teasing one day when a smear of tobacco tar appeared on my pink T-shirt right over my left breast. "Looks like somebody tried to grab a handful," my sister-in-law grinned.

I muttered something about the tractor's tar-gummy steering wheel, but I changed shirts at lunchtime and for the rest of the summer I wore the darkest T-shirts in my dresser drawer.

Now Barry Blackman was a preacher man running to fat, the father of two little boys and a new baby girl, while Deborah Knott was a still-single attorney running for a seat on the court bench, a seat being vacated against his will by old Harrison Hobart, who occasionally fell asleep these days while charging his own juries.

As Barry drew parallels between Old Testament Israel and modern Colleton County, I plotted election strategy. After the service, I'd do a little schmoozing among the congregation—

Strike "schmoozing," my subconscious stipulated sternly, and I was stricken myself to realize that Lev Schuster's Yiddish phrases continued to infect my vocabulary. Here in rural North Carolina schmoozing's still called socializing, and I'd better not forget it before the primary. I pushed away errant thoughts of Lev and concentrated on lunch at Beulah's. For that matter, where was Beulah and why weren't she and J.C. seated there beside me?

Beulah had been my mother's dearest friend, and her daughter-in-law, Helen, is president of the local chapter of Mothers Against Drunk Driving. They were sponsoring a meet-the-candidates reception at four o'clock in the fellowship hall of a nearby Presbyterian church, and three of the four men running for Hobart's seat would be there too. (The fourth was finishing up the community service old Hobart had imposed in lieu of a fine for driving while impaired, but he really didn't expect to win many MADD votes anyhow.)

Barry's sermon drew to an end just a hair short of equating a vote for Deborah Knott as a vote for Jesus Christ. The piano swung into the opening chords of "Just as I Am," and the congregation stood to sing all five verses. Happily, no one accepted the hymn's invitation to be saved that morning, and after a short closing prayer we were dismissed.

I'm not a member at Bethel, but I'd been a frequent visitor from the month I was born; so I got lots of hugs and howdies and promises of loyal support when the primary rolled around. I hugged and howdied right back and thanked them kindly, all the time edging toward my car.

It was starting to bother me that neither Beulah nor J.C. had come to church. Then Miss Callie Ogburn hailed me from the side door, talking sixty to the yard as she bustled across the grass.

"Beulah called me up first thing this morning and said tell you about J.C. and for you to come on anyhow. She phoned all over creation last night trying to let you know she's still expecting you to come for dinner."

That explained all those abortive clicks on my answering machine. Beulah was another of my parents' generation who wouldn't talk to a tape. I waited till Miss Callie ran out of breath, then asked her what it was Beulah wanted to tell me about J.C.

"He fell off the tractor and broke his leg yesterday, and he's not used to the crutches yet, so Beulah didn't feel like she ought to leave him this morning. You know how she spoils him."

I did. J.C. was Beulah's older brother, and he'd lived with her and her husband Sam almost from the day they were married more than forty years ago. J.C. was a born bachelor, and except for the war years when he worked as a carpenter's helper at an air base over in Goldsboro, he'd never had much ambition beyond helping Sam farm. Sam always said J.C. wasn't much of a leader but he was a damn good follower and earned every penny of his share of the crop profits.

Although I'd called them Cousin Beulah and Cousin Sam till I was old enough to drop the courtesy title, strictly speaking, only Sam Johnson was blood kin. But Beulah and my mother had been close friends since childhood, and Beulah's two children fit into the age spaces around my older brothers, which was why we'd spent so many Sundays at Bethel Baptist.

When Sam died seven or eight years ago, Sammy Junior took over, and J.C. still helped out even though he'd slowed down right much. At least, J.C. called it right much. I could only hope I'd feel like working half days on a tractor when I reached seventy-two.

Five minutes after saying good-bye to Miss Callie, I was turning off the paved road into the sandy lane that ran past the Johnson home place.

The doors there were closed and none of their three cars were in the yard, but Helen's Methodist and I'd heard Beulah mention the long-winded new preacher at her daughter-in-law's church.

Helen and Sammy Junior had remodeled and painted the shabby old two-story wooden farmhouse after old Mrs. Johnson died, and it was a handsome place these days: gleaming white aluminum siding and dark blue shutters, sitting in a shady grove of hundred-year-old white oaks.

Beulah's brick house—even after forty years, everyone in the family still calls it the "new house"—was farther down the lane and couldn't be seen from the road or the home place.

My car topped the low ridge that gave both generations their privacy, then swooped down toward a sluggish creek that had been dredged out into a nice-size irrigation pond beyond the house. As newlyweds, Sam and Beulah had planted pecans on each side of the lane, and mature nut trees now met in a tall arch.

The house itself was rooted in its own grove of pecans and oaks, with underplantings of dogwoods, crepe myrtles, redbuds, and flowering pears. Pink and white azaleas lined the foundation all around. On this warm day in late April, the place was a color illustration out of *Southern Living*. I pulled up under a chinaball tree by the back porch and tapped my horn, expecting to see Beulah appear at the screen door with her hands full of biscuit dough and an ample print apron protecting her Sunday dress against flour smudges.

A smell of burning paper registered oddly as I stepped from the car. It wasn't cool enough for a fire, and no one on this farm would break the fourth commandment by burning trash on the Sabbath.

There was no sign of Beulah when I crossed the wide planks of the wooden porch and called through the screen, but the kitchen was redolent of baking ham. J.C.'s old hound dog crawled out from under the back steps and wagged his tail at me hopefully. The screen door was unhooked, and the inner door stood wide.

"Beulah?" I called again. "J.C.?"

No answer. Yet her Buick and J.C.'s Ford pickup were both parked under the barn shelter at the rear of the yard.

The kitchen, dining room, and den ran together in one large L-shaped space, and when a quick glance into the formal, seldom-used living room revealed no one there either, I crossed to the stairs in the center hall. Through an open door at the far end of the hall, I could see into Donna Sue's old bedroom, now the guest room.

The covers on the guest bed had been straightened, but the spread was folded down neatly and pillows were piled on top of the rumpled quilt as if J.C. had rested there after Beulah made the bed. He wouldn't be able to use the stairs until his leg mended, so he'd probably moved in here for the duration. A stack of *Field and Stream* magazines and an open pack of his menthol cigarettes on the nightstand supported my hypothesis.

The house remained silent as I mounted the stairs.

"Anybody home?"

Beulah's bedroom was deserted and as immaculate as downstairs except for the desk. She and Sam had devoted a corner of their bedroom to the paper work connected with the farm. Although Sammy Junior did most of the farm records now on a computer over at his house, Beulah had kept the oak desk. One of my own document binders lay on its otherwise bare top. I'd drawn up her new will less than a month ago and had brought it out to her myself in this very same binder. I lifted the cover. The holographic distribution of small personal keepsakes she had insisted on was still there, but the will itself was missing.

For the first time since I'd entered this quiet house, I felt a small chill of foreboding.

Sammy Junior's old bedroom had been turned into a sewing room, and it was as empty as the bathroom. Ditto J.C.'s. As a child I'd had the run of every room in the house except this one, so I'd never entered it alone.

From the doorway, it looked like a rerun of the others: everything vacuumed and polished and tidy; but when I stepped inside, I saw the bottom drawer of the wide mahogany dresser open. Inside were various folders secured by brown cords, bundles of tax returns, account ledgers, bank statements, and two large flat candy boxes, which I knew held old family snapshots. More papers and folders were loosely stacked on the floor beside a low footstool, as if someone had sat there to sort through the drawer and had then been interrupted before the task was finished. Beulah would never leave a clutter like that.

Thoroughly puzzled, I went back down to the kitchen. The ham had been in the oven at least a half hour too long, so I turned it off and left the door cracked. The top burners were off, but each held a pot of cooked vegetables, still quite hot. Wherever Beulah was, she hadn't been gone very long.

Year round, she and J.C. and Sam, too, when he was alive, loved to walk the land, and if they weren't expecting company, it wasn't unusual to find them out at the pond or down in the woods. But with me invited for Sunday dinner along with Sammy Junior and Helen and their three teenagers? And with J.C.'s broken leg?

Not hardly likely, as my daddy would say.

Nevertheless, I went out to my car and blew the horn long and loud.

Buster, the old hound, nuzzled my hand as I stood beside the car indecisively. And that was another thing. If J.C. were out stumping across the farm on crutches, Buster wouldn't be hanging around the back door. He'd be right out there with J.C. It didn't make sense, yet if there's one thing the law has taught me, it's that it doesn't pay to formulate a theory without all the facts. I headed back inside to phone and see if Helen and Sammy Junior were home yet, and as I lifted the receiver from the kitchen wall, I saw something I'd missed before.

At the far end of the den, beyond the high-backed couch, the fireplace screen had been moved to one side of the hearth, and there were scraps of charred paper in the grate.

I remembered the smell of burning paper that had hung in the air when I first arrived. I started toward the fireplace, and now I could see the coffee table strewn with the Sunday edition of the Raleigh *News and Observer*.

As I rounded the high couch, I nearly tripped on a pair of crutches, but they barely registered, so startled was I by seeing J.C. lying there motionless, his eyes closed.

"Glory, J.C.!" I exclaimed. "You asleep? That must be some painkiller the doctor—"

I suddenly realized that the brightly colored sheet of Sunday comics over his chest was drenched in his own bright blood.

I knelt beside the old man and clutched his callused, work-worn hand. It was still warm. His faded blue eyes opened, rolled back in his head, then focused on me.

"Deb'rah?" His voice was faint and came from far, far away. "I swear I plumb forgot . . ."

He gave a long sigh and his eyes closed again.

❖ ❖ ❖

Dwight Bryant is detective chief of the Colleton County Sheriff's Department. After calling the nearest rescue squad, I'd dialed his mother's phone number on the off chance that he'd be there in the neighborhood and not twenty-two miles away at Dobbs, the county seat. Four minutes flat after I hung up the phone, I saw his Chevy pickup zoom over the crest of the lane and tear through the arch of pecan trees. He was followed by a bright purple TR, and even in this ghastly situation, I had to smile at his exasperation as Miss Emily Bryant bounded from the car and hurried up the steps ahead of him.

"Damn it all, Mother, if you set the first foot inside that house, I'm gonna arrest you, and I mean it!"

She turned on him, a feisty little carrottop Chihuahua facing down a sandy-brown Saint Bernard. "If you think I'm going to stay out here when one of my oldest and dearest friends may be lying in there—"

"She's not, Miss Emily," I said tremulously. J.C.'s blood was under my fingernails from where I'd stanched his chest wound. "I promise you. I looked in every room."

"And under all the beds and in every closet?" She stamped her small foot imperiously on the porch floor. "I won't touch a thing, Dwight, but I've got to look."

"No." That was the law talking, not her son; and she huffed but quit arguing.

"Okay, Deborah," said Dwight, holding the screen door open for me. "Show me."

♣ ♣ ♣

Forty-five minutes later we knew no more than before. The rescue squad had arrived and departed again with J.C., who was still unconscious and barely clinging to life.

Sammy Junior and Helen were nearly frantic over Beulah's disappearance and were torn between following the ambulance and staying put till there was word of her. Eventually they thought to call Donna Sue, who said she'd meet the ambulance at the hospital and stay with J.C. till they heard more.

A general APB had been issued for Beulah, but since nobody knew how she left, there wasn't much besides her physical appearance to put on the wire.

Dwight's deputies processed the den and J.C.'s room like a crime scene. After they finished, Dwight and I walked through the house with Sammy Junior and Helen; but they, too, saw nothing out of the ordinary except for the papers strewn in front of J.C.'s bedroom dresser.

Sammy Junior's impression was the same as mine. "It's like Mama was interrupted."

"Doing what?" asked Dwight.

"Probably getting Uncle J.C.'s insurance papers together for him. I said I'd take 'em over to the hospital tomorrow. In all the excitement yesterday when he broke his leg, we didn't think about 'em."

He started to leave the room, then hesitated. "Y'all find his gun?"

"Gun?" said Dwight.

Sammy Junior pointed to a pair of empty rifle brackets over the bedroom door. "That's where he keeps his .22."

Much as we'd all like to believe this is still God's country, everything peaceful and nice, most people now latch their doors at night, and they do keep loaded guns around for more than rats and snakes and wild dogs.

Helen shivered and instinctively moved closer to Sammy Junior. "The back door's always open, Dwight. I'll bet you anything some burglar or rapist caught her by surprise an forced her to go with him. And then J.C. probably rared up on the couch and they shot him like you'd swat a fly."

I turned away from the pain on Sammy Junior's face and stared through the bedroom window as Dwight said, "Been too many cars down the lane and through the yard for us to find any tread marks."

Any lawyer knows how easily the lives of good decent people can be shattered, but I'll never get used to the abruptness of it. Trouble seldom comes creeping up gently, giving a person time to prepare or get out of the way. It's always the freakish bolt of lightning out of a clear blue sky, the jerk of a steering wheel, the collapse of something rock solid only a second ago.

From the window I saw puffy white clouds floating serenely over the farm. The sun shone as brightly as ever on flowering trees and new-planted corn, warming the earth for another round of seedtime and harvest. A soft wind smoothed the field where J.C. had been disking before his accident yesterday, and in the distance the pond gleamed silver-green before a stand of willows.

My eye was snagged by what looked like a red-and-white cloth several yards into the newly disked field. Probably something Buster had pulled off the clothesline, I thought, and was suddenly aware that the others were waiting for my answer to a question I'd barely heard.

"No," I replied. "I'd have noticed another car or truck coming out of the lane. Couldn't have missed them by much, though, because the vegetables on the stove were still hot. Beulah must have turned them off just before going upstairs."

"It's a habit with her," Sammy Junior said. He had his arm around Helen and was kneading her shoulder convulsively. It would probably be bruised tomorrow, but Helen didn't seem to notice.

"Mama burned so many pots when we were kids that she got to where she wouldn't leave the kitchen without turning off the vegetables. She'd mean to come right back, but then there was always something that needed doing, and you know how Mama is."

We did. We surely did. "Whatsoever thy hand findeth to do" must have been written with Beulah in mind. She always reacted impulsively and couldn't pass a dusty surface or a dirty windowpane or anything out of place without cleaning it or taking it back to its rightful spot in the house.

Maybe that's why that scrap of red-and-white cloth out in the field bothered me. If I could see it, so would Beulah. She wouldn't let it lie out there ten minutes if she could help it, and it was with a need to restore some of her order that I slipped away from the others.

Downstairs, the crime scene crew had finished with the kitchen; and for lack of anything more useful to do, Miss Emily had decided that everybody'd fare better on a full stomach. She'd put bowls of vegetables on the counter, sliced the ham, and set out glasses and a jug of sweet iced tea. At this returning semblance of the ordinary, Helen and Sammy Junior's three anxious teenagers obediently filled their plates and went outside under the trees to eat. Their parents and Dwight weren't enthusiastic about food at the moment, but Miss Emily bullied them into going through the motions. Even Dwight's men had to stop and fix a plate.

No one noticed as I passed through the kitchen and down the back steps, past the Johnson grandchildren, who were feeding ham scraps to Buster and talking in low worried tones.

The lane cut through the yard, skirted the end of the field, then wound circuitously around the edge of the woods and on down to the pond; but the red-and-white rag lay on a beeline from the back door to the pond and I hesitated about stepping off the grass. My shoes were two-inch sling-back pumps, and they'd be wrecked if I walked out into the soft dirt of the newly disked field.

As I dithered, I saw that someone else had recently crossed the field on foot.

A single set of tracks.

With growing horror I remembered the red-and-white hostess aprons my aunt Zell had sewed for all her friends last Christmas.

I ran back to my car, grabbed the sneakers I keep in the trunk, and then rushed to call Dwight.

❖ ❖ ❖

It was done strictly by the book.

Dwight's crime scene crew would later methodically photograph and measure and take pains not to disturb a single clod till every mark Beulah had left on the soft dirt was thoroughly documented; but the rest of us hurried through the turned field, paralleling the footprints from a ten-foot distance and filled with foreboding by the steady, unwavering direction those footsteps had taken.

Beulah's apron lay about two hundred feet from the edge of the yard. She must have untied the strings and just let it fall as she walked away from it.

The rifle, though, had been deliberately pitched. We could see where she stopped, the depth of her footprints where she heaved it away from her as if it were something suddenly and terribly abhorrent.

After that, there was nothing to show that she'd hesitated a single second. Her footprints went like bullets, straight down to the pond and into the silent, silver-green water.

As with most farm ponds dredged for irrigation, the bottom dropped off steeply from the edge to discourage mosquito larvae.

"How deep is it there?" Dwight asked when we arrived breathless and panting.

"Twelve feet," said Sammy Junior. "And she never learned how to swim."

His voice didn't break, but his chest was heaving, his face got red, and tears streamed from his eyes. "Why? In God's name, *why*, Dwight? Helen? Deb'rah? You all *know* Uncle J.C. near 'bout worships Mama. And we've always teased her that J.C. stood for Jesus Christ the way she's catered to him."

❖ ❖ ❖

It was almost dark before they found Beulah's body.

No one tolled the heavy iron bell at the home place. The old way of alerting the neighborhood to fire or death has long since been replaced by the telephone, but the reaction hasn't changed much in two hundred years.

By the time that second ambulance passed down the lane, this one on its way to the state's medical examiner in Chapel Hill, cars filled the yard and lined the ditch banks on either side of the road. And there was no place in Helen's kitchen or dining room to set another plate of food. It would have taken a full roll of tinfoil to cover all the casseroles, biscuits, pies, deviled eggs, and platters of fried chicken, sliced turkey, and roast pork that had been brought in by shocked friends and relatives.

My aunt Zell arrived, white-faced and grieving, the last of three adventuresome country girls who'd gone off to Goldsboro during World War II to work at the air base. I grew up on stories of those war years: how J.C. had been sent over by his and Beulah's parents to keep an eye on my mother, Beulah, and Aunt Zell and protect them from the dangers of a military town, how they'd tried to fix him up with a WAC from New Jersey, the Saturday night dances, the innocent flirtations with that steady stream of young airmen who passed through the Army Air Forces Technical Training School at Seymour Johnson Field on their way to the airfields of Europe.

It wasn't till I was eighteen, the summer between high school and college, the summer Mother was dying, that I learned it hadn't all been lighthearted laughter.

We'd been sorting through a box of old black-and-white snapshots that Mother was determined to date and label before she died. Among the pictures of her or Aunt Zell or Beulah perched on the wing of a bomber or jitterbugging with anonymous, interchangeable airmen, there was one of Beulah and a young man. They had their arms around each other, and there was a sweet solemnity in their faces that separated this picture from the other clowning ones.

"Who's that?" I asked, and Mother sat staring into the picture for so long that I had to ask again.

"His name was Donald," she finally replied. Then her face took on an earnest look I'd come to know that summer, the look that meant I was to be entrusted with another secret, another scrap of her personal history that she couldn't bear to take to her grave untold even though each tale began, "Now you mustn't ever repeat this, but—"

"Donald Farraday came from Norwood, Nebraska," she said. "Exactly halfway between Omaha and Lincoln on the Platte River. That's what he always said. After he shipped out, Beulah used to look at the map and lay her finger halfway between Omaha and Lincoln and make Zell and me promise that we'd come visit her."

"I thought Sam was the only one she ever dated seriously," I protested.

"Beulah was the only one *Sam* ever dated seriously," Mother said crisply. "He had his eye on her from the time she was in grade school and he and J.C. used to go hunting together. She wrote to him while he was fighting the Japs, but they weren't going steady or anything. And she'd have never married Sam if Donald hadn't died."

"Oh," I said, suddenly understanding the sad look that sometimes shadowed Beulah's eyes when only minutes before she and Mother and Aunt Zell might have been giggling over some Goldsboro memory.

Donald Farraday was from a Nebraska wheat farm, Mother told me, on his way to fight in Europe. Beulah met him at a jitterbug contest put on by the canteen, and it'd been love at first sight. Deep and true and all-consuming. They had only sixteen days and fifteen nights together, but that was enough to know this wasn't a passing wartime romance. Their values, their dreams, everything meshed.

"And they had so much fun together. You've never seen two people laugh so much over nothing. She didn't even cry when he shipped out because she was so happy thinking about what marriage to him was going to be like after the war was over."

"How did he die?"

"We never really heard," said Mother. "She had two of the sweetest, most beautiful letters you could ever hope to read, and then nothing. That was near the end when fighting was so heavy in Italy—we knew he was in Italy though it was supposed to be secret. They weren't married so his parents would've gotten the telegram, and of course, not knowing anything about Beulah, they couldn't write her."

"So what happened?"

"The war ended. We all came home, I married your daddy, Zell married James. Sam came back from the South Pacific and with Donald dead, Beulah didn't care who she married."

"Donna Sue!" I said suddenly.

"Yes," Mother agreed. "Sue for me, Donna in memory of Donald. She doesn't know about him, though, and don't you ever tell her." Her face was sad as she looked at the photograph in her hand of the boy and girl who'd be forever young, forever in love. "Beulah won't let us mention his name, but I know she still grieves for what might have been."

After Mother was gone, I never spoke to Beulah about what I knew. The closest I ever came was my junior year at Carolina when Jeff Creech dumped me for a psych major and I moped into the kitchen where Beulah and Aunt Zell were drinking coffee. I moaned about how my heart was broken and I couldn't go on and Beulah had smiled at me, "You'll go on, sugar. A woman's body doesn't quit just because her heart breaks."

Sudden tears had misted Aunt Zell's eyes—we Stephensons can cry over telephone commercials—and Beulah abruptly left.

"She was remembering Donald Farraday, wasn't she?" I asked.

"Sue told you about him?"

"Yes."

Aunt Zell had sighed then. "I don't believe a day goes by that she doesn't remember him."

The endurance of Beulah's grief had suddenly put Jeff Creech into perspective, and I realized with a small pang that losing him probably wasn't going to blight the rest of my life.

❖ ❖ ❖

As I put my arms around Aunt Zell, I thought of her loss: Mother gone, now Beulah. Only J.C. left to remember those giddy girlhood years. At least the doctors were cautiously optimistic that he'd recover from the shooting.

"Why did she do it?" I asked.

But Aunt Zell was as perplexed as the rest of us. The house was crowded with people who'd known and loved Beulah and J.C. all their lives, and few could recall a true cross word between older brother and younger sister.

"Oh, Mama'd get fussed once in a while when he'd try to keep her from doing something new," said Donna Sue.

Every wake I've ever attended, the survivors always alternate between sudden paroxysms of tears and a need to remember and retell. For all the pained bewilderment and unanswered questions that night, Beulah's wake was no different.

"Remember, Sammy, how Uncle J.C. didn't want her to buy that place at the beach?"

"He never liked change," her brother agreed. "He talked about jellyfish and sharks—"

"—and sun poisoning," Helen said with a sad smile as she refilled his glass of iced tea. "Don't forget the sun poisoning."

"Changed his tune soon enough once he got down there and the fish started biting," said a cousin as he bit into a sausage biscuit.

One of Dwight's deputies signaled me from the hallway, and I left them talking about how J.C.'d tried to stop Beulah from touring England with one of her alumnae groups last year, and how he'd fretted the whole time she was gone, afraid her plane would crash into the Atlantic or be hijacked by terrorists.

"Dwight wants you back over there," said the deputy and drove me through the gathering dark, down the lane to where Beulah's house blazed with lights.

Dwight was waiting for me in the den. They'd salvaged a few scraps from the fireplace, but the ashes had been stirred with a poker and there wasn't much left to tell what had been destroyed. Maybe a handful of papers, Dwight thought. "And this. It fell behind the grate before it fully burned."

The sheet was crumpled and charred, but enough remained to see the words *Last Will and Testament of Beulah Ogburn Johnson* and the opening paragraph about revoking all earlier wills.

"You were her lawyer," said Dwight. "Why'd she burn her will?"

"I don't know," I answered, honestly puzzled. "Unless—"

"Unless what?"

"I'll have to read my copy tomorrow, but there's really not going to be much difference between what happens if she died intestate and—" I interrupted myself, remembering. "In fact, if J.C. dies, it'll be exactly the same, Dwight. Sammy Junior and Donna Sue still split everything."

"And if he lives?"

"If this were still a valid instrument," I said, choosing my words carefully, "J.C. would have a lifetime right to this house and Beulah's share of the farm income, with everything divided equally between her two children when he died; without the will, he's not legally entitled to stay the night."

"They'd never turn him out."

I didn't respond and Dwight looked at me thoughtfully.

"But without the will, they could if they wanted to," he said slowly.

Dwight Bryant's six or eight years older than I, and he's known me all my life, yet I don't think he'd ever looked at me as carefully as he did that night in Beulah's den, in front of that couch soaked in her brother's blood. "And if he'd done something bad enough to make their mother shoot him and then go drown herself . . ."

"They could turn him out and not a single voice in the whole community would speak against it," I finished for him.

Was that what Beulah wanted? Dead or alive, she was still my client. But I wondered: when she shot J.C. and burned her will, had she been of sound mind?

❖ ❖ ❖

By next morning, people were beginning to say no. There was no sane reason for Beulah's act, they said, so it must have been a sudden burst of insanity, and wasn't there a great-aunt on her daddy's side that'd been a little bit queer near the end?

J.C. regained consciousness, but he was no help.

"I was resting on the couch," he said, "and I never heard a thing till I woke up hurting and you were there, Deb'rah."

He was still weak, but fierce denial burned in his eyes when they told him that Beulah had shot him. "She never!"

"Her fingerprints are on your rifle," said Dwight.

"She never!" He gazed belligerently from Donna Sue to Sammy Junior. "She never. Not her own brother. Where is she? You better not've jailed her, Dwight!"

He went into shock when they told him Beulah was dead. Great sobbing cries of protest racked his torn and broken body. It was pitiful to watch. Donna Sue petted and hugged him, but the nurse had to inject a sedative to calm him, and she asked us to leave.

I was due in court anyhow, and afterwards there was a luncheon speech at the Jaycees and a pig-picking that evening to raise funds for the children's hospital. I fell into bed exhausted, but instead of sleeping, my mind began to replay everything that had happened Sunday, scene by scene. Suddenly there was a freeze-frame on the moment I discovered J.C.

Next morning I was standing beside his hospital bed before anyone else got there.

"What was it you forgot?" I asked him.

The old man stared at me blankly. "Huh?"

"When I found you, you said, 'Deborah, I swear I plumb forgot.' Forgot what, J.C.?"

His faded blue eyes shifted to the shiny get-well balloons tethered to the foot of his bed by colorful streamers.

"I don't remember saying that," he lied.

❖ ❖ ❖

From the hospital, I drove down to the town commons and walked along the banks of our muddy river. It was another beautiful spring day, but I was harking back to Sunday morning, trying to think myself into Beulah's mind.

You're a sixty-six-year-old widow, I thought. You're cooking Sunday dinner for your children and for the daughter of your dead friend. (*She's running for judge, Sue. Did you ever imagine it?*) And there's J.C. calling from the den about his insurance papers. So you turn off the vegetables and go upstairs and look in his drawer for the policies and you find—

What do you find that sends you back downstairs with a rifle in your hands and papers to burn? Why bother to burn anything after you've shot the person who loves you best in all the world?

And why destroy a will that would have provided that person with a dignified and independent old age? Was it because the bequest had been designated "To my beloved only brother who has always looked after me," and on this beautiful Sunday morning J.C. has suddenly stopped being beloved and has instead become someone to hurt? Maybe even to kill?

Why, *why,* WHY?

I shook my head impatiently. What in God's creation could J.C. have kept in that drawer that would send Beulah over the edge?

Totally baffled, I deliberately emptied my mind and sat down on one of the stone benches and looked up into a dogwood tree in full bloom. With the sun above them, the white blossoms glowed with a paschal translucence. Mother had always loved dogwoods.

Mother. Aunt Zell. Beulah.

A spring blossoming more than forty-five years ago.

I thought of dogwoods and spring love, and into my emptied mind floated a single *what if—?*

I didn't force it. I just sat and watched while it grew from possibility to certainty, a certainty reinforced as I recalled something Mother had mentioned about shift work at the airfield.

It was such a monstrous certainty that I wanted to be dissuaded, so I went to my office and called Aunt Zell and asked her to think back to the war years.

"When you all were in Goldsboro," I said, "did you work days or nights?"

"Days, of course," she answered promptly.

The weight started to roll off my chest.

"Leastways, we three girls did," she added. "J.C. worked nights. Why?"

For a moment I thought the heaviness would smother me before I could stammer out a reason and hang up.

Sherry, my secretary, came in with some papers to sign, but I waved her away. "Bring me the phone book," I told her, "and then leave me alone unless I buzz you."

Astonishingly, it took only one call to Information to get the number I needed. He answered on the second ring and we talked for almost an hour. I told him I was a writer doing research on the old Army Air Forces technical schools.

He didn't seem to think it odd when my questions got personal.

He sounded nice.

He sounded lonely.

❖ ❖ ❖

"You look like hell," Sherry observed when I passed through the office. "You been crying?"

"Anybody wants me, I'll be at the hospital," I said without breaking stride.

❖ ❖ ❖

Donna Sue and Helen were sitting beside J.C.'s bed when I got there, and it took every ounce of courtroom training for me not to burst out with it. Instead I made sympathetic conversation like a perfect Southern lady, and when they broke down again about Beulah, I said, "You all need to get out in the spring sunshine for a few minutes. Go get something with ice in it and walk around the parking lot twice. I'll keep J.C. company till you get back."

J.C. closed his eyes as they left, but I let him have it with both barrels.

"You bastard!" I snarled. "You filthy bastard! I just got off the phone to Donald Farraday. He still lives in Norwood, Nebraska, J.C. Halfway between Omaha and Lincoln."

The old man groaned and clenched his eyes tighter.

"He didn't die. He wasn't even wounded. Except in the heart. By you." So much anger roiled up inside me, I was almost spitting my words at him.

"He wrote her every chance he got till it finally sank in she was never going to answer. He thought she'd changed her mind, realized that she didn't really love him. And every day Beulah must have been coming home, asking if she'd gotten any mail, and you only gave her Sam's letters, you rotten, no-good—"

"Sam was homefolks," J.C. burst out. "That other one, he'd have taken her way the hell away to Nebraska. She didn't have any business in Nebraska! Sam loved her."

"She didn't love *him*," I snapped.

"Sure, she did. Oh, it took her a bit to get over the other one, but she settled."

"Only because she thought Farraday was dead! You had no right, you sneaking, sanctimonious Pharisee! You wrecked her whole life!"

"Her life wasn't wrecked," he argued. "She had Donna Sue and Sammy Junior and the farm and—"

"If it was such a star-spangled life," I interrupted hotly, "why'd she take a gun to you the minute she knew what you'd done to her?"

The fight went out of him and he sank back into the pillow, sobbing now and holding himself where the bullet had passed through his right lung.

"Why in God's name did you keep the letters? That's what she found, wasn't it?"

Still sobbing, J.C. nodded.

"I forgot they were still there. I never opened them, and she didn't either. She said she couldn't bear to. She just put them in the grate and put a match to them and she was crying. I tried to explain about how I'd done what was best for her, and all at once she had the rifle in her hands and she said she'd never forgive me, and then I reckon she shot me."

He reached out a bony hand and grasped mine. "You won't tell anyone, will you?"

I jerked my hand away as if it'd suddenly touched filth.

"Please, Deb'rah?"

"Donald Farraday has a daughter almost the same age as Donna Sue," I said. "Know what he named her, J.C. ? He named her Beulah."

❖ ❖ ❖

Dwight Bryant was waiting when I got back from court that afternoon and he followed me into my office.

"I hear you visited J.C. twice today."

"So?" I slid off my high heels. They were wickedly expensive and matched the power red of my linen suit. I waggled my stockinged toes at him, but he didn't smile.

"Judge not," he said sternly.

"Is that with an *N* or a *K*?" I parried.

"Sherry tells me you never give clients the original of their will."

"Never's a long time, and Sherry may not know as much about my business as she thinks she does."

"But it *was* a copy that Beulah burned, wasn't it?"

"I'm prepared to go to court and swear it was the original if I have to. It won't be necessary though. J.C. won't contest it."

Dwight stared at me a long level moment. "Why're you doing this to him?"

I matched his stare with one about twenty degrees colder. "Not me, Dwight. Beulah."

"He swears he doesn't know why she shot him, but you know, don't you?"

I shrugged.

He hauled himself to his feet, angry and frustrated. "If you do this, Deborah, J.C.'ll have to spend the rest of his life depending on Donna Sue and Sammy Junior's good will. You don't have the right. Nobody elected you judge yet."

"Yes, they did," I said, thinking of the summer I was eighteen and how Mother had told me all her secrets so that if I ever needed her eye-witness testimony I'd have it.

And Deborah was a judge in the land

Damn straight.

A Woman's Eye, 1991
Winner, Agatha Award for Best Short Story of 1991

Fruitcake, Mercy,
And Black-Eyed Peas

This is another story that grew out of a colleague's request. Charlotte MacLeod was putting together her second Christmas anthology and asked me to send her a story. I hastily dashed something off, and she sent it right back with a gentle note suggesting I could do better. This story met her high standards. A few months later, our county's first baby of the year turned out to be the child of an unwed black teenager. Their picture appeared in the local newspaper and for several issues afterwards, every letter to the editor could have been written by either Billy Tyson or Deborah's Aunt Zell.

Marnolla's first question after I bailed her out of jail was, "What's a revisichist?" Her second was, "Ain't you getting too old for a squinchy little shoe box like this?"

"You wanted a Cadillac ride home, you should've called James Rufus Sanders," I told her, referring to the most successful black lawyer in Colleton County, North Carolina. I switched on the heater of my admittedly small sports car against the chill December air and helped pull the seat belt across her broad hips, an expanse further broadened by her bulky winter coat. "You mean recidivist?"

"I reckon. Something like that. Miz Utley said I was one and I won't going to give her the satisfaction of asking what it was. Ain't something ugly, is it?"

"Miz Utley never talks ugly and you know it," I said as I pulled out of the courthouse parking lot and headed toward Darkside, the nearest thing Dobbs has to a purely black section. "Magistrates have to be polite to everybody, but under the habitual-offender statutes—"

"Don't give me no lawyer talk, Deb'rah," she snapped. "I wanted that, I *would've* called Mr. Sanders."

"It means this isn't the first time Billy Tyson's caught you shoplifting in his store, and this time he wants to put you under the jail, not in it," I snapped back.

She leaned back and loosened the buttons of her dark-blue coat. "Naw, you won't let him do that."

It was three days past Christmas, but she still wore a sprig of artificial holly topped by two tiny yellow plastic bells that had been dipped in gold glitter and sparkled gaily in the low winter sun.

Marnolla Faison was barely ten years older than me, yet her short black hair was almost half gray and her callused hands had worked about twenty years harder than mine. In truth our families had worked for each other more years than either of us could count and it looks like it's going to go on another generation, even though Marnolla left the farm before she was full grown.

"What in God's name made you think you could walk out with all that baby stuff?" I asked. "Two boxes of diapers? Who's had a baby now?"

"Nobody," she said.

I stopped for the light and we waved to Miss Sallie Anderson, waiting to cross at the corner.

Miss Sallie motioned for Marnolla to roll down her window and she leaned in to greet us. Her white curls were covered by a fuzzy blue scarf that exuded a delicate fragrance of rose sachet and talcum. "Did y'all have a nice Christmas?"

"Yes, ma'am," we chorused. "How 'bout you?"

"Real nice." Her face was finely wrinkled like a piece of thin white tissue paper that's been crumpled around a Christmas present and then smoothed out by careful hands. "Jack and Caroline were down with their new baby, and he's the spitting image of his great-granddaddy. They named him after Jed, you know."

The driver behind us tapped his horn. Not ugly. Just letting us know the light was green and he couldn't get by with us in the middle of the lane, so if we didn't mind . . .

It was nobody I knew, but Miss Sallie thought he was saying hello and she waved to him abstractedly. "I better not hold y'all up," she said. "I just wanted you to tell Zell that we sure did appreciate that fruitcake. It was so moist and sweet, just the best I've had since your mother died, honey."

"I'll tell her," I promised, easing off the brake. "And that reminds me," I told Marnolla as she closed the window and we drove on. "Aunt Zell sent you a fruitcake, too."

"That's mighty nice of her. She still making them like your mama used to?"

"Far as I know."

Slyness needled Marnolla's chuckle. "No wonder Miss Sallie thought it was so good."

She always knew how to zing me.

"Never mind Aunt Zell's fruitcakes," I told her. "We were talking about you stealing baby diapers for 'nobody.' Nobody who?"

"Nobody you ever met."

Her face took on a stubborn set and I knew there was no point trying to pry a name. Didn't matter anyhow. Whoever the mother was, she wasn't the one who tried to walk out of Billy Tyson's Bigg Shopp with a brand-new layette. It isn't that Marnolla wants to steal or even means to steal; it's that her heart is bigger than her weekly paycheck from the towel factory and sometimes she gets impulsive. With her daughter Avis engrossed in a fancy job out in California and nobody of her own to provide for, she tries to mother every stray that wanders in off the road.

"What's Avis going to think when she hears about this?" I scolded.

"She ain't never going to hear," Marnolla said firmly.

Avis is a little younger than me, born when Marnolla was only fourteen. She was the first baby I'd had much to do with and I'd hung over her crib every chance I got, gently holding her tiny hands in mine, marveling over every detail, right down to the little finger on her left hand that crooked at the tip just like Marnolla's. I really mourned when Marnolla and Sid moved into Dobbs while Avis was still just a toddler. Sid split to California a few years later; and when Avis was fifteen and going through a wild stage in school, she took thirty dollars from Marnolla's purse and hitchhiked out to live with him.

Marnolla grieved over it at first, but eventually reckoned that Avis needed her daddy's stronger hand to keep her in line. Every time I saw Marnolla and remembered to ask, she had only good things to say about the way Avis had turned her life around: Avis was finishing high school; Avis was taking courses at a community college; Avis had landed a real good job doing something with computers, Marnolla wasn't quite clear what.

"Not married yet," Marnolla keeps reporting. "She's just like you, Deb'rah. Working too hard and having too much fun to bog herself down with menfolk and babies."

I'm glad Avis is doing so good, but it is too bad she can't find the time to come visit her own mother. Not that I'd ever say that to Marnolla, she being so proud of Avis and all. I can't help thinking, though, that if Marnolla had somebody she was special to, she might not keep trying to help more people than she could afford. Loneliness is a big hole that takes a lot of filling sometimes.

I pulled up and parked in front of her little shotgun, three rooms lined up one behind the other so that if you fired through the front door, the pellets would go straight out through the back screen. The wood frame house was old and needed paint, but the yard was raked and tidy and the porch railing was strung with cheerful Christmas lights. A wreath of silver tinsel hung on the door.

"I'd ask you in," Marnolla said, "but you're probably in a hurry."

"You got that right," I agreed. "I need to get up with Billy Tyson before all his Christmas spirit evaporates. Maybe I can talk him out of it one more time, but I swear, Marnolla, you can't blame him for being so ill about this after you promised on a stack of Bibles you'd never take another penny's worth from his store."

"Tell him I'm sorry," she said as she stood with the car door open. A gust of chill December wind caught the gold bells pinned to her coat and they twinkled in the afternoon sunlight. "Tell him I won't do it never again, honest."

❖ ❖ ❖

She didn't look all that repentant to me and Billy Tyson didn't look to be all that full of Christmas spirit when I entered his office back of the cash registers at the Bigg Shopp. He gave me a sour glance and went on crunching numbers on his calculator.

"You here about Marnolla Faison?"

"Well, your ad did say bargains so good they're practically a steal."

It didn't get the grin I'd hoped for.

"Forget it, Deb'rah. I'm not dropping charges this time."

He'd gained even more weight than Marnolla over the years, and the bald spot on the top of his head had grown bigger since the first time I'd stood in his office and talked him out of prosecuting Marnolla for shoplifting.

"How come she always steals from me anyhow?" he growled. "How come she don't go to K mart or Rose's?"

"You're homefolks," I said. "She wouldn't steal from strangers."

"That's because strangers would've put her in jail the first time she tried it with them. That's what I should've done." He glared at me. "What I would've done, too, if you hadn't talked me out of it. Well, no more, missy. This time when the judge asks me if I've got anything to say, you're not going to hear me ask him to let her off with some piddly little fine. This time she gets to see the inside of a jail, if I have anything to say about it. And I will, by damn! As president of the Merchants' Association, I've got an example to set."

"And you set a fine example, Billy," I wheedled. "Everybody says so, but it's Christmas and a little baby needed a few things and—"

"Dammit, Deb'rah, you can't talk about Christmas like the Merchants' Association don't do their part. We're civic-minded as hell and we give and we give and—"

"And everybody appreciates it, too," I assured him. "But you know how Marnolla is."

"What Marnolla is is a common thief and she's gonna go to jail like one! Every time she wants to act like a big shot with some poor soul, she comes in here and steals something from me to give to them."

"Oh, come on, Billy. How much did she actually try to take? Thirty dollars' worth? Forty?" I reached for my wallet, but he waved me off.

"Don't matter if it wa'n't but a nickel. It's the principle of the thing."

"Principle or not, you know she won't get more than a couple of weekends at the most."

"Not if Perry Byrd hears the case," he said shrewdly.

He had me there. Judge Perry Byrd adores the principle of things. Especially if the defendants are black or Hispanic.

"I expect you're just tired out with too much Christmas," I said. "You have a nice New Year's and we'll talk some more next week."

"You can talk all you want." He had a mule-stubborn look on his face. "You're not gonna get around me this time."

❖ ❖ ❖

I made a quick walk through Bigg Shopp's shoe racks before leaving just in case something nice had been marked down. There was a darling pair of green slingbacks. I didn't have a single winter thing to go with them at the moment, but Aunt Zell had made me several floral-print sundresses last summer and they'd match those dresses.

Besides, they were only $18.50.

Billy had come out of his office to help out at the express lane. I smiled at him sweetly as I gave him the shoes and a twenty. "Unless you'd rather I shopped at K mart or Rose's?"

"*Paying* customers are always welcome at Bigg Shopp," he said and handed me my change.

But at least he finally smiled. I dropped the change into the crippled children's jar beside the cash register and went out to the parking lot with a happier heart, figuring if I kept working on him, I could maybe soften him up before Marnolla's case was called.

As I put my new shoes in the trunk, I saw the fruitcake Aunt Zell had sent Marnolla.

For just a minute, I thought about running back in the store and giving it to Billy. In his mood, though, he'd probably consider it a bribe instead of a present in keeping with the holidays.

For some reason, people like to poke fun at Christmas fruitcake and joke about how there's really probably only a hundred or so in the whole United States and they just get passed around from one year to the next.

Those people never tasted Aunt Zell's.

For starters, she uses Colleton County nuts. Not those puny dried-up English walnuts you get in the grocery store, but thick, meaty pecans and rich black walnuts. She goes easy on the citron and heavy on her home-dried apples and figs. When the dark dense loaves come out of the oven in late October, the first thing Aunt Zell does, before they're even cool, is wrap them up in cheesecloth and slosh on a generous splash of what she euphemistically calls "Kezzie's special apple juice." They get basted like that every week till Christmas.

(She says Kezzie hasn't run any white whiskey since Mother died and he moved back to the main farm. The applejack he brings her every fall is some private stock he's had stashed back somewhere aging all these years. Or so he tells her.)

I live in town with Aunt Zell, my mother's sister, and I'm touchy about discussing my daddy, but it *is* the best fruitcake in Colleton County and that's not idle bragging. The one time she entered it at the state fair ten years ago, they gave her a blue ribbon.

❖ ❖ ❖

Dusk was falling when I got back to Marnolla's. The lights on her porch blinked colorfully in the twilight and the calico cat curled on the railing came over to meet me as I mounted the two steps and knocked on the door.

When Marnolla opened it, the cat twined around and through her ankles. She scooped it up and stood in the doorway stroking its sleek body.

Her own body was encased in a long woolly red robe that looked warm and Christmassy. "What'd he say?" she asked.

It was cold on the porch and I could smell hot coffee and cornbread inside. "Let's go in the kitchen and I'll tell you."

"No."

I thought she was joking. "Come on, Marnolla. I'm freezing out here."

"I let you in, you'll start asking questions and fussing," she said.

"What's to fuss about?"

"See? Asking questions already," she grumbled, but she stood aside and let me step into her living room. It was dark except for the multi-colored glow of her Christmas tree. Normally the room was neat as a pin; that night, in addition to the expected clutter of opened presents at the base of the tree, there was a stack of quilts folded at the end of the couch and a pillow on top.

"You got somebody staying here?" I asked, as the cat trotted from the living room on through her bedroom and out to the kitchen.

Before she could answer, I heard someone speak to it. The next minute, a young girl stepped into view and I suddenly knew why Marnolla had tried to steal baby items.

She didn't look a day over twelve. (I later learned she was fifteen.) Except for her swollen abdomen, she was slender and delicately formed, with a childish face. But her lovely almond-shaped eyes were the eyes of a fearful adult as if she'd already seen things no child in America should have had to see.

"Her name's Lynette and she's going to be staying with me awhile," said Marnolla in a voice that warned me off any nosy questions. "Lynette this here's Miss Deborah Knott. My daddy used to sharecrop with hers."

She nodded at me shyly from the kitchen, but neither joined us nor spoke as she picked up the cat and moved out of my sight. Marnolla was giving off such odd vibes that I briefly described Billy Tyson's determination to see her in jail, handed over the fruitcake, and edged my way out the front door again.

Marnolla followed me onto the porch and shut the door. "Lynette's why you can't let them put me in jail," she said. "She's just a baby her own self and she's got nobody else, so I need to be here, Deb'rah. You hear?"

"I hear," I sighed and drove home in the darkness through side streets still festive with Santa Claus sleds and wooden reindeer, although the Rudolph spotlighted on a neighbor's roof was beginning to look a bit jaded.

❖ ❖ ❖

Aunt Zell had made chicken pastry for dinner and she was pleased to hear Miss Sallie's pretty words about her fruitcake, but worried over Marnolla.

"Maybe Billy Tyson's right," I said as she passed the spinach salad. "Maybe it is going to take a few days in jail to get her to quit taking stuff out of his store."

"But if there's a baby coming—"

Aunt Zell paused and shook her head over a situation with no easy solutions. "I'll pray on it for you."

"That'll be nice," I said.

❖ ❖ ❖

While I did care about Marnolla's problems, she was only one client among many, and none of them blighted my holiday season.

Court didn't sit the week between Christmas and New Year's, so we kept bankers' hours at the law office. I made duty calls on most of my brothers and their wives during the day, did some serious partying with friends over in Raleigh by night, and, since I was getting low on clean blouses and lingerie, skipped church on Sunday morning so I could sneak in a quick load of wash while Aunt Zell was out of the house.

She swears she isn't superstitious; all the same, if I want to wash clothes between new Christmas and old Christmas, she starts fussing about having to wash shrouds for a corpse in the coming year. I've tried to tell her it's only if you wash bedclothes, but she won't run the risk. Or the washer.

Rather than argue about it every year, I just wait till she's gone.

She came home from church rather put out with Billy Tyson. "I entreated him in the spirit of Christian fellowship to turn the cheek one more time and give Marnolla another chance, but he kept asking whether the laborer wasn't worthy of his hire."

I looked at her blankly.

"Well, it sort of made sense when he was saying it." She grinned and for a moment looked so like my mother that I had to hug her.

❖ ❖ ❖

On New Year's Eve, I ran into Tracy Johnson at Fancy Footwork's year-end clearance sale. She's one of the D.A.'s sharpest assistants, tall and willowy with short blond hair and gorgeous eyes, which she downplays in court with oversized glasses. I caught her wistfully trying on a pair of black patent pumps with four-inch stiletto heels.

Regretfully, she handed the shoes back to the clerk and slipped into a pair with low French heels. They were okay, but nothing dazzling. Tracy walked back and forth in front of the mirror and sighed. "When I was at Duke, I almost married a basketball player."

I tried to imagine life without high heels. "It might have been worth it," I said. "Most of Duke's players at least graduate, don't they?"

"Eventually. Or so they say. Wouldn't matter. Judges aren't crazy about tall women either."

Her eyes narrowed as I tried on the shoes she'd relinquished and I instantly knew I'd made a tactless mistake.

"I see Marnolla Faison's going to be back with us next week," she said sweetly. "Third-time lucky?"

Hastily, I abandoned the patent leathers. It was not a good sign that the D.A.'s office remembered Marnolla.

"Woodall plans to ask for ninety days."

Three months! My heart sank. I could only hope that Judge O'Donnell would be hearing the case.

As if she'd read my mind, Tracy gave the clerk her credit card for the low-heeled shoes and said, "Perry Byrd's due to sit then."

✤ ✤ ✤

Layers of pink and gold clouds streaked the eastern sky as a designated driver delivered me back to the house on New Year's Day. I forget who designated him. The carload of friends that came back to Dobbs weren't all the same ones I'd left Dobbs with and I couldn't quite remember where the changeovers had come because we hit at least five parties during the night. I recall kissing Randolph Englert in Durham just as the ball dropped in Times Square, and I know Davis Reed and I had an intimate champagne breakfast with grits and red-eye gravy around 3 a.m. somewhere between Pittsboro and Chapel Hill. Further, deponent sayeth not.

I'd been asleep about four hours when the phone rang beside my bed. A smell of black-eyed peas and hog jowl had drifted up from the kitchen to worry my queasy stomach, and Billy Tyson's loud angry voice did nothing to help the throbbing in my temples.

"If this is your idea of a joke to make the Merchants' Association look shabby," he roared, "we'll just—"

Before he could complete his sentence, I heard Aunt Zell's voice in the background. "You give me that phone, Billy Tyson! I told you she had nothing to do with this baby. Deb'rah? You better come on over here, honey. I need you to help pound some sense in his head."

It took a moment till my own head quit pounding for me to realize that Aunt Zell wasn't downstairs tending to her traditional pot of black-eyed peas.

"Where are you?" I croaked.

"At the hospital, of course. The first baby was born and it's that Lynette's that's staying with Marnolla and Billy's saying they're going to disqualify it."

"Why?"

"Because it's"—her voice dropped to a whisper—"illegitimate."

"I'll be right there," I said.

Despite headache and queasy stomach, I stepped into the shower with a whistle on my lips. Sometimes God does have a sense of humor.

Every January, amid much local publicity, the Merchants' Association welcomes Dobbs's first baby of the New Year with a Santa Claus bagful of goodies: clothes and diapers from Bigg Shopp or K mart, a case of formula or nursing bottles from our two drugstores, a pewter cup from the Jewel Chest, birth announcements from The Print Place, a nightlight from Webster's Hardware, several pounds of assorted pork sausages from the Dixie Dew Packing Company.

Integration had officially arrived in North Carolina before I was born, but I was twelve before Colleton County finally agreed that separate wasn't equal and started closing down all the shabby black schools. I was driving legally before a black infant qualified as Dobbs's first baby of the year.

I had a hard time believing this was the first illegitimate first baby the stork had ever dropped on Dobbs Memorial Hospital, but this was Aunt Zell's first year as president of the Women's Auxiliary and she has a strong sense of fair play.

She'd make Billy do the right thing and then maybe I could pressure him to drop the charges against Marnolla.

❖ ❖ ❖

"Forget it," Billy snarled. "She's not getting so much as a diaper pin from us."

We three were seated at a conference table in the Women's Auxiliary meeting room just off the main lobby. A coffee urn and some cups stood on a tray in the middle and Aunt Zell pushed a plate of her sliced fruitcake toward me. I hadn't stopped for any hair of the dog before coming over and I wondered if my stomach would find fruitcake soaked with applejack an acceptable substitute.

Billy bit into a fresh slice as if it were nothing more than dry bread. "Anyhow, what do we even know about this girl? What if she's a prostitute or a drug addict? What if the baby was born with AIDS? It could be dead in three months."

"It won't," Aunt Zell said. "I sneaked a look at her charts. Lynette tested out healthy when they worked up her blood here at our prenatal clinic."

"I don't care. The Merchants' Association stands for good Christian values, and there's no way we're going to reward immorality and sinful behavior by giving presents to an illegitimate baby."

"Why, Billy Tyson," my aunt scolded. "What if the Magi had taken that attitude about the Christ Child? Strictly speaking, by man's laws anyhow, He was illegitimate, wasn't He?"

"With all due respect Miss Zell, that's not the same as this and you know it," said Billy. "Anyhow, Mary was married to Joseph."

"But Joseph wasn't the daddy," she reminded him softly.

"Bet the *Ledger*'ll have fun with this." I poured myself a steaming cup of coffee and drank it thirstily. "Talk about visiting the sins of the father on the child! And then there's that motor mouth out at the radio station. Just his meat."

"Damn it, Deb'rah, the girl's not even from here!" Billy howled. "You can't tell me Lynette DiLaurenzio's a good old Colleton County name."

"Jesus wasn't from Bethlehem, either," murmured Aunt Zell.

I can quote the Bible, too, but I decided maybe it was time for a little legal Latin. Like ex post facto.

"What's that?" asked Billy.

"It means that laws can't be changed retroactively."

"In this case, unless you can show me where the Merchants' Association ever wrote it down that the first baby has to be born in wedlock, then I'd say no matter where Lynette DiLaurenzio is from, her baby's legally entitled to all the goods and services any first baby usually gets. And if there's too much name-calling on this, it might even slop over into a defamation of character lawsuit."

"Oh, Christ!" Billy groaned.

"Exactly," said my aunt.

As long as we had him backed to the wall, I put in another plea for Marnolla. "After all," I said, "how's it going to look when you give that girl all those things in the name of the Merchants' Association and then jail the woman who took her in?"

"Okay, okay," said Billy, who knew when he was licked. "But this time, you're paying the court costs."

Aunt Zell leaned across the table and patted his hand. "I'd be honored if you'd let me do that, Billy."

The three of us trooped upstairs to the obstetrics ward to tell Marnolla and the new mother the good news.

✣ ✣ ✣

Lynette was asleep, so Marnolla walked down the hall with us to the nursery to peer through the glass at the brand-new baby girl. Red-faced and squalling lustily, she kicked at her pink blanket and flailed the air with her tiny hands. Billy's spontaneous smile was as foolish as Aunt Zell's, and I knew an equally foolish smile was on my own face. What is it about newborn babies? Looking over Marnolla's shoulder, I found myself remembering that long-ago wonder when she first let me hold Avis. For one smug moment I felt almost as holy as one of the Magi, figuring I'd helped smooth this little girl's welcome into the world.

Nobody had told Marnolla that the baby had won the annual derby, and her initial surprise turned to a deep frown when Billy said he'd call the newspaper and radio station and arrange for coverage of the presentation ceremony sometime that afternoon.

"It's going to be in the paper and on the radio?" she asked.

"And that's not all," I caroled. "Since it'd sound weird if people heard you were going to be punished for trying to provide some of those very same things for the baby, Billy's very kindly agreed to drop the charges." I tried not to gloat in front of him.

"No," said Marnolla.

"*No?*" asked Billy.

"What do you mean, 'No'?" I said.

"Just no. N, o, no. We don't want nothing from the Merchants' Association." Marnolla turned to Billy earnestly. "I mean, it's real nice of y'all, but let somebody else's be first baby. You were right in the first place, Billy. What I done was wrong and I'm ready to go to jail for it."

I found myself wondering if the Magi would have felt this dumbfounded if Joseph had told them thanks and all that, but he'd just as soon they keep their frankincense and myrrh.

"What about Lynette?" asked Aunt Zell. "Shouldn't she have some say in this? You're asking that young mother to give up an honor worth at least three hundred dollars."

"More like five hundred," Billy said indignantly.

For a moment, Marnolla wavered; then she drew herself up sharply. "She'll be all right without it. I'll take care of her and the baby, too. So y'all just keep those reporters away from her, you hear?"

I grabbed her by the arm. "Marnolla, I want to speak to you."

She tried to pull away, but I said, "Privately. As your lawyer."

Reluctantly, she followed me down to the Women's Auxiliary room. As soon as we were alone with the door closed, I sat her down and said, "What the devil's going on here? First you say for me to do whatever I can to keep you out of jail, and now, when the next thing to a miracle occurs, you say you *want* to go."

"I didn't say I want to," Marnolla corrected me. "I said I was ready to if that's what it takes to get people to leave Lynette alone."

"Same thing," I said, pacing up and down as if I were in a courtroom in front of the jury.

But then what she'd said finally registered and I realized it wasn't the same thing at all.

"How come you don't want Lynette's name in the paper or on the radio?" I asked.

Marnolla cut her eyes at me.

"Who don't you want to hear? The baby's daddy? Has she run away from some abusive man?"

There was a split second's hesitation, then Marnolla nodded vigorously. "You guessed it, honey. If he finds out where she's run to, he'll—"

"You lie," I said. "She's not from the county, nobody outside ever reads the *Ledger*, and WCYC barely reaches Raleigh."

As I spoke, Aunt Zell came in uninvited. That wasn't like her, but I was so exasperated with Marnolla, I barely noticed.

"Deb'rah, honey, why don't you run home and look in my closet and bring me one of those pretty new bed jackets? Get a pink one. Pink would look real nice when they take Lynette's picture with the baby, don't you think so, Marnolla?"

Marnolla had always shown respect for Aunt Zell, but nobody was going to roll over her without a fight this morning. Before she could gather a full head of steam, though, Aunt Zell advanced with fruitcake for her and a stern look at me. "Deborah?"

When she sounds out all three syllables like that, I don't usually stay to argue.

"And take a package of turnip greens out of the freezer while you're there," she called after me.

Most of my brothers married nice women and they all seem real fond of Aunt Zell, but they sure were in a rut with giving her presents. I bet there were at least a dozen bed jackets in her closet, half of them pink, and all in their original boxes. I chose a soft warm cashmere with a wide lacy collar, then went downstairs to take the turnip greens out of the freezer.

After my overindulging on rich food all through the holidays, New Year's traditional supper was always welcome: peas and greens and thin, skillet-fried cornbread.

As I passed the stove, I snitched a tender sliver from the hog jowl that flavored the black-eyed peas and gave the pot an experimental stir. There was no sound of the dime Aunt Zell always drops in. Even if you don't get the silver dime that promises true prosperity, the more peas you eat, the more money you'll get in the new year. I hoped Marnolla'd cooked herself some. Her troubles with Billy were about to be over, yet worry gnawed at the back of my brain like a toothless hound working a bone and I couldn't think why.

When I returned to the hospital, I could tell by Marnolla's eyes that she'd been crying. Aunt Zell, too; but whatever'd been said, Marnolla had agreed to let everything go on as we'd originally planned. We fixed Lynette's hair and got her all prettied up till she really did look like a young madonna holding her baby.

Billy had rounded up the media and Aunt Zell got some of the obstetrical nurses to stand around the bed for extra interest.

My own interest was in how Marnolla and Aunt Zell between them had managed to keep everybody's attention fixed on the baby's bright future and away from the shy young mother's murky past.

As everybody was leaving, I heard Aunt Zell tell Marnolla that by the time the baby had been home a week, people would've forgotten all about the hoopla and stopped being curious. "But the baby'll still have all the presents and she and Lynette will have you."

"I sure hope you're right, Miss Zell."

I drove Marnolla home and neither of us had much to say until she was getting out of the car. Then she leaned over and patted my face and said, "Thanks, honey. I do appreciate all you did for me."

I clasped her callused hands in mine as love and pity welled up inside of me. And yes, maybe those hands had stolen when they were empty, and maybe her altruism was even tinged by a less than lofty pride—which of us can plead differently before that final bar of justice? What I couldn't forget was that those selfsame hands had once suckered my daddy's tobacco and ironed my mother's tablecloths. And I remembered them holding another baby girl thirty years ago; a baby girl whose left little finger crooked like her own.

As did the left little finger of that baby back at Dobbs Memorial.

Aunt Zell must have remembered, too. I wondered what had really happened to Avis. The lost, scared look in Lynette's eyes did not bespeak a rosy, stable childhood. Drugs? Violence? Was Avis even still alive? I couldn't ask Marnolla how her pregnant granddaughter had fetched up here in Dobbs, and I knew Aunt Zell wouldn't betray a confidence.

"I hope you cooked you some black-eyed peas," I said.

She nodded. "A great big potful while I was timing Lynette's labor pains."

"Better eat every single one of 'em," I said. "You're going to need all the money you can lay your hands on these next few years."

"Ain't that the truth!" Her tone was rueful but her smile was radiant as she gave my hand a parting squeeze. "Happy New Year, Deb'rah, and God bless you."

"You, too, Marnolla."

"Oh, He has, honey," she told me. "He already has."

Christmas Stalkings, 1991

Lieutenant Harald
And the Impossible Gun

Chronologically, this was the first Sigrid Harald short story, but for some reason, it got stuck in my files and was forgotten till Marilyn Wallace was putting together her fourth anthology, which is why it's here rather than several stories earlier.

The calendar said late September, but summer hung on in the city like a visiting uncle who'd overstayed his welcome and sat out on the front stoop in a smelly sweatshirt, scratching his belly and smoking a cheap cigar all day. The unseasonable heat had blanketed New York for so long that the air felt stale and grimy, as if every wino in the city had breathed it before, replacing oxygen with cheap muscatel and sewer fumes. Even the trees along the street and scattered through dozens of vest pocket parks drooped beneath a sun that held in check the cleansing autumn storms that should strip away wilted, half-turned leaves and leave the clean grace of bare limbs.

In the air-conditioned coolness of her office, Lieutenant Sigrid Harald looked up from a report she was typing to see Detective Tildon standing in the open doorway.

"Could we talk to you a minute, Lieutenant?" His normally cheerful round face wore a look of serious worry. Behind him, equally solemn, stood a younger uniformed patrolman of similar height and the same sandy-colored hair.

Sigrid pushed the typing stand aside, swung her chair back around to face them and motioned to the chairs in front of her neatly ordered desk. Tildon hesitated a moment before electing to close the door. "Lieutenant, this is my cousin. Officer James Boyle."

As he named his cousin's current Brooklyn posting, the woman acknowledged the introduction with a formal nod.

"Glad to meet you, ma'am," said Boyle, but his heart had sunk at first glance. Tillie had made the lieutenant sound like Wonder Woman and here she was, thin, mid-thirties probably, taller than average, with a long neck and a wide unsmiling mouth. Her thick dark hair was skinned back into a utilitarian knot without even a stray wisp to soften the strong lines of her face.

Boyle was irresistibly reminded of Sister Paula Immaculata, his third grade teacher. Where Sister Paula had worn a long dark habit, Lieutenant Harald wore an equally concealing pantsuit of a shapeless cut which did nothing to flatter. Similar, too, was the way she sat motionless, her slender ringless fingers lightly laced on the desk before her as her wide gray eyes studied him dispassionately. Thus had Sister Paula Immaculata sat and weighed his tales of why he hadn't handed in his arithmetic homework or who had thrown the first punch in that kickball fracas at recess.

"What can I do for you?" asked Lieutenant Harald in her low cool voice; and for the first time since Tillie had proposed coming, Boyle felt hopeful. He remembered now that Sister Paula Immaculata had always known when he was telling the truth.

"A man named Ray Macken was shot last night," said Tildon, "and Jimmy—I mean, Officer Boyle thinks he's going to be charged with it."

"Not think, Tillie. *Know!*" said Boyle. "My sergeant gave me the name of a lawyer to get in touch with. A guy who specializes in cases of police shootings."

"And did you shoot this Ray Macken?" she asked mildly.

"Ma'am, I've never fired a gun at all except on the pistol range; but they've got the .38 that killed Ray and it has my fingerprints on it."

"Your own piece?"

"No, ma'am, but it was locked up tight in a property cabinet at the station house and everybody says I had the only key."

Sigrid Harald lifted an eyebrow. "Explain," she said, leaning back in her chair.

The uniformed Boyle looked helplessly at his plainclothes older cousin. His professional training faltered before such intensely personal involvement, as if he simply didn't know where to begin. Sigrid almost smiled as Detective Charles Tildon—Tillie the Toiler to his coworkers—took over with one of his inevitable thick yellow legal pads.

To compensate for his lack of imagination, a lack he was humbly aware of, Tillie followed the book to the letter and was scrupulous about detail. His reports could be a superior's despair, but Sigrid knew that if any vital clues were present at the scene of any crime or had been elicited in a witness's interview, they would appear somewhere in his meticulous notes; and she preferred his thorough plodding to the breezier hotshots in the department who were sloppy about detail and who bordered on insubordination when required to take her orders.

Now she listened quietly as Tillie described Ray Macken, a swaggering native of Boyle's Brooklyn precinct, who'd married the neighborhood beauty and moved to Texas to cash in on the sunbelt boom. His glib and easy manner had started him up half a dozen ladders, but alcohol and an aversion to hard work kept knocking him off.

Three months ago his mother had died and left him the two-family house of his childhood. Since he'd exhausted all the unemployment benefits Texas had to offer, the rental from the top floor and his mother's small insurance benefits were enough to bring him back north to Flatbush with his wife and son.

"He promised her a mansion," growled Boyle, "then he brought her back to an old house that hasn't had a new stick of furniture in thirty years. No air conditioner, no dishwasher in the kitchen, just a beat-up stove and refrigerator from the fifties!"

He lapsed into moody silence.

Sigrid fished four linked silver circles from a small glass bowl on her desk and toyed with them as Tillie resumed his narrative. It was a new Turkish puzzle ring which someone, knowing her fondness for them, had sent to her disassembled. She hadn't quite found the trick of fitting these particular sinuous circlets back into a single band, but it was something to occupy her eyes as she waited for what she suspected was coming.

Emotion always embarrassed her and this was the old familiar tale of high school sweethearts reunited, of a still-beautiful wife who realizes she picked the wrong man, of a young police officer who suddenly falls in love all over again: the secret meetings, the husband's suspicion and jealousy, the bruises where he's hit her in drunken rages.

Then, last night, the tenants upstairs had overheard a loud abusive argument, followed by the banging of the back door as Liz Macken fled to a friend's house. Afterwards, only silence until Ray Macken's body was found early this morning with a .38 bullet lodged just under his heart. As a woman, Sigrid had remained curiously untouched by love or hate, but as a police officer she knew its motivating force. "Involuntary manslaughter?" she asked.

Tillie shrugged.

"Hey, no way!" cried Boyle. "Liz isn't a killer and anyhow, she couldn't have used that particular gun."

He slumped back down in his chair dispiritedly. "Nobody could have used it except me and I swear I didn't."

"Tell me about that gun," Sigrid said.

"It was four days ago," Boyle began. "Friday, and St. Simon's kindergarten class."

♣ ♣ ♣

Even though Labor Day had marked the official end of summer vacation, everyone at Boyle's precinct house kept finagling for extra leave time while the heat wave continued and beach weather held. Sergeant Fitzpatrick, the duty officer, had juggled rosters until his temper frayed and he'd made it profanely clear when he tacked up the month's final version that no officer would be excused from duty unless he could produce a death certificate signed by three doctors and an undertaker.

Unfortunately, he'd forgotten about Sister Theresa, which is how Boyle got yanked from patrol duty that hot September morning.

"You'll take over for Sergeant Hanley until further notice," Fitzpatrick had informed him at morning shape-up.

"Hanley?" Boyle was puzzled. Hanley was a real oldtimer who was trying to finish out thirty years on the force. He was nearly crippled with arthritis and, as far as Boyle knew, only puttered around the station house and kept the coffee urns full. He'd been on sick leave all week and, except for grousing about coffee, no one seemed to miss him. Boyle was incautious enough to voice that thought to the sergeant.

This earned him a blistering lecture about macho motor jockeys who thought riding around in an air-conditioned patrol car was all there was to being a policeman.

An hour later, a sweaty Jimmy Boyle stood before a blackboard in the briefing room, clutching Hanley's keys, and faced the true reason Fitzpatrick needed a sacrificial goat: Sister Theresa, nineteen wide-eyed five-year-olds, and two of their mothers.

One of those mothers was Liz Macken, cool and lovely in a simple cotton sundress that he'd slipped from her tanned shoulders only a few days earlier in one of their stolen mornings together in his bachelor apartment. As his lover, she made his blood course wildly; today, however, was the first time that he'd seen her in her maternal role and it'd taken him several minutes before he could meet her mischievous smile with a casual smile of his own.

Luckily a fight broke out over a lecture pointer just then and Sister Theresa clucked in dismay as he tried to separate the combatants. Mrs.

DiLucca, a six-time grade mother, confiscated the pointer and promised the two kids she'd rap it over their heads if they didn't settle down.

Every September, Sister Theresa taught a unit called "Our Community Helpers" to her kindergarten class at St. Simon's.

Already they had trooped over to the clinic on Arrow Street where a nice nurse had taken their blood pressure and given them tongue depressors, to the local firehouse where they'd slid down the pole and clambered over a pumper truck, and to the branch post office where they'd seen mail sorted and had their hands postmarked with a rubber stamp.

"And today," chirped Sister Theresa, "this nice Officer Boyle is going to show us exactly what policemen do to help our community."

Nineteen pairs of skeptical eyes swung to him and Jimmy Boyle scrapped any thought of giving them a comprehensive view of the department. No way were these kids going to sit still for a lecture on hack licensing, housing violations and the other unexciting details policemen have to keep tabs on. Besides, with Liz sitting there he couldn't concentrate, so he yielded to the kids' appetite for sensationalism and passed out handcuffs for them to examine before herding them upstairs.

The drunk tank was empty for once and a deceptively fragile-looking child got herself wedged between the bars while another shinnied up to the ceiling and swung from the wire-caged light fixture.

He heard Liz say firmly, "Tommy Macken, you get down from there this minute!" and he looked closely at the little acrobat who could have been his son if things had gone differently.

If Liz hadn't thought him dull and square seven years ago.

If Ray hadn't dazzled her with a silky line and visions of the rich life in Texas.

The rest of the hour was just as hectic. In the basement, Boyle showed the children the small outdated lab that no longer got much use since all the complex needs were handled by a central forensic lab elsewhere. They compared hairs under a microscope—Tommy yanked a few from the small blond girl beside him and Liz gave him a quick swat on the bottom. He demonstrated how litmus paper works, then fired several shots from an old .38 into a cotton mattress and retrieved the slugs to show how the markings matched up for positive identification.

"Did that gun ever kill somebody?" they asked eagerly.

Boyle knew they'd be bored with the true story of two derelicts arguing over a bottle of cherry brandy, so he improvised on a television program he'd seen the week before and they ate up the blood and gore. Several grubby little hands had clutched at the pistol, but he put it back in the property cabinet and locked it securely. Of that he was positive. He had capped the tour by taking every child's fingerprints and warning them mock-ferociously that if any crimes were committed, the department would know whom to pick up. There was a moment of sheepish shuffling and a sudden emptying of pockets.

"Oh dear!" said Sister Theresa as ink pads, handcuffs, a set of picklocks and Sergeant Hanley's keys were returned to him. Liz laughed outright, but Mrs. DiLucca pursed her lips in disapproval.

Upstairs, he had passed out some lollipops from Hanley's desk and managed to wave back as the children filed down the front steps onto a sidewalk shimmering with heat. Sister Theresa had chirped again, "Now aren't policemen *nice?*"

Liz had smiled back at him then, the memory of their last meeting in her eyes, but Boyle didn't think Lieutenant Harald would be interested in that particular detail.

❖ ❖ ❖

"So you're positive the key to the gun cabinet was still on the ring when the kids gave it back?" asked Tillie.

"It had to be, Tillie, because it was sure there when Sergeant Fitzpatrick asked for the keys this morning. Ballistics got a make on the gun right away and they knew where to go for it. Ever since the kids left, those keys've been locked in my own locker at the station. I stuck them there Friday afternoon and forgot to return them when the sarge said I could go back to my own beat. Nobody needed them. Hanley's still out." Boyle twisted his blue hat in his hands and shook his head. "I just don't see how the gun was taken and then put back."

"No sign of the cabinet's lock or hinges being tampered with?" asked Sigrid.

"No, ma'am," he said unhappily.

"Do you have the M.E.'s report?" she asked Tildon.

Tillie shook his head. "Too soon. But I talked to Dr. Abramson, who did the autopsy. He said the bullet entered about here—he demonstrated an area just under his left midriff—and traveled up at an angle to nick the heart and lodge in the pleural cavity. The actual cause of death was internal hemorrhaging. Macken might have lived if he'd been rushed to a hospital in time; instead, he drowned in his own blood, so to speak."

Sigrid looked up from her puzzle ring. "The bullet traveled upward? That means he was standing while the killer sat or—"

"Or the killer stood over him and fired down?" asked Boyle eagerly. "Liz said they had a fight in the kitchen while she was trying to fix herself a glass of iced tea. That old icebox ought to be in a museum the way the frost builds up around the freezer so fast. Ray'd been drinking and he grabbed her. She twisted away and he slipped on a piece of ice and was lying on the floor half-zonked as she ran out the door. What if he never got up? Just lay there till someone who hated him came along and shot him. Liz certainly didn't stop to lock the door. Anybody could've—"

He saw the lieutenant's imperceptible frown. "Yeah," he said, slumping again. "That damn gun."

"Did the tenants or neighbors hear the shot?" asked Sigrid.

Young Boyle shook his head. "No. The neighbors on either side had their windows closed with air conditioners running and the tenants said they slept with a fan that was so noisy it could drown out fire engines."

"Abramson said Macken wasn't shot from close range," said Tillie, reading from his notes. "No powder burns and the fact that the bullet only penetrated four or five inches show that; but there's a bruise around the wound that puzzles him. Maybe he fought with his killer first and got punched there? And all Abramson can give us is an approximation of when the shooting occurred since, like I said, Macken didn't die as soon as he was shot."

Sigrid nodded and resumed her manipulation of the silver circles. Young Boyle looked at his cousin and started to speak, but Tillie signaled for silence. After a moment she lifted those penetrating gray eyes and said to Boyle, "What did Tommy Macken give back?"

Boyle looked blank. "Give back?"

Her tone was coldly patient. "In describing the tour you gave those unruly children, you said that several of them pocketed different items which your remark about fingerprints caused them to give back. What did Tommy Macken take?"

Boyle thought hard, visualizing the scene in his mind. "Nothing," he said finally. "He never touched the keys, if that's what you're thinking. It was the other kids who took things, not Tommy."

"I rather doubt that a child as agile and inquisitive as you've described would have gone home empty-handed," she said dryly.

Three of the silver circles lay perfectly stacked between her slender fingers. Delicately, she inserted a knob of fourth circlet between the first two and gently rotated it until all four locked into place and formed one ring. She examined it for a moment, then returned it to the glass bowl on her desk with a small sigh of regret at how easy it had been to solve.

Equally regretful was the look she gave Tillie's young cousin. "I'm sorry, Boyle, but my first opinion stands. I really don't see how anyone else could have killed him except Mrs. Macken."

"You're nuts!" cried Boyle. He pushed up from his chair so hard that it scraped loudly against the tiled floor. He glared at Detective Tildon angrily. "You said she could help, Tillie. Is this how? By pinning it on Liz?"

"Sit down, Boyle." There was icy authority in Sigrid Harald's voice. She pushed her telephone toward him. "Someone must still be posted at the Macken house. Call."

Resentfully he dialed and when one of his fellow officers from the precinct answered, he identified first himself and Lieutenant Harald, who gave crisp suggestions as to where he should search and what he should search for. She held on to the receiver and only a few minutes had elapsed before the unseen officer returned to his end and admiringly reported, "Right where you thought, Lieutenant—stuck down one of the garbage pails in the alley. It's already on its way to the lab.

✤ ✤ ✤

"An ice pick?" whispered Jimmy Boyle. "He was *stabbed* first?"

"First and only, I'm afraid," said Sigrid. "It was hot last night. You said she was trying to make iced tea when the fight began. A lot of those old refrigerators only make chunks of ice, not cubes, so it's logical to assume she had an ice pick in her hand. Afterwards, she must have remembered your lecture on rifling marks and pushed that slug into the wound to make it look as if an impossible gun had shot her husband."

"And the blow when she stabbed him with the pick must have made the bruise that bothered Abramson," Tillie mused.

She nodded. "Of course, someone will have to question the boy— make him admit he palmed one of those demonstration slugs and that his mother confiscated it. He may have bragged about it to some of the other children."

"Sorry, Jimmy, " Tildon said, awkwardly patting the stunned young patrolman's shoulder.

Boyle stood up and he still wore a dazed expression. "Not your fault, Tillie." Purpose returned to his face. "I'm still going to call that lawyer the sarge told me about. If Liz did stab Ray, it's got to be self-defense, right?"

"Right," Tillie answered sturdily; but after his cousin had departed, he turned back to Sigrid. "What do you think, Lieutenant?"

She shrugged. "The stabbing might not have been premeditated, but driving the slug into him definitely was. And didn't Abramson say Macken didn't die immediately? The prosecution's bound to bring that up."

Sigrid pulled the typing stand back in place and scanned the half-completed report Tillie had interrupted.

He started to leave, then paused in the doorway. "I didn't think you knew much about kids. What made you guess Tommy took that slug?"

"I have cousins, too," Sigrid said grimly. "They all have children. And all the children have sticky little fingers."

Her own slender fingers attacked the keyboard in slashing precision and Tillie was careful not to grin until he'd pulled the door closed behind him.

Sisters in Crime 4, 1991

Hangnail

I love the old dying clue mysteries and Ellery Queen's Challenge to the Reader almost as much as I enjoy anagrams and double-crostics. This story began with a Brooklyn setting, went nowhere, and was shoved into a file drawer unfinished till I realized it might work if I changed the setting and brought it south.

The first call for police help came approximately four and a half minutes after Toni and Pete Bledsoe arrived for breakfast at their nearly finished house out at Tinker's Landing, one of Colleton County's newest residential developments.

The house was supposed to have been ready in time for them to move in as soon as they came back from their honeymoon in Hawaii; but what with rain delays, mix-ups in materials orders, and an unreliable sheetrock crew, it was now seven weeks past the wedding and looked to be at least another week more before the painters and electricians would be through and they could install the wedding presents, which were currently taking up one whole room at Toni's mother's house.

At least the cedar deck was finished, and they had been out the night before to take delivery on the white wrought-iron patio table with its glass top and four matching chairs that Pete's aunt from Georgia had sent them.

Everything was fine then, they told the deputy.

That morning, they'd driven over shortly after sunrise with a thermos of coffee and a takeout order of sausage and biscuits from Hardee's, intending to enjoy a romantic breakfast on their brand-new deck at their brand-new table before heading off to their jobs in the Research Triangle.

❖ ❖ ❖

Now that I-40 had put Dobbs within easier commuting distance from Raleigh, the whole western part of Colleton County was growing. Tinker's Landing lay three miles west of the little county seat, but it had adopted big-town upscale zoning regulations. The smaller lots began at two acres and each custom-built house had to contain at least twenty-five hundred square feet, set back no less than seventy-five feet from the road.

Unlike the new trailer parks and budget developments creeping like kudzu vines across one-time tobacco fields, treeless and bare of all vegetation except wiregrass and cockleburs, Tinker's Landing lay along the river in a lush stand of second-growth hardwoods. The doctors, lawyers, or young professionals who bought lots here were, like the Bledsoes, affluent enough to bring in clever architects and landscapers who would incorporate the natural into their designs and cut no more trees than were absolutely necessary.

Poplars, oaks, and black gums flamed with September's gold and scarlet, but few leaves had actually fallen. Red-berried hollies, ironwoods, and huckleberries formed bushy barriers; honeysuckle, Virginia creeper, and poison ivy added their thick curtains; and bracken filled in the few bare patches that sloped down to the river.

A twisty road ambled artfully from the four-lane highway down to the old ferry landing that gave the development its name. Trees overhung ditch banks thick with Queen Anne's lace, purple-stemmed pokeberries, bright yellow coreopsis, and pink-flowered beggar's-lice. There were no streetlights to compete with the stars at night, and utility lines had been buried so that nothing spoiled the daytime illusion.

If not for the anachronistic sound of power saws and electric hammers that were due to shatter the morning stillness as soon as various building crews began work in another hour, this could be the archetypal backcountry road. Any minute now Andy and Opie might come strolling around the next curve with their cane poles, heading for the old fishing hole.

At 6:30, though, Pete and Toni Bledsoe had found the morning every bit as quiet and beautiful as they'd expected. A light haze hung over the river like a gauzy bridal veil, birds twittered in the tulip poplars, and as the newlyweds walked around to the side steps with their picnic basket, a young rabbit reared up on its haunches and watched until they were almost near enough to touch before scampering off in the tall grass.

"I'll get the cushions," Toni said as Pete poured steaming coffee into new hand-thrown pottery mugs and unwrapped the savory sausage biscuits.

She'd left the mauve chair cushions on top of their new shiny black washing machine the night before, but when she unlocked the French doors and entered the hi-tech utility room off the kitchen, she was at first puzzled to see the cushions tumbled on the marble tiles. It took a minute to register that the reason they were lying on the floor was because the washer was no longer there.

Nor was its matching dryer.

Upon hearing her startled yelp, Pete rushed inside and immediately realized that not only were washer and dryer gone, so was their oversized upright freezer. A hasty check of the house revealed a forced lock on the basement door. Also missing were an electric stove and refrigerator that had been delivered two days earlier and hadn't even been uncrated yet.

"Mama's gonna have a hissy," moaned Toni. The missing kitchen equipment had been a wedding present from her mother. "We like to've *never* found a black freezer."

"Don't touch anything," Pete cautioned his bride.

He spoke to an empty room. Toni was already storming for the front door and the cellular phone in their BMW.

Less than ten minutes later, a deputy from the Colleton County Sheriff's Department pulled into their new drive.

Carefully, he listened to their account of how the theft had been discovered. He followed them into the house, took a close-up picture of the tool marks on the forced door, and dutifully looked at the empty utility room where expensive major appliances were no longer sitting. He shook his head over the empty doorway between the formal dining room and butler's pantry where the thieves had carefully removed a custom-made stained glass door from its hinges. Then the three of them sat down at the new wrought-iron table out on the deck and the deputy accepted the offer of a cup of coffee as he filled out his report, because by that time they'd discovered that Toni's older brother and Deputy Raeford McLamb had played on the same high school baseball team the year they made the state playoffs.

"I'll be honest with you," McLamb told them. "I can send for our crime scene unit if you want me to, and they'll smear fingerprint powder all around, but as many people as go in and out of a new house, I doubt we'll get anything helpful."

He described the difficulties of removing grimy graphite from fresh white enamel or gleaming marble tiles, and both Bledsoes told him not to bother.

The deputy had barely finished both his coffee and his report when the two-way radio clipped to his belt crackled with an order to check out a second house three lots away. More new appliances had disappeared.

"Looks like you folks aren't the only ones got hit," said McLamb as he left the Bledsoes after telling them to tell Toni's brother that he said hey. Before he reached the second house, his radio squawked again with reports of a third.

And then a carpenter on the Hardin job called in and all hell broke loose.

♣ ♣ ♣

Lieutenant Dwight Bryant, Detective Chief of the Colleton County Sheriff's Department, read again from the form in his hand: *Jennifer Paula Hardin (Mrs. K. C.), née Brantley, Cauc. fem., 26, blk hair, brn eyes.*

That's how Deputy Raeford McLamb, first deputy on the scene nearly two hours ago, had listed her on the new checkoff form recently approved by Sheriff Bowman Poole.

Chapel Hill would eventually submit a fuller report, thought Dwight as he surveyed the unfinished sun-filled room where she'd been murdered. The state's medical examiner would give them her height and weight, a description of her multiple injuries, an itemized analysis of her internal organs, and the results of a dozen laboratory tests; and all would do their bit to describe Jenny Paul Hardin's physical makeup at the time of her death. Yet nowhere on any of their report forms were there spaces to mention pixie features, the swing of her dark hair, the tilt of her head when she listened, or the infectious laugh, which, according to Curtis Weill, got more work out of the men than two hard-nosed foremen or double wages ever could.

"She was a real lady," Weill said sadly. The head carpenter on the Hardins' nearly completed house was a lankily muscular man in his mid-forties. The gnawed stub of a toothpick perpetually resided in the corner of his mouth. It was he who'd found the body and sent one of his men out to the highway to phone the sheriff's department. "Gutsy, too," he added.

Dwight Bryant didn't need his years of homicide experience to read the trail of blood across the new living room's wide-planked floor. Jenny Paul Hardin had been setting nails in the baseboard when she was attacked last night. J. V. Pruitt, the local undertaker who acted as Colleton County's coroner, hated to be pinned down to specifics, but before he took away her slender body, he'd made an educated guess that death occurred sometime between seven and midnight.

Blood had splattered against the unpainted sheetrocked walls and pooled on the floor. The young woman's steel nail setter still shared that crimson puddle with an open tube of wood putty; but her hammer was on its way to the lab, its bright head caked with blood and hair after her killer had left her for dead.

Except that she hadn't died.

Not immediately anyhow.

Gutsy wasn't a strong enough word for her, Dwight thought. Her right hand smashed when she tried to ward off the blows, her head a pulpy mass, where on God's green earth had she found the strength of will to crawl more than twenty feet across the unfinished floor?

And what muddled logic had flickered through her dying brain and propelled her to the raised hearth now jumbled with new nails of all sizes? Surely so much determination signaled an intelligent reason. Several of the heavy brown paper sacks that stored the nails bore bright red stains, and three of the bloodiest were upended altogether.

"She spent a lot of time keeping them nails sorted," said Weill, whose eyes had also followed the ghastly trail to the hearth. "Made it one of her special jobs."

"You knew Mrs. Hardin pretty good?" asked Dwight.

Since returning to Colleton County after resigning from D.C.'s Capitol City Police Department two years ago, he'd occasionally seen her picture in the Dobbs *Ledger.* She had chaired United Appeals, presented awards at high school graduations, given blood when the hospital's bloodmobile visited her neighborhood, and appeared alongside other socially prominent women as they went through the socially aware motions Dobbs expected of its socially prominent families. (Dwight's ex-wife came from such a family in a small Virginia town and he regarded the species with sour wariness these days.)

In those grainy black-and-white photographs, however, there'd been something about Mrs. Kevin Charles Hardin that set her off from the other women. Jenny Paul Hardin had lacked the glossy surface sheen and easy complacency of the town's more fashionable Merediths and Dardens and Glenns. Her backbone was always a little too straight, her smile a shade anxious, as if she were uncomfortable in the Junior Women's Club role thrust upon her simply because her jack-of-all-trades father had left her a fortune larger than most in Dobbs.

"She took a couple of shop courses I once taught at the high school," said Weill, confirming Dwight's impression that she'd found blue jeans more comfortable than silk dresses. "Guess she was her daddy's daughter, all right. They say Paul Brantley could've built a tree if he'd a mind to, and Jenny Paul was real good with her hands, too. She didn't just work hard, she worked smart. I used to tell her if she ever needed a job, I'd take her on as a journeyman. Wasn't fooling, neither. All that money, yet if you didn't know, you'd never think it. Not like that banty-cock husband of hers, *Doctor* K. C. Nit-picking Hardin. Good thing State College keeps him busy or he might've accidentally got himself beaned with a two-by-four."

"He get in y'all's hair a lot?" asked Jack Jamison. He was young, new to the force, and didn't talk much, but Dwight suspected he was going to shape into a shrewd detective.

Weill gave a noncommittal shrug and Dwight filed the animosity for later examination. "But you didn't mind Mrs. Hardin being underfoot?" he asked.

"She wasn't," Weill said flatly. "She'd show up with a cold six-pack for our lunch and then pitch right in wherever she could help—not just me, but Vic or Neal or Billy, too—asking a million questions and listening to the answers. She wanted to learn it all and she wasn't afraid to get her hands dirty either. Why would a bunch of sneak thieves hurt a lady like that?" he asked angrily. "You reckon they walked in on her, not knowing she was here, and she recognized one of 'em?"

Dwight sighed and wished the room could speak.

The body was gone now, but a chalk outline remained near the hearth where Jenny Paul Hardin had finally died. Fingerprint powder lay like gray dust on every surface his crime scene unit had tested after they'd collected the usual fiber samples and other bits and scraps. Theoretically the detritus they collected would link a killer to this particular scene; in reality, as many different workmen who'd swarmed over this place the last month, it was probably a useless exercise.

Dwight eyed the jumbled nails. "What'd you mean when you said she made them her special job?"

Weill spat out the toothpick he'd chewed down to a nub and pulled a fresh one from the bib pocket of his denim overalls. "See, during the day your nail apron fills up with different types. Most jobs, you just dump 'em all in a box. By the time a house is finished, you could have forty or fifty pounds of nails mixed up. It's wasteful, but you can't pay a man carpenter's wages to sort nails; so every evening, Jenny Paul'd put 'em back in the right sacks. She kept 'em lined up from threepenny finishing nails"—he gestured with his toothpick to the left of the long hearth where several sacks stood undisturbed—"up to twentypenny stud-setters."

On the right, more sacks remained standing. Between the untouched sacks were those that were bloodstained or had been overturned.

Dwight had grown up out in the country where every farmer kept a supply of big nails on hand, but he'd never given much thought to the different types. "And each nail has its own specific job?"

"Sure. See this?" Curtis Weill parked the toothpick in the corner of his mouth and held up two slender headless nails, identical in size and length except one was brighter. "Both are eightpenny finishing nails, but the shiny one's galvanized so it won't rust. It's for outside trim. The other's for inside, where you don't have to worry about rain."

Weill handed Dwight another nail of similar length and girth except that it had a duller finish and a large flat head. "That's an eightpenny, too; easier to hammer, but you have to use it in the underwork where it won't show. There's nails for wood, masonry, grooved ones for sheet-rock, roofing tacks—"

His callused hands reached in and out of the bags as he explained the differences.

"And Mrs. Hardin knew all the names and uses?" asked Jamison.

"I said she listened, didn't I?" he growled.

From the pocket of his gray corduroy sports jacket, Dwight drew out an envelope that held a single nail and handed it to Weill. "What would a nail like this have meant to her?"

Three inches long and a quarter-inch wide at the head, the nail was flat and it tapered very slightly to a squared point, rather like an extremely skinny wedge of chess pie with the point nipped off.

Weill held it delicately in his rough fingers. "This what was clenched up in her hand so tight?"

Dwight nodded. The bloodiest sack still crumpled on the hearth had held others of this type.

"Well, it's a sixpenny cut nail," Curtis Weill said, choosing his words with obvious care. "It's made flat so it won't twist and split the wood when you nail it. This type gets put through a special heat treatment at the factory so's to harden the outer casing for extra strength. They'll go through concrete, but we used 'em for the flooring here. It's hundred-year-old heart pine we salvaged from an old house over in Raleigh, back of the governor's mansion. Hard as a rock."

The two detectives looked down at the mellow brick-toned floor, but could see no nails in the wide planks.

"Tongue-and-groove," Weill explained. "Each row's nailed on the tongue and the groove of the next board hides it."

Even though the floor still needed to be sanded and sealed with varnish, it was a beautiful piece of work, and Curtis Weill gave it a professional's accolade: "Best job Billy ever did. Old flooring's like doing a jigsaw puzzle the way you have to piece and fit, but he didn't face-nail one single plank."

"Billy Partin do the whole floor by himself?" Dwight asked.

Weill's eyes flicked over the deputy's face and looked away. "We all gave him a hand when he needed it—Vic, Neal, even Jenny Paul."

"But here in this house, on this job, this particular nail means flooring and flooring means Billy Partin, right?"

Curtis Weill nodded reluctantly.

Dwight slipped the nail back in the envelope and tucked it in his jacket pocket. "Did she always work here alone at night?"

"Sometimes. She said it was relaxing. Gave her a chance to think."

"About what?"

Weill shrugged. "Couldn't say. But her husband was away this week, down at the coast—Wilmington, I believe—at some sort of conference for college professors, so she'd been staying late. Sometimes till ten or eleven."

"Who knew that?"

"Hell, all of us did. Wasn't no secret."

"She wasn't worried about being out here alone?" asked Dwight.

He knew every construction site was subject to minor pilfering, but up until last night, nothing very major had gone missing from Tinker's Landing. They should have realized it was just a matter of time, he thought. Last night's haul had been the biggest and most methodical yet —in all, four houses had suffered an estimated combined loss of nearly thirty thousand dollars—but all across the county there had been sporadic instances in which expensive plumbing fittings and newly installed appliances suddenly sprouted legs and walked off.

Until last night, though, there'd been no incidents of physical violence.

"No, being alone never seemed to bother her," Weill told them. "And we rigged her up a light she could move around easy." He gestured toward the rough tripod of slender one-by-twos that supported a drop cord and a bare light bulb.

The room was flooded with bright September sunshine, but the bulb was still lit, just as Weill's crew had discovered it when they arrived at 7:15. There had been no sign of forced entry, but the front door was unlocked.

Dwight Bryant could understand the appeal of virgin landscape; unfortunately, all that natural foliage had allowed the thieves—Jenny Paul's killers?—to slip in and out of the houses unseen. With sight lines almost nonexistent, a dozen vehicles could have come and gone unnoticed. Nevertheless, two deputies had patiently begun to canvass the other building sites scattered through Tinker's Landing.

Now he sent Jamison to question the Hardins' housekeeper and to radio back when Dr. Hardin returned. It had been nearly ten o'clock before the murdered woman's husband had been located at a large educational conference down at Wilmington, so they couldn't expect him much before noon or 1:00 p.m.

❖ ❖ ❖

While he waited for that call to come, Dwight turned his attention to Billy Partin, Vic Lincoln, and Neal Cutler, the other three carpenters. If there had been any friction between Jenny Paul Hardin and the men, it wasn't immediately apparent.

Billy Partin seemed bewildered that anyone could have hurt such a nice lady, and even after Dwight rephrased his questions in simpler language, the forty-year-old laborer appeared not to understand that every workman in the development was a potential suspect.

Vic Lincoln, an easygoing, husky blond with muscular forearms, admitted he'd once made a pass at her, but claimed that she'd handled it as a flattering joke and that they'd become friends.

Neal Cutler, dark and close-faced, chain-smoked through the whole interview and denied any knowledge of anything.

A disconsolate Curtis Weill reduced half a dozen toothpicks to splinters with his callused fingers as he listened to his crew answer questions about his young client's death. When Dwight was finished, Weill had the men gather up their tools. There'd be no more work on this house probably until after the funeral.

If then.

❖ ❖ ❖

Dwight left a patrol officer posted at the house and drove back to his office in the basement of the new courthouse. As he passed between the stone pillars at the entrance of Tinker's Landing, he saw several cars and trucks backed up in front of the roadblock they'd established earlier to screen out the curious. There were work crews in dusty pickups coming back from early lunches; architects in shiny imported sports cars; a huge yellow backhoe; a delivery truck from Pennywise Discount Appliances in town; another delivery truck from Heigh's Building Supplies out on Highway 70; a green-and-beige furniture van from The Gallery, a high-priced decorator over in Raleigh; and a nursery truck with a large flatbed that held an expensive array of half-grown rhododendrons, azaleas, and other flowering shrubs that were going to give some new home owner an instant splash of color next spring.

"You can pack it in," Dwight told the two uniformed officers who were manning the checkpoint. Within minutes, the intersection was deserted as the vehicles rumbled through the gates unrestrained and disappeared around tree-lined curves. For a moment, Dwight stared after the green-and-beige van, trying to recall where he'd last seen the driver's face. And now that he thought about it, wasn't Tinker's Landing a little more upscale than Pennywise Discount Appliances' usual clientele?

Something else to file for future reference, he thought, and headed back to town.

❖ ❖ ❖

Word had spread through Dobbs and already the Hardin house was beginning to fill as shocked friends and neighbors came with hushed voices and platters of food. Dr. K. C. Hardin might not be Curtis Weill's favorite client, but he was a respected member of the town's intellectual community, and Jenny Paul's Brantley roots went back to the earliest settlers in the county, so there were many to mourn her death.

Dwight arrived at the house shortly before one p.m. and was met by young Deputy Jamison, who'd spent the last hour with Miss Lily Freeman, the Hardins' grief-stricken housekeeper. The two men walked out onto a deserted side porch to confer. Hardin had called from Clinton and was due to return in less than twenty minutes.

"You learn much?" asked Dwight.

Jack Jamison gave a noncommittal shrug.

He was a tubby youngster with a quiet, good-natured demeanor that put most people instantly at ease, which was why Dwight had started sending him first to a victim's bereaved family. As usual, Jamison's sympathetic murmurs at the right places had elicited from the housekeeper more background information on the murdered woman.

Her father, Paul Brantley, had possessed a wide-ranging curiosity about the way things worked in the building industry, and among his innovations to streamline production, he'd patented a cheaper method of making concrete blocks. Jenny Paul was his only child and he'd left her a fortune. She planned to build an industrial arts center in his memory to train high school dropouts, "but Dr. Hardin wanted her to endow a Chair of Education at his college with guess who as the first holder?"

The housekeeper wasn't just a hired woman, but also a distant cousin who had raised Jenny Paul in this very house after her mother died in childbirth, and she was clearly jealous of the man her charge had married.

"And what was so wrong with this house?" she'd asked Jamison tearfully. "If he hadn't of had to have a big fancy house to impress his friends from Raleigh, Jenny Paul would've been safe at home here last night."

Dwight glanced about them. The house was typical of this section of Dobbs. Built in the early twenties, in a neighborhood then peopled by skilled workmen and white-collar clerks, the comfortable unpretentious bungalow had large rooms and was wrapped in broad porches. Now that the tall Victorian houses a few blocks over were in short supply, tradition-minded Yuppies had begun to snap up these solidly built houses and to restore them with loving care. Even so, the contrast between this shabby old house and the luxurious new one out at Tinker's Landing was striking.

"Mrs. Hardin didn't want a new house?" asked Dwight.

"Not necessarily," Jamison said. "Miss Lily says she didn't, but she also let on that Mrs. Hardin kept talking about how nice it'd be for Miss Lily to have more privacy. I get the feeling it wasn't just Miss Lily's privacy she was interested in."

"Any hanky-panky on either side?"

"Not on Mrs. Hardin's part," said Jamison. "Leastways, not according to Miss Lily. And as much as she doesn't like him, I bet she'd be the first to tell it if Dr. Hardin was catting around. She says his idea of a big time's to have a bunch of guys from the college over for dinner to talk about how the country's educational system's going down the slop chute."

His tone was regretful. Both men knew that more murders were committed by friends and relatives than by total strangers, but except for Hardin and Miss Freeman, Jenny Paul had had no close family.

"I talked to the deputy who went over to Hardin's motel to break the news this morning," said Dwight. "She sounds pretty sharp. Says the night clerk's positive that Hardin's Volvo didn't leave the parking lot last night after nine o'clock and that a Professor B. L. Arnault had dinner with him from eight to ten."

Even with I-40 now open all the way, it still took more than two hours to drive to Wilmington.

"Say two hours here, two hours back, and a half hour to do it," mused Dwight. "Even if he left there at ten on the dot, it'd be midnight before he got here."

"And the coroner said she died between seven and midnight." Jamison reluctantly relinquished Hardin as a suspect. "What about the carpenters?"

"No simple solutions there, either," Dwight said. "Weill was at church and the other three were in a bowling-league playoff till after ten last night, and then they all say they went home alone, so where do we start?"

"With the nail?" Jamison suggested. "Miss Lily says she really loved word games. Scrabble. Balderdash. And you should see the puzzle magazines in her bedroom—codes, puns, anagrams, you name it."

"So it really does mean something?" The big-framed detective leaned against a porch post and studied the slender flat nail with bemusement. "Twelve years a policeman and this is my first honest-to-goddamn dying clue. I thought they only happened in those old Ellery Queen stories."

A stir from the front of the house drew their attention, and when they walked around the corner, they saw Dr. Hardin step out of his Volvo to be enfolded by several women from the church he and Jenny Paul had attended.

From the way he was dressed, Kevin Hardin could have gone straight to the church for the funeral, thought Dwight. His three-piece suit was dark and conservatively cut, his tie was subdued, every hair was smooth. But his handsome face seemed to have aged; his eyes were red-rimmed and bloodshot, and his voice broke when he first tried to speak to his friends.

The two deputies waited till after the first crush of condolences and then kept their interview short.

"A sixpenny cut nail?" asked Hardin when they were alone.

They had diplomatically elicited the address and phone number of the colleague with whom Hardin had dined the night before, and now that formalities were out of the way, they invited him to speculate on what that nail could have meant to his wife.

" 'For want of a nail, a battle was lost'?" Hardin shook his head and seemed genuinely puzzled. "My wife wasn't a great intellectual, but she did have a quick flair for puns and wordplay. If this is one of them . . ." His voice trailed off as he turned the nail in his smooth hands. "All I can think of is that old marriage rhyme: 'Something old, something new; something borrowed, something blue; and a sixpence for her shoe.' "

✤ ✤ ✤

The rhyme echoed in Dwight's head all the way back to the court-house.

. . . and a sixpence for her shoe.

For her shoe?

For Hersh Shue!

Jack Jamison pulled into the next parking space and glanced over with curiosity.

"Hershell Shue," Dwight told him. "He's a driver for Pennywise Discount Appliances. I thought it was odd to see their truck in a place like Tinker's Landing."

Jamison caught the implication instantly. "A delivery van sure makes a good cover for unscheduled pickups. Want me to ask him to stop by?"

✤ ✤ ✤

It was easier said than done.

According to Pennywise's dispatcher, Hersh Shue had gone to pick up a special order at their warehouse in Sanford and wasn't expected back till after their shift was over.

"And his delivery to Tinker's Landing this morning was legit," Jamison reported.

"Guess that's what I get for jumping to conclusions," said Dwight. "Just the same, though, let's put out the word to all patrol units: they're to keep an eye on any furniture vans roaming around after normal business hours. Especially anywhere near half-finished construction sites."

Routine procedure filled the rest of the afternoon. Jamison called the bowling alley to see exactly when the three carpenters had left, and he checked with someone from Weill's church to learn when prayer meeting had ended.

Dwight called around town and discreetly shook the grapevine of mutual acquaintances. No ripe juicy grapes of scandal fell into his lap.

"They were already into separate bedrooms, but that's life, Dwight," said a young woman who'd known Jenny Paul fairly well. "People like them don't get divorced, they get hobbies. Hers were word puzzles and working with her hands."

"What was his?"

"Work?" she hazarded.

"Sounds dreary," he said.

"Tell me, sugar," she needled. "Is divorce any better?"

"Touché," he said, only he slipped back into their childhood banter and pronounced it "touchy."

Nevertheless, even after he'd hung up, he continued to toy with the possibility that B. L. Arnault, Hardin's main alibi and the colleague with whom he'd dined the night before, might be a sex-starved little blondie named Betty Lou. Neither the Wilmington deputy nor Hardin had referred to Arnault by pronoun.

He pulled the phone over and punched in the Raleigh number Hardin had given them. A breathy female voice answered on the third ring.

"Arnault residence."

Bingo! thought Dwight. "Professor Arnault?" he asked. "B. L. Arnault?"

"I'm sorry. He's not here at the moment. Take a message?"

Dwight explained that he was a sheriff's deputy from the next county. "Is this Mrs. Arnault?"

"Good Lord, no!" The voice was amused. "I live next door and feed his cats when he has to be out of town. That's where he is now. In Wilmington. I have the number if you need it."

Disappointed, Dwight wrote it down. He heard a cat's mew in the background. "How many cats does Professor Arnault have?"

"Four young toms," she answered, and laughter bubbled just beneath her words.

Over the telephone, Arnault sounded rather young himself when Dwight ran him to earth at the conference on higher education. He answered questions hesitantly, with an upward inflection at the end of each sentence, even though his choice of words was that of a pedant-in-training. Nevertheless, he did confirm that he and Dr. Hardin had discovered a mutual appetite for she-crab soup and had availed themselves of a restaurant that served it down on Wilmington's restored waterfront.

"We drove back to the motel in my car shortly after ten and I then retired for the night," he said, his words as precise as if he were reading from a tome of lecture notes.

Jamison got no further with the carpenters. All could be accounted for by independent witnesses until ten o'clock. After that, it was either a wife (Curtis Weill and Neal Cutler) or elderly mother (Billy Partin).

Vic Lincoln didn't even have that much.

A clerk stuck her head into the room. "You know those names you gave me, Lieutenant? I got a hit on two of 'em."

She laid the printouts on Dwight's desk and he scanned them quickly. Eight years earlier, Billy Partin had served a sixty-day sentence for breaking and entering and stealing a color television.

That would have been interesting enough in view of the stolen appliances, but it was outweighed by the second report.

Fifteen months ago, Neal Cutler had been arrested for beating up his wife. According to the complaint she'd signed at the emergency room, he'd broken two ribs and her nose, but when the case came to trial, she refused to testify and so was charged with malicious prosecution and fined for costs.

Three months ago, he'd blackened both her eyes. Again she refused to press charges when court convened.

"A habitual wife-beater doesn't have much respect for any woman," Dwight said grimly.

"Neal Cutler," Jack Jamison mused. "Cut nail?"

Dwight found a clean legal pad and listed in block letters and alphabetical order the name of every man they'd yet encountered in the case: Neal Cutler, Dr. K. C. (Kevin Charles) Hardin, Vic (Victor) Lincoln, Billy (William) Partin, Hersh (Hershell) Shue of Pennywise Discount Appliances, and Curtis Weill.

He tried to think himself into the mind of a woman he'd never known. A down-to-earth young woman who'd delighted in puns. Would she have chosen something too arcane to decipher?

"She was dying, Jack. Yet she crawled across that floor on her hands and knees to get one particular nail. She thought it would be as obvious as writing us a name. Yet what've we got? Her shoe and cut nail."

Suddenly something caught his eye. "Hey, wait a minute! When you think of a penny, you think of Lincoln's head, right? And the first two letters of Vic make the Roman numeral six. *VI Lincoln—sixpenny!*"

"But why this sixpenny nail?" argued Jack Jamison. "There were at least four more types—with heads, without. Remember the bloodstains. She even had her hands on some of the others, so why this one if she didn't mean Billy Partin or Neal Cutler?"

They worried with Jenny Paul's riddle another twenty minutes and then called it a day.

✤ ✤ ✤

Next morning, when Dwight arrived at his office in the basement of the courthouse, Curtis Weill was waiting for him. Dwight almost didn't recognize him. Weill was dressed in a suit and tie and without his coveralls. The grim tiredness on the man's face didn't fit either. Only the toothpick in the corner of his mouth was familiar.

"I don't care how it looks," Weill said, "he didn't kill Jenny Paul."

"Huh?"

"Vic Lincoln," Weill said impatiently.

Dwight was puzzled. "You want to back up and tell me what you're talking about?"

Jack Jamison entered the office. He stood silently but Dwight sensed a suppressed excitement.

"What?" he asked.

"McLamb arrested Vic Lincoln and his brother Danny about six this morning," Jack said. "You know that fancy decorating place over in Raleigh? Danny Lincoln's a deliveryman for The Gallery. Only, he and Vic make pickups from some of the same houses. They've been stashing the stuff at a potato house over in Little Creek Township and then selling it at a flea market down in Georgia."

"You knew about this?" Dwight asked Weill.

The carpenter shook his head, but his eyes shied away from Dwight's as he dropped the gnawed toothpick in the wastebasket and pulled a fresh one from his pocket. "I didn't know," he said, "but, yeah, I guess I was starting to wonder. Every place we worked, it'd either be the house we were working on or someplace nearby. Soon as new appliances got delivered, they'd get ripped off. First two or three times I thought it was coincidence. But Vic was always wandering off to check things out during lunchtime—he was friendly with everybody."

He took a deep breath. "He called me this morning to see if I'd help with his bail. And he's scared y'all are going to say he killed Jenny Paul. He might could steal, but I promise you he couldn't kill."

"No?" Dwight said sardonically. "What about this?"

He showed Curtis Weill the list of names he'd doodled with the afternoon before, including what they'd worked out for Vic Lincoln.

Weill's eyes leaped from Vic's name to his own. "You really believe one of us did it?"

"I really believe that nail means something. Don't you?"

"Well . . . yeah, I guess I do," Weill said slowly. "That's the way Jenny Paul's mind worked, all right. Lucky for me she stayed away from the little ones."

"Why do you say that?"

Curtis Weill pulled out a small gold brad. "When we started the house, she gave me this for good luck. Seems some guy with my name wrote a play called *The Threepenny Opera*."

"Kurt Weill!" Chagrined that he'd missed that coincidence, Dwight pointed to the rest of the list. "We can make Vic Lincoln and Neal Cut fit if we have to, and there's always Billy Partin. He's the main one who used those heat-treated cut nails and—"

"Not 'heat-treated' cut nails," the carpenter corrected with a faint smile for their laymen's ignorance. "They're 'case-hardened' nails."

His flat country drawl drew out the "case" and clipped off the "hardened."

The three men stared at each other and Weill's jaw tightened angrily as he suddenly realized what the young murdered woman had tried to tell them.

Dwight Bryant cupped the nail in his hand, the only case-hardened type in Jenny Paul Hardin's new house. Now that its message was finally clear, it shouldn't be too hard to break down the colleague who'd alibied Dr. K C. Hardin. Maybe B. L. Arnault was going to turn out to be Hardin's little sex-starved blondie after all.

"I hope you hang his hide on the jailhouse wall," Weill growled.

"Don't worry," said Dwight. "She's already nailed him herself."

Deadly Allies, 1992

That Bells May Ring
And Whistles Safely Blow

Every time a whistle-blowing public servant gets the ax while the blow-ee gets to keep his job or gets promoted, I want to fire all the politicians.

"**D**eck the halls?" snarled Jane as she untied a rope of tinsel from a file cabinet and added it to the pile growing beside her reception desk. "I know one Hall I'd love to deck."

"And I know where I'd like to stick a few boughs of holly," Sheila agreed. She stood atop a step stool and unhooked the cluster of shiny stars that dangled from an overhead light.

I didn't speak. I believe actions speak louder than words and I was using all my breath to stuff our four-foot artificial fir tree into a huge plastic bag—lights, ornaments, icicles, and all.

'Twas two nights before Christmas, and we were three angry middle-aged mice as we stripped the office of every decoration. Santa Claus was a bully, Scrooge had triumphed, why continue the peace-on-earth-goodwill-to-men charade?

The annual Christmas party downstairs had put us in such a bleak mood that when we came back up for our coats, the jingle-bell festivity of our office repelled us. As one woman, we decided to bundle every-thing up and give it to someone deserving. The way our boss's bosses had reacted to Bridget's whistle-blowing, a shelter for battered women seemed the most appropriate.

Not that Sheila wasn't put out with Bridget herself.

"If she hadn't gone off half-cocked—" She tossed the stars atop Jane's pile of tinsel and paused to help me close the top of the tree bag.

"She's young," I said. "Things are more black and white when you're nineteen."

In truth, Bridget reminded me of myself at that age, which was more years ago than I like to contemplate: naive, idealistic, and full of youthful misconceptions.

Here in the Budget Department of the City Planning Commission, she'd soon learned that very few public officials actually serve the public.

Clerical staff does most of the work while department heads hide incompetence, gross negligence, and outright dishonesty by playing the bureaucratic shell game: You cover my rear, I'll cover yours, and Santa will fill both of our stockings with sugarplums.

Our boss was one of Santa's best little helpers. Nicholas T. Hall exuded an air of confident ability. He spoke the jargon. He had an endless fund of risqué stories that were clean enough to be told in mixed company, and he knew to the millisecond when to cut through the laughter with a "But seriously, guys, this problem we have here means we're gonna need to . . ."

As a result, he'd been promoted two notches above his level of competency. Nothing terribly unusual about that. We "girls" were used to covering our bosses' worst blunders. But then he began to muddle ineptitude with greed. Before his arrival, most contracts were still awarded to the lowest or most efficient bidder. Now reports had their figures padded or deflated depending on what was needed and what could be glossed over, and kickbacks ranged from bottles of scotch to God knew what.

Business as usual, right? It was only taxpayer dollars. Who gave a happy damn?

Well, as it turned out, Bridget did.

❖ ❖ ❖

She'd seemed as militant as dandelion fluff when she first floated into our department right out of high school back in May. We soon learned that she'd fudged her application form and that she had no burning desire to work her way up from file clerk to senior administrative aide in the city's civil service system. She merely wanted to earn more than a student's usual summer job paid and she planned to quit at the end of August and go off to college.

Jane was a bit ticked because it would mean training someone else in the fall, but Bridget proved a quick learner and, though clearly not a dedicated worker, was at least willing to follow directions, so Jane kept her mouth shut to Mr. Hall.

Which was lucky because in mid-June, Bridget's parents and three perfect strangers were killed in a car crash that was clearly her father's fault. Funeral expenses and settling two messy civil lawsuits out of court took the house and most of her parents' modest estate. There were no relatives and Bridget's college plans had to be put on hold. She did manage to salvage some of her mother's furniture and a few family keepsakes from the sale of the house, and Jane and Sheila helped her find a cozy little apartment near enough so she didn't need a car to get to work.

Bridget changed overnight. She'd been an adored only child and was very close to her parents. After their death, the lightness went out of her steps; and all through the fall, she threw herself into the job with a passion that gave a whole new meaning to the term workaholic. We knew her reaction wasn't completely healthy, but compulsive dedication was certainly easier to deal with than the crying jags that had gone before.

Jane was pleased with her new thoroughness, Sheila was skeptical as to how long it could last, while I, keeping to the real agenda, was indifferent.

There were other, younger women in the department, but for some reason Bridget attached herself to the three of us even though we did little to encourage her. At coffee breaks she brought her hot chocolate to my cubicle, or she tagged along at lunch. Occasionally, she and I were even mistaken for mother and daughter. I'd seen pictures of Bridget's mother and knew there was a vague resemblance, but it wasn't something I wanted to promote. I had two perfectly satisfactory Siamese cats, thank you, and I certainly didn't want an emotional involvement with anyone's orphaned child. Nevertheless, there were times when something I said would remind her of happier times and tears would spill down her smooth cheeks. That's when it got hard to stay completely aloof.

❖ ❖ ❖

Early in December, when Mr. Hall's Christmas booty began pouring in, Bridget started to notice. Soon she had matched the names on the gift cards with names on certain city contracts, and she came to us in outright indignation.

"Look at this!" she cried. "Davis Corporations's original bid. Here are their first figures and this is how Mr. Hall let them change it. And now they've sent him two bottles of scotch? They're going to get an extra four thousand a month from the city for two bottles of scotch?"

Sheila and Jane and I exchanged glances. We knew the scotch was but a socially acceptable token of Davis Corp's real appreciation, which was delivered every month in an unmarked envelope.

"And see what Mainline's done! They—"

"And just where did you get those contracts?" Jane asked sternly, snatching them out of her hands. "You have no business rummaging in those particular files."

Bridget's big blue eyes had opened even wider. "Don't you care that they're robbing the city blind?"

"Small potatoes," Sheila said heartlessly, "compared to what some others are doing."

I gave Sheila a cold glare and she shut up as I pulled on my boots against the snow falling outside. "I'm going to spend my lunch hour Christmas shopping," I announced. "Anyone interested?"

❖ ❖ ❖

"I'll come," said Jane. She quickly refiled the contracts and closed those drawers with a crisp finality. "Rowan's has a sale on men's flannel shirts."

"Maybe I'll get one for Bill," said Sheila.

"How can you shop when—" Bridget's outraged protest broke off as the inner door swung open and our boss breezed through in his overcoat, heading out for his usual two-hour lunch.

He smiled at us in genial bonhomie. "Going Christmas shopping, girls?"

"Yes, Mr. Hall," I said.

If he ever remembered how long it took me to teach him his job here, and if he ever realized he still couldn't handle it without me, he never showed it. I could appreciate the irony, and unlike Sheila and Jane, I didn't resent the institutional unfairness of the situation. Might as well resent December for not being June. Makes as much sense. So what, if I still knew more about how the department functioned than he ever would? Clerical experience wasn't worth a reindeer's damn to the hierarchy. The job description for department head specified a college degree.

I didn't have one.

Nicholas T. Hall did.

That's why we called him Mr. Hall and he called us "girls."

"You got some Christmas presents," Bridget said, thrusting the beribboned boxes toward him. Unexpected acid etched her voice.

Mr. Hall held one up to his ear and beamed happily as he heard the expected liquid slosh from the bottle inside. "Good old Davis!" he chuckled. "Why don't you help me put these in my office, little lady?"

Davis Corp knew their man. He would probably take a quick nip before leaving and two or three more nips when he came back from his three-scotch lunch. Then he'd shove a few papers around his desk, sign the ones I'd left there, and about midafternoon ask us to hold his calls.

At times like that, the rest of the staff thought he was concentrating on a project. Only Jane and Sheila and I knew that he sneaked long naps on the couch in his office, and he trusted us to cover for him. Four years of such indulgence had added an extra chin and puffed the bags beneath his eyes.

Indignation still burned in Bridget's eyes as Mr. Hall held the door for the three of us; and when we returned an hour later with our shopping bags crammed with gaily wrapped bundles, she spoke not a word but went straight on with her work on the far side of the office.

We let her sulk. December was hurtling past, the year was coming to an end, and we were so pressed for time on our own special project that we had none to spare for her. In fact, we used her sulks to rationalize our neglect. That was the guilt that gnawed at us and had sent us back up to the office to rip down the Christmas decorations that afternoon.

"If only we'd paid attention!" said Jane. "We could have headed her off."

"Who'd expect someone that young to get so uptight about morality?" asked Sheila.

"It's the young who do," I said slowly. "Once they get our age, most of them are too cynical to care anymore."

"They didn't have to fire her though," Sheila muttered.

Jane snorted and I gave Sheila a jaundiced look.

"Okay, okay," Sheila said. "You're right. But . . . I mean— Well, darn it all, it *is* Christmas."

"That's what *they* said," I reminded her.

As senior administrative aide in this department, I'd had to stand and listen that morning while Nicholas T. Hall and G. W. Parry, Hall's superior, fired Bridget.

When the flow of Christmas bottles reached its crest, that naive little bit of dandelion fluff had carefully listed all the donors and keyed their names to various contracts Hall had awarded. This morning, bright and early, she'd marched down to Parry's office, handed him the list, and stood there expecting to be told what a good little girl she was for blowing the whistle on crooked contractors.

Instead, she'd gotten a rude blast of reality and orders to clean out her desk before five o'clock.

"What else did you expect?" I'd asked her as we climbed the stairs back to our office. She was shaking in nervous reaction and trembling on the verge of tears, and I'd chosen stairs over the elevator so she'd have time to collect herself. "Okay, so city employees aren't supposed to take gifts. Nobody considers a few bottles of hooch a bribe. You're lucky they're satisfied just to fire you. You could have been sued for slander."

"Sued?" she whimpered. "Again?"

She'd endured agonies when everything her parents amassed had gone to settle the lawsuits over her father's car wreck. I hated to touch a hurt that had almost healed, but she needed to understand the consequences of going off half-cocked.

"Do you know what this is going to do for morale in our department?"

Tears did stream from her eyes then. "Oh, Glenna. I'm so sorry. I wasn't thinking."

I sighed and put my arms around her and let her cry. Inside, I burned with white-hot rage and impotence, but I kept my voice soothing as I patted her back and told her everything was going to be fine, just fine. She was such an emotionally fragile kid and here she was, being cut adrift at Christmas with no immediate job prospects and no shoulder to go home and cry on. Not even a cat.

When we reached our landing, the humiliation of having to clean out her desk while the whole department watched was more than she could take at the moment and she clutched at my hand.

"Don't make me go in there. Please, Glenna?"

I offered to do it for her, but she shook her head and began to edge down the stairs. "No, I'll come back this afternoon while everyone's at the Christmas party, okay?"

Reluctantly, I agreed but made her promise to wait while I got her coat. She seemed ready to bolt off into the snowy day with nothing on her arms but a thin pink sweater, and I didn't want her pneumonia on my conscience, too.

My return to the office coincided with Mr. Hall's. It was his year to play Santa Claus, to hand out the gag gifts and Christmas bonuses, and he had his red suit and wig in one hand and the white beard in the other.

"Damn shame," he said, fluffing out the beard. He'd decided to be noble and magnanimous, more sinned against than sinning, this hurts me more than it hurts her. "Such a pretty little thing. I thought Parry was a bit hard on her, but he seemed to think we had no choice."

What G. W. Parry had said, with more force than originality, was that when an apple (i.e., Bridget) turned rotten, it had to be plucked out before it spoiled the whole barrel (the Budget Department).

"And I agree," I told him with more sincerity than he realized.

"You do? Ah, Glenna, you girls always surprise me. Will you tell the others?"

"I thought I'd wait till just before the party, if that's all right with you?"

"Good thinking. The party will take their minds off it, and then with the whole Christmas weekend— You're right. By Tuesday morning they'll have forgotten this whole unpleasant situation."

✣ ✣ ✣

On the whole, he probably hadn't underestimated his staff's compassion. In an announcement shortly before the party was due to start at two-thirty, I explained that Bridget had made certain unfounded accusations against Mr. Hall and that she'd been asked to resign in light of her poor team spirit. Rumors would fly, but except for Sheila, Jane, and me, Bridget had made no close friends among the other ten women in the department. Unless we discussed her actions in public, there'd be nothing to keep the rumors going.

Of course I'd told Jane and Sheila everything over lunch and by the time we'd had a few cups of the spiked punch down in Central Planning, the three of us had gone from rage to despair to a melancholy pity for poor Bridget. As the others drifted off early to their varied merry Christmases, we went back upstairs and found that Bridget had been and gone. Her desktop was bare, the empty drawers stood ajar, but everything that had made the desk hers—nameplate, coffee mug, even a cloisonné brass pot full of pencils, pens, and scissors—had been dumped in the nearest trash can as if she'd suddenly changed her mind about taking anything with her.

That's when we got angry all over again and attacked the Christmas decorations. We were almost finished when Nicholas T. Hall staggered in, beard awry, reeking of scotch, and slurring his words. He made a half-hearted joke about mistletoe and pretty girls as he shucked off his red jacket, hat, and attached wig, and slung them toward the nearest coat rack.

We ignored him.

Wounded, he retreated to his office and a moment later we heard the tinkle of glass, then the whooshing sound that his leather couch always makes when he sprawls upon it full length. By the time we'd bagged all the decorations to take over to the women's shelter, muted snores were drifting through our boss's half-open door.

It was only a little past four, but the sky had darkened and a fifty-percent probability of fresh snow was predicted. The telephone rang just as we were putting on our coats.

"Glenna? Oh good. This is Louise Hall. Is my husband still there? He promised he'd be home early."

Automatically I spoke the sort of lies Mr. Hall had instructed me to speak in such circumstances. "I'm sorry, Mrs. Hall. He left about a half hour ago. I think he planned to do some Christmas shopping on the way home. I was just leaving myself."

As I opened my desk drawer for my purse, I found a small gaily wrapped package with my name on it.

"I thought we agreed no presents," I said. Then, across the room, I saw that Sheila and Jane had discovered similar boxes.

I looked again at the name tag and recognized the handwriting.

"From Bridget," I said.

"Oh, gee," said Jane, ripping the paper from hers. "With all her troubles, she went and did this for us?"

She lifted the lid from the box and gasped with delight. Inside was a beautiful snow dome, one of those glass balls filled with water and white flecks that create a swirling snowstorm when shaken. This one was old, almost an antique. I knew because I was there the day Bridget showed it to Jane, who collects snow domes. It held a miniature elf who trudged across the snowy field carrying a decorated tree on his shoulders. It had belonged to Bridget's grandmother.

My gift was a sterling silver bracelet I'd once admired. Her mother's. Even Sheila was touched. "I can't take this," she said though she tenderly cradled the old-fashioned gold pocket watch in her hand and traced the intricate initials with the tip of her finger. "It was her great-grandfather's. Almost a hundred years old. She loves this watch."

Jane inverted the snow dome and watched the white flecks dance inside its polished glass. "This is one of her favorite things."

The thin silver bracelet suddenly felt like a sliver of ice on my wrist. "These *are* her favorite things. Why has she given them away?"

I looked into their faces and saw my own startled apprehension reflected.

❖ ❖ ❖

My reserved parking space was nearest the back entrance and Sheila and Jane piled into the car with me. Bridget's apartment was only a few short blocks away and though we made it in minutes, we were at least a half hour too late.

She'd left the door unlocked.

She was still wearing the pink sweater, but now the front was drenched in blood. She must have come home and sat down in her mother's wingback chair then pressed a needlepoint cushion against her chest before pulling the trigger, as if the cushion would somehow soften the shot.

Nicholas T. Hall's gun.

Every once in a while he had to go out and inspect deserted job sites in the rougher sections of the city. Legally registered. We recognized the fancy bone handle. He kept it in his desk drawer and whenever he cleaned the damn thing, he'd leave his office door open so that we *girls* could catch a glimpse of the he-man in action, ready and willing to face all dangers, the city's very own rootin', tootin' gunslinger.

And now his gun had finally notched its first kill.

Bridget's blue eyes stared into eternity. With infinite tenderness, Jane leaned over and closed them; then, almost wordlessly, we did what had to be done.

✤ ✤ ✤

Christmas arrived two days later and that morning, the police apologetically summoned the three of us back to the office. They had a search warrant.

Mr. Hall was there, too. He looked as if he'd discovered rats and spiders in his Christmas stocking.

"Tell them, girls," he said hoarsely. "Tell them how I fell asleep on the couch night before last and didn't wake up till after eight. Jane? Sheila? You were here when I came back from the party and—Glenna! You were still working when I woke up. Remember?"

We looked at him blankly.

"I'm sorry, Mr. Hall," I said. "You left the office immediately after the party. If you came back again, it must have been after we'd gone."

"Besides," added Jane, "why would Glenna work late that night? It was the beginning of our Christmas holiday."

"Fits with what Mrs. Hall said," one of the detectives muttered to another. "Let's get on with it."

They soon found the gun behind the couch where it'd dropped from Mr. Hall's comatose fingers. (Jane's idea, and a nice touch, I thought.)

They were equally pleased with the red jacket and white beard still dangling from the back of Mr. Hall's door. "The old lady across the hall said she saw a Santa ringing the girl's bell."

So many people had worn the company's Santa costume over the years, it wouldn't matter whose hairs they found on the cap and wig as long as one or two of them belonged to Mr. Hall.

The detectives were very good at their job. Within hours after the anonymous call late Christmas Eve, they'd also found the computer disks I'd hidden in Bridget's lingerie drawer as well as the papers I'd stashed in her flour canister.

Taken together, the papers and floppies documented four years of corruption that stretched from the Budget Department right up to the City Council itself. There were names and dates and bank account numbers and xerox copies of dated deposit slips. Every allegation wasn't backed with solid proof, of course. Not as much as Sheila and Jane and I'd hoped to provide before Bridget so abruptly forced our hand, but more than enough to fuel the public investigation we'd been planning for almost a year—especially when linked to the shooting of a pretty young city clerk.

Bridget's death, an apparently cold-blooded murder so she wouldn't go public with her tale of bureaucratic corruption, wasn't the sort of thing that could be glossed over like a few bottles of complimentary Christmas booze. Not if that television van parked downstairs meant what I hoped it did.

Scotch had fogged Mr. Hall's perceptions more than he realized. It was closer to nine than eight when he woke up and found me still stripping the electronic data of all links to the three of us and transferring it to the sort of floppies that Bridget's computer used. Sheila and Jane had families so they had washed the sulfites from Bridget's hands, taken away the cushion, and gone straight home. The rest was up to me; and if it'd taken longer than any of us expected, if Bridget's delicate young face kept coming between my tear-blurred eyes and the numbers on my computer screen, who would know? Siamese cats can't tell time. Can't testify.

Open and shut, said the detectives. "The kid let slip what she had on you; you got her fired. Then she threatened to blow an even bigger whistle and you got drunk and shot her."

"No!" whimpered Nicholas T. Hall.

"Drunkenness is no longer a defense against murder," warned the younger detective.

"Why won't you girls tell them?" Mr. Hall asked plaintively as they hauled him away like a defective Christmas present.

I pulled on my gloves and my own Christmas present gleamed against the soft leather, a slender shining hoop too delicate for everyday wear. Too easily crushed.

If Sheila and Jane and I had been younger, less cynical, perhaps we could have trusted her.

As soon as Cameron Jewelry begins its January clearance sale next week, I shall buy a tiny gold whistle to hang on Bridget's silver bracelet.

I shall blow it every Christmas.

Santa Clues, 1993

What's a Friend For?
(With Susan Dunlap)

This story came almost intact from the lips of Dorothy Cannell's husband; and the moment we finished laughing, I asked if I could have it. "Well," Julian said, "it happened eight years ago, and Dorothy's never used it, so, yes." Susan Dunlap and I had talked about collaborating on something ever since she told me that her character, Kiernan O'Shaughnessy, took a grad course at UNC-Chapel Hill, Deborah Knott's alma mater. Using Julian's anecdote as the framework, the story almost wrote itself.

My elderly cousin Lunette got off the plane apologizing from the moment she spotted me waiting at the tinsel-draped gate at our Raleigh-Durham airport. "Oh, Deborah, honey, I'm so frigging sorry."

Even though I was now a duly sworn district court judge, Aunt Zell still thought I had plenty of time to pick up some of the aunts, uncles, and cousins coming in for Christmas from Ohio, Florida, New Orleans, or, in Lunette's case, Shady Palms, California.

Her hair was Icy Peach, her elegantly slouchy green sweatshirt had an appliquéd Rudolph with a red nose that really did light up, and her skintight stretch pants seemed to be fashioned from silver latex. Nevertheless, for all the holiday joy in her twice-lifted face you'd have thought it was the first day of Lent instead of the day before Christmas Eve.

Lunette's of my mother's generation. We're first cousins once removed, which, if you're into genealogy, means that she and Mother shared a set of grandparents on our Carroll side.

But whereas most of the Carrolls have stuck right here in Colleton County ever since our branch got booted out of Virginia and wound up in North Carolina in the early 1800's, Lunette was born without a dab of tar on her heels. She became an airline stewardess in the early fifties, married a Jewish sales exec from California, and crisscrossed the country with him for twenty years till he took early retirement. Then they became semi-rooted in Shady Palms, where Lunette's continued to live since his death six years ago.

The family's tried to get Lunette to come home, but she says all her friends are there, the gaming tables of Las Vegas are just a short drive away, and anyhow, she's too old to exchange blue language for blue hair or give up the Hadassah and join the Women's Missionary Union.

But she does come back for Christmas now that Jules is gone. They never had children, and Lunette says, "If I'm going to have to listen to foolish old women burble on about their blippity-blip grandchildren, it might as well be kids I'm kin to. Besides, you can't get decent sweet potato pie out in California."

We made our way downstairs through the holiday throng to the baggage claim area and while we waited for the carousel to start turning, I finally grasped that Lunette was half-crying, half-cursing because her condo had been ripped off less than a week ago.

Through Aunt Zell, I'd heard most of the details when she called two days earlier to confirm what time her flight was due. Over the phone, Aunt Zell said Lunette had sounded almost matter-of-fact: Half her friends have been robbed, she guessed she was overdue; she was sorry to lose Jules's wedding ring, but she'd been wearing most of the jewelry she cared about and she wasn't all that sad to be rid of the ugly pieces she'd inherited from Jules's mother. "Everybody coos over marcasite these days, but when I was a girl, it was old-lady stuff. Yuck!"

The stereo and color TV were brand new, but insurance would replace them, too. Mostly she'd seemed annoyed because the thief had left such a mess and because the local police didn't seem all that concerned.

She was still blueing the air around us with her views on the boys in blue—a prissy young mother glared at Lunette and made a point of leading her child away—when a loud bell sounded and the carousel rumbled into motion. Soon everyone was grabbing for luggage, and Lunette wasn't the only passenger with several shopping bags of brightly wrapped presents.

"Oh, is this young lady your cousin?" asked a middle-aged black woman when she and Lunette reached for the same shiny red shopping bag. They had been seatmates on the plane. "You're a judge, I believe? Your cousin told me about your loss. Such a shame."

Loss? Loss of what? My virginity? Last year's runoff? My freedom now that I was on the bench? Or had somebody died while I wasn't looking? No time to ask Lunette because she'd trotted off after someone who'd mistaken her garment bag for his.

We finally got it all sorted out, carried everything out to my sports car, and belted ourselves in somehow without smashing anything. As I zipped through the exit lanes and pointed the car toward Raleigh, Lunette switched my radio from a country music station to one that was rapping out carols with new lyrics that gave a whole other meaning to the term "blue Christmas." I compromised by switching it off completely.

"What did that woman mean about my loss?" I asked in the ensuing silence.

"I swear, you're as hard of hearing as Jules used to be. What the hell do you think I've been trying to tell you? Last night when I was packing, I was going to wrap it up and give it to you for Christmas. And that's when I realized that that double-damned SOB had taken it, too."

"The *locket?*" I was aghast. "The Carroll locket?"

Lunette's surgically smooth face almost crumpled again. "Two hundred years it's been in our family and I was the one to lose it," she mourned tearfully. "I *meant* to get the chain mended and send it to you when you won the election, but then—"

She didn't have to finish. I'd actually lost the runoff election and getting appointed was almost anticlimactic. What with one thing and another, I had forgotten that Lunette had promised to give me the Carroll locket if I ever made it to the bench.

The heavy gold octagon-shaped locket was the only family treasure salvaged when our branch left Virginia. It had been passed down in the family from generation to generation, always going to the oldest son's bride until Lunette turned out to be her father's only child. There were two male Carroll cousins in her generation, but she hadn't liked either of their wives and steadfastly ignored all hints that the Carroll locket should go back to someone with the Carroll name.

More than its age and monetary worth, the locket was valued in our family because of the myths that had grown up around it. It had been pawned at least a dozen times, given as surety in exchange for fertilizer money or to meet a mortgage payment, and more than once it had been lost forever. Or so its then-owner thought. But always the locket came back, redeemed by bounteous crops or recovered through miracles.

In 1822, it had fallen into a deep well. Three months later, it was pulled up in a wooden bucket.

In 1862, Anne Carroll tucked it inside her husband's uniform when he went off to Yorktown. "It'll bring you back to me," she whispered. He fell in battle, but a Yankee soldier sent the locket home to her with his condolences, one corner of the hinged lid nicked by the Minié ball that had pierced the young rebel's heart.

In 1918, while a new bride frolicked on the beach with her groom, it had slipped into the sand unnoticed. Two years later, as she helped her firstborn build a sand castle, the tot's bright red tin shovel clinked against something metallic and there was the locket, a bit pitted by the salty sand but otherwise intact.

Lunette herself had lost it last March at a movie theater. Her friends found the broken chain, but the locket had completely disappeared. Yet when she undressed that night, it fell out of her bra. "And I know I shook my clothes out thoroughly," she swore. "The bloody thing's like the monkey's paw. You couldn't throw it away if you tried."

Nevertheless, she'd stowed it in her jewelry box till she could remember to get the chain mended.

Now as we took the bypass around the south side of Raleigh, she seemed disconsolate.

"It'll never come back this time," she predicted gloomily.

"Maybe the police will get lucky," I comforted her.

My words only set her off again. Those lazy SOBs? They didn't even want to come out because her losses were less than five thousand dollars. And when they did come, they didn't bother to try to find fingerprints. "They said whoever took my things had probably already pawned them. I didn't really care till I realized the locket was gone. Hell! They didn't even question the neighbors very well. Mrs. Katzner across the street said she saw somebody loading a stereo in the back of his car, and she even took down the license number and gave it to me."

She rummaged in her silver shoulder bag and pulled out a crumpled slip of paper which she shoved under my nose. "See? A California state license."

I glanced at the digits and then pulled around a pickup with two dogs and a shabby-looking fir tree in the back.

"Did you tell the police detectives?"

"Of course I did. Know what those brother-buckers said?" Her voice dripped sarcastic venom. " 'Ma'am, the plates were probably stolen last week. Nobody rips off a house in broad daylight using his own plates.'"

She was so upset that I asked her to let me have the license number. "I'll get someone to run a check," I told her.

"Why bother? The cops are probably right, damn their eyes. Too bad Maria Vincelli died."

She lost me there. "Who?"

"Maria Vincelli. Her brother was connected. Nobody came near our building while Maria was living there. But she died four years ago and that's when we started getting ripped off."

"Connected? You mean mob connected?"

"Mob, schmob. She never really said, but he used to come once a month to visit her in one of those shiny black cars with the tinted windows so you can't ever tell how many people are inside. Everybody felt so safe."

By the time we reached Dobbs, Lunette had begun to brighten up a little. Then we turned into Aunt Zell's drive and several Carroll women appeared on the veranda to welcome her back. Lunette clasped my hand. "Promise you won't say a word about it till after Christmas," she implored. "Some of those old biddies would peck my eyes out if they knew the locket's gone for good."

Jeeter and Gloria would be sympathetic, but Lib and Mary Frances had such sharp tongues that I promised I'd hold mine. Relieved, Lunette jumped out of my car, held out her arms to the advancing cousins, and cooed, "Oh, you sweet things, I'm just so glad to *see* you!"

Nevertheless, while Aunt Zell pressed coffee and fruitcake on everybody, I slipped upstairs to my private quarters and called a friend in the highway patrol. In almost no time, she called back to say that she'd tracked it down and found it'd been issued to a certain Samuel James Watkins in San Diego. No report that it'd been stolen. She then called a friend of hers in San Diego who ran his name through files out there and discovered a long string of petty larcenies. Was it really going to be that simple?

I pulled out a Rand-McNally and traced the distance between Shady Palms and San Diego. An easy drive.

My finger continued another short distance up the map along the California coast and the name La Jolla jumped out at me. Probably wouldn't do a bit of good. She was probably busy. Or gone for the Christmas holidays.

Nevertheless, I flipped to the O's in my Rolodex and started dialing.

❖ ❖ ❖

When the phone rang, Kiernan O'Shaughnessy was dropping into a back bend. "Damn!" she grumbled, as her hands hit the floor. She walked, crablike on all fours across to the desk and lifted up one arm to reach the receiver. Instead of the "hello" she intended, it came out "Huruhhh"

"Kiernan?"

"Yes?"

"It's Deborah Knott. Did I catch you at a bad time?"

"As a matter of fact, yes," she said, holding the back bend, but now in control of her breath. "Fortunately, I can still do two things at once. And even if I couldn't, I'd choose talking to you. So how're things in the wilds of Colleton County?"

"It's Christmas. Something you probably don't have to bother with out there, but relatives are flocking in here like homing pigeons to Capistrano."

"Swallows," Kiernan corrected.

"Whatever. Listen, I'm calling about my cousin Lunette. She's on my mother's Carroll side. I need to ask a professional favor now that you're a licensed detective. Unless you're too busy?"

Smiling at the way her former housemate's voice still went up at the end of sentences, Kiernan pushed herself erect and pulled down the hem of her T-shirt. "Gee, Deb, I'd love to help, but I'm really busy at the moment. I need to do some more back bends, then catch some sun on my beachfront deck. After that it'll be time to watch bronzed young men amble over the rocks or balance on their body boards out on the waves."

Before Deborah could laugh, she said, "Actually, what I'm doing is waiting for the one thing that will make this duplex on the beach in La Jolla perfect."

"Which is?"

"A servant. I'm running an ad for a housekeeper/cook. Someone like your cousin Lunette, who'll run the house, cook great meals, and love my dog."

Deborah laughed. "If that's your standard, forget Lunette because she's forgot every bit of raising she ever had. She hasn't lifted a mop in half a century, she uses the oven for storage, and if she took your dog out, it'd probably be to sell him."

"Then it's just as well that I've found the perfect woman. At least I think I have. Listen to this: She managed an inn for ten years, planned the menus herself, is so tidy she straightened the kitchen counter while we talked, and best of all, she speaks in monosyllables. I'll hardly know she's here."

Kiernan's voice had not dropped at the end of her sentence. Even so, Deborah asked, "But—?"

"But I'd hoped for someone who could spell me with Ezra when I'm on a case," Kiernan admitted. "Mrs. Pritchard looks to be sixty-some years old. A very matronly sixty-some. I can't see her loping along the beach with an Irish wolfhound. Still, she likes Ezra and that's what counts in the end, isn't it?"

"So you hired her? That's nice. Now, my cousin—"

"I have one more applicant to screen," Kiernan interjected smoothly. "A man. Might be interesting to have a real butler, don't you think? Remember those old Mr. Belvedere movies they used to run on Channel 5? Who was that actor? Robert Young? David Niven?"

"I really don't remember."

"Not David Niven . . . Clifton Webb! But unless this guy's actually a gentleman's gentleman, Mrs. Pritchard will get the job."

"I'm sure she'll do just fine."

Deborah hadn't interrupted, or *said* anything to indicate impatience, but that impatience was clear to Kiernan. While finishing up some postgrad work in Chapel Hill, the two women had shared an apartment off-campus. It had taken almost half the summer for Kiernan, a Northerner from a family that made silence a life form, to discern the slight hesitation before responses, and to realize that when Deborah flattened her tones like this, she might as well be screaming, "Dammit! Stop interrupting and let me get to my point!"

Once Kiernan understood, she had taken devilish pleasure in lengthening her descriptions, slipping into circuitous conversational byways and sluggish swamps of supposition as long and drab as the Great Dismal, all the time waiting to see how long good southern manners would last. By September, Deborah's record stood at thirty-eight minutes. Kiernan went back to California without ever revealing the game, but she did wonder what Deborah made of her and those rambling half hours.

"So, Deborah," she said with a grin, "what's this favor?"

Kiernan was still listening to her friend's tale of Cousin Lunette and the Carroll locket when the doorbell rang. "Can you hang on a minute, Deb? I'll just glance over this last applicant's résumé and unless he's better than Niven or Webb, he'll be on his way before he gets as far as the sofa."

She put the phone on the table and opened the door.

"Brad Tchernak," the applicant said, extending a hand the size of Rhode Island. The man didn't fill the entire doorway, but he didn't leave room for anyone else to squeeze through. "Everyone calls me Tchernak."

"You're a chef?" she asked amazed. "I would have taken you for a linebacker."

"Line*man. Former* offensive lineman with the Chargers."

"A lineman rather than a cook," she said, not moving from the door.

"Not a professional cook, but a great one, and a great housekeeper."

Maybe, Kiernan thought. He might not match Mrs. Pritchard's professional qualifications, but this guy was definitely a hunk. A tall, athletic, wiry-haired, bearded honest-to-God hunk. If she were merely decorating the duplex, she'd grab him. But she didn't need a live-in hunk; she needed a housekeeper, a nice middle-aged lady with the legs of a miler.

"Don't jump to conclusions," Tchernak said. "And don't say no before you let me whip up a dinner that will answer all your questions. Where's your kitchen? Through there?"

"No. I've already—"

Toenails scratched on stairs, a furry rump hit the wall, and a moment later the Irish wolfhound clambered down the last step. Momentarily he stood nearly shoulder to shoulder with Kiernan, assessing the intruder. At this point in introductions, the other applicants had edged out the door.

Tchernak didn't move.

Ezra's mouth opened slightly. Tchernak stepped forward, a grin twitching his wiry brown beard. Ezra leaped, paws landing on Tchernak's shoulders, tongue lathering both of Tchernak's cheeks. Tchernak scratched the huge dog's stomach. "Am I hired?"

"Not so fast," she said, the haloed picture of Mrs. Pritchard in her mind. "But go ahead and check out the kitchen."

"Kiernan!" The voice shouting from the receiver came in loud and clear and there wasn't a drop of graciousness, southern or otherwise, in it.

She picked up the phone. "Sorry, Deb. This interview's a bit more complicated than I expected."

"So I gather."

Ignoring Deborah's sarcastic tone, she said, "You were just about to ask me for a favor?"

"Damn straight. You've got a slimeball out there in California and
he's got the Carroll locket. *My* locket. The one Cousin Lunette was
going to give me when I won the election. You reckon you could find
out where he pawned it and buy it back? I've got his name, address, and
phone number."

Kiernan couldn't gracefully refuse. Not after leaving Deborah on the
phone till she was actually screaming. Anyhow, how hard could it be to
find a small-time thief who steals from little old ladies?

"If the locket hasn't been melted down, I'll find it," she promised.

She put down the phone and stood in the doorway that separated her
flat from the large kitchen and small studio that would soon be Mrs.
Pritchard's. With Ezra in there and with Tchernak opening and closing
cabinets—apparently searching for some cooking paraphernalia she didn't
have—the kitchen seemed smaller than a child's playhouse, and she began
to comprehend fully just how big Tchernak was. Together, both craggy
faces surrounded by shaggy gray brown hair, he and Ezra looked not
unlike a pair of oversized werewolves whipping up a snack.

But this was no time to be pondering the physical attributes of a man
who would be out of her life in an hour. The man she needed to assess
was Samuel James Watkins, and she needed to get on him now if
Deborah's cousin Lunette was going to have a happy Christmas.

Kiernan wasn't crazy about leaving a stranger in her house, but she
told herself that while burglars may answer ads, they don't usually offer
to make dinner. And there was something she trusted about Tchernak.
Maybe it was just because he resembled the world's best dog. Or maybe
she was just after a free meal. Still, she asked, "How long will you be
cooking, Tchernak?"

"An hour if I hurry. Why?"

"I have to run an errand. It might keep me two hours. I don't want
to hold you up."

Tchernak smiled. "That's okay. I'll just take him for a run on the
beach before I start dinner."

Mrs. Pritchard, she thought. *Quiet, competent Mrs. Pritchard. If I pass
up a gem like her . . .*

✣ ✣ ✣

Kiernan called the number for Samuel James Watkins twice on her
way to his house and got only a noncommittal answering machine: "*This
is 555-8782. Leave a message.*"

A careful man who didn't want associates to know how long he'd been gone or when he'd be back?

A careful man in a distinctly downscale San Diego neighborhood, she decided as she drove past the auto repair shop at Watkins's address. His house would be in the back.

Darkness comes early in December and covers a lot of illicit activity. Nevertheless, Kiernan parked a block away and kept to the shadows. She knew that housebreaking was not the way to begin a career as a licensed private investigator, but she'd just slip in this once and she'd be careful.

And she'd never do it again.

Absolutely never.

Kiernan made her way along the tall threadbare hedge beside the auto repair shop and pushed through it into the backyard—a few square feet of hard-packed dirt with one dead jade plant in the far corner. Watkins's "house" at the rear of the lot was two stories tall and maybe twelve feet square, probably two rooms one atop the other. All the windows were closed, Kiernan moved into the shadows, weighing her options. Even with tools, this assemblage of locks could consume more time than was reasonable for the entire search. She couldn't afford to be caught, and certainly not before she even got inside. But the little house was hers now, asking to be entered. She was damned if she'd give up.

She circled around back, checking each window, finding each locked. Watkins was indeed a very careful man.

But even careful men can make mistakes and his was a second-floor bathroom window, opened eight inches from the top. Logic would have told him no one could get to the window without dragging a two-story ladder back past the auto repair shop. And once at the window, no one could enter without breaking the glass.

But he hadn't counted on a woman barely five feet tall, not quite a hundred pounds, who had spent her entire adolescence practicing gymnastics. For Kiernan, climbing a tree to the roof, lowering herself over the edge and into the window was nothing like the challenge of the uneven bars or the balance beam. Or even dropping back into a back bend.

On this roof, she thought as she positioned herself above the window, the main danger was loose shingles, or a rain gutter too fragile to support her. But she would have to trust it. Grasping the gutter with both hands, she lowered her feet over the edge of the roof and slid them down the side of the house till she felt the space left by the open window.

She shifted to ease her legs inside. The rain gutter creaked. She caught her feet inside the window and pulled. The rain gutter snapped free of the roof. She fell back, hanging in air. Frantically she pressed with her legs, locking the muscles of her legs, her butt, her back, to keep from slamming down into the glass. She shifted her hands to the window, took a thankful breath, and slid down inside, her flashlight banging against the sill.

Best if I don't fall, she thought. *Watkins isn't likely to have insurance.*

The bathroom was so small the sink was over the toilet tank. No place to hide contraband here. In the bedroom there was barely room for the bed and the stairs. A couple of blankets were on the bare mattress, but no sign of clothing. Two stereos were piled in the corner along with three electric typewriters and a dusty computer monitor. They looked like rejects from a tag sale.

Feeling her way in the dark, she walked down the steps. The stairs creaked; the leaves of the tree scraped the windows. Headlights shone in the path from the auto repair shop. Watkins could come back anytime. With any number of nasty associates.

She froze, listening. For the first time it occurred to her she couldn't go back out the bathroom window and up onto the roof, not with no rain gutter to grab onto. If all the windows were not just locked, but dead bolted . . .

The headlights disappeared.

She eased down the remaining steps and flashed her light quickly around the tiny room, at a stove, fridge, water heater, sink, tiled counter, a door on wooden sawhorses that passed for a desk with a worn leather swivel chair next to it, and a phone and answering machine atop it. She pressed the play button and cryptic voices whispered in the darkness: *"Mickey says yeah." "Eddie says he's got more, so call him." "That shipment from Fresno's due in on time."*

Beneath the desk, something glittered in the flashlight's narrow beam. It was a jet-and-crystal earring and Kiernan eased open a nearby carton. It held several brand-new blenders, but no records or files. And definitely no TVs, stereos, marcasite jewelry, or octagonal gold lockets.

Reluctantly, Kiernan faced the facts. This was just his accommodation address, a transfer point. His cache could be in the auto repair shop out front. Or in self-storage anywhere in San Diego County. Or Riverside, Orange, or Imperial counties. With someone this organized,

Deborah's cousin's things could be scattered around the whole Southwest. The odds of getting anything back were astronomical.

A wasted trip.

And she could probably waste more time watching this place, trailing Samuel James Watkins to his real home, trying to track down all his fences, and still not come up with the locket.

She walked up the stairs, slid out through the window, and dropped to the ground—a long dismount, but not one of Olympic quality. It went with her mood. How embarrassing it was going to be to have to tell Deborah that she'd failed.

✤ ✤ ✤

"Look, don't worry about it," I told Kiernan when she called a couple of hours later and described how she'd spent the time since I phoned her. I was horrified to think she'd actually broken and entered, yet quite touched that she would take such a risk for me.

"Too bad we can't sic Maria Vincelli's brother on him," I said lightly.

"Who?"

I repeated Cousin Lunette's speculations about her former neighbor's mob connections and heard Kiernan laugh across the miles.

"Maybe it's not too late," she said and hung up without another word.

✤ ✤ ✤

Tchernak was pulling popovers from the oven when Kiernan got off the phone.

"And from the broiler," he said with a flourish, "shish kebabs of fresh-from-the-dock Ahi tuna, marinated green tomatoes, shiitake mushrooms, and Walla Walla onions—frozen because they're only available one month a year, but lovingly thawed. Ideally the tomatoes should be flown in fresh from Jersey, but—" He shrugged.

With his paw, Ezra tapped Tchernak's leg.

"He wants his offering," Kiernan explained.

Tchernak waited a moment, then turned, pulled an all-tuna kebab from the broiler and put it on the counter to cool.

Ezra let out a gleeful yip. She hadn't heard one of those since he was a puppy.

That did it, Kiernan thought. *Mrs. Pritchard is going to have to find other employment.*

She was halfway through the gooseberry/kiwi sorbet before she could divert her attention from the food and ask, "Tchernak, I have another brief and totally different job that I could use your help on. Tonight."

Tchernak's face seemed to freeze. He was waiting.

"Whether or not you do it will have no effect on my decision about hiring you. Really."

He nodded noncommittally.

"And it's only fair to warn you that it's slightly illegal."

Tchernak grinned. "What do I do?"

They worked out the script over espresso. Twenty-five minutes later, Tchernak was growling into Samuel James Watkins's answering machine with a very credible Chicago accent. "Listen up, scuzzbag, 'cause this is the voice of Christmas present—"

"You did what?" I asked sleepily when Kiernan's second call of the evening woke me around two a.m. Eastern Standard Time.

Incoherent with laughter (and maybe five or six glasses of California chardonnay), Kiernan O'Shaughnessy described how her new butler? houseboy? dog walker?—Californians certainly do give themselves interesting Christmas presents—had recorded a message for Watkins. As I understood it, this Tchernak person pretended to be a Mafia hit man who resented the hell out of Watkins ripping off his old Aunt Lunette in Shady Palms.

"I'm sorry I can't take a month off and track down his whole operation," Kiernan apologized, "but if it's any consolation, we've probably put the fear of the Celestial in him. With a little luck, he'll be jumping at every shadow and wondering how much longer his kneecaps will be intact."

I had to laugh. It wasn't the Carroll locket, but it certainly was a unique Christmas present.

"Have a merry," I told her.

"I plan to." She laughed and I heard Ezra barking happily in the background.

Court reconvened on the third of January, so I couldn't drive Lunette to the airport. Just as well since it was a long, exhausting session as I handed out fines and suspended sentences to those who'd celebrated the holidays not wisely, but too well. It was nearly eleven and I was ready to fall into bed when my telephone rang.

Across three thousand miles, I heard Lunette's excited voice. "It's the weirdest freaking thing you ever saw!" she cried. "I unlocked my front door and everything was piled in the middle of the living room floor—stereo, TV, my silverware, all that blinking marcasite, Jules's ring—and oh, Deborah! The locket! It's back. I'm going to send it to Dennis's son first thing tomorrow. Did I tell you? He's getting married Valentine's Day."

"Wait a minute," I protested. "You promised it to me."

"Oh, honey, I'd love to give it to you, but don't you see? The only reason it's come back is so it can go to a Carroll bride. How 'bout I send you a diamond necklace instead?"

"Diamond necklace? I didn't know you had one."

"I didn't." She giggled. "But now I have two. And a sapphire ring. And a string of pearls. Whoever brought my things back, he left a lot of extra stuff. A ruby brooch. Some silver bracelets. A—"

As my cousin rattled on like a four-year-old detailing every item in her Christmas stocking, I sighed, reached for my Rolodex, and flipped to the O's.

Partners in Crime, 1994

With this Ring

The whole subject of bridesmaid's dresses amuses me immensely. No one dress could be equally flattering to any bride's six best friends, so someone's nose is always out of joint. And as for their usefulness as a party/cocktail dress? In my lifetime, I have only seen two that might actually be worn after the wedding.

"Detective Bryant," said Dwight's voice when he finally picked up his extension at the Colleton County Sheriff's Department.

"Can you still button the pants of your army dress uniform?" I asked.

"Say what?"

I was out at your mother's last week." I let a hint of mischief slip into my tone. "She said that picture of you at the White House was taken only three years ago, but I reckon you've put on a few pounds since you came home and started eating regular."

As if a district court judge has nothing better to do with her time than call just to needle him about his thickening waistline, Dwight bit like a largemouth bass suckered by some plastic feathers and shiny paint.

"Listen," he said. "I bet I can fit into my old clothes a lot better'n you could fit into yours."

I reeled him in. "It's a bet. Loser pays for the tickets."

"Wait a minute. You want to back that mule up and walk her past me again?"

"The Widdington Jaycees are putting on a charity ball for Valentine's Day," I explained. "I know you don't own a tuxedo, but—"

"You and that Chapin guy have a fight?" Dwight growled. "Or don't he know how to dance in a monkey suit?"

For the life of me, I can't understand Dwight's attitude. It's not like Kidd's the first man he's ever seen me with, and it's certainly not like he's interested in me himself. Our families have known each other five or six generations, and Dwight's always treated me like he's one of my older brothers. One of my *bossy* older brothers. Unfortunately, small-town social life resembles the Ark—everything two by two. So when I need an escort and don't have one on tap, I just call Dwight, who's divorced and still unattached. By choice, he says.

Yet ever since I met Kidd Chapin down at the coast last spring, Dwight's done nothing but snipe at him. Dwight's a chief of detectives; Kidd's a game warden. Both like to hunt and fish and stomp around in the woods. Wouldn't you think they'd mesh together tight as Velcro?

Oil and vinegar.

I've decided it's a guy thing and nothing worth bothering *my* pretty little head with.

"Kidd has to be at a conference down in Atlanta that weekend. Look, if you don't want to come dancing and help me act the fool, fine. I'll call Davis, see if he's free that night."

Davis Reed's a good-timing, currently unmarried state representative from down east, and Dwight hates his politics. (Hey, I'd never actually sleep with a Republican, but that doesn't mean I won't let one buy me dinner.)

"Act the fool how?" Dwight asked cautiously, and I knew I had him flopping in my net.

"It's a bridesmaids ball," I said. "Everybody's supposed to wear something we've worn in a wedding."

"What's so foolish about that?"

"Dwight Bryant, have you ever *looked* at one of those dresses?" I was torn between amusement and exasperation.

Men.

But that's not fair. Why should I bad-mouth men when it's women that keep putting four to eight of their best friends into some of the most ridiculous dresses known to polite society?

Was it a man who thought it'd look really darling to send us down the aisle one Christmas wearing red plaid over enormous hoop skirts and carrying tall white candles?

Lighted white candles that dripped wax all down the front of our skirts?

No, that was Missy Randolph.

Was it a man who put us in skin-tight sheaths of bright pink satin so that the bride looked like a silver spoon pink surrounded by six Pepto-Bismol bottles?

No, that was Portland Smith.

"What about this one?" said Aunt Zell as we prowled the far end of her unheated attic, where several long gowns hung like ghosts from the rafter nails, each Cinderella fantasy shrouded in a white cotton sheet.

"You girls were just precious in these picture hats."

"The hats were okay," I conceded, shivering in the February chill, "though that shade of lavender made me took downright jaundiced. It was the scratchy lace mitts. My wrists itched for a week. And Katy's parasol kept poking all the ushers in the eye."

"Such a pretty garden wedding," Aunt Zell sighed as she pulled the sheet back over that gown. "Too bad they split up before the first frost. Now where's the dress you wore when Seth and Minnie married? You were cute as a june bug in it."

"That was a flower-girl dress," I reminded her. "And have you ever seen a flower girl who *wasn't* cute as a june bug?"

Here in Colleton County, if a groom has a sister, she *will* be in the wedding even if she and the bride despise each other. For the record, I never exactly despised any of my brothers' brides (some of the boys got married before I was even born), but scattering rose petals can get awfully tiresome after you've done it four or five times.

The attic was too chilly for lingering, and I quickly narrowed my choices down to two.

The ball committee promised us prizes in various categories. If total tackiness were a category, surely the dress I'd worn in Caroline Corbett's wedding would be an automatic winner: moss green lace over a moss polyester sateen that had already started mutating toward chartreuse before the first chord of Mendelssohn was ever played. The neckline dipped so low in front that only a cluster of green chiffon roses preserved our maiden modesty. Droopy shoulder flounces were tied up with dangling sateen ribbons that had tickled my arms just enough to keep me slapping for a fly or a mosquito. Accessories included a floppy picture hat big as a cartwheel and a wicker basket filled with more chiffon roses. What finally decided me against wearing it to the ball were the tiered net petticoats that shredded panty-hose and legs indiscriminately.

Besides, the frosty air made bare-armed summer frocks look even more inane than usual. I was drawn instead to a wintry blue velvet concoction.

Janelle Mayhew's idea of Victorian began with a high, tight white lace collar, descended to pouf sleeves that had to be stuffed with tissue paper to hold their balloon shape, and was topped (or should I say *bottomed?*)

by an enormous bustle. The white plumed fan had barely begun to molt and it ought to amuse Dwight. Besides, the dark blue velvet, bustle and all, actually flattered my sandy blond hair and turned my blue eyes sapphire. As a thirty-something judge, maybe it'd be more dignified to go for pretty instead of comic.

More politic, too, because Janelle and Glenn Riggsbee were Widdington Jaycees and certain to be at the ball. Their restaurant has prospered over the years, and they contributed to my last campaign by hosting a big reception for me out there in the country.

The old-fashioned dress had been a little on the loose side twelve years ago; now it needed a whalebone corset with power lacing. Even with a girdle, I was going to have to sit up straight all evening and remember to laugh no harder than Queen Victoria.

❖ ❖ ❖

When Dwight came to pick me up that Saturday night, he was wearing a borrowed black tuxedo and the fuchsia sateen cummerbund and clip-on bow tie that had been dyed to match the bridesmaids's dresses when he ushered for a friend in D.C.

"Aw, and I was really looking forward to your sword," I teased.

"Mama could've let out the pants," Dwight said sheepishly, "but she said she'd rather pay for the damn tickets herself than try to get that dress jacket to fit."

Before he'd write me a check for the cost of the tickets, he rousted Aunt Zell from upstairs where she and Uncle Ash were watching the news and made her swear she hadn't added a gusset of blue velvet in my side seams.

"No gloating, okay?"

"I *never* gloat," I told him, tucking the check away in my beaded evening bag.

He and Aunt Zell both snorted.

❖ ❖ ❖

Widdington's about thirty-five minutes east of Dobbs, and we drove over with Avery and Portland Brewer. Portland is Uncle Ash's sister's daughter and therefore Aunt Zell's niece by marriage, which makes us courtesy cousins. Not that a family connection is needed. We laugh at the same things and have been friends since junior girls class in Sunday school.

When Dwight opened the rear door of their car, she twisted around in the front seat and said, "Oh, shoot! I told Avery I *knew* you were going to wear that pig-pink thing Mother made y'all buy for our wedding."

She had a winter coat draped over the droop-shouldered horror of Caroline Corbett's green lace. In Portland's case, the polyester underlining had gone past chartreuse, right on into an acid yellow. "I'm competing in the 'Most Unusual Color Combination' category," she giggled.

"Where's your hat and garden basket?"

"In the trunk," said Avery. "The brim's so wide she couldn't fit in the car."

Before the interior light went off, Portland noticed my pearl earrings. "I thought we wore red-and-blue rhinestone hoops with that dress?"

"We did. That's why Elizabeth thought you stole the ring, remember? When she caught a flash of sparkling stones in your hand?"

"She just said that to throw suspicion off herself," said Portland. "I still think she's the one who took it."

"They never did get it back, did they?" asked Avery as he waited for a pickup to pass before pulling away from the curb.

"Huh?" said Dwight.

"Oh, that's right," I remembered. "You were probably stationed in Panama or someplace when Janelle Mayhew married Glenn Riggsbee. This is the dress Portland and I and their three sisters wore in their wedding."

"All five of you?" he asked dryly. "No wonder you can still squeeze into it."

I fluttered my ostrich-plume fan under his chin. "Why, Rhett, honey, you just say the sweetest *thangs*? Don't y'all pay him no nevermind," I told Portland and Avery. "He's still pouting 'cause he couldn't get into his little ol' dress uniform."

"You said you never gloat," Dwight reminded me. "What ring?"

Avery sailed through the last stoplight in Dobbs and headed east along a backcountry road. As we drove through the cold winter night, stars blazing overhead, we took turns telling Dwight about Janelle's godawful engagement ring and how it disappeared in the middle of her wedding to Glenn Riggsbee.

"It all began with Elizabeth and Nancy—Glenn's two sisters," said Portland. "Both of them wanted the ring he gave Janelle."

Dwight might not've gone to college, but he knows about Freudian complexes. "Isn't that a little unnatural?"

"We're talking greed, not Greek," I told him, "and strictly speaking, it really began with Glenn's great-uncle."

Glenn Riggsbee was named for his mother's favorite uncle, a larger-than-life character who ran away from home at fifteen and went wild-catting in Texas back in the twenties. Unlike most kids who go off to seek their fortunes and slink home a few years later hoping nobody'll notice their tails dragging in the mud, Great-Uncle Glenn hit a gusher before he was eighteen, married a flashy dance-hall blonde before he was twenty, and lived high, wide, and handsome for the next fifty years.

He and his wife never had children, so when she died and the big money ran out, he came back to Colleton County, bought a little house next door to his niece, and settled down to bossing Glenn and his sisters around like they were his own grandchildren. Portland and I never even heard of him till our good friend Janelle Mayhew started dating Glenn, but we heard plenty after that because Janelle was terrified of him.

With good reason.

True, he'd been a Daddy Warbucks to Mrs. Riggsbee and her children when he had lots of money, lavishing her with expensive treats and setting up trust funds so Glenn and his two sisters could go to college in style. And yes, he continued to be generous with the dregs of his fortune, helping Glenn buy a first car, for instance, or doling out to the girls some of his late wife's gold and silver baubles.

But in old age, he was just as opinionated and short-tempered as he'd been in his youth. Any help he gave was on his terms and any gifts he gave came with stretchy elastic attached. For such a renegade, he had a surprisingly wide streak of conservatism.

He had expected both of Glenn's sisters to become schoolteachers and to stop work once they had babies. When Elizabeth majored in accounting and had a chance to buy into a new insurance brokerage firm soon after graduation, he refused to help. Said it wasn't fitting for an unmarried woman to be in a position to boss around married men.

The same thing happened when Nancy wanted to become a minister. A woman preacher? The very concept shocked him to the core. "Be damned if I'll bankroll such blasphemy!" Somehow he found a legal loophole that let him tie up Nancy's college trust fund until she tearfully promised not to take any theology courses.

As a male, Glenn was, theoretically, free to major in whatever he wanted, but you can imagine Great-Uncle Glenn's reaction when he finally realized that Glenn planned to use his shiny new degree in restaurant management to turn an old dilapidated farmhouse into a restaurant.

"A restaurant out in the middle of the country? Stupidest damn thing I ever heard of," he snorted. "Don't expect me to help finance it."

In vain did Glenn point out that I-40 was going to dot the county with housing developments full of wage-earning commuters happy to pay someone else to fix supper.

Nor did it open Great-Uncle Glenn's wallet when he heard that Janelle was taking cooking courses at the local community college. Indeed, he took to wondering audibly if she was good enough for young Glenn. After all, what kind of trashy mama did Janelle have that wouldn't teach her own daughter how to fry chicken and make buttermilk biscuits?

While it's true that the Mayhews were even poorer than the Riggsbees, they were by no means trash, and Janelle was always a hard worker. She also has lovely manners and yes-sirred and no-sirred Great-Uncle Glenn till, when Glenn said he was going to ask her to set a date, the old man went to his lockbox at Dobbs First National and gave Glenn the platinum-and-diamond ring he'd bought to woo his dance-hall wife.

We'd never seen anything quite like it: a huge rose-cut yellow diamond surrounded by forty tapered baguette diamonds, sapphires, and rubies in a ballerina mount.

"What's a ballerina mount?" asked Dwight.

"Picture a big yellow golf ball surrounded by a red-white-and-blue-ruffle," I said.

"Sounds sort of ugly to me," he ventured.

"It was beyond ugly," Portland assured him.

"But the diamond was what they call a flawless fancy yellow and was supposed to have been insured for eighty thousand dollars," I recalled.

"Supposed to be?"

"That's why I'm sure Elizabeth took it," said Portland. "Where else did she get the money to buy a partnership?"

"Circumstantial evidence," Avery murmured. Like Portland, he's an attorney, too.

"Not entirely," she argued. "See, Dwight, Elizabeth hadn't bought in with Bob McAdams yet, but she'd been working there a couple of years and she was supposed to have written up a policy for the ring once it went from Great-Uncle Glenn's lockbox to Janelle's finger—"

"But Elizabeth assumed the Mayhews had household insurance," I said. "And since Janelle was still living at home to save money for the restaurant, Elizabeth thought that would protect it up to the wedding."

"That's what she *claimed*," said Portland, "but even if the Mayhews did have insurance, no piddly little renters' policy would ever cover an eighty-thousand-dollar ring. Uh-uh, Deb'rah. She knew there'd be hard-nosed investigators swarming all over the place if Janelle filed a claim for eighty thousand. No policy, no claim. No claim, no serious investigation."

"No policy?" asked Dwight from the darkness beside me.

"Elizabeth dated it to take effect at twelve noon, which was when the ceremony took place and when Janelle's residence would officially change from her parents' house. The last time anybody saw the ring was at eleven-thirty when Janelle stuck it in her makeup bag in the choir robing room next to the vestibule."

I took up the tale. "And before you ask, no, nobody was seen going into that room between the time we finished dressing until after the ceremony. Miss Louisa Ferncliff directed the wedding and she was right there in the vestibule the whole time, making sure the ushers knew whether the guests were bride's side or groom's and then sending us down the aisle spaced just right. If anybody'd gone back in, she'd have seen them."

"Who was last out of the robing room?"

"Janelle and me," Portland answered. "Her sister Faye was maid of honor and I was matron of honor. Deb'rah went first, then Nancy, Elizabeth, Faye, and me. The room was empty after Janelle and I went out to the vestibule and I pulled the door shut."

"So who was first back in?"

I shrugged. "All of us. There was a receiving line with the parents right after the recessional, then we all went to put on fresh lipstick for the formal pictures and that's when Janelle discovered the ring was gone."

"And the only ones in the robing room the whole time were you six?"

"Are you kidding?" said Portland. "Both mothers were in and out, as well as Miss Louisa, the photographer, the minister's wife—"

"Don't forget Omaleen Grimes," I said. "She was dating one of Glenn's ushers, and she acted like that gave her a right to stick her nose in everywhere."

With This Ring

219

"But between the time Janelle took off the ring and the time she realized it was gone?"

Portland and I had to admit it. During the crucial time, there were just us five bridesmaids, Mrs. Mayhew, Mrs. Riggsbee, and Janelle herself.

Everybody had been sweet as molasses pie, but Portland and I and seventeen-year-old Faye Mayhew had hovered protectively around Janelle because Elizabeth and Nancy still had their noses out of joint. Glenn Riggsbee was damn lucky to find someone as fine as Janelle, but in their minds—particularly Elizabeth's—their brother was marrying down. The Mayhews were too poor to own their own home, Janelle hadn't gone to college, and on top of that, she had somehow dazzled Great-Uncle Glenn into parting with the last substantial piece of jewelry in his possession.

Both sisters had been allowed to wear the ring on special occasions in the past, and each had hoped that Great-Uncle Glenn would leave it to her someday: Elizabeth because she was the oldest, Nancy because she was the baby of the family and had already been given his wife's garnet necklace. No matter how nice Janelle was to them, it was all they could do to maintain a polite façade, though a stranger wouldn't have known it for all the "sugars" and "honeys" being thrown around the choir robing room that morning.

A moment or two before eleven-thirty, Mrs. Mayhew had set the veil on Janelle's hair. When Janelle lifted her hands to adjust it, the gaudy ring flashed in the pale January sunlight.

"Don't forget to take that ring off before you start down the aisle," said Mrs. Mayhew. "Your finger needs to be bare when Glenn puts on your wedding band."

As if in chorus, Elizabeth and Nancy both offered to hold it for her.

"That's okay," said Janelle.

She slipped the yellow diamond into the same worn gray velvet box Great-Uncle Glenn had given his wife sixty years earlier. It was so old, the domed lid no longer closed with a tight snap, but she tucked the box into her makeup bag. Her eyes met ours nervously in the mirror. "Glenn's ring! Por?"

Portland waggled her thumb and there was the wide gold wedding band that Janelle would slip onto Glenn's finger in less than an hour.

At that instant, Miss Louisa stuck her head in and hissed, "Sst! Mothers! Places!"

The clock above the mirrors said 11:31.

We'd been primping and preening since ten o'clock, so you'd think we could have sat with our hands folded quietly and discussed the weather or something, wouldn't you? Instead we all dived back into our own makeup bags, touching up mascara and lipstick, adjusting our bustles, adjusting Janelle's veil, reminding each other how to hold the white plumed fans at identical angles, then a final spritz of hairspray before Miss Louisa herded us all out into the vestibule.

Afterwards, none of us could say who had or hadn't touched which makeup bag.

But that was later, when Sheriff Poole questioned us.

At the beginning, Janelle was sure the ring must have somehow worked its way out of the loose-lidded velvet box and slipped down among her cosmetics. Then, that it must have fallen out while we all made last-minute touch-ups. Surely on the floor, beneath the dressing table, under a chair . . . ?

Nothing.

"Somebody's taken it!" Portland said dramatically.

"Don't be silly," said Janelle, anxiously uncapping all her lipsticks, as if that ring could possibly fit inside a slender tube. Her sister Faye was down on her hands and knees searching beneath the choir robes. "We were the only ones here and . . ."

Her voice trailed away as she saw Portland and me staring at her new sisters-in-law.

Elizabeth and Nancy both turned beet red.

"If you think for one minute—!" Elizabeth huffed indignantly. "You can search me if you like."

"Me, too!" said Nancy.

"Don't be silly," Janelle said again.

"Girls, girls!" Miss Louisa stood in the doorway. "The photographer is waiting."

"Miss Louisa," I said. "Did anybody come in here during the ceremony?"

"No, of course not, dear. Why do you ask?"

Janelle broke in. "Miss Louisa, could you please tell the photographer we'll be right there?"

As Miss Louisa tottered away on her little high heels, Janelle twisted her brand new wedding band nervously and said, "Look, if one of you took it as a joke . . ."

Instant denial was on all our lips.

"It's okay if it's a joke," she continued doggedly. "Let's go out like nothing's happened, and if whoever took it will just drop it on the floor, that will be the end of it, okay?" Her voice trembled. "Just don't tell Glenn or our folks, okay? It'd spoil our wedding day. Please?"

Subdued, we promised to keep quiet.

Without looking around, Janelle swept out to the sanctuary and we trailed along after. During the next half hour, as the photographer grouped and regrouped various components of the wedding party, Janelle managed to send each bridesmaid back to the robing room alone. Would Elizabeth fetch her lipstick? Would Nancy be a dear and find a comb? A tissue, Faye? Oh goodness, Por, she'd forgotten her blue garter!

Before she could invent a task for me, the photographer decided to take a shot of the newlyweds' hands, and Great-Uncle Glenn said, "Take me one with her engagement ring, too."

"I'll go get it," I said brightly, absolutely positive that I'd find the stupid thing back on the robing room dressing table.

Wrong.

Nor had it been dropped on the floor as Janelle suggested. I searched every square inch.

After that, a bit of discreet hell broke loose. Mrs. Riggsbee managed to keep Great-Uncle Glenn reined in till after the reception was over. Fortunately, it was only punch and wedding cake in the church's fellowship hall and as soon as the cake was cut, Janelle and Glenn pretended to leave in a shower of rice. Actually, all they did was drive over to their new apartment, change clothes and sneak back into the church robing room where Sheriff Bo Poole was questioning the rest of us.

"I'm surprised I never heard anything about this," Dwight said as we entered the outskirts of Widdington.

"They pretty much hushed it up when it was clear nobody was going to confess," said Portland. "Janelle insisted that someone had to've sneaked into the robing room while Miss Louisa was watching the ceremony because there was no way that a sister or friend could have done her that shabby."

I smoothed the plumes on my fan. "Great-Uncle Glenn was furious, of course."

"But Janelle faced him down," Portland said. "She told him it was her ring and she was the one who'd been careless with it and it was her loss, not his."

"Remember his face when Elizabeth admitted that there was no insurance? I thought he was going to hit her with his walking stick."

"So what happened next?" asked Dwight.

"I think Sheriff Poole put a description on the wire, but I never heard that anything came of it," said Portland. "Great-Uncle Glenn died a few months later, and when Janelle and Glenn got back from the funeral, they found the ring in their mailbox. All the little diamonds and sapphires and rubies were still there, but the big yellow diamond was gone."

"No one ever confessed?" asked Dwight.

"Not that we ever heard," we told him.

What we left unsaid was the suspicion that maybe Janelle thought Portland or I had taken the ring because after that, we were never quite as close again.

"I don't *care* what happened to it!" she stormed when Portland pressed her about the theft a few months later. "If one of y'all needed the money that bad, then that was a better use for that darned old ring than on my finger."

Portland had called me the minute she got back to Dobbs. "She thinks you or I took it."

"She probably heard about our new mink coats and all our trips to Bermuda," I said dryly.

So we dropped it after that. Janelle was still friendly with us when we saw her, but as time passed, those occasions were less frequent. She and Glenn threw themselves into the restaurant, which took off like a rocket from opening day, and Portland and I were both caught up in our own careers back in Dobbs. Anyhow, loyalties always realign when you marry outside your own crowd. Janelle had made her bed among Riggsbees and from that day forward, it was as if Elizabeth and Nancy had never acted ugly to her. Or stolen from her and Glenn.

"Well, one good thing came out of it," Portland said, paralleling my thoughts. "Elizabeth was so grateful to Janelle for understanding about the insurance mixup that they became real friends from then on."

❖ ❖ ❖

The Widdington Jaycees were holding their ball at the new Shrine club and as Avery drove into the parking lot, laughing couples streamed toward the entrance.

Heaven knows there was plenty to laugh at. I haven't seen that much organdy, chiffon, and taffeta froufrou since I helped judge a Little Miss Makely beauty contest last year.

Inside, the club was decorated in valentines of every size and jammed to the walls, but friends had saved space at a table for us. While Dwight and Avery went off to fight their way to the bar, lights played across the dance floor and I saw a lot of familiar faces.

And one familiar dress.

Nancy Riggsbee was much heavier now. The seams on her blue velvet had clearly been let out and her bustle rode on hips even more ample than mine, but she beamed with seeming pleasure when she spotted me and came right over.

"Deborah Knott! How you been, lady?"

We kissed air, and half screaming to be heard above the music and talk, I said, "Where's your fan? And don't tell me Elizabeth's here in this same dress, too? And Faye?"

"No, Faye's living in Boston now and Elizabeth's little girl came home from school sick with the flu yesterday, so I'm here on her ticket. In her dress. Mine was cut up for a church pageant years ago. Mary and one of the Magi, I think. The fans went for angel wings."

So Elizabeth had porked up a bit, too, since I last saw her? Mean of me to be smug about it. To atone, I told Nancy I'd heard about her getting a church out in the country from Durham and how was she liking it after so long in Virginia?

It was too loud for small talk though, and after a few more shouted pleasantries, Dwight and Avery came back with our drinks. I introduced Dwight to Nancy, who said she was going to go find Janelle and tell her we were there.

Fortunately someone got the band to turn down their speakers about then and conversation became possible again.

"So she got to be a preacher after all?" Dwight asked.

I nodded. "After Great-Uncle Glenn died, the others encouraged her to go to divinity school. It was a struggle because he didn't leave much, but Janelle and Glenn pitched in. Elizabeth, too, even though she was scraping every penny to buy into the firm about then."

"Notice Nancy's ring if she comes back," Portland told him. "After the ring came home without the yellow diamond, Glenn had the diamond baguettes set into a sort of engagement ring. They gave Elizabeth the sapphires and Nancy the rubies. Janelle told me that's pretty much what they would've done anyhow if he'd left both girls the ring—sell the big stone and make two rings out of the little ones. In the end, it made three."

I was tired of that stupid ring. The band was playing a lively two-step and I wanted to shake my bustle. Despite his size, Dwight dances surprisingly well, and I didn't mean to waste the music talking about something over and done with. We moved out onto the dance floor and were soon twirling with the best.

A couple of slow numbers followed, then the spotlight fell on the emcee who announced the first category of the evening: Hearts and Flowers, i. e., fussiest dress. To the strains of "Here Comes the Bride," nine women glided across the dance floor, as if down an aisle, to a makeshift altar behind the emcee. The clear winner was a stiff yellow net covered with row upon row of tight little ruffles.

Amid the laughter and applause, I felt a light touch on my arm and there was Janelle smiling at Portland and me. She gave us each a hug and said to me, "Nancy said you signed up in the prettiest dress category? I'm so flattered. It *was* a beautiful wedding, wasn't it?"

She herself was wearing ice blue satin from her sister-in-law Elizabeth's wedding. "That's the only time I was a bridesmaid," Janelle said regretfully. "I was always big-as-a-house pregnant when everybody else was getting married."

One of the Widdington Jaycees dragged her away to help with something, and she made us promise we wouldn't leave without speaking again.

The next category was My Funny Valentine for the most unusual gown, and it was a tie between a Ronald McDonald clown (the bride managed a local franchise) and a gold lamé jumpsuit (the skydiving bride and groom were married in free-fall).

Portland didn't win the Purple Heart Award (the most unusual color actually went to a hot-pink velvet bodice, orange organza skirt, and lime green sash), but she was persuaded to enter Kind Hearts and Coronets for the most accessories and won handily with her huge picture hat, arm-length lace mitts, and wicker basket full of chiffon roses.

In between, as groups of contestants were assembled for their march down the mock aisle, we danced and chatted and filled several bedoiled sandwich plates with the usual array of finger foods found at a typical wedding reception: raw vegetables and herb dip, cheese straws, cucumber sandwiches, tiny hot rolls stuffed with ham and melted pimiento cheese, salted nuts, and heartshaped butter mints.

Despite all the laughter, wearing the dress brought back memories of Janelle and Glenn's wedding, and seeing Nancy around the room in the same garb only emphasized the feeling. I knew Portland was flashing on it, too, because she kept going back to the missing ring. Faye, Nancy, or Elizabeth. Who had taken it? (Loyally, we'd each long since cleared the other.)

If Faye had eventually lavished money around, we'd never heard of it.

It had to be Elizabeth or Nancy.

"Nancy's a preacher," Portland said.

"That wouldn't have mattered," I argued. "They both felt entitled to the ring. Don't forget, she came up with tuition to divinity school."

"Elizabeth helped her though. And so did Glenn and Janelle. Janelle didn't buy any new clothes for three years, till long after Elizabeth bought a partnership with Bob McAdams. Where did Elizabeth get enough money if not from pawning the ring?"

"I thought Glenn cosigned a loan with her?" said Avery.

"Yes, but—"

"You gals have gone at it all wrong," said Dwight. "From what you've told me, there's only one person who could have taken the ring without being caught or even suspected."

I hate that superior air he puts on when he's being Dick Tracy, but all of a sudden, I realized he was right.

"Who?" asked Avery.

"The woman who directed the wedding, of course."

"Miss Louisa Ferncliff?" Portland exclaimed.

Dwight lifted his glass to her. "The only person alone out in the vestibule while everyone else was taking part in the ceremony. Anybody ever take a look at *her* lifestyle after the wedding?"

Avery cocked his head. "You know something, ol' son? I sort of remember when she died, Ed Whitbread was the one who drew up her will, and when he came over to file it at the courthouse, seems like he said he was surprised how much money she did have to leave that sorry nephew of hers down in Wilmington."

Portland was looking doubtful. "Miss *Louisa?*"

I spread my fan and drew myself up in a most judicial manner. "It's unfair to slander the name of a good woman who can no longer defend herself, but"—I used the fan to shield my voice from the rest of the table —"one thing's for sure. Miss Louisa Ferncliff directed just about every single wedding at that church for years. She sure would know that brides take off their engagement rings and leave them somewhere in the robing room, but that was the first ring really worth taking, wouldn't you say?"

"I'll be damned," said Portland. "Miss Louisa!"

She jumped up from the table. "Come on, Deb'rah! Let's go tell Janelle."

Protesting that we had no proof, I followed her around the edge of the dance floor until we found Janelle, who, as one of the ball's organizers, had just presented the Heart of Carolina prize for the most denim or gingham in a bridesmaid's dress.

Quickly, we maneuvered her into the lobby where it was quieter and Portland laid out Dwight's theory and my supporting logic.

Janelle was flabbergasted. "Miss *Louisa* stole my ring?"

"She certainly had plenty of opportunity," I said cautiously, "but I don't see how you'd ever prove it. She left everything to that sorry nephew and what he didn't sell off, he either burned or threw out."

"I don't care!" A radiance swept across Janelle's sweet face and she hugged Portland. "We never once thought of Miss Louisa. I can't wait to tell Glenn. If you could know what it means that we can say it was her and not—"

She broke off and hugged us both again, then whirled away back into the ballroom.

"Well, I'll be blessed," said Portland, standing there with her mouth hanging open. "Not you or me after all, Deb'rah. She really did think it was one of Glenn's sisters."

"Or they could have accused her own sister," I reminded her. "For all they knew, Faye could have been the thief."

"Oh, I'm so glad Dwight finally figured it out. Let's go buy him a drink."

"You go ahead," I told her.

✜ ✜ ✜

The band was playing a suburban version of "Hometown Honeymoon" when I caught up with Janelle.

"You and Glenn went to New York on your honeymoon, didn't you?"

Surprised, she nodded.

"Is that where you sold the diamond?"

"*What?*"

"The biggest diamond market in the country's right there on Forty-seventh Street. You'd have gotten better money for it there than anywhere here in North Carolina."

There was a door off to the side and Janelle pulled me through it into an empty office, the club manager's by the look of it.

"You said Miss Louisa must've taken it."

"I said she had lots of opportunity," I corrected. "You had the most though."

"That's crazy! Why would I steal my own engagement ring? It wasn't even insured."

"I think that's exactly why you did," I said. "You're not really a thief and you wouldn't have pretended it was stolen if it meant the insurance company was going to be defrauded of eighty thousand dollars. But the ring was legally yours, you and Glenn needed money, and that was the simplest way to get it without ticking off his uncle. All you needed to do was go through that charade."

Janelle was shaking her head. "No, no, *NO!*"

"Oh, get real," I told her. "How else did you and Glenn have enough to get the restaurant off to such a good start? How'd Glenn have enough collateral to cosign a loan for Elizabeth's partnership so quick?"

"Uncle Glenn—"

"Uncle Glenn didn't leave that kind of money. I was nosy enough to look up the records when his estate was settled even though I never put two and two together. The house went to Glenn's mom and what was split between Glenn and his sisters wouldn't have bought a partnership in a hot dog stand at the fair. That's why we were so sure one of them took it."

Her eyes fell.

"It was mean of you to let Portland think you suspected us all these years."

Janelle threw up her hands in exasperation. "I didn't want to, but it was the only way I could make her quit talking about it. I was afraid if she kept on, she'd finally figure it out."

That dog-with-a-bone tenacity makes Portland a good lawyer, but it's a real pain in the neck for some of her friends, and I couldn't help grinning.

"Are you going to tell her?" Janelle asked.

"And spoil the fun she and Dwight are having, thinking Miss Louisa did it?"

Janelle giggled and I had to laugh, too. "You know, I bet Miss Louisa would love it if people remembered her for pulling off a slick jewel theft."

Better than not being remembered at all, I judged, and clasped Janelle's hand. We both looked down at the circle of diamond baguettes that sparkled modestly above her wedding band.

"It really was the tackiest ring in the whole world," she said.

"Something that trashy deserved to get itself stolen," I agreed.

❖ ❖ ❖

As we stepped back into the room a few minutes later, someone yelled, "Here she is!" and immediately pushed me into the final lineup of the evening. Queen of Hearts. The prettiest dress of weddings past.

Nancy, in her sister's dress, had entered this category, too, and there was a truly gorgeous Scarlett O'Hara confection of pale green organza, plus a couple of sophisticated black silks, but none of them had a fan of white ostrich plumes and none of them was as shameless at working a crowd.

The prize was a five-pound, red satin, heart-shaped box of chocolates.

I won by a landslide.

Crimes of the Heart, 1995

Prayer for Judgment

Certain smells take you back in time as quickly as any period song. One whiff of Evening in Paris *and I am a child again, watching my mother get dressed up. The smell of woodsmoke, bacon, newly turned dirt, a damp kitten, shoe polish, Krispy Kreme doughnuts—each evokes anew its own long sequence of memories . . . like gardenias on a summer night.*

The late June evening was so hot and humid, and the air was so still, that the heavy fragrance of gardenias was held close to the earth like layers of sweet-scented chiffon. I floated on my back at the end of the pool and breathed in the rich sensuous aroma of Aunt Zell's forty-year-old bushes.

More than magnolias, gardenias are the smell of summer in central North Carolina and their scent unlocks memories and images we never think of when the weather's cool and crisp.

Blurred stars twinkled in the hazy night sky, an occasional plane passed far overhead and lightning bugs drifted lazily through the evening stillness. Drifting with them, unshackled by gravity, I seemed to float not on water but on the thick sweet air itself, half of my senses disoriented, the other half too wholly relaxed to care whether a particular point of light was insect, human or extraterrestrial.

The house is only a few blocks from the center of Dobbs, but our sidewalks roll up at nine on a week night, and there was nothing to break the small town silence except light traffic or the occasional bark of a dog. When I heard the back screen door slam, I assumed it was Aunt Zell or Uncle Ash coming out to say goodnight, but the man silhouetted against the house lights was too big and bulky. One of my brothers?

"Deb'rah?" Dwight Bryant moved cautiously down the path and along the edge of the pool, as if his eyes hadn't yet adjusted to the darkness.

"Watch out you don't fall in," I told him. "Unless you mean to."

I didn't reckon he did because my night vision was good enough to see that he had on his new sports jacket. As chief of detectives for the Colleton County Sheriff's Department, Dwight seldom wears a uniform unless he wants to look particularly official.

He followed my voice and came over to squat down on the coping and dip a hand in the water.

"Not very cool, is it?"

"Feels good though. Come on in."

"No suit," he said regretfully, "and Mr. Ash is so skinny, I couldn't get into one of his."

"Oh, you don't need a bathing suit," I teased. "Not dark as it is tonight. Besides, we're just home folks here."

Dwight snorted. Growing up, he was in and out of our farmhouse so much that he really could have been one more brother, but my brothers never went skinny-dipping if I were around. (Correction: not if they *knew* I was around. Kid sisters don't always announce their presence.)

"You're working late," I said. "What's up?"

"A young woman over in Black Creek got herself shot dead this morning. They didn't find her till nearly six this evening."

"Shot? You mean murdered?"

"Looks like it."

"Someone we know?"

"Chastity Barefoot? Everybody called her Chass."

Rang no bells with me.

"She and her husband both grew up in Harnett County. His name's Edward Barefoot."

"Now that sounds familiar for some reason." I stood up—the lap pool's only four feet deep—and Dwight reached down his big hand to haul me out beside him. I came up dripping and wrapped a towel around me as I tried to think where I'd heard that name recently. "They any kin to the Cotton Grove Barefoots?"

"Not that he said."

I finished drying off and slipped on my flip-flops and an oversized tee-shirt and we walked back to the patio to sit and talk. Aunt Zell came out with a pitcher of iced tea and said she and Uncle Ash were going upstairs to watch the news in bed so if I'd lock up after Dwight left, she'd tell us goodnight now.

I gave her a hug and Dwight did, too, and after she'd gone inside and we were sipping the strong cold tea, I said, "This Edward Barefoot. He do the shooting?"

"Don't see how he could've," said Dwight. "Specially since you're his alibi."

"Come again?"

"He says he spent all morning in your courtroom. Says you let him off with a prayer for judgment."

"I did?"

Monday morning traffic court is such a cattle call that it's easy for the faces to blur and if Dwight had waited a week to ask me, I might not have remembered. As it was, it took me a minute to sort out which one had been Edward Barefoot.

As a district court judge, I had been presented with minor assaults, drug possession, worthless checks and a dozen other misdemeanor categories; but on the whole, traffic violations had made up the bulk of the day's calendar. Seated on the side benches had been uniformed state troopers and officers from both the town's police department and the county sheriff's department, each prepared to testify why he had ticketed and/or arrested his share of the two hundred and five individuals named on my docket today. Tracy Johnson, the prosecuting ADA, had efficiently whittled at least thirty-five names from that docket and she spent the midmorning break period processing the rest of those who planned to plead guilty without an attorney.

At least 85% were male and younger than thirty. There doesn't seem to be a sexual pattern on who will come up with phony registrations, improper plates or expired inspection stickers, but most sessions have one young lead-footed female and one older female alcoholic who's blown more than the legal point-oh-eight. Yeah, and every week I get at least one middle-aged man who thinks it's his God-given right to keep driving even though his license has been so thoroughly revoked that for the rest of his life it'll barely be legal for him to get behind the steering wheel of a bumper car at the State Fair.

As I poured Dwight a second glass of tea, I remembered seeing Edward Barefoot come up to the defense table. I had wondered whether he was a first-time speeder or someone on the edge of getting his license revoked. His preppie haircut was so fresh that there was a half-inch band of white around the back edges where his hair had kept his neck from tanning, and his neat charcoal gray suit bespoke a young businessman somewhat embarrassed at finding himself in traffic court and eager to make a good impression. His pin-striped shirt and sober tie said, "I'm an upstanding taxpayer and solid citizen of the community," but his edgy good looks would have been more appropriate on one of our tight-jeaned speed jockeys.

Tracy had withdrawn the charge of driving without a valid license, but Barefoot was still left with a 78 in a 65 speed zone.

I nodded to the spit-polished highway patrolman and said, "Tell me about it."

It was the same old same old with a slight variation. Late one evening, about a week earlier, defendant got himself pulled for excessive speed on the interstate that bisects Colleton County. According to the trooper, Mr. Barefoot had been cooperative when asked to step out of the car, but there was an odor of an impairing substance about him and he didn't have his wallet or license.

"Mr. Barefoot stated that his wife was usually their designated driver, so he often left his wallet at home when they went out like that. Just put some cash in his pocket. Mrs. Barefoot was in the vehicle and she did possess a valid license, but she stated that they'd been to a party over in Raleigh and she got into the piña colladas right heavy so they felt like it'd be safer for him to drive."

"Did he blow for you?" I asked.

"Yes, ma'am. He registered a point-oh-five, three points below the legal limit. And there was nothing out of the way about his speech or appearance, other than the speeding. He stated that was because they'd promised the babysitter they'd be home before midnight and they were late. The vehicle was registered in both their names and Mr. Barefoot showed me his license before court took in this morning."

When it was his turn to speak, Barefoot freely acknowledged that he'd been driving 'way too fast, said he was sorry, and requested a prayer for judgment.

"Any previous violations?" I asked the trooper.

"I believe he has one speeding violation. About three years ago. Sixty-four in a fifty-five zone."

"Only one?" That surprised me because this Edward Barefoot sure looked like a racehorse.

"Just one, your honor," the trooper had said.

"Another week and his only violation would have been neutralized," I told Dwight now as I refilled my glass of iced tea, "so I let him off. Phyllis Raynor was clerking for me this morning and she or Tracy might have a better fix on the time, but I'd say he was out of there by eleven-thirty."

"That late, hmm?"

"You'd like for it to be earlier?"

"Well, we think she was killed sometime mid-morning and that would give us someplace to start. Not that we've heard of any trouble between them, but you know how it is—husbands and boyfriends, we always look hard at them first. Barefoot says he got a chicken biscuit at Bojangles on his way out of town, and then drove straight to work. If he got to his job when he says he did, he didn't have enough time to drive home first. That's almost fifty miles. And if he really was in court from nine till eleven-thirty—?"

"Tracy could probably tell you," I said again.

According to Dwight, Chastity Barefoot had dropped her young daughter off at a day care there in Black Creek at nine-thirty that morning and then returned to the little starter home she and her husband had bought the year before in one of the many subdivisions that have sprung up since the new interstate opened and made our cheap land and low taxes attractive to people working around Raleigh. She was a part-time receptionist for a dentist in Black Creek and wasn't due in till noon; her husband worked for one of the big pharmaceuticals in the Research Triangle Park.

When she didn't turn up at work on time, the office manager had first called and then driven out to the house on her lunch hour because "And I quote," said Dwight, " 'Whatever else Chass did, she never left you hanging.' "

"Whatever else?" I asked.

"Yeah, she did sort of hint that Miz Barefoot might've had hinges on her heels."

"So there *was* trouble between the Barefoots."

"Not according to the office manager." Dwight slapped at a mosquito buzzing around his ears. "She says the poor bastard didn't have a clue. Thought Chass hung the moon just for him. Anyhow, Chass's car was there, but the house was locked and no one answered the door, so she left again."

He brushed away another mosquito, drained his tea glass and stood up to go. "I'll speak to Tracy and Phyllis and we'll check every inch of Barefoot's alibi, but I have a feeling we're going to be hunting the boyfriend on this one."

That would have been the end of it as far as I was concerned except that Chastity Barefoot's grandmother was a friend of Aunt Zell's, so

Aunt Zell felt she ought to attend the visitation on Wednesday evening. The only trouble was that Uncle Ash had to be out of town and she doesn't like to drive that far alone at night.

"You sure you don't mind?" she asked me that morning.

On a hot Wednesday night, I had planned nothing more exciting than reading briefs in front of the air conditioner in my sitting room.

I had originally moved in with Aunt Zell and Uncle Ash because I couldn't afford a place of my own when I first came back to Colleton County and there was no way I'd have gone back to the farm at that point. I use the self-contained efficiency apartment they fixed for Uncle Ash's mother while she was still alive, with its own separate entrance and relative privacy. We're comfortable together—too comfortable say some of my sisters-in-law who worry that I may never get married—but Uncle Ash has to be away so much, my being there gives everybody peace of mind.

No big deal to drive to the funeral home over in Harnett County, I told her.

✤ ✤ ✤

It was still daylight, another airless, humid evening and even in a thin cotton dress and barefoot sandals, I had to keep the air conditioner on high most of the way. As we drove, Aunt Zell reminisced about her friend, Retha Minshew, and how sad it was that her little great-grand-daughter would probably grow up without any memory of her mother.

"And when Edward remarries, that'll loosen the ties to the Minshews even more," she sighed.

I pricked up my ears. "You knew them? They weren't getting along?"

"No, no. I just mean that he's young and he's got a baby girl that's going to need a mother. Only natural if he took another wife after a while."

"So why did you say 'even more'?" I asked, as I passed a slow-moving pickup truck with three hounds in the back.

"Did I?" She thought about her words. "Maybe it's because the Minshews are so nice and those Barefoots—-"

Trust Aunt Zell to know them root and stock.

"They say Edward's real steady and hard-working. Always putting in overtime at his office. Works nine or ten hours a day. But the rest of his family—" She hesitated, not wanting to speak badly of anybody. "I think his father spent some time in jail for beating up on his mother.

Both of them were too drunk to come to the wedding, Retha says. And Retha says his two younger brothers are wild as turkeys, too. Anyhow, I get the impression the Minshews don't do much visiting back and forth with the Barefoots."

Angier is still a small town, but so many people had turned out for the wake that the line stretched across the porch, down the walk and out onto the sidewalk.

Fortunately, the lines usually move fast, and within a half-hour Aunt Zell and I were standing before the open casket. There was no sign that Chastity Minshew Barefoot had died violently. Her fair head lay lightly on the pink satin pillow, her face was smooth and unwrinkled and her pink lips hinted at secret amusement. Her small hands were clasped around a silver picture frame that held a color photograph of a suntanned little girl with curly blond hair.

A large bouquet of gardenias lay on the closed bottom half of the polished casket and the heavy sweet smell was almost overpowering.

Aunt Zell sighed, then turned to the tall gray-haired woman with red-rimmed eyes who stood next to the coffin. "Oh, Retha, honey, I'm just so sorry."

They hugged each other. Aunt Zell introduced me to Chastity's grandmother, who in turn introduced us to her son and daughter-in-law, both of whom seemed shellshocked by the murder of their daughter.

As did Edward Barefoot, who stood just beyond them. His eyes were glazed and feverish looking. Gone was the crisp young businessman of two days ago. Tonight his face was pinched, his skin was pasty, his hair disheveled. He looked five years older and if they hadn't told me who he was, I wouldn't have recognized him.

He gazed at me blankly as Aunt Zell and I paused to give our condolences. A lot of people don't recognize me without the black robe.

"I'm Judge Knott," I reminded him. "You were in my courtroom day before yesterday. I'm really sorry about your wife."

"Thank you, Judge." His eyes focussed on my face and he gave me a firm handshake. "And I want to thank you again for going so easy on me."

"Not at all," I said inanely and was then passed on to his family, a rough-looking couple who seemed uncomfortable in this formal setting, and a self-conscious youth who looked so much like Edward Barefoot that I figured he was the youngest brother. He and his parents just nodded glumly when Aunt Zell and I expressed our sympathy.

As we worked our way back through the crowd, both of us were aware of a different pitch to the usual quiet funeral home murmur. I spotted a friend out on the porch and several people stopped Aunt Zell for a word. It was nearly half an hour before we got back to my car and both of us had heard the same stories. The middle Barefoot brother had been slipping around with Chastity and he hadn't been seen since she was killed.

"Wonder if Dwight knows?" asked Aunt Zell.

"Yeah, we heard," said Dwight when I called him that evening. "George Barefoot. He's been living at home since he got out of jail and—"

"Jail?" I asked.

"Yeah. He ran a stop sign back last November and hit a Toyota. Totaled both cars and nearly killed the other driver. He blew a ten and since he already had one DWI and a string of speeding tickets, Judge Longmire gave him some jail time, too. According to his mother, he hasn't been home since Sunday night. He and the youngest brother are rough carpenters on that new subdivision over off Highway Forty-eight, but the crew chief says he hasn't seen George since quitting time Friday evening. The two brothers claim not to know where he is either."

"Are they lying?"

I could almost hear Dwight's shrug over the phone. "Who knows?"

"You put out an APB on his vehicle?"

"He doesn't have one. Longmire pulled his license. Wouldn't even give him driving privileges during work hours. That's why he's been living at home. So he could ride to work with his brother Paul."

"The husband's alibi hold up?"

"Solid as a tent pole. It's a forty-mile roundtrip to his house. Tracy says he answered the calendar call around nine-thirty—that's when his wife was dropping their kid off at the day care—and you entered his prayer for judgment between eleven-fifteen and eleven-thirty. Lucky for him, he kept his Bojangles receipt. It's the one out on the bypass, and the time on it says twelve-oh-five. It's another forty minutes to his work, and they say he was there before one o'clock and didn't leave till after five, so it looks like he's clear."

More than anybody could say for his brother George.

Poor Edward Barefoot. From what I now knew about that bunch of Barefoots, he was the only motivated member of his family. The only one to finish high school, he'd even earned an associate degree at the community college. Here was somebody who could be the poster child for bootstrapping, a man who'd worked hard and played by the rules, and what happens? Bad enough to lose the wife you adore, but then to find out she's been cheating with your sorry brother who probably shot her and took off?

Well, it wasn't for me to condemn Chass Barefoot's taste in men. I've danced with the devil enough times myself to know the attraction of no-'count charmers.

✤ ✤ ✤

Aunt Zell went to the funeral the next day and described it for Uncle Ash and me at supper.

"That boy looked like he was strung out on the rack. And his precious little baby! Her hair's blond like her mama's, but she's been out in her wading pool so much this summer, Retha said, that she's brown as a pecan." She put a hot and fluffy biscuit on my plate. "It just broke my heart to see the way she kept her arms wrapped around her daddy's neck as if she knew her mama was gone forever. But she's only two, way too young to understand something like that."

From my experience with children who come to family court having suffered enormous loss and trauma, I knew that a two-year-old was indeed too young to understand or remember, yet something about Aunt Zell's description of the little girl kept troubling me.

For her sake, I hoped that George Barefoot would be arrested and quickly brought to trial so that her family could find closure and healing.

✤ ✤ ✤

Unfortunately, it didn't happen quite that way.

Two days later, George Barefoot's body was found when some county workers were cleaning up an illegal trash dump on one of the back roads just north of Dobbs. He was lying on an old sofa someone had thrown into the underbrush, and the high back had concealed him from the road.

The handgun he'd stuck in his mouth had landed on some dirt and leaves beside the sofa. It was the same gun that had killed Chastity Barefoot, a gun she'd bought to protect herself from intruders. There was a note in his pocket addressed to his brother:

E — God, I'm so sorry about
Chass. I never meant
to hurt you. You know
how much you mean
to me.
　　Love always,
　　George

A rainy night and several hot humid days had mildewed the note and blurred the time of death, but the M.E. thought he could have shot himself either the day Chastity Barefoot was killed or no later than the day after.

"That road's miles from his mother's house," I told Dwight. "Wonder why he picked it? And how did he get there?"

Dwight shrugged. "It's just a few hundred feet from where Highway 70 crosses the bypass. Maybe he was hitchhiking out of the county and that's where his ride put him out. Maybe he got to feeling remorse and knew he couldn't run forever. Who knows?"

I was in Dwight's office that noonday, waiting for him to finish reading over the file so that he could send it on to our District Attorney, official notification that the two deaths could be closed out. A copy of the suicide note lay on his desk and I'm as curious as any cat.

"Can I see that?"

"Sure."

The original was locked up of course, but this was such a clear photocopy that I could see every spot of mildew and the ragged edge of where Barefoot must have torn the page from a notepad.

"Was there a notepad on his body?" I asked idly.

"No, and no pencil either," said Dwight. "He must have written it before leaving wherever he was holed up."

I made a doubtful noise and he looked at me in exasperation.

"Don't go trying to make a mystery out of this, Deb'rah. He was bonking his sister-in-law, things got messy, so he shot her and then he shot himself. Nobody else has a motive, nobody else could've done it."

"The husband had motive."

"The husband was in your court at the time, remember?" He stuck the suicide note back in the file and stood up. "Let's go eat."

"Bonking?" I asked as we walked across the street to the Soup 'n' Sandwich Shop.

He gave a rueful smile. "Cal's starting to pick up language. I promised Jonna I'd clean up my vocabulary."

Jonna is Dwight's ex-wife and a real priss-pot.

"You don't talk dirty," I protested, but he wouldn't argue the point. When our waitress brought us our barbecue sandwiches, I noticed that her ring finger was conspicuously bare. Instead of a gaudy engagement ring, there was now only a thin circle of white skin.

"Don't tell me you and Conrad have broken up again?" I said.

Angry sparks flashed from her big blue eyes. "Good riddance to bad rubbish."

Dwight grinned at me when she was gone. "Want to bet how long before she's wearing his ring again?"

I shook my head. It would be a sucker bet.

Instead, I found myself looking at Dwight's hands as he bit into his sandwich. He had given up wearing a wedding band as soon as Jonna walked out on him, so his fingers were evenly tanned by the summer sun. Despite all the paperwork in his job, he still got out of the office a few hours every day. I reached across and pulled on the expansion band of his watch.

"What—?"

"Just checking," I said. "Your wrist is white."

"Of course it is. I always wear my watch. Aren't you going to eat your sandwich?"

My appetite was fading, so I cut it in two and gave him half. "Hurry up and eat," I said. "I want to see that suicide note again before I have to go back to court."

Grumbling, he wolfed down his lunch; and even though his legs are much longer than mine, he had to stretch them out to keep up as I hurried back to his office.

"What?" he asked, when I was studying the note again.

"I think you ought to let the SBI's handwriting experts take a closer look at this."

"Why?"

"Well, look at it," I said, pointing to the word *about*.

"See how it juts out in the margin? And see that little mark where the *a* starts? Couldn't that be a comma? What if the original version was just *I'm sorry, Chas*?" What if somebody also added that capital *E* to make you think it was a note to Edward when it was probably a love letter to Chastity?"

"Huh?" Dwight took the paper from my hand and looked at it closer.

We've known each other so long he can almost read my mind at times.

"But Edward Barefoot was in court when his wife was shot. He couldn't be two places at one time."

"Yes, he could," I said and told him how.

❖ ❖ ❖

I cut court short that afternoon so that I'd be there when they brought Edward Barefoot in for questioning.

He denied everything and called for an attorney.

"I was in traffic court," he told Dwight when his attorney was there and questioning resumed. "Ask the judge here." He turned to me with a hopeful look. "You let me off with a prayer for judgment. You said so yourself at the funeral home."

"I was mistaken," I said gently. "It was your brother George that I let off. You three brothers look so much alike that when I saw you at the funeral home, I had no reason not to think you were the same man who'd been in court. I didn't immediately recognize you, but I thought that was because you were in shock. You're not in shock right now, though. This is your natural color."

Puzzled, his attorney said, "I beg your pardon?"

"He puts in ten or twelve hours a day at an office, so he isn't tan. The man who stood before my bench had just had a fresh haircut and he was so tanned that it left a ring of white around the hairline. When's the last time you had a haircut, Mr. Barefoot?"

He touched his hair. Clearly, it was normally short and neat. Just as clearly, he hadn't visited a barber in three or four weeks. "I've— Everything's been so—"

"Don't answer that," said his attorney.

I thought about his little daughter's nut-brown arms clasped tightly around his pale neck and I wasn't happy about where this would end for her.

"When the trooper stopped your wife's car for speeding, your brother knew he'd be facing more jail time if he gave his right name. So he gave your name instead. He could rattle off your address and birthdate glibly enough to satisfy the trooper. Then all he had to do was show up in court with your driver's license and your clean record and act respectable and contrite. Did you know he was out with Chastity that night?"

Like a stuck needle, the attorney said, "Don't answer that."

"The time and date would be on any speeding ticket he showed you," said Dwight. "Along with the license number and make of the car."

"She said she was at her friend's in Raleigh and that his girlfriend had dumped him and he was hitching a ride home," Edward burst out over the protest of his attorney. "Like I was stupid enough to believe *that* after everything else!"

"So you made George get a haircut, lent him a suit and tie, dropped him at the courthouse, with your driver's license, and then went back to your house and killed Chastity. After court, you met George here in Dobbs, killed him and dumped his body on the way out of town."

"We'll find people who were in the courtroom last Monday morning and can testify about his appearance," said Dwight. "We'll find the barber. We may even find your fingerprints on the note."

Edward Barefoot seemed to shrink down into the chair.

"You don't have to respond to any of these accusations," said his attorney. "They're just guessing."

Guessing?

Maybe.

Half of life is guesswork.

The little Barefoot girl might be only two years old, but I'm guessing that she'll never be allowed to forget that her daddy killed her mama.

Especially when gardenias are in bloom.

Mystery Novels and Short Stories by Margaret Maron: A Checklist

BOOKS

One Coffee With. Raven House 1981. Reprinted by Bantam 1988 and Mysterious Press 1995.
Sigrid Harald novel.
Death of a Butterfly. Doubleday 1984. Reprinted by Bantam 1991.
Sigrid Harald novel.
Death in Blue Folders. Doubleday 1985. Reprinted by Bantam 1992.
Sigrid Harald novel.
Bloody Kin. Doubleday 1985. Reprinted by Bantam 1992 and Mysterious Press 1995.
Deborah Knott prequel novel.
The Right Jack. Bantam 1987. Reprinted by Mysterious Press 1995.
Sigrid Harald novel.
Baby Doll Games. Bantam 1988. Reprinted by Mysterious Press 1995.
Sigrid Harald novel.
Corpus Christmas. Doubleday 1989. Reprinted by Bantam 1991.
Sigrid Harald novel.
Past Imperfect. Doubleday 1991. Reprinted by Bantam 1992.
Sigrid Harald novel.
Bootlegger's Daughter. Mysterious Press 1992. Reprinted as a Mysterious Press paperback 1993.
Deborah Knott novel.
Southern Discomfort. Mysterious Press 1993. Reprinted as a Mysterious Press paperback 1994.
Deborah Knott novel.
Shooting at Loons. Mysterious Press 1994. Reprinted as a Mysterious Press paperback 1995.
Deborah Knott novel.
Fugitive Colors. Mysterious Press 1995. Reprinted as a Mysterious Press paperback 1996.
Sigrid Harald novel.
Up Jumps the Devil. Mysterious Press 1996. Reprinted as a Mysterious Press paperback 1997.
Deborah Knott novel.

Killer Market. Mysterious Press 1997. Reprinted as a Mysterious Press paperback 1998.
Deborah Knott novel.
Shoveling Smoke, Selected Mystery Stories. Crippen & Landru, Publishers 1997. Reprinted in 1998 and 2000.
Short story collection, including cases solved by Sigrid Harald and Deborah Knott.
Home Fires. Mysterious Press 1998. Reprinted as a Mysterious Press paperback 2000.
Deborah Knott novel.
Storm Track. Mysterious Press 2000.
Deborah Knott novel.

Mystery and Crime Short Stories

* Story collected in *Shoveling Smoke.*

*"The Death of Me," *Alfred Hitchcock's Mystery Magazine,* January 1968.
"The Compromised Confessional," *Alfred Hitchcock's Mystery Magazine,* January 1969.
"The Roots of Death," *Alfred Hitchcock's Mystery Magazine,* August 1969.
*"A Very Special Talent," *Alfred Hitchcock's Mystery Magazine,* June 1970.
"The Early Retirement of Mario Called,"*Mike Shayne Mystery Magazine,* December 1970.
*"The Beast Within," *Alfred Hitchcock's Mystery Magazine,* July 1972.
"Side Trip to King's Post," *Alfred Hitchcock's Mystery Magazine,* October 1972.
"To Hide a Tree," *Alfred Hitchcock's Mystery Magazine,* May 1973.
"Bang! You're Dead!" *Alfred Hitchcock's Mystery Magazine,* February 1974.
*"When Daddy's Gone," *The Executioner Mystery Magazine,* August 1975.
"Lady of Honor," *Alfred Hitchcock's Mystery Magazine,* November 1975.
*"Deadhead Coming Down," *Mike Shayne Mystery Magazine,* April 1978.
*"Guy and Dolls," *Alfred Hitchcock's Mystery Magazine,* June 1979.
*"Let No Man Put Asunder," *Mike Shayne Mystery Magazine,* May 1980.
*"A City Full of Thieves," *Skullduggery,* June 1980.
*"Mrs. Howell and Criminal Justice 2.1," *Alfred Hitchcock's Mystery Magazine,* May 1984.

*"On Windy Ridge," *Alfred Hitchcock's Mystery Magazine*, Mid-December 1984.

"Lost and Found," *Woman's World*, February 16, 1988.

*"Out of Whole Cloth," *Sisters in Crime 2*, ed. Marilyn Wallace, 1989.

*"Lieutenant Harald and the *Treasure Island* Treasure," *Alfred Hitchcock's Mystery Magazine*, September 1989.

*"My Mother, My Daughter, Me," *Alfred Hitchcock's Mystery Magazine*, March 1990.

*"Small Club Lead, Dummy Plays Low," *New Crimes II*, ed Maxim Jakubowski, 1990.

*"Deborah's Judgment," *A Woman's Eye*, ed. Sara Paretsky, 1991.

*"Fruitcake, Mercy, and Black-Eyed Peas," *Christmas Stalkings*, ed. Charlotte MacLeod, 1991.

*"Lieutenant Harald and the Impossible Gun," *Sisters in Crime 4*, ed. Marilyn Wallace, 1991.

*"Hangnail," *Deadly Allies*, ed. Marilyn Wallace and Robert Randisi, 1992.

". . . That Married Dear Old Dad," *Malice Domestic II*, ed. Martin Harry Greenberg, 1993.

*"That Bells May Ring and Whistles Safely Blow," *Santa Clues*, ed. Ed Gorman and Martin Harry Greenberg, 1993.

*"What's a Friend For?" with Susan Dunlap, *Partners in Crime*, ed. Elaine Raco Chase, 1994.

*"With This Ring," *Crimes of the Heart*, ed. Carolyn G. Hart and Martin Harry Greenberg, 1995.

"No, I'm not Jane Marple, But . . . ," *Vengeance Is Hers*, ed. Mickey Spillane and Max Allan Collins, 1997.

"Shaggy Dog," *Funny Bones*, ed. Joan Hess and Martin Harry Greenberg, 1997.

"The Stupid Pet Trick," *Murder She Wrote 2*, ed. Elizabeth Foxwell and Martin Harry Greenberg, 1997.

*"Prayer for Judgment," *Shoveling Smoke: Selected Mystery Stories*, 1997.

"Half of Something," *Irreconcilable Differences*, ed. Lia Matera and Martin Harry Greenberg, 1999.

"Growth Marks," *Mom, Apple Pie, and Murder*, ed. Nancy Pickard, 1999.

"Roman's Holiday, *Mary Higgins Clark Mystery Magazine*, Summer 1999.

CRIPPEN & LANDRU, PUBLISHERS

P. O. Box 9315
Norfolk, VA 23505
E-mail: info@crippenlandru.com; toll-free 877 622-6656
Web: www.crippenlandru.com

Crippen & Landru publishes first edition short-story collections by important detective and mystery writers. The following books are currently in print in our regular series; see our website for full details:

The McCone Files by Marcia Muller. Trade softcover, $19.00.

Who Killed Father Christmas? by Patricia Moyes. Signed, unnumbered cloth overrun copies, $30.00. Trade softcover, $16.00.

My Mother, The Detective by James Yaffe. Trade softcover, $15.00.

In Kensington Gardens Once . . . by H.R.F. Keating. Trade softcover, $12.00.

Shoveling Smoke. Trade softcover, $19.00.

The Ripper of Storyville by Edward D. Hoch. Trade softcover. $17.00.

Renowned Be Thy Grave by P.M. Carlson. Trade softcover, $16.00.

Carpenter and Quincannon by Bill Pronzini. Trade softcover, $16.00.

Not Safe After Dark and Other Stories by Peter Robinson. Trade softcover, $17.00.

All Creatures Dark and Dangerous by Doug Allyn. Trade softcover, $16.00.

Famous Blue Raincoat by Ed Gorman. Signed, unnumbered cloth overrun copies, $30.00. Trade softcover, $17.00.

The Tragedy of Errors by Ellery Queen. Trade softcover, $19.00.

McCone and Friends by Marcia Muller. Trade softcover, $16.00.

Challenge the Widow Maker by Clark Howard. Trade softcover, $16.00.

The Velvet Touch: Nick Velvet Stories by Edward D. Hoch. Trade softcover, $16.00.

Fortune's World by Michael Collins. Trade softcover, $16.00.

Long Live the Dead by Hugh B. Cave. Trade softcover, $16.00.

Tales Out of School by Carolyn Wheat. Trade softcover, $16.00.

Stakeout on Page Street by Joe Gores. Trade softcover, $16.00.

The Celestial Buffet by Susan Dunlap. Trade softcover, $16.00.

Kisses of Death by Max Allan Collins. Trade softcover, $17.00.

The Old Spies Club and Other Intrigues of Rand by Edward D. Hoch. Signed, unnumbered cloth overrun copies, $32.00. Trade softcover, $17.00.

Adam and Eve on a Raft by Ron Goulart. Signed, unnumbered cloth overrun copies, $32.00. Trade softcover, $17.00.

The Sedgemoor Strangler by Peter Lovesey. Trade softcover, $17.00.

The Reluctant Detective by Michael Z. Lewin. Signed, numbered clothbound, $42.00. Trade softcover, $17.00.

Nine Sons by Wendy Hornsby. Trade softcover, $16.00.

The Curious Conspiracy by Michael Gilbert. Signed, numbered clothbound, $42.00. Trade softcover, $17.00.

The 13 Culprits by Georges Simenon, translated by Peter Schulman. Trade softcover, $16.00.

The Dark Snow by Brendan DuBois. Signed, unnumbered cloth overrun copies, $32.00. Trade softcover, $17.00.

Jo Gar's Casebook by Raoul Whitfield, edited by Keith Alan Deutsch [Published with Black Mask Press]. Trade softcover, $20.00.

Come Into My Parlor by Hugh B. Cave. Trade softcover, $17.00.

The Iron Angel and Other Tales of the Gypsy Sleuth by Edward D. Hoch. Signed, numbered clothbound, $42.00. Trade softcover, $17.00.

Cuddy – Plus One by Jeremiah Healy. Trade softcover, $18.00.

Problems Solved by Bill Pronzini and Barry N. Malzberg. Signed, numbered clothbound, $42.00. Trade softcover, $16.00.

A Killing Climate by Eric Wright. Signed, numbered clothbound, $42.00. Trade softcover, $17.00.

Lucky Dip by Liza Cody. Signed, numbered clothbound, $42.00. Trade softcover, $17.00.

Kill the Umpire: The Calls of Ed Gorgon by Jon L. Breen. Signed, numbered clothbound, $42.00. Trade softcover, $17.00.

Suitable for Hanging by Margaret Maron. Signed, unnumbered cloth overrun copies, $32.00 Trade softcover, $17.00.

Murders and Other Confusions: The Chronicles of Susanna, Lady Appleton, Sixteenth-Century Gentlewoman, Herbalist, and Sleuth by Kathy Lynn Emerson. Signed, numbered clothbound, $42.00. Trade softcover, $17.00.

Byline: Mickey Spillane by Mickey Spillane, edited by Max Allan Collins and Lynn F. Myers, Jr. Signed, numbered clothbound, $48.00. Trade softcover, $20.00.

FORTHCOMING TITLES IN THE REGULAR SERIES

The Confessions of Owen Keane by Terence Faherty
The Adventure of the Murdered Moths and Other Radio Mysteries by Ellery Queen
Murder – Ancient and Modern by Edward Marston
Murder! 'Orrible Murder! by Amy Myers
More Things Impossible: The Second Casebook of Dr. Sam Hawthorne by Edward D. Hoch
14 Slayers by Paul Cain, edited by Max Allan Collins and Lynn F. Myers, Jr. Published with Black Mask Press
Tough As Nails by Frederick Nebel, edited by Rob Preston. Published with Black Mask Press
The Mankiller of Poojeegai and Other Mysteries by Walter Satterthwait
A Pocketful of Noses: Stories of One Ganelon or Another by James Powell
You'll Die Laughing by Norbert Davis, edited by Bill Pronzini. Published with Black Mask Press
Hoch's Ladies by Edward D. Hoch
Quintet: The Cases of Chase and Delacroix, by Richard A. Lupoff

CRIPPEN & LANDRU LOST CLASSICS

Crippen & Landru is proud to publish a series of *new* short-story collections by great authors who specialized in traditional mysteries. Each book collects stories from crumbling pages of old pulp, digest, and slick magazines, and most of the stories have been "lost" since their first publication. The following books are in print:

Peter Godfrey, *The Newtonian Egg and Other Cases of Rolf le Roux*, introduction by Ronald Godfrey
Craig Rice, *Murder, Mystery and Malone*, edited by Jeffrey A. Marks
Charles B. Child, *The Sleuth of Baghdad: The Inspector Chafik Stories*
Stuart Palmer, *Hildegarde Withers: Uncollected Riddles*, introduction by Mrs. Stuart Palmer
Christianna Brand, *The Spotted Cat and Other Mysteries from the Casebook of Inspector Cockrill*, edited by Tony Medawar
William Campbell Gault, *Marksman and Other Stories*, edited by Bill Pronzini; afterword by Shelley Gault
Gerald Kersh, *Karmesin: The World's Greatest Criminal — Or Most Outrageous Liar*, edited by Paul Duncan

C. Daly King, *The Complete Curious Mr. Tarrant*, introduction by Edward D. Hoch

Helen McCloy, *The Pleasant Assassin and Other Cases of Dr. Basil Willing*, introduction by B.S. Pike

William L. DeAndrea, *Murder – All Kinds*, introduction by Jane Haddam

Anthony Berkeley, *The Avenging Chance and Other Mysteries from Roger Sheringham's Casebook*, edited by Tony Medawar and Arthur Robinson

Joseph Commings, *Banner Deadlines: The Impossible Files of Senator Brooks U. Banner*, edited by Robert Adey; memoir by Edward D. Hoch

Erle Stanley Gardner, *The Danger Zone and Other Stories*, edited by Bill Pronzini

T.S. Stribling, *Dr. Poggioli: Criminologist*, edited by Arthur Vidro

Margaret Millar, *The Couple Next Door: Collected Short Mysteries*, edited by Tom Nolan

Gladys Mitchell, *Sleuth's Alchemy: Cases of Mrs. Bradley and Others*, edited by Nicholas Fuller

FORTHCOMING LOST CLASSICS

Philip S. Warne/Howard W. Macy, *Who Was Guilty? Two Dime Novels*, edited by Marlena Bremseth

Rafael Sabatini, *The Evidence of the Sword*, edited by Jesse Knight

Michael Collins, *Slot-Machine Kelly*, introduction by Robert J. Randisi

Julian Symons, *Francis Quarles: Detective*, edited by John Cooper; afterword by Kathleen Symons

Lloyd Biggle, Jr., *The Grandfather Rastin Mysteries*, introduction by Kenneth Biggle

Max Brand, *Masquerade: Nine Crime Stories*, edited by William F. Nolan, Jr.

Hugh Pentecost, *The Battles of Jericho*, introduction by S.T. Karnick

Erle Stanley Gardner, *The Casebook of Sidney Zoom*, edited by Bill Pronzini

Mignon G. Eberhart, *Something Simple in Black and Other Mysteries*, edited by Rick Cypert and Kirby McCauley

Victor Canning, *The Minerva Club, The Department of Patterns and Other Stories*, edited by John Higgins

Elizabeth Ferrars, *The Casebook of Jonas P. Jonas and Others*, edited by John Cooper